Silver
Hands

Silver
Hands

Elizabeth Hopkinson

**TOP HAT
BOOKS**

Winchester, UK
Washington, USA

First published by Top Hat Books, 2013
Top Hat Books is an imprint of John Hunt Publishing Ltd., Laurel House, Station Approach,
Alresford, Hants, SO24 9JH, UK
office1@jhpbooks.net
www.johnhuntpublishing.com

For distributor details and how to order please visit the 'Ordering' section on our website.

Text copyright: Elizabeth Hopkinson 2012

ISBN: 978 1 78099 872 5

A CIP catalogue record for this book is available from the British Library.

Design: Stuart Davies

Printed and bound by CPI Group (UK) Ltd, Croydon, CR0 4YY

We operate a distinctive and ethical publishing philosophy in all
areas of our business, from our global network of authors to
production and worldwide distribution.

CONTENTS

In loving memory:
David Macrae Cumming (Grandad)
Winifred Mavis Clark (Aunty Mavis)
"Every dream is within your reach."

Acknowledgements

I consulted many books, websites and museums during my research for *Silver Hands*. I would like to acknowledge my particular indebtedness to: *The East India Company: Trade and Conquest from 1600* by Antony Wild; *1688: A Global History* by John E Wills; *Edo Japan: A Virtual Tour* (www.us-japan.org/edomatsu); the Captain Cook Memorial Museum, Whitby; and the *Grand Turk* Frigate (now the *Étoile du Roy*).

I would also like to thank:

Yumiko Sugai and Oxalis Holidays for the dream-come-true "Shoguns and Samurai" tour of central Japan

Alan Humpries at the Thackray Medical Museum, Leeds, for letting me read the 18th century medical textbooks

Royal Armouries Oriental Gallery, Leeds, for their brilliant Oriental Weekend

Yuki Aruga and Mr. Aruga for help with the Japanese names and translations

Everyone at Swanwick Writers' Summer School

Autumn Barlow and Top Hat Books for taking a chance on me

All my family and friends for their love and support, especially Mick and Anna

July 1706

Until the day Mr. Van Guelder came, I had never once done anything adventurous or defiant. The nearest I came was telling a French lace merchant that his cargo would be delayed because of storms. This was only what Father had told me to say, but since I was keen to show off my French at the time, I might have got a bit carried away in the translation. The Frenchman said a very rude word (which unfortunately I also understood) and refused to use Father's ships ever again.

After that all the French went home anyway, since their famous Sun King had decided to make another war on England, and Father set me to learning Dutch instead.

My sister Susanna – one year my junior – could never understand how I could live as I did and not go mad.

"You're always studying, Margaret," she said. By this time I had become reasonably fluent in Dutch so that Peg Brown, our housekeeper, said it quite frightened her when I practiced it over the laundry. "Always reading books, and for what? Father has enough apprentices, you know. And I'm sure we do enough in this house as it is."

"It's…" I shrugged. How could I explain it to Susanna, who thought that reading through an overly long letter from an aunt was tedium beyond belief? "It's a challenge. It gives me something to think about, something different and interesting."

"Interesting?" Susanna rolled her eyes. "An old Dutch grammar and a book of sermons? Don't you ever dream of another life, Margaret? Haven't you once in sixteen years thought there could be something other than this?" She waved her arms over the small-beer she was brewing at the time.

"Such as what?" I said. "Be careful; you're going to fall into it."

"What do you think? Romance. Adventure." Her cheeks flushed as they always did when she grew excited, reminding me yet again why the women of Hollyport considered her the family beauty. "Don't you ever look out to sea and wish you could be sailing to the Indies like a boy?"

"Not really. Ships smell, you know, and you have to sleep hanging above cannon."

"Well, not that then. I shouldn't like to sleep among a lot of rough sailors either," she said, in a tone that suggested otherwise. "But there are other things to long for. Adventures of the heart." She lowered her long eyelashes. "Don't tell me you never think of that. I know you had a sweetheart once, even if you did send him away. I wouldn't have."

"Don't be ridiculous, Susanna."

The truth was I had once been handed a sprig of flowering rosemary by an apprentice named Harry with a pockmarked face and the personality of a boiled egg. Father had seen fit to tan his backside for it, but he needn't have wasted his energy. It may have been Susanna's constant hope to have verses written about her in the attic by candlelight, but I greatly doubted that the sort of cross between Mr. Greatheart, Adonis and Robin Hood who was my idea of a suitor would be found among a group of lanky boys with appetites like pigs at a country fair and clothes that were always too small.

"It doesn't matter what I dream or don't dream about," I said seriously. "The fact is that Father is the head of this household and he decides what happens. Our role is to be his dutiful daughters, just like it says in Scripture: *Children, obey your parents in the Lord: for this is right.*" I gave my best motherly look. Susanna shrugged impatiently. "You must know that by now. That's just the way it has been ordained. There's no escaping it."

"Well, you don't have to be such a prig about it," Susanna said into the beer.

I bit back the choice Dutch word that came into my mind. I knew I was right and I wasn't going to be drawn into a pointless argument. Girls like us – or girls like anyone else – had no choice at all over what happened in our lives. We did as our fathers, and then as our husbands, told us to. At fifteen, Susanna ought to have seen plainly how fortunate we were to have had such an active place in the business, ever since Mother died. We could just as easily have been confined to sewing and spinning." Count your blessings," I said with a grin. "And then hurry up and finish that. We need to do the kitchen accounts."

Had I known then exactly what Father was planning for me, I might have been less certain what my blessings were. But that surprise was still to come.

It came on a warm day in July. I was sitting in the small parlor with Martha – the youngest of us three sisters – listening to her read from a well-worn book of instructional verse that had belonged to each of us in turn. The shutters were open and the sun hadn't yet come round to this side of the house. A bright but cool light touched the pale blue paintwork and rested gently on the wall-mounted candlesticks with their mirror backings. It played over Father's chair with its leather back and heavy brass studs. A smell of salt and seaweed wafted in through the open window, along with the cries of gulls and dock workers. This side of the house looked onto the west harbor; the other side overlooked the street and let in some rather more unpleasant smells at this time of year.

"Can I go and play yet?" Martha was saying. "I've read 'In Praise of Prudence' three times over now."

"You still have your chores to do after this," I said. "Peg needs a hand with the..."

I broke off as the door opened and a familiar figure came in. The hint of a rolling gait to his walk showed that he had never forgotten the sea.

3

"Father." I got to my feet and dropped a small curtsey. "I hope you're well today. Do you need me to help with something?"

"Sit down, child, sit down." Father waved the cuff of the somber brown coat he preferred to wear. "Where is Peg Brown?"

"Filling the linen presses with Susanna," I said. "And Mercy and Hannah are shelling peas." (Mercy and Hannah were the maidservants).

"What have you ordered for dinner?" Unsurprisingly, Father took no interest in either linen or peas. But then it was unusual for him to take a hand in ordering dinner either. I started to wonder if something was troubling him. His face was unusually red beneath his grey wig and he kept fiddling with his waistcoat buttons.

"I've got the cold mutton ham from yesterday," I began. "And I told Peg to do an herb pudding because the apprentices always get so hungry, you know…"

"No, no; that won't do at all." Father waved his hand again. "I shall send John out for a lobster. And do we have any claret?"

"I…don't think so. Father, is something the matter? Are we expecting a guest?"

Father muttered to himself for a moment, as if doing additions in a vexing sum. Martha sat silent at the other side of the table, all brown eyes and it-wasn't-me.

"The apprentices must dine in their lodgings today," he said eventually. "I have told them so already. And I will speak to Peg Brown myself. We must have a lobster. And a soup. And John must wait at table. Margaret, child, why are you sitting there?"

"You told me to sit here yourself. Father, are you quite well?" I was starting to become worried.

"Perfectly well, child. But you must not sit around. I want you to go and put on your Sunday dress and make your hair…well, I'm sure one of your sisters can help you arrange it in a suitable manner. And tell Susanna I wish to speak with her. Go, child, go."

I got up slowly, feeling as if I must give him space.

"May I ask who you are expecting, Father?"

Father gave a snort of exasperation. "Hurry and change your dress, child. Mr. Van Guelder will be here shortly and we do not wish to keep him waiting."

"Mr. Van Guelder?" I had never heard the name before. And I thought I knew all Father's clients. "Does he wish to do business with us?"

"Business?" Father blinked as if he had no knowledge of the word. "Mr. Van Guelder is a gentleman-merchant. A traveler. From Amsterdam. And there is much to be done before his arrival. Now go."

Looking back, I think that we all did the very best we could at such short notice. Father was not generally given to announcing unexpected dinner guests, but Peg Brown was a good house-keeper and I felt sure she would rise to the occasion with her usual vigor. From my seat before the looking glass in the chamber I shared with Susanna, I could hear her brisk orders. They mingled together with repeated grumblings from Mercy and the tread of John and Thomas as they ran here and there with baskets and platters. Outside the window, the sea sparkled and glared between the dark shapes of fishing cobles, as the sun rose to its highest point. It was going to be another hot afternoon. I was glad not be in the kitchen, but rather to be changing into a light print dress, which was cool and comfortable, in spite of the many whalebones beneath its bodice. But I couldn't help wondering why I was doing it at all. Surely I would have been of more use supervising the servants while they laid the table, instead of sitting here like Queen Anne on her throne, having the last touches put to my hair by Susanna.

"I hope he is a real gentleman and not just another dull old pottery merchant." My sister paused to inspect her handiwork before ramming another bone pin straight into my skull. "That would be so exciting. We could have cultured conversation, talk

5

of gardening and architecture." I could almost feel her romantic imagination surging into my scalp through her busy fingers. "I'm so sick of boring conversations about revenue and all that."

"He'll have come to talk to Father about business and religion, like everyone else," I said. Father was at heart a Puritan, although he had no desire to go all the way and become an Anabaptist. He was too sound a businessman to stand out from the establishment. But he liked his religion plain and his preaching Bible-based, just as many of the Dutch did. It didn't bode well for a light dinner-time chat. I had sat in on enough conversations with Dutch merchants to know that the table-talk was likely to be as stodgy as the herb pudding I wanted to feed to the apprentices.

"Susanna, are you sure that pin should go there?"

"Trust me." Susanna put another pin between her teeth and took a handful of my hair between her hands. "This is quite the look of the season. Of course, if we were only allowed a few false curls…"

"Well, we're not." My hair may have been unfashionably all my own, but along with the womanly curves I had finally managed to achieve by the age of sixteen, it was my best feature, thick and the glossy color of conkers. The rest of me, I could live without. Susanna and Martha had inherited the large eyes and heart-shaped face that I think had been my mother's. I was left with a strong jaw and a snub nose, neither of which I liked anyone to look at for very long. In fact, I started to wonder if Father had sent me up to get ready early simply because I was naturally the least presentable.

Susanna thrust in the last pin with a final, excruciating stab, and tucked a lace cap firmly into position. I looked at the result in the uneven surface of the glass and felt the usual feeling of deflation. Nothing had improved. The lock of hair left to trail artfully over my neck only seemed to emphasize how long my face was. I grimaced as Susanna peered round over my shoulder with a look of smug satisfaction.

"Exquisite," she said, blowing herself a kiss. I sighed.

"Whoever this Mr. Van Guelder is," I said, "I just hope he appreciates all the fuss he's causing."

Whatever he did or did not appreciate, Mr. Van Guelder turned out to be a surprise.

For a start, he quite obviously was a real gentleman. His bearing and his clothes spoke that at once. Not the English sort of gentleman, with a lavishly embroidered and skirted coat, and a wig curling halfway down his back. Instead he was a rather more sober-looking Dutch variety in a close-fitting dark coat and breeches, long fair hair tied with a black ribbon, and unmistakable silk stockings set off by spotless buckled shoes. For another thing, he was young. No more than five-and-twenty was my guess. Certainly no contemporary of Father's.

And for a third thing, he was heart-stoppingly handsome.

"Oh my goodness!" Susanna breathed in my ear as we came down stairs into the parlor. "Forget conversation. I'll just be looking."

For a moment, I entirely agreed with her. Mr. Van Guelder had the most piercing blue eyes, the straightest nose and the most strikingly sculpted cheekbones I had ever seen. I started to wonder if I had met my Adonis after all. But, as we got closer and the light from the window fell on him more clearly, I noticed just how cold those blue eyes were, and how they rested on me with a look almost like hunger.

"My eldest daughter, Mistress Margaret Rosewood." Father bustled me towards our guest with what felt like embarrassing pride.

"Mistress Rosewood." Mr. Van Guelder kissed my hand, producing a sigh of jealousy from Susanna. "An honor."

"Mr. Van Guelder." I made a deep curtsey and greeted him courteously in Dutch, keeping my eyes low and demure. He had a small sword or hangar at his side with an ivory hilt carved in

7

the likeness of a two hounds devouring a hart. Ivory. An exotic substance. It suggested a connection with the *Vereenigde Oost-Indische Compagnie*: the Dutch East-India Company. And there was something else, I noticed, something less obvious. Something about the smell of him. I couldn't figure out what it was.

And I had no chance to do so. Susanna and Martha had to be introduced and John could be seen hovering in his footman's waistcoat.

"Shall we sit to table?" said Father, indicating the open door to the dining room. "Mr. Van Guelder, do have this seat next to Mistress Margaret".

The business of settling ourselves to dine soon took over from everything else. There were seats to be taken, glasses to be filled, dishes to be passed. Looking up and down the table, I was struck with admiration. Peg and the servants had surpassed themselves in what must have been the hastiest preparation of a guest meal on the English coast. The dining table was covered with a damask cloth, and the best antler-horned knives and forks laid out. A jug of our finest home-brewed ale graced the center. The lobster had made a glorious appearance, along with dishes of peas, beans, pastries and a miraculous soup. The humble mutton ham was disguised with herbs, the suet pudding banished to the apprentices' attic. The sideboard was piled high with plums, raspberries and nuts from the cellar. I thought of the weekly accounts and cringed.

Not only was the food impressive, but the conversation was not what I expected either. Almost as soon as Father had finished saying Grace, it became clear that Mr. Van Guelder had not come to discuss the shipping news or the authority of the Bible.

"I see your boast was true, Master Rosewood," he said after the first dishes had been passed around. His English was excellent, with no trace of a Dutch accent. "You have extremely well-educated daughters." He leaned towards me. "Your father has a rare belief in the education of women, does he not?"

"He believes a good daughter should be taught her father's business," I said. "And his religion." I hadn't expected to be questioned like this.

"And so you read the Bible and your father's account book?" Mr. Van Guelder took a sip of ale.

I felt my face flush. I did indeed read both those venerable texts, but I had the distinct feeling that Mr. Van Guelder was testing me and I didn't like it. I wondered again what it was about the smell of him that was so strange.

"Not only those. I am very fond of *Pilgrim's Progress*. And Father let me borrow *Paradise Lost* from the circulating library. There is much in it that is hard to understand but there is such imagination and awe in it." I had never forgotten the scene in which Satan came upon the world hanging by a golden chain in the midst of the stars; it took my breath.

"Ah, yes, *Paradise Lost. Which way I fly is Hell; myself am Hell.* An unexpected choice for an innocent young girl."

There was something about the way he said the quotation that made me uncomfortable. He put far too much feeling into it than seemed appropriate for the dinner table. And I didn't like the way he kept twisting everything I said. I tried to think of a way to change the subject but, before I had the chance, Martha changed it for me.

"What's that?" she said, pointing to something around Mr. Van Guelder's neck.

Instantly, Susanna and I both kicked her under the table for bad manners, but Mr. Van Guelder merely smiled.

"This?" He drew out a pendant on a brass chain. Contained in a brass setting worked to look like a flaring sun, was an uneven, rough-looking stone that glittered here and there as though sprinkled with diamond dust. "I should imagine your father can answer that."

Father leaned forward, peering under his wig. "It looks like some kind of lodestone. A magnetic rock, child, of the sort our forefathers used to make their compasses and guide their ships. Before our modern age." He smiled.

"Indeed. Once the possession of my own father, now no longer with us." I thought I detected a slight sneer to his lip as he spoke. "If you will believe it, Mistress Rosewood," (I noted he turned his attention immediately back to me), "this rock represents the very pinnacle of Dutch exploration. A trophy brought back from the lands that lie beyond the edge of the map. Those lands that cannot be reached except by those who are seeking something else." He waited until Martha's eyes had grown as large as her own dinner plate before adding: "For those who care for such travelers' tales."

Susanna and I exchanged glances. As was to be expected, a fair amount of travelers' tales had passed around this very table over the years. And despite what I told my sister, part of me had always wanted to believe they were true.

"Would you like to play a little game?" Mr. Van Guelder leaned across the table towards Martha, the pendant still hanging from his finger. "Shall we see if our lodestone can locate your sister?" There was a gasp of anticipation from Susanna, but I already knew which sister he meant.

"I'm not sure I care for games, Mr. Van Guelder."

"Oh, come." His blue eyes glittered as the stone swung lazily. "It is the simplest thing. Touch your finger to the stone. I shall close my eyes. Then stand anywhere you wish in the room and we shall see whether the magnetic pull of the rock is drawn towards you."

The way he looked at me was making me feel more uncomfortable by the minute, and I had no wish to be singled out in some ridiculous game, but Martha was already crying: "Oh go on, Margaret, do!" and even Father said quietly: "Oblige our guest, Margaret."

"Very well, then." There was no other choice. I put the tip of my finger on the lodestone. It felt smoother than it looked and surprisingly warm. My finger prickled; it was the sort of sharp stab you can sometimes get from stroking a cat too long.

"Anywhere in the room?" I said. Mr. Van Guelder closed his eyes. "Anywhere at all."

I eased my way over to the window, as quietly as possible, feeling the sea breeze across my lower back. My chest rose and fell beneath the constricting whalebones. Slowly, Mr. Van Guelder pushed his chair back from the table, rose, and without the slightest falter or slip, walked over to the window and took my hand.

Susanna decided to get in her bid for attention.

"That is a wonderful demonstration, Mr. Van Guelder. Truly amazing."

"Nonsense." Mr. Van Guelder was still holding my hand, rather more firmly than I would have liked. I could feel a shudder building up somewhere across my shoulder blades. "It is as I suspected. Your sister is naturally attractive."

The rest of the meal passed without incident. We ate the nuts and raspberries, and then Father and Mr. Van Guelder retired to Father's study to smoke their pipes or discuss the shipping forecast, or do whatever it is men do when women are not present. I busied myself trying to work some embroidery for when they returned and to ignore Susanna's swooning over our guest's features.

"So tall, so distinguished. And those eyes, Margaret, did you see?"

"Yes."

There were times I heartily wished my sister would be silent. I was still cringing over that hideous game. I kept remembering the feel of his hand closing round mine, his mocking of my obvious plainness by comparison to my sister. The way he had found me with his eyes shut had been nothing more than a trick for a gentleman's amusement, I was sure, but I still couldn't believe Father had permitted it. To let him touch me, come so near. He had been close enough to...

To smell. Suddenly it struck me what it was about the smell of Mr. Van Guelder that I found so odd. He had no smell. Not of pomanders, nor snuff, nor bodily odors, nor sea spray, nor anything else. Mr. Van Guelder smelled of nothing at all.

"Margaret, child, I must speak with you in my study."

I scarcely noticed that Father had come back into the parlor. He was alone. Our guest, it seemed, had left. I made a curtsey and followed him across the hallway into the small room next to his business chamber. The bizarre realization I had come to a moment ago still buzzed around my mind as I went. It seemed to color the most familiar objects with an eerie unreality. Father's writing desk with his quills, knife, ink and sander. The drawers below it containing his certificate from the Guild of Master Mariners, his precious maps and the apprentices' indentures. The calf-bound books in locked bookshelves, and clay pipes ranged on the window ledge. All looked in that moment like curiosities at a fair, things I could hardly name the use of.

"Take a seat, Margaret." Father, I noticed, had chosen to stand and was half-gazing out the window to where the front of the house opposite almost met ours. "Mr. Van Guelder has taken his leave of us for today, but he has asked me to convey to you that you are everything he expects of a young woman. Modest, intelligent...well, I am sure he can tell you the rest himself. In short, Margaret, he has asked for your hand in marriage."

The very dust in the air seemed to stop falling.

"Mr. Van Guelder is a wealthy man, with property in Amsterdam and in the East Indies. He asks no dowry and will provide everything you need." My father swallowed, as if struggling with emotion. It was not like him and it frightened me. "This is more than I expected for any of you girls. Much more. My dear, I have accepted his proposal. You are to be married in one month's time."

2

The Mysterious Bridegroom

"I don't believe it," said Susanna. "Margaret, you are so lucky. I hate you."

"Your turn will come, Mistress Susanna," said Peg Brown. "Oh, but it will be a grand day for this house. I must start on the wedding cake just as soon as some raisins come into harbor. Hannah, where is that recipe book?"

It seemed that my forthcoming marriage had created a holiday atmosphere in the house. The servants were transformed. Mercy almost smiled as she offered her grim congratulations and John actually winked at me. And if they were bad, the rest of the household was terrible. Martha begged to be allowed to throw her own shoes at the wedding, and a deputation of apprentices, led by a red-haired, scrawny fellow called James, burst into, "Oh hark! I hear the church bells ringing," at the top of the stairs before running away with much hooting and laughter.

"High spirits; that's all," said Father, when I tried to complain. "We shall all be celebrating shortly."

No one seemed to expect that I should be anything but overjoyed with my sudden change in situation. And since I had barely been able to summon a single word on the subject beyond, "Yes, Father," and "Thank you," they had no reason to think otherwise. I wasn't trying to deceive them. I hardly knew what to think myself. My thoughts had become frozen in my brain the minute Father had spoken the word *married*. Just one small word now loomed larger than my entire existence. Married. Married. That uncanny man's wife. And with no warning either. Of course, I had known that a marriage would probably be arranged for me at some stage, but this...this... Nothing had prepared me for it. As early as tact allowed, I got out of the way and sought refuge in a goose-feather pillow and sleep.

When I woke the next morning, the world looked much the same as it had before. The boats stood on the shale at low tide, and the earthenware jug and bowl were there on the washstand as usual. It didn't seem credible that the events of yesterday had happened. It was only the tense feeling in my stomach that told me all was about to change beyond recognition. And I didn't want to think about it. As soon as breakfast was over, I went out into the small garden between the main house and the kitchen buildings, as if work and the sea air could somehow blow my betrothal away.

It was not such a warm day as the previous one. The sea breeze ruffled my skirts and apron and made my cap strings flutter. I had taken a knife and a basket to cut lavender. I leaned over to drink in its timeless scent, as fuzzy bees bobbled around the pale purple flowers.

"I need to get a good basketful," I told myself. "Enough to hang for the winter. That way, there'll be some for pomanders, some for the linen chest, a little for Martha's pillow..."

But I wouldn't be here in winter. I would be... Where would I be, I wondered? In Amsterdam? In Mr. Van Guelder's bedchamber? I slashed determinedly at the lavender stalks, trying to erase the memory of cold blue eyes and a hand closing over mine. I passed bunches from the flowerbed to the basket as though I were operated by clockwork. One more handful. Another. Another. Keep going. Don't think of anything beyond the garden.

"Master Rosewood said I'd find you here," said a soft bass voice behind me. "Haven't you a kind word for an old sailor, then?"

"Kit!"

I spun round to face a lean man of mid-twenties in a short jacket and breeches of blue-grey. His hair was the color of cornfields and tied in a pigtail. He burst into a grin all over his sun-browned face, revealing teeth that were crooked in the extreme.

"How do you do, sweetheart?"

He held out his arms and I threw myself into them like a child. His clothes held a faint smell of tarred oak and tobacco, but I didn't care. Father's first ever apprentice and adopted heir to the business had been the closest thing we girls had had to a brother growing up. All his visits had been occasions of celebration ever since he got his first posting as a lowly yard captain. I held on tight while Kit gently patted my back, and then let me go, looking me up and down with brotherly pride.

"Just take a look at you! Anyone would think you were bound to be a bride soon."

So he had heard the news already. I scowled and suppressed a shudder.

"Must we speak of that?"

"Easy, Queen Mab!" Kit spread his hands. The calluses of a mariner used to rope-work ran across the palms. "I thought it you girls were all for weddings. Lace and ribbons and all. And off to be a gentlewoman in Amsterdam, too." He caught the look in my eye and his voice softened. "Too sudden, hey? Don't fret; Master Rosewood's ships are always going to Amsterdam. You won't be lonely. I might even show my ugly face if I get back from China in one piece."

"China? Why? What's your news?" I almost knocked over the lavender basket in my eagerness.

Kit grinned. "Came here to tell Master Rosewood myself. I've got my first commission with the East India Company. Second mate on the *Hopewell* bound for Canton. Sailing on the fifth of August. I collect my new uniform from London at the start of next week."

"Oh, Kit, that's wonderful!" I said. "But you'll stay till then, won't you?" Any hint of normality – or indeed anything that would take the focus off me and stop the servants from going on about bridal blessings – was more than welcome. "I'll get Hannah to make up your bed in the back chamber. John and Thomas can squeeze upstairs. It's such a joy to see you, Kit."

It was a joy; there was no doubt of that. Within moments of our meeting in the herb garden, the whole household had descended and my wedding was temporarily forgotten. Poor Kit could barely stand for the flurry all about him. Susanna and Martha were proudly showing how much they'd grown, and the four apprentices were a veritable cacophony of new skills and hero-worship. It took a Herculean effort on the part of John and Thomas to simply bring in Kit's trunk and set him up in his old room again.

I was soon so swept along in it all that I forgot my betrothal myself for a time. Everyone was talking at once and drinking one another's health over dinner. Father was asking for news of this ship and that captain; Kit speaking of the Straits of Gibraltar and the Afric coast. By the time we had eaten, it felt like a merry and ordinary house once more. So the last thing I expected – once Father had taken Kit to assist the apprentices in their lesson with the sextant – was to be informed by Hannah, as she bobbed a curtsey in the doorway:

"If you please, Mistress Margaret, Mr. Van Guelder is here."

"Already?" I leapt to my feet before the words had even left my mouth. I think for a moment I fancied he was coming to take me to the church immediately.

"Yes, Mistress Margaret, and your father said you were to dress for a walk if he called today." She beamed. "It's a fine day for it."

Mr. Van Guelder was waiting for me in the parlor by Mother's old harpsichord. He was wearing the same dark coat and breeches as the day before, and a three-cornered hat to match, which he took off to me as I arrived.

"My love," he said with a formal bow.

I glanced around anxiously, fiddling with the bow on my own straw hat.

"Won't we need a chaperone?" I would have given anything just then for Susanna's ceaseless chattering, or even Mercy's grim silence.

Mr. Van Guelder smiled; a radiant smile that would have turned most girls' legs to water.

"My dear Margaret, we are shortly to be man and wife. It is hardly improper. Besides, we should get to know one another."

"Yes." My voice came out as a strangled squeak. The thought of knowing Mr. Van Guelder better turned my blood cold. Susanna had spent much of the night making suggestive comments about bedchambers, which I now found hard to drive from my mind. And then there was that eerie lack of smell. Had I imagined that?

"Perhaps a stroll along the sea front?" My betrothed suggested. "The tide is going out at present."

I managed a sort of nod, and Mr. Van Guelder took my arm. Out on the street, the closely-built houses cast oppressive shadows and the gully running down the middle of the road threw back an unpleasant smell. Despite my predicament, I was almost glad to walk downhill to the sea front. Here the breeze blew a fresh taste of salt in our faces, bringing with it the hiss of the turning waves and the screams of the gulls. Boats large and small stood slantwise on the damp sand, with carts and horses in between to carry the goods back and forth. Customs men came in and out of the round house; holds were opened; loads were hauled. This was the west harbor, home to my father's own ships, and people were bound to know me here. I couldn't decide if the hideous embarrassment of being seen with a man would be worse than taking another route and having no familiar acquaintance within easy call.

Mr. Van Guelder helped me down the stone steps to the beach

and we walked between the scattered ships, out towards the edge of the town. On an ordinary day with Susanna, I might have gathered shells here or stopped to examine rock pools, but now the experience of having to link arms with a man I barely knew turned my movements stiff. I saw nothing but the wooden pattens over my shoes going up and down as I walked, and my petticoat trailing in the sand. The rank smell of seaweed was strong in the sun. Had Mr. Van Guelder brought me this way to disguise his own lack of smell? And what sort of man had no smell anyway?

"I trust you are in good health," Mr. Van Guelder was saying.

"Excellent," I lied. I felt sick to my stomach. "And you?"

My escort gave a snort as if the topic were not worth mentioning.

"It is the gaining of an intelligent and beautiful wife that will complete me. For which I suppose I must offer you my thanks, Mistress Margaret."

"I'm not beautiful." The words slipped out before I realized, but I thought I might as well carry on once I'd started. "So there's no need to tease me. If I am to be your wife, we ought to be honest with one another."

"Not beautiful? I think you deceive yourself, my love. I see many beauties in you. Innocence, gentleness, dutifulness..." He raised his fingers to my cheek. I flinched. That look of fierce hunger was in his eyes again. "No, I will not be disappointed in you, Margaret."

I didn't like the way this conversation was going. I walked a little faster, trying to think of something else to talk about.

"So what brought you to England, Mr. Van Guelder? The spice trade, perhaps?" I stabbed a guess, remembering the ivory sword-hilt and his property in Batavia.

"The search for a wife, naturally." The way he spoke, I couldn't tell if he was teasing or not. "And a little other – ah – business. I have taken rooms above the Magpie; do you know it?"

I knew it well. Hollyport's first coffee house was a gannets' roost of news and opinion for ship owners and merchants. Father spent time there every day, except the Sabbath. "Your father has been a most informative and helpful acquaintance. I was glad to offer him this alliance."

"I see." The sudden swing from intimate gestures to gentlemen's agreements left me more confused than ever. I supposed this was how betrothals worked, but something seemed very odd.

"We are all most grateful to you, Mr. Van Guelder," I said to my shoes.

His hand caressed my wrist. I could hear my own pulse in my ears.

"Call me Holman, my love."

"Perhaps when we're wed." I took a step back. As I did, I thought I felt a slight pull in the air, something like having one's finger caught in a cobweb. Only this was something I could feel through my whole body, very faint but definitely there. My eyes caught the glint of the brass chain round Mr. Van Guelder's neck, partly hidden by his cravat. He was still wearing the lodestone. What was it he had said about it yesterday? Something about the magnetic pull of the rock being drawn towards me. But that had been just a trick, hadn't it? An excuse to hold my hand.

Mr. Van Guelder saw where I was looking and smiled.

"A remarkable thing, is it not? I can see it fascinates you, my love. Touch it again if you wish."

Did I wish it? I hadn't thought I did, but then why was I still looking at it? And what was that strange feeling I had felt just then? Cautiously, I moved my free hand closer to the stone, and there it was again: a small but insistent tug as though my hand was pulled by a current at sea. Mr. Van Guelder gave a soft laugh. I snatched my hand away and put it behind my back.

"Attraction, you see," he said, with a roguish smirk. "It ought to be mutual between man and wife, don't you think? And I believe, Margaret, that we will be deeply attracted to one another. Shall we walk?"

There were walks every day after that. While the rest of the household was busily quizzing Kit about the East Indies or seeking recipes for a wedding breakfast, I found myself thrown into a bizarre new life of leisure that was far from relaxing. There was no time for reading or languages now. Mr. Van Guelder called each afternoon. I soon learned to go straight from dinner to change out of my working cap and apron in order to meet him in the parlor. I had to leave Susanna in charge of the household, and James and Henk – the older apprentices – responsible for my business tasks, under Kit's temporary supervision. I supposed this new arrangement was the way things would be after I had left home, but I didn't give it too much thought. Too often the fear of walking with my betrothed chased everything else from my mind.

We took various routes: sometimes along the sea front, sometimes up through the town and onto the cliffs, sometimes following the stream to the woodland on the edge of our local squire's land. The betrothal had been announced now, and every-where we went, I was stopped by congratulations. Captains' widows and trade guild wives, girls my own age and everyone we dined or went to church with: all had to torment me with their good wishes.

"Such a handsome husband! If you'll permit the compliment, sir."

"A pity you're to leave so soon. But a good match can't wait. Your father must be delighted."

"And will you have a carriage in Amsterdam, Mistress Rosewood? And a lady's maid?"

I tried to answer the questions as best I could, but the truth was, I still knew no more about my new life than they did. I kept trying to ask Mr. Van Guelder about Amsterdam. What did it look like? Was it really the mass of canals and warehouses I had heard about? How many rooms had his house? What were my domestic duties to be? But he seemed strangely reluctant to answer. He would turn all my questions with replies like: "There is no need to concern yourself with that," or, "One place is much like another," until I daren't press the matter any more.

I got little further trying to ask him about his business interests in the East Indies. Since Kit was about to go there, I thought he might have told us something of the Spice Islands or the Dutch colony on Batavia but he made no mention of either. When I once mentioned the Dutch East India Company, he turned to me with what looked like a snarl.

"The *Vereenigde Oost-Indische Compagnie*! Curse it for a tyrant! Forgive me, my love, but there are things you cannot understand. My father may have gloried in nutmeg and cloves, but if the Spice Islands keep me in food and clothing, that is as much as I wish to think of them."

"But I imagine spice will be keeping both of us in our new life," I ventured. I had already had a hint of Mr. Van Guelder's true wealth. In the hurry to prepare for our wedding, he had paid the local seamstresses and milliners twice the usual amount to have my wedding clothes ready by the appointed day. He had hinted, too, at a visit to the goldsmith's. His wealth must have been far in excess of Father's. "You know the verse: *Remember the Lord thy God: for it is he that giveth thee power to get wealth.* It applies to us all, does it not? We should all be grateful for what we have to live on." I smiled nervously.

Mr. Van Guelder gave a hollow laugh, as though I had made a ridiculous statement.

"Living, my love, is an over-rated activity." He kissed my hand, almost violently. "Our union will be so much more."

I didn't like him kissing me. On our walks, I did everything I could to avoid it. It was not so difficult in the town. Propriety dictated that we keep a modest distance from one another, and

Mr. Van Guelder would have been a fool to tarnish my honor in front of all the neighbors. But up on the cliff top or in the woods, on the lonelier paths out of sight of sailors and tradespeople, the hunger in his cold blue eyes was unmistakable. I tried my best to show no fear, but his expression showed that my attempts were feeble at best.

"Blushes become you," he said in his half-mocking way. Then he seized my hand and pressed his lips to the inside of my wrist. "Such a pure, innocent bride. How I have longed for this."

"Mr. Van Guelder!" I tried to release my hand, but his strength was three times my own. "Our wedding day."

"Indeed." He released my hand and breathed deeply, looking out to sea. "We must be fully united in every sense, as man and wife. It is the only way to gain true peace."

I didn't know what he meant, but I didn't really care if I could manage to stem the kisses. The lodestone, however, was another matter. Each day when Mr. Van Guelder called on me, there it was at his neck, rough and glittering in its brass setting. And each day as we walked, I felt the same pull as I had on the first day, every time a fraction stronger. I was sure I was not imagining it. I kept thinking back to the "game" in my father's dining-room, and the way Mr. Van Guelder had found me so quickly. On our walks too, my betrothed seemed to have an ability to keep very close to me. If ever I should wander off – to look at a pretty bunch of ribbons, say, or a starfish in a rock-pool – there he was at my shoulder again, however far from his sight I had gone. Perhaps he just had quick instincts. Perhaps not.

Back at home, the wedding preparations rolled unstoppably ahead. Peg finally had the raisins for her cake, and was now fretting that a few weeks was much too short a time to produce a decent flavor. Susanna kept fluttering her eyelashes and puckering up in my direction every time she thought Father wasn't looking, and making suggestive jokes when he was out of the room. As for Father himself, he was in his element.

"You make me very proud, child," he said, taking my hand in the parlor one night. "My only regret is that your dear mother is not here to see this day. But I am sure she looks down on us from glory and approves this happy circumstance."

He wiped away a tear as he spoke. I could think of no reply. How could my mother – who I remembered as only good and kind – want me to be a wife to Mr. Van Guelder? I couldn't understand why no one else could see anything strange in my future husband. He had no smell. Could no one else detect that? When I had tried to suggest as much to Father, he merely said, "Don't be ridiculous, child," and began giving me a most unwanted lecture on The Wife of Noble Character. Susanna had simply laughed, and Peg had felt my forehead and given me an herbal tonic. Was I living in a houseful of people missing one of their five wits? Or was I gradually being driven witless myself? I sincerely hoped not.

One night, Kit and I were sitting up alone in the parlor. Father had just said prayers and everyone else had turned in for the night. I was in no hurry to get to the chamber I shared with Susanna. Since the betrothal, fraught dreams or sweaty sleeplessness were all I could look forward to at bedtime.

"Doesn't anything strike you as odd about Mr. Van Guelder?" I said. He had dined or supped with us a couple more times since Kit came home, and Father's heir had had as much chance to observe him as anyone else. "Something eerie. I don't want to marry him, Kit. It's not just nerves; I think there's something wrong about him. Can't you speak to Father?"

Kit was filling his pipe and stretching his legs across the chimney corner. Red light glowed on the fire brasses. He put the tobacco pot down and looked at me seriously.

"No, I can't. And it makes me sad to hear you talk that way. It's not like you, Margaret. I'm going to sea soon. I want to think of you as a happy bride who made her father proud." He sighed. "Master Rosewood only wants the best for you, just as he does for everyone else in this house. I know it's a big thing for a girl to marry and you're bound to be fearful, but if your father approves of Van Guelder then he must be a decent man. Don't you think?"

"But..." I was starting to sound like an infant now. After all the lectures I'd given Susanna and Martha on duty, now it looked like I was disobeying my own lessons. But there was something seriously untoward going on. I knew it.

"But Kit, he has this stone. He said it came from the lands beyond the map. That it can attract people, the way a lodestone attracts iron."

"I know; Susanna told me." I got the feeling Kit was trying to end the conversation. Was he so desperate for a smoke that he couldn't be bothered to hear me out? I scrunched up my fists in frustration. He gave a tilt of his head, making his pigtail loom as a shadow on the wall. "See, there you go. He's quite the man, wouldn't you say? Wooing a bride and entertaining her sisters at the same time. I'd say that counts in his favor."

This was getting nowhere. "But what if it's real? The stone."

Kit gave me a stern look. "Stop it, Margaret. That's gone far enough. You know your father doesn't hold with superstitions and I didn't think you did either. If I didn't know better, I'd say you've been reading too much poetry. Now, maybe this isn't the match you wanted, and maybe it isn't what I expected either, but Mr. Van Guelder is to be your husband and you've got to respect him. For Master Rosewood's sake. This match means everything to him. I said the same thing to Henk and James."

"Henk and James?" My heart quickened. Had the apprentices noticed something no one else had? "Why? What did they say?"

"Only some nonsense about seeing Mr. Van Guelder lying drunk outside the Dolphin Inn by the east harbor. The other afternoon when he was walking with you. I told them they shouldn't be anywhere near the east harbor and they were lucky it was me they told and not your father or he'd tan their hides."

"While he was out walking with me?" This was getting stranger by the minute.

"Which is why it's utter nonsense." Kit went back to stuffing his pipe. "Believe me, sweetheart, you've made the safest match in Hollyport. You're going to be set up for life. A gentlewoman with your own home. So stop worrying and start enjoying it."

But I couldn't stop worrying. I lay awake that night in the bed I shared with Susanna. I listened to the creak of the heavy bedstead as she turned in her sleep and I thought about Mr. Van Guelder: his sneeringly handsome face, his lack of smell, and that stone swinging round his neck, pulling, pulling. Was all this really just nerves? Maybe all girls betrothed to be married felt as I did. I remembered the tales Peg used to tell us round the fireside in winter: tales of girls married to monsters who turned out to be princes in disguise. But what if the prince turned out to be a monster? I shuddered.

I thought about what Kit had said: of Henk and James saying they'd seen Mr. Van Guelder while he'd actually been elsewhere. That was a strange tale. The Dolphin Inn had a terrible low reputation. It was hardly the place for a respectable Dutch gentleman. Perhaps the apprentices had taken a drop to drink themselves before seeing that particular vision. But I couldn't be sure of anything any more. All I had to go on were feelings and hearsay. I needed proof.

I pushed aside the bed curtains and dropped my feet to the sand-scrubbed boards. The shutters of the windows were still closed, but a few lines of sunlight pushed through and made mathematical patterns on the painted wall behind me. I would test the lodestone. I would do it today. Then I would know for myself if I was imagining its powers or not.

I waited until we were well into our daily walk. We had taken a path upwards through the streets of the town, away from the sea. The mid-day smell of cabbage leaves, fish heads and other unsavory matter was at its height. As we walked past the shop fronts – apothecary, drapers, shoemaker – their overhanging upper storeys looked as if they were closing in on us.

"I feel stifled," I said, plucking at my bodice. What I was about to do made my heart pound. I hardly needed to act the part of being hot and flustered. "Holman, dear, may I let go of your arm for a moment?"

Holman, dear. The words stuck in my throat. I wondered for a minute if I had gone too far in my act, but Mr. Van Guelder looked down on me with one of his radiant smiles.

"Of course, my love. But perhaps you would prefer to sit down?"

"But where would I sit?" I released my arm and began flapping a painted fan Mr. Van Guelder had given to me only two days previously.

"Oh, some shopkeeper will oblige. Leave that to me."

I waited until the moment his attention was taken from me, and then I picked up my skirts and ran as hard as I could up the hill, dodging townsfolk, children and sheep as I went. It was the first time I had gone anywhere unchaperoned, but I knew exactly which path to take. Dust kicked up from the dry streets and dirtied my hems. I turned up a flight of stone steps and, gasping, made for the churchyard on the top of the cliff. If I was to try this mad experiment, at least I would go somewhere respectable.

My chest felt like it would burst by the time I reached the lych-gate. Whalebone corsets and all-out sprints did not make a good combination. But there had been something else hindering me too: a force trying all the time to drag me back, so that my run resembled those in dreams where you struggle to reach some important destination but never manage to arrive. I could feel it now as I leaned against the inside of the gate, the back of my neck going hot and cold. The recoil of something that had been stretched out tight and was now closing in. Closer and closer. I rubbed my hand across my eyes.

"Well, you have proved yourself a healthy bride, at least." I looked up. Mr. Van Guelder was standing directly in front of me, one hand resting casually on his sword hilt. He did not seem remotely out of breath. "But I rather doubt this little episode has achieved much, except to shorten your wind." His free hand reached up to finger the lodestone. "I do not advise you to try that again. Not now that you realize how much – shall we say attraction – exists between us?"

My gaze flickered from the stone to the sword and back. I took a step nearer the church, vaguely wondering if I could claim sanctuary.

Mr. Van Guelder's lip curled. "Do you imagine I would harm you? Oh no, my love. You are too valuable to me for that. Now come here." He held out his hand. "I have something to give you."

I looked around me, wishing desperately that someone else would come along. They didn't. I was alone in the churchyard with Mr. Van Guelder and my worst fears were coming true. My betrothed husband was in possession of a stone from God-knew-where and he was using it to gradually draw me to himself, day by day, hour by hour. If I didn't do something, eventually there would be no escape.

"I said: come to me, Margaret."

I lowered my eyes and took a step towards my future husband. I felt like I was sealing my own doom. Mr. Van Guelder took something from inside his waistcoat and held it towards me.

"In honor of our betrothal. I have had the goldsmith engrave it with a quotation from your favorite *Paradise Lost*. To express all that I hope for in our future together."

It was a gold ring, of heavy foreign make, obviously an heirloom. I held out my hand as Mr. Van Guelder dropped it into my palm, willing his fingers not to touch mine at all.

"I never said it was my fav..." I began feebly, but my voice faded away as I held up the ring and read the inscription the skilled master craftsman had toiled into the night to put there. The expression of our future life.

One flesh, one heart, one soul.

My heart sank.

3

A Terrifying Revelation

By the time I got home, my legs could barely hold me up. This was not simply my imagination. The lodestone did have power; my betrothed had as good as admitted it. My innards recoiled as I was forced to go through all the parting bows and courtesies with him. I didn't want Mr. Van Guelder anywhere near me, let alone kissing my hand and giving his best wishes for my father's health. The moment he left, I collapsed back against the doorframe, my palms sweating. I couldn't take it any more. I didn't care how disappointed Father would be. I would go to his study and tell him that my betrothal was a terrible mistake. He couldn't allow his daughter to go through marriage to a man who had such inhuman power. Whatever honorable agreement he had made, he must see that. I took a deep breath and squared my shoulders. I would do it now, before I lost my nerve.

I opened the inner door and almost ran straight into Martha. She came hurtling towards me with a grin that looked set to crack her face in two.

"Guess what? Guess what? We're to see Kit off from the East India Docks when he sails!"

"Beg your pardon?" I said; my thoughts scattered. Martha began dancing round me as if I were a maypole.

"Father's arranged it all this afternoon. Just think: a visit to London and a wedding in one month!"

"Don't be silly, Martha. We can't afford that." But a growing worry was nagging away at my stomach. The next moment, Susanna came across the hallway with Hannah.

"Margaret; you're back. Ooh, you've got a ring! Look, Hannah. Isn't it gorgeous? Mr. Van Guelder has such exquisite taste."

"Never mind that," I said. "What's all this about going to

London?"

"Martha!" Susanna scowled. "I was going to tell her that. Well." She leaned forward confidentially. "It's all down to Mr. Van Guelder. He's such a patron, Margaret! His house must be all over silver and gold. He wouldn't take no for an answer, Thomas says. He heard it last night. Not that I condone servants listening at doors, but it's such fun, isn't it? He's paid for the whole trip. Kit is overjoyed. And Father, of course. He's been longing to see Kit as first mate, although you know he'd never say. And now it's all happening! Mr. Van Guelder is a marvel. He's coming to join us on horseback for a tour of the sights, and he's promised us all new clothes. We'll be parading in silk gowns through Amsterdam next."

"I don't want a silk gown. I like my white petticoat," said Martha.

"Enough!" I said, putting my hand to my midriff. I could feel myself swaying again. How dare Mr. Van Guelder do this? It was a deliberate act; I knew it. He was buying the whole household with generous gifts, so that I couldn't possibly speak against him. If the betrothal were called off, the visit to the East India docks would be too. I could see in an instant what that would mean to both Kit and Father. It would be an unspeakable blow, and all my fault. Kit was going to the other side of the world, for crying out loud! It was a year's voyage at least, in dangerous waters too. No one wanted to speak of the possibility we would never see him again, but it was there. My family would never forgive me if I denied him a final farewell.

"It's wonderful news," I forced myself to say. "Kit will appreciate it so much."

Martha tugged at my sleeve.

"Susanna says I mayn't sit next to her in the post-chaise, but that's not fair, is it, Margaret? I can sit with you, can't I?"

"Of course, darling," I said, faking a smile. I wondered how many more smiles I would have to fake before long.

The night of Kit's departure for London came at last. To my relief, Mr. Van Guelder was not present for the occasion, and everyone made an effort to make it as merry as possible. The servants and apprentices were permitted in the parlor (though it was something of a squash) and we all enjoyed the familiar hymns and tales before the fire. The old tunes had never sounded as moving as they did that night. Susanna played the harpsichord and Father the hautboy, and Kit sang in his fine bass voice. When they were done, we all listened, rapt, as Kit told us of his ship, the *Hopewell*, and its cargo of gold and silver bullion, bound for lands of tea and ginger, of monkeys and bright birds. Nobody mentioned storms or shipwrecks.

"Real gold and silver?" said Martha. "You'll be sailing on a treasure ship?"

"Of course, silly." Kit touched her on the nose. "How else do you expect the captain to pay for all that tea and silk?"

"But what if someone tries to steal it?"

Kit took up a manly pose, making Martha and the rest of us giggle.

"Any man caught stealing on my watch will have to run the gauntlet, young lady, and be whipped on the backside by the entire crew. And as for pirates, why, that's what the cannon and the marines are for."

I laughed at the time, but by morning everyone was a little red-eyed, despite our promise to meet Kit in London in a fortnight. As for me, once the house was back to usual, thoughts of Mr. Van Guelder returned even more strongly. Peg had set aside the morning to help me begin to pack my trunks for the journey to Amsterdam. We had decided to lay in storage the cloaks and winter dresses I would not need for some months, with bunches of lavender squeezed between them to keep out the moths. Garments for the more immediate future had begun to take shape too. I now had the blue silk garters compulsory for every bride tucked away in the corner of a small chest. Picturing the moment when Mr. Van Guelder would untie them made me nearly sick with fear. I opened the box to peep at them and had to clasp my hand over my mouth to stop myself from retching.

"Oh, don't you worry yourself," Peg said, seeing the tightness of my features. "It's just bride nerves, that's all. Lord knows I was as frightened as a rabbit in a trap the day I wed Goodman Brown, God rest his soul, and we had many a happy year together. It'll be just the same for you, you'll see." She patted my hand and smiled.

But after she had left the room, I slammed down the lid of the trunk and sat on it, willing the panic to be as easily contained as the yards of woolen and flannel within. Fear was taking over my whole body; my chest actually ached with it. I couldn't just sit here and wait for dinner time to come round again; and with it the inevitable knock at the door and the appearance of that cold-eyed, cold-hearted man. I had to do something.

Was there no weakness in Mr. Van Guelder that I could exploit? Nothing that would give me back the peaceful life I had known before? I thought back over the previous couple of weeks and shivered. There was no advantage to be had. In this game, Mr. Van Guelder held all the cards and the dice too.

Cards. Dice. Disreputable pastimes. The Dolphin Inn! I could follow the rumor Henk and James had suggested to Kit. Maybe there was nothing in it after all, but I must at least try something.

I got up and threw the trunk lid open. Somewhere in here was a thin, black head-shawl. I pulled it out and, despite the summer weather, wrapped it round my head. I hoped it would disguise my features. It would never do to be recognized where I was going. I left my chamber and crept down the narrow stairs as silently as I could. By now, all the servants would be occupied in the kitchen buildings across the garden, and Susanna would be busy taking Martha's lesson. I opened the front door and eased it closed behind me with only the faintest scrape. Then I hurried down the street and towards the shore as fast as I was able.

I did not go down the stairs at the west harbor this time. I turned in the opposite direction and hurried along by the sea wall. Soon I was passing piles of lobster pots. The smell of fresh shellfish mingled in the air with the cries of those trying to sell it. This was the east harbor, home of the fishing fleet. Their cobles and the scraps of flag marking sunken pots could be seen out in the bay. Along the wet beach, groups of fishwives and their children picked their way between the rocks, looking for limpets and bait. Not one in ten of them had any shoes. Further along, someone was pegging out some grubby-looking washing on the sea front. I quickened my pace and kept going. This was no place for an unchaperoned girl of my class, and I knew I was inviting all sorts of trouble, but I wanted to get to the truth of what Henk and James had said. It was my only hope of getting any kind of proof against Mr. Van Guelder.

I didn't quite know where to find the place I was looking for, but I knew it would be somewhere near the harbor. Ignoring the whistles and bawdy name-calling from the boats, I pulled my shawl tighter and turned into what passed for a main street in this part of town. All the houses were in sore need of new paintwork, not to mention new shutters and roof slates. If I thought our street smelled terrible, this was even worse. There was a reek of gin and something that might have been death. Too late I thought about the possibility of smallpox, or even worse.

"All right, maidy?" said a male voice behind me.

I picked up my pace and didn't answer. What did I think I was doing? From narrow alleys, dogs whose bones you could see through their fur barked at me. One young mother with a baby in her arms muttered something I couldn't understand at all, and then slid down the wall to sit in the dust, baby and all. I had been a fool to come here alone. I should have asked James or Henk to come with me. A sensible person would have turned round and run for her life now. Part of me wanted to do it too, but at that moment I saw what I was looking for. Ahead of me stood a graying building with narrow bay windows and a signboard outside displaying a rather underfed dolphin. The creature leaped through waves that the artist seemed to have drawn while actually sampling the inn's brew. Outside it were a couple of tables where sailors of a very different sort from Kit were sitting staring grimly over tankards of something. It was almost unbearably seedy, and it took all the courage I had to take a step or two closer.

"Wha' d'you want?" said a man who had just stepped outside the tavern door. By his apron, I guessed he was the innkeeper. He was red-nosed and unshaven and looked as if he might have used his wig to wipe up spilled beer.

The small courage I had left me. I took a step back, shaking my head. With any luck, he might think I was a poor idiot who had lost the power of speech.

"Well, clear off, then," was his remark. He turned to another, thinner man who had followed him out. "And what exactly am I supposed to do with His Lordship here? Can't pay me in that state and no one's rushing forward to claim him."

"Sexton?" suggested the thin man with a shrug.

"Very funny." The innkeeper took off his wig and wiped his forehead with it. "Even in this miserable hole, sextons don't bury them unless they're dead." He put the wig back on, not very neatly, and gave a sigh. "Just throw another jug of water over him. Today might be our lucky day."

At first I couldn't imagine what they were talking about. It was only after the innkeeper and the thin man had gone back inside that I noticed a third figure in the doorway. He lay slumped with his head back and one arm round an ugly wooden dolphin that served as a second sign. His clothes were stained and may well have had several jugs of water thrown over them, dried out, and then thrown over again. But they were expensive clothes. There was lace at his throat and cuffs – albeit dirty lace – and the coat buttons alone must have cost some guineas. He was wearing tall riding boots up to the thigh that looked as if they had been coated in several months' worth of mud and wet sand. He didn't move. Had it not been for the innkeeper's words, I would have been certain he was dead.

The sight of him made me more nervous than ever. Nothing could be more eerie than a dead man who isn't really dead. But I felt curious too. There was something about the size and shape of him that was oddly familiar. The grim sailors seemed preoccupied with their tankards just then and the thin man hadn't returned to throw his water. I dared to shuffle just a little closer, keeping half an eye out for the red-nosed innkeeper. As soon as I did so, I wished I hadn't, because I could see the man's face and it was a face I knew.

It was Mr. Van Guelder.

That is to say, it was and it wasn't. I had never seen Mr. Van Guelder unshaven or without the black ribbon that kept his long hair in place. Nor had he appeared in anything but the best of health. The face I was looking at was unhealthily pale and covered in blond stubble. The eyes were sunken and shadowed, the mouth hanging open. And his hair, which had probably once been shaven to accommodate an expensive wig, had now grown back in short, fine strands of no particular style. If he was handsome – and he still was – his beauty was in danger of being lost to neglect.

And he stank. Of gin, of mold, of his own bodily functions. The stench of him made me want to retch. I couldn't understand how such a transformation had occurred. It was almost more frightening to see him like this than upright and in control of his faculties. How could he have got like this in so short a space of time? He had called on me only the day before. How could he have been lying here as well? It was not possible.

"I thought I told you to clear off."

I started. The innkeeper had come back, accompanied by the thin man, now carrying a pewter jug. The grim sailors raised their heads, and one of them nudged the other with a look I didn't like at all. For the first time, I noticed an unsheathed cutlass lying on the table.

"Looks like this one's got stuck," said one of the sailors, in a voice that could have belonged to Davy Jones himself. "Perhaps we should offer her some assistance." He raised himself up, leaning on the table. His hand was inches from the cutlass hilt. "Reckon she could do with some, don't you?"

I opened my mouth to scream, but nothing came out. Instead, the sound I heard was that of a sword being drawn behind me, and a familiar voice saying, "I'd thank you to leave my wife unharmed, as you value your lives."

To say the sailors and the inn folk looked like they'd seen a ghost would have been an understatement. They moved so quickly that the cutlass was left abandoned on the table and the poor chap sprawling in the doorway had his hands trodden on. I wished I could run away as well, but I couldn't. My rescuer's hand came down possessively on my shoulder. I could feel the pressure of the middle finger against the bone.

"That was foolishly done, my love," said the voice in my ear. The breath against my neck had no smell.

"How did you know I was here?" It was a stupid question to ask in the circumstances, but the first that came into my mind. In front of me, I could still see the unconscious Van Guelder in the doorway. I daren't turn to look at the one standing behind me.

"I think we both know the answer to that, Margaret. Perhaps now you finally realize that there is nowhere you can hide from your appointed husband. I will always know where you are."

A shudder ran through my body. Mr. Van Guelder chuckled softly. "You will come to appreciate that in time. Trust me."

"Trust you?" I couldn't help blurting the words out. "Which one of you? How do I know I'm not betrothed to…?" I waved my hand vaguely in the direction of the filthy figure in the doorway. "How can…?" There simply weren't words for what I was seeing and hearing. Even with what I had experienced in the past couple of weeks, it defied explanation.

"Him?" I had seldom heard such contempt in the human voice. "He is nothing. A worthless English aristocrat who wastes his inheritance and himself on drink and opium. His sort is ludicrously easy to control, since they have no self-control of their own. I mastered him in a day. He doesn't deserve the body he stands up in." He snorted. "On the few occasions when he does stand."

My brain was aching from trying to piece together the evidence of my senses.

"You control him? With the lodestone?"

He put a hand on my other shoulder and turned me to face him. I kept my eyes low, still not wanting to look at his face. If it even *was* his face.

"I was right about you, Margaret. You are an intelligent young woman. I like that. Yes, with the lodestone. The only heirloom of my father's that has afforded me any pleasure in this life. In time you will come to discover, as I did, its remarkable properties. Studying its use has been my life's work. Truly, it is an extraordinary substance. What uses it had in its own land, we can scarcely imagine. It must have ruled worlds."

He sounded as if he was some kind of Locke or Newton presenting a discovery for the benefit of humankind. It made me sick. This was the man who was using a plundered stone to control people and destroy their lives. To control me.

"Would you believe, my love, that a magnet could channel the will?" he went on. "I can see you are shocked by that, and so you should be: a virtuous young girl like you. But it is true nonetheless. The lodestone attracts what I will and repels what I will. With a little effort and manipulation, of course. The results can be...interesting." He turned his head in the direction of the sprawling man.

My gaze followed his. I was shivering now, in spite of the

shawl and the summer heat. I had an idea in my head about what Mr. Van Guelder had done here, but it didn't seem possible.

"You...have taken his form?" My voice came out hoarse and feeble.

Mr. Van Guelder gave a supercilious smile.

"As I said, he does not deserve it. And for wooing a wife, I'm sure you will agree it is ideal. Unfortunately for him, he will not be able to regain consciousness so long as I share his features. But he was scarcely ever conscious anyway. I doubt anyone can tell the difference."

I swallowed hard, thinking how easily Mr. Van Guelder could dismiss the life of another human being. This was the man I was to marry in less than two weeks. What was it he was planning to do with me?

"Mr. Van Guelder. When we are wed..." I hardly dared ask the question. My thoughts were racing like skittish horses and the possibilities that were coming to my mind were as unspeakable as they were fantastic. "Do you mean to do the same to me? To take my form?"

Mr. Van Guelder threw back his head and laughed. In such a place, in front of such a terrible sight as that poor ruined heir, it seemed hideous. Then he drew me a little closer with his left hand. His right hand reached up to my temple, teasing at a few strands of chestnut hair that had escaped my cap. I shuddered.

"Oh no, my love. What we share will go deeper than that. Much deeper. I will be you and you will be me. One flesh. One heart. One soul. Forever. The perfect marriage."

He tilted my chin upwards with a finger. My nostrils filled with his unreal lack of smell. With horror, I realized he was about to kiss me. Properly, on the lips. This inhuman man, who wanted to swallow me up into himself until I ceased to exist. Here in these dirty backstreets, no one would care for propriety. And besides, he had called me his wife. Who would dare to stop him?

Of all things, I did not expect to be saved by my corset. But as my pulse pounded in my ears and sweat prickled all over my scalp, the pressure on the whalebones just became too great. I felt a wave of dizziness sweep over me like high tide. My legs crumpled. Mr. Van Guelder cursed in Dutch and braced his left arm against my fall. He was indeed strong; I knew that. He put out his other hand to steady me and raised me back up. My black shawl was trailing in the dust; he tossed it over the crook of his arm. I drew in a ragged breath. The moment was broken.

Mr. Van Guelder scowled and breathed heavily through his nose.

"Too soon, too soon, curse it! You flout me at every turn, my love. But it will not be long now." He gave a sigh from deep within his chest. "Would that I was one with you now and this agony would be over."

There was something in his frosty eyes that I didn't understand: a kind of longing or suffering. But it only flickered there for a moment. Then he straightened his shoulders and tucked my arm firmly into the crook of his.

"Come, my love, I cannot have my bride unwell. Allow me to escort you home. You need to rest."

I resented the fact that I was forced to lean on his arm as we turned away from the Dolphin Inn and made our way down the alley towards the sea once more. My head was still swimming and my stomach was in horrible pain from my near-faint. I had to put all my concentration into keeping conscious. Not for anything would I pass out completely and be helpless in the arms of Mr. Van Guelder. We wove our way through the seafront market, with its last baskets of whelks being cried and the gulls rivaling the calls and swooping in as low as they could to steal the wares. My thoughts slipped back to that poor unconscious man at the Dolphin. How long would he lie there? A month? A year? Forever? And, however sinful he was, did he really deserve to lose his freedom, his life, his very self? I didn't know him: he must have come a long way to our little port town.

Was anyone waiting for him to return?

I was thinking so hard I barely realized where we were until I found Mr. Van Guelder knocking on the nail-studded door of our house. An astonished John answered, only to be told that I had been touched by the sun and must be put to bed immediately. Within moments, the household swung into action. Everything was a whirl of fussing and fanning and iced cloths to my forehead. Thomas was lifting me upstairs; the maidservants were traipsing in and out with this and that trusted cure. I didn't need them. I needed to be alone. I pushed Peg away and pulled the curtains closed around my bed.

"Go away," I said. "Just leave me."

"Suit yourself, Miss Impudence, but I'll be in the back chamber when you change your mind."

She shut the door with a click. I turned and put my face to the goose feather pillow.

Tears burst from me like a summer storm. My chest heaved. My nose streamed. I stuffed the pillow into my mouth to stifle the sound, but nothing could stop the wailing in my heart. I sobbed and sobbed and sobbed until there was nothing inside me but a hollow ache. There was no way out of my marriage. No proof. No argument. Mr. Van Guelder was far more powerful than I could even have imagined, and much more evil. He had arranged things so that no one would ever believe me if I told of his crimes. They would think me insane and commit me to the madhouse. And I couldn't take a step without his knowledge. I had no means of escaping him. My only choice was to become his bride. For hours I wept in the sure knowledge that my life was about to end in less than a fortnight's time.

4

The Sailing of the *Hopewell*

I pleaded indisposition for the rest of the day, and the day after that. Part of it was faked, but not all, by a long way. I had cried for a good two hours at least, and my head ached something dreadful. Martha tried to cheer me up by showing me improvements in her embroidery, and Peg brought me possets to drink, but as neither of these two things could take away the horror of becoming Mistress Van Guelder, they didn't make me feel much better.

I had pondered a hundred times over what *One flesh, one heart, one soul* actually meant, and each conclusion I came to was more terrifying than the last. I wanted to throw the betrothal ring away – I hated the way it was always there to remind me of my fate – but the heat had embedded it into my finger and every effort to remove it only caused worse pain. The wedding was getting nearer and nearer, the wedding that would end my life before it had even begun. With a churning stomach, I realized that I didn't even know what my fiend of a future husband really looked like.

"You're doing this on purpose to spoil everything," Susanna said on the second day. "I was going to ask for new hats when Mr. Van Guelder came to meet us in London, but he won't come at all if you're still here in bed. Now we'll just have to stand and wave goodbye to Kit's ship. Without you." She glared. "And then hurry home to our poor, ailing sister. And we won't get to see the markets or the new houses or anything. Mary Trevellyan went last Whitsun and she said it was marvelous. You would hardly know it for the same place since all the re-building work around the river."

"You wouldn't know it anyway; you've never been," I said, but she carried on without as much as drawing breath. "And just look at these beautiful oranges Mr. Van Guelder sent you. He calls twice a day to ask after your health like a true gentleman and you barely send him even a line of a message. I bet you're only staying in bed so he'll end up coming to your bedside."

"Will you please be quiet, Susanna," I said. The thought of Mr. Van Guelder at my bedside made me sick with revulsion. I had already started to believe that I could feel the pull of the lodestone from my bedchamber. It might have just been a sick fancy, but there again it might not. I had to get away from him. I simply had to. I couldn't go through with the marriage. But how was that possible when he could find me everywhere? Anywhere I tried to go, he would catch up with me, and the thought of his anger was terrifying.

"And you're letting Kit down." Susanna continued, regardless.

A sudden thought flashed across my mind. A picture of how I could escape. Was it just too crazy to be attempted? I didn't know, but to find out, I was going to have to get well: well enough to go to London. And I was going to have to be exceptionally brave.

Susanna looked at me, waiting for an answer. I picked up an orange.

"If you don't annoy me today, I think I may start feeling better," I said. "And then we'll see about those new hats."

Father had hired a post-chaise for our journey to London. It was bottle green and very narrow. There was barely enough room for us girls to squeeze inside with Father, and we all felt a little queasy after the first couple of miles. John was riding postilion on Father's horse (the one pulling the carriage) and Thomas was standing on the back plate. I thought that they had the best of it, since at least they had the benefit of fresh air and a little peace and quiet. Inside, it quickly became sweaty as we bumped together over the dry summer roads. Above us, the trunks bounced on the roof. From the way the carriage swayed, it seemed as if my middle sister had brought more luggage than Kit was taking to the East Indies.

"Cheer up," she said, as we juddered over the packhorse bridge that marked the county boundary. I hadn't spoken since we'd left our house at dawn, unceremoniously walking the first bit while the horses got up the steep road out of town. As narrow streets had given way to hay fields, ricks and flocks of shorn sheep, I was sure I could feel a thread stretched out thinner and thinner, yearning to pull me back. I kept waiting for the point at which it would snap – or snatch me backwards.

"It's not meant to be a cheerful journey," I pointed out. "Kit's leaving for distant eastern seas. Anything could happen to him."

Susanna just rolled her eyes.

"He's advancing his career, silly. Father, tell Margaret not to be so miserable. It's a special occasion. And we're going to London. London!"

Father did have to speak then, but only to tell Susanna to stop rocking the carriage because Martha looked like she was going to be sick. She did settle down a bit after that, but if it hadn't been for the ruts in the road and the prospect of Kit's dangerous voyage, her limitless cheer would have made my silence stand out starkly. My mind was racing. One day in London before Mr. Van Guelder came on horseback to join us. One opportunity to get away from him. Had the thread of magnetism broken yet? Was it still there?

We changed horses three times on the first day and twice on the second. Apart from that, we passed through the countryside without incident and with increasing stiffness. The roads were good for the time of year, and such things as thrown shoes and highwaymen might not have existed, for all we knew. The first day's journey took us to the edge of the royal hunting forest, with its smell of burning charcoal. The second took us through villages, villages, coming closer and closer upon each other as we neared the capital. Over and again, we heard church bells, saw the smoke from blacksmith's forges, and smelled new-mown hay as teams of reapers swung their scythes for the last harvest of the year. We sat sore-bottomed at coaching inns, sipping watery ale while John bargained with the ostlers, and kicked one another in scratchy beds to the sound of squeaking mice.

The second day was drawing to an end when at long last the road gradually became busier and busier. Men rode by on horseback and goose girls drove their wares for tomorrow's market. As fields and farms gave way to ever more tightly-packed and taller-built houses, we leaned out of the narrow window to see men leaning likewise from loaded carts and crowded stage-coaches, bellowing red-faced at the ever-growing crowd of walkers weaving their way between the wheels and the horses' heads. Susanna nudged me in the ribs as one coachman took a riding whip to a cooper's boy whose barrels were holding up the whole street, both of whom then let fly with a sharp volley of words, spoken much more harshly than they ever would have been in Hollyport.

We crossed the groaning causeway of shops and houses that is London Bridge. It heaved with sailors on shore leave, beggars with sticks, pigs, dancing bears, chalky stonemasons, stray dogs, toy hoops and sedan chairs. In the red sunset, we could see the spires and domes and scaffolding of brand-new buildings not even finished. Then Father pulled down the blinds against the dreadful August stench rising from the Thames, and we had to imagine the rest of the journey from the bumps in the road. I honestly thought Susanna's excitement would explode the carriage – right to the point where Martha finally threw up in her lap and she was forced to sit like a stone until we got to the inn.

It was a very different inn from the Dolphin: a house so tall and thin it looked as if it had been squashed, wedged in between a tea-merchant's and a law building. But it was a bustling, friendly place with good clean sawdust on the floor and good clean stables for the horses in a communal yard you got to by driving under an archway by the main door. Our host greeted us with a smile (despite the smell of Susanna's gown) and showed us to an upstairs room where Kit and a hearty supper were waiting for us.

"Bless you, you've arrived at last!" were Kit's first words. "I took the liberty of ordering some vittles: pease porridge, black pudding, bread, cheese, small beer. There's plenty for us all. My, but it is good to see you!"

After such a long day, none of us really had the stomach for it (particularly Susanna, although the hostess had wiped down her petticoat as best she could). But we tried our best for Kit's sake, toasting him several times and wishing him God-speed around the Cape and the Straits of Malacca. Father said a few prayers and we said *amen* louder than usual. The danger of the voyage was beginning to sink in; the thought of it made stomaching black pudding a near-impossibility. But there was no dampening Kit's spirits. He was radiant in his East India Company uniform; the buttons engraved with the famous 'cat and cheese' fairly glowed. His pigtail looked jauntier than ever.

"I'll bring you each a gift from the Indies," he said, giving each of us girls a gentle hug. "A monkey: how would you like that?" He pinched Martha's cheek.

"Just travel safely," I said. My whole body was tense. Kit gave a crooked smile and whispered in my ear:

"Don't fret about me. I'm like a bad penny; I always show up. I'll be in Amsterdam sooner than you know. You just keep your chin up. Everything's going to be fine and you'll have a lovely wedding day."

But after he was gone to his ship, and we had finally got into our chamber – Susanna, Martha and I squashed into an ancient four-poster with scarcely any air – there no longer any cause for jollity. Susanna's ruined petticoat had put a damper on her enthusiasm for London, and Martha spent half the night sobbing that Kit would drown and be eaten by sharks. As for myself, despite the exhaustion of traveling, I could scarcely close my eyes. There were rocks in my chest. Tomorrow was the day. The day when, if I was to save myself, I was going to have to break the heart of everyone I loved, and maybe risk never seeing them again. And how did I know if it would even work? Courage. I prayed for courage all night. And determination. I was going to need both those things like never before.

The East India Fleet docked between Tower Bridge and London Bridge. Father's plan was that we should go there to wave the *Hopewell* off, and then repair to one of the city's many churches to offer prayers for Kit's safe passage. Susanna's request that it be the new St Paul's Cathedral was met by only grunts from my father and an observation from Martha that it was nowhere near finished yet. My second sister had managed to recover her enthusiasm overnight (whereas I was in a state of sleep-deprived agitation). Only now she had completely reversed her ideas of the occasion and was determined not only that she should cry buckets on Kit's departure, but that Martha and I should as well.

"But what if the tears don't come?" Martha clutched the three handkerchiefs Susanna had insisted she carry, as if the future of England was at stake.

"It won't matter." I took her hand and stepped out briskly, avoiding Susanna's glare. "Kit knows we all love him, and he won't see us from the deck anyway."

It was not far to the docks from the inn, but to get there we had to fight our way through streets ten times busier and more confusing than those of Hollyport. It was not just that the streets were crowded; many of them were still being rebuilt after the Great Fire. We would turn a corner between tall warehouses, to find men taking their morning beer from a half-built roof on one side of the street and others chiseling stone cherubs on the other. Everyone seemed to be in a hurry about some kind of business. Butchers hauled mutton sides for the meat market. Heavy-loaded carts went past with no regard for those walking. A number of well-dressed men swaggered by, gold-topped canes in hand, the wide skirts of their embroidered coats swinging. It would be terribly easy to get lost in this crowd. Father had insisted on bringing his old hangar with him, grasping the hilt at all times and saying, "Stay by me, child," to whichever one of us happened to catch his eye. I don't think he trusted a single person and neither did I. But where he saw only threat, I was beginning to see opportunity.

The port of the city of London was even busier than its streets: a very forest of tall masts all along the Thames, with swarms of small boats dodging in between. Covered wagons came and went with cargo (the famous gold and silver coming from the Bank of England itself, Martha decided on the spot). Men drenched with sweat loaded and unloaded. Inside the open doors of warehouses, customs officials checked and counted; crates were opened, examined, nailed shut again. From the decks, bo'suns barked commands, men sang out a reply with one voice and a sail would unfurl. Here and there an officious-looking gentleman in a long, curling wig would step aboard to make sure all was in order. We saw detachments of marines marching to the sound of pipes and drums, and even the awful sight of a pirate hung on a gibbet. But none of these were what we were looking for, and when Father cried, "Here we are, children," we hurried through the crowd as quickly as possible to catch sight of the *Hopewell*.

She was a barquentine: a three-masted ship with square-rigged sails and ports for twenty-eight guns, painted a brave red and blue, and flying the striped ensign of the East India Company. At her bows was a figurehead of a woman wearing a Roman helmet, who stared fiercely at the other ships as if she would like to blast them from the water.

"She ought to be able to keep the ship in order, even if Kit can't," Susanna whispered to me.

By the looks of things, she wasn't quite ready to make sail yet.

The hatches were still open, and not only was the customary be-wigged gentleman still aboard, but so were a vast number of other people, many of them women. Some were no more than girls. That they were the sailors' wives and sweethearts was obvious from the fact that there was a great deal of kissing and crying going on. Some of the women were holding up children for the men to kiss; one resolute girl was halfway up in the rigging, apparently sucking the life out of a dark-haired boy.

"There's Kit!" Susanna screamed in my ear.

She was right. Kit was standing on the quarter-deck, deep in conversation with a thickset man in a tricorn hat. Another man approached him. Kit gave a brisk order and the man saluted. It was strange to see him about his work; he looked like a different person.

"Do we have to start crying now?" Martha plucked at my elbow.

Her little face was so earnest. I couldn't keep all my memories of her from elbowing their way into my mind. Martha nursing her wooden dolls, skipping in the kitchen garden, sitting on Father's lap. Any second it would be now-or-never for my plan, and after that I didn't know when I would ever see my baby sister again. Tears wobbled in my eyes and I kissed her forehead.

"Of course not, dearest. There's nothing to cry about."

"You're crying," she pointed out.

"My eyes are just watering in the wind," I said, taking out a handkerchief. "Go and hold Father's hand like a good girl."

The moment had come. It was now. I wiped my eyes and gripped Susanna by the shoulder. I faked a jolly enthusiasm I was far from feeling.

"Let's go and kiss Kit goodbye. It will be such a surprise for him."

Susanna's eyes brightened in surprise and eagerness. She giggled.

"Do you think we should? What fun it will be!"

A stab of guilt went through me. My impulsive sister was so easy to persuade. I suddenly felt the urge to apologize for every argument we'd ever had. I hoped I'd always remember her like this, smiling and bubbling with life. I hoped she'd make a good mistress of the house and comfort Father and never have to be with a man like Van Guelder.

"Hush! Not so loud. Come on; let's go quickly while Father's looking away. Don't let him see us."

We caught hands and dodged between dock workers, merchants and beggars, down to the water's edge. I didn't even look back. The gang-plank connecting the *Hopewell* to the riverbank was up ahead. I could see it through the crowd. I pushed Susanna in front of me.

"Go on!"

"It's steep. Take your pattens off," she called back.

I tugged them from my shoes and shoved them down my bosom, using my hands to balance. The Thames was hardly the open sea, but I didn't fancy the fall nevertheless. Below us, small rowing craft were being fastened to the ship by ropes, the men at the oars grunting and straining to maneuver. Susanna hitched up her skirts and clambered over the bulwarks between the ropes.

"Kit!" she screamed across the amidships. "Kit, it's us!"

I had one brief moment to enjoy the look of mixed shock and shame that crossed Kit's face. My sister went hurtling towards him, her petticoats flying so wildly you could see her stockings. I just about had time to hear the laughter and whistles from the men in the rigging who obviously appreciated seeing their second mate accosted. I heard Kit, struggling to keep his calm say: "Susanna, go back to your father now," and a hoarse voice from the quarter-deck yell: "Mr. Blackthorn! Resume control there!" But that was all I had time to enjoy, because while so much attention was focused on Susanna, no one on board was looking at me.

This was the moment of opportunity. This or nothing. I had to get to a hatch, and quickly. Preferably the one to the hold or the manger, and definitely one without a man standing watch by it. I squeezed myself as subtly as I could between the sobbing sweethearts, looking left and right through the giant cobweb of ropes.

"Well, I think you're being jolly miserable, Kit," came Susanna's voice. "It's not mutiny or anything."

"Susanna, for heaven's sake!"

I'd heard that tone in Kit's voice before. If she didn't leave, he was going to make her. They mustn't start looking for me. I had to hurry. I edged across the main deck.

The thunderous shot of a musketoon made my heart strike against my ribs.

"Clear the deck!" the hoarse voice roared. "Clear the deck! Batten down the hatches! All hands to stations!"

No time! All around me, I was hearing, "Don't leave me, Hob!" and, "I won't forget you, Mekuria!" The girl in the rigging wailed as a copper-topped man prized her off and carried her down to the gangplank. I had to hide *now*. Wasn't that a hatch there? No time to think. I ran and threw myself down it, slipping on the stairs and bashing my shins right to the bottom.

For the first few eye blinks, everything was dark. Where was I? I rubbed my sore shins and tried to get used to the dim light below deck. This wasn't the hold. It was a gun deck. I knew it well enough from descriptions, although I'd never seen one before, nor smelled its choking smell of candles, powder and tar. By the smoky light of hanging lanterns, I could make out run-in cannons, fire buckets, tables suspended by ropes, and hammocks tied up like cocoons. It was a place to fight, work, eat and sleep. Men could be through here any minute. If I listened, I could hear deep voices echo along the length of the ship. There was no telling from which direction they came. I was too exposed here. I had to go deeper into the belly of the ship and find a place where no one would spot me.

Another hatch. This time on the deck where I stood, leading

down to a lower level. It looked as dark as the pits of Hell down there, and felt as hot. I lowered myself a bit more cautiously this time, struggling to keep my skirts from tangling in the ladder. Then I listened. No good. There were voices getting closer. I heard, "Secure that hatch," and, "Better check the cockpit." Picking my skirts up again, I blundered along the deck, tripping over gun carriages and catching my hem on frayed timbers. At this rate, I would be better ripping my dress off altogether. Men – I thought – had no idea what they were saved from in not having to wear petticoats or corsets. I had to get to the hold or somewhere quiet to hide, but I no longer had any idea where I was going. Everything looked the same: smoky-dark decks of cannon and hammocks and painted sea-chests. To my horror, I heard more voices coming from below. They were going to find me and catch me. Whatever happened, I must not get thrown off the ship.

I heaved myself up another ladder. By now I was panting hard and sweating so my bodice clung to my back. The air was so close. I mustn't pass out now; that would be the end of every-thing. Deep breaths. I must take deep breaths and take stock of my position. My neck throbbing, I looked round to see where I'd come to this time.

Not a gun deck, that was for certain. Here the lanterns were brighter and the walls were paneled in polished wood, just like in Father's study. I looked up and down a narrow corridor. Set into the panels were several doors at regular intervals. Between them, shields were displayed, with what looked like trade guild coats of arms.

"Look lively, Mr. Solomons" said a voice alarmingly near.

My heart shot into my mouth as I realized one of the doors was opening. A voice screamed, deep inside me. *Hide now!* Quick as thought, I seized the handle of another door and flung it open, threw myself through the gap and shut it behind me. I pushed my back against the door, straining with my feet. My heart was going so hard; I could feel it bumping against the woodwork.

The voices were still talking outside, their words muffled. I was not safe yet. Not by a long way. What would I do if they tried to come in? I quickly scanned the cabin I had taken refuge in. There was a small, square window, against which water was lapping gently on the outside. Two teakwood cabinets, bound to the floor; a chair likewise. All this I might have expected in the quarters of an East India officer. But heaped on top of them – and on top of each other, right to the ceiling – were the most incredible piles of paraphernalia I had ever seen. They filled every available space and appeared to cover every conceivable occupation, and several I could not conceive. From a writing desk and piles of papers to a pocket watch and magnifying lens; from a washstand to a saw to a pair of scales with half a dozen lemons rolling beside it: the cabin's occupant had clearly thought of everything. Had I had the leisure to be curious, I might have wondered who on earth would bring such an odd collection of things to sea.

But to one side of the cabin was something far more to my purpose: a built-in cabin bed with drawers beneath it and a patterned curtain across it. It was my perfect hiding place. I climbed in: shoes, pattens and all, and pulled the curtain across to hide me. On the ceiling of the cabin, lanterns and a brass pail swung close enough to clang together. I prayed for them to make no noise. I lay back on the bed and took my pattens out of my bodice, waiting for my heart to stop hammering like an overactive blacksmith's forge. I could still hear voices somewhere outside, fainter now. How long should I wait? How would I know when it was safe to leave and make for the hold? Best wait a little longer, I reckoned. I shut my eyes. My bodice was so tight and I was so hot. I went back to taking deep breaths. The last thing I wanted was to faint. I would lie still and try to be calm...

I should have known what would happen next. Lying on a soft mattress, exhausted from my flight and short on sleep, it ought to have been obvious. I didn't even feel myself nodding off. The very next thing I knew was queasiness in my stomach and a feeling that the world was swaying, followed by the oily smell of a burning lantern. Then came the sound of the curtain being drawn back and a man's voice, clear and educated, saying:

"Well, Mr. Solomons, this is an unexpected surprise."

5

Bound for the East Indies

I opened my eyes. The man looking back at me raised one eyebrow very slowly. Both his eyebrows, I noticed, were very thick and very dark. They gave his face a severity that made him look as if he was angry with me. But there was a sparkle in his eyes that suggested otherwise.

"I think perhaps I should add it to my collection of curiosities."

He was speaking to another, much younger man behind him, a man with a long nose and round spectacles. The young man blinked rapidly and gave an awkward smile. I grabbed a handful of blanket for comfort. Could stowaways be keel-hauled? I wished I had come up with a fuller plan. I had only thought as far as hiding aboard the ship until it was out at sea. That, I saw now, had been extremely foolish.

The first man leaned closer. His hair, as dark and thick as his eyebrows, fell over his face a little, escaping from the brown ribbon that held it back. He was not a young man, but younger than Father, and had remarkably good teeth.

"And does it speak, I wonder?"

Now would have been the right moment to make a convincing speech and gain the man's sympathy, but fear had made my mind go blank, and the first thing I actually said was the most embarrassing imaginable.

"I'm going to be sick."

Down came the pail from where it clanked against the lantern. I leaned over it, just as my guts began to wrench. The dark-haired man held back my hair and wiped my mouth with a cloth. The touch of his hands was surprisingly gentle.

"I see we have a lubber, Mr. Solomons," he commented. "If she can't cope with the Channel, how is she to deal with the eastern typhoons?"

Mr. Solomons seemed not to know what to do about the typhoons either. He suggested, in a barely audible voice, that perhaps the captain should be informed.

"Excellent notion, Mr. Solomons." My discoverer continued to regard me as if I were some interesting new species of tropical bird. "Tell Captain Robinson that Mistress..." He tilted his head, waiting.

"Margaret Rosewood." I felt my face flush.

"Charming. That Mistress Margaret Rosewood has seen fit to grace us with her presence. I shall make the introduction shortly." He indicated the pail. "And send our friend Frenchie along for this."

Mr. Solomons seemed only too pleased to leave. I shrank against the cabin wall, concentrating on keeping the contents of my stomach down. The dark-haired man turned to an iron-bound chest full of square drawers, opened the lid and began to select various glass vials from it. I heard the chink of glass on metal. Shortly, he turned to me with a small cup of liquid in his hand.

"Not the most pleasant of cordials, but it ought to help with the sea legs. All in one draught, Mistress Rosewood, if you will."

It was a command, not a suggestion. The cordial tasted terrible, with a backbite of ginger that caught in my throat. But immediately after swallowing it, my mouth felt less bitter and in a few moments my forehead stopped sweating. By this time, the fabled Frenchie had arrived. He turned out to be an extremely pretty lad of about twelve with a stunted figure and fine, sandy hair. He opened his eyes wide when he saw me, but after picking up the pail, flashed me a conspiratorial grin over his shoulder.

"That will do for now, Frenchie. Find out the barber's case for when Mr. Solomons returns."

"Aye, Dr Lemuel." Frenchie grinned again.

"Shall we?" Dr Lemuel held out his hand to me as if we were

at a private dance. He pulled me up from the cabin bed, supporting me with a hand under my elbow. The eyebrow slid up again as he bent his head towards my ear.

"No need to look quite so nervous. I believe the captain has already dined tonight. He won't be requiring you for second course."

Despite Dr Lemuel's arm, it was a lot more difficult to walk in a straight line than it had been before my unfortunate sleep. The deck seemed not to stay where it was put, but to be a different distance from my foot every time I took a step. Around me, invisible things clanked and creaked. The cordial appeared to have done its job. My stomach was no longer heaving but it still felt as though it was stuffed with rocks. The captain was bound to be angry. I may not be keel-hauled or flogged around the fleet, but I could well be confined to quarters and sent straight back to England at the next port. In view of Mr. Van Guelder, I'd rather be hung from the yard-arm.

The doctor helped me up a ladder to another wood-paneled corridor, even more proudly decked out than the one we had come from. We wobbled past an arsenal of weapons and two petty officers at work counting them. I kept my eyes down at the sight of the men, but Dr Lemuel seemed to find nothing amiss and greeted them cheerily with: "Good evening." A set of double oaken doors at the end of the corridor indicated the captain's private quarters. The doctor knocked at them with a light double rap. I felt absolutely certain I would be set adrift with the tide, without so much as a hearing. There was no point concealing anything, I thought. Someone would find out I was a runaway bride sooner or later. May as well tell the truth and be thought mad than lie and be thought unnatural.

Captain Robinson was sitting behind an oaken table, the great bay windows of the ship's stern behind him and the remains of a good supper in front of him. His uniform was buttoned up in what looked to me like an imposing manner. He did not stand as we entered. I took that for a bad sign.

"Thank you, Dr Lemuel." He waved away a manservant who was standing behind him with a decanter. Then his eyes flashed up at me, with the sort of look that could make seventy men jump to order.

"I trust you have a good explanation for this, young woman. Your actions this day could put the entire ship and crew in jeopardy. The reputation of the East India Company will not tolerate being tarnished by low behavior. Passengers pay. They do not skulk in officer's cabins."

His eyes were boring into me; deep green and stormy as the sea itself. He had a hooked nose, like a bird of prey. I couldn't think of anything to say to him. All the explanations I had thought of outside the door melted away.

"I do take it there was some manner of purpose to this foolish enterprise."

"Begging your pardon, Captain." I dropped the best curtsey I could manage with the swaying floorboards. Dr Lemuel steadied me with a hand. "I was...that is to say, I am..."

There was another knock at the door.

"Come in, Mr. Blackthorn!" the captain barked.

Kit! I had never been so glad to hear his name. He could speak up for me. He was second mate, after all. A word from him had to count in my favor. Relief coursed through me. I looked back over my shoulder to watch him enter, hat in hand, and bow to the captain. My sigh of relief stopped in mid-flow. Kit looked odd; his face was as white as flour and he was shaking. Was he afraid for me? Surely he wasn't seasick too? I tried to catch his eye. He looked back with a glare that shot fire, then turned away from me and stared out the window.

Captain Robinson cleared his throat.

"As you were saying, Mistress Rosewood."

I looked back at Kit. His jaw was tight. He didn't even give me one look. My heart sank. He wasn't going to speak for me after all. I alone was responsible for my action. I had to try and get my thoughts together.

"I was lately betrothed to be married..." My voice trembled and squeaked as I tried to get out the story of Mr. Van Guelder and the lodestone. But my mind kept going blank at crucial points and I was sure it was all coming out in the wrong order. I couldn't take my mind off Kit, standing behind me, as silent as an effigy. And I could feel Dr Lemuel's hand squeezing at my elbow. Meanwhile, the captain tapped with his fork and breathed heavily through his nose. He was losing patience. Any minute now and it would be the brig for me.

"Yes, I think we're heard enough," he said, as I stumbled my way through the episode at the East India Dock. "Mr. Blackthorn, you are connected with the family I believe? What do you know of this?"

"Nothing, Captain." His voice was toneless. My throat tightened. Now I knew why he was so white. Kit was angry with me. He was angry with what I'd done by sneaking on board. He was going to get me thrown off the ship and sent back to Mr. Van Guelder.

"What is your opinion, Dr Lemuel?" the captain said. "Some form of brain malady?"

I looked up at the doctor, expecting an immediate committal to Bedlam. Of course my story sounded like nonsense. I had probably provided him with enough interesting case-notes to keep him busy for the entire voyage. But strangely, the ship's surgeon looked more as if a vivid dream he had almost forgotten had turned out to be true. He shook his head vigorously and ran a hand through his dark hair.

"I wonder, Captain, if I may presume upon our long friendship and take Mistress Rosewood under my protection for the time being? I will write to her father, of course, with Mr. Blackthorn's assistance. We make port at Madeira, do we not? A letter may be sent from there."

"That is quite a presumption." The captain glared over his hawk-like nose.

"Indeed. And I would not make it without the best of reasons. If I may…"

He let go of my elbow and went to stand nearer the captain, where they continued a conversation I could only hear in part. Something about the ship from Bristol in 1699 and, "not the sort of thing one spoke of." And then a rather more heated discussion about length of voyage and the men and what the men might do and, "could lose my commission." I backed up against a paneled door to keep my balance. Kit, still not officially dismissed, stood two paces away with his hands behind his back. He was still looking out of the window. It was fogged up, with the pale colors of a summer evening behind.

"Kit, I'm sorry about…" I caught at the doorknob against a sudden swell. "About having to trick you and show you up and all. It wasn't Susanna's fault; she didn't know. It was me. I had to get away from him. He's not the man you think."

"Don't." He didn't even turn his head. "Do you hear me? Just don't."

"Kit, please. Don't you even believe me a bit?" Only last night he had been smiling and embracing me. Now he was just a glowering statue. "Don't you, Kit?"

"I don't believe you could do that to Master Rosewood." He spat the words. "That's what I don't believe. I thought you were better than that, Margaret."

I didn't know what to say. I hadn't meant to hurt Father, I really hadn't. But no one else but me could know the horror of Mr. Van Guelder's cold eyes, his gripping fingers. Even if the ship flew like a stooping peregrine, it could not go fast enough to take me away from him. Dr Lemuel mustn't write to Father. I looked back to where he and the captain were still in debate. The captain leaned back in his chair and pinched the bridge of his hooked nose. Dr Lemuel looked at me, his expression unreadable beneath the dark eyebrows.

"Mistress Rosewood." The captain fixed me with those commanding eyes. "Thanks to Dr Lemuel's extreme generosity, I have agreed to take you as far as the Cape, where he will make arrangements for your future care. You may use the guest cabin, under his direct supervision, on condition that you in no way interfere with the running of this ship. I trust you are sufficiently grateful. Mr. Blackthorn, you will be relieved to hear that I do not hold you responsible. You may resume your duties."

"Aye, Captain." Kit saluted and left the room without even a glance in my direction. I suddenly felt like crying. Dr Lemuel came and took my arm again.

"Thank the captain and let's be about our business," he whispered in my ear.

I knew full well that I had no business whatsoever aboard the *Hopewell*, but now was not the time to argue. Somehow or another, Dr Lemuel had saved my neck. As to why: I couldn't rightly tell. I managed a curtsey and, "Your very humble servant, sir," to Captain Robinson. He had turned to his sea charts and didn't even look up. The deck rolled and swayed again as we left the room. I tried to swallow back the tears. Kit was nowhere to be seen.

"Well, you are a curiosity indeed, Mistress Rosewood." From the tone of the doctor's voice, the conversation with the captain might never have taken place. "I look forward to observing your manners and disposition in due course."

I had no idea what he was talking about. "I think you saved my life, sir. But I don't know why you should." I could hear my voice going quavery again.

"Let's just say that birds of a feather must flock together. My experience of travel has made me open to the...unusual. Your story interests me."

"So you believe me, then?" My voice cracked. He believed me?

A learned doctor and physician trusting me when my own family wouldn't? I still couldn't get over the disdain in Kit's face. "Please don't write to my father. Please."

Dr Lemuel stopped walking and put his hands on my shoulders. The quizzical, eyebrow-sliding look had gone out of his face; he looked kindly and sympathetic. I wondered if he was a father with children at home.

"I have reason to believe you, yes. You have no cause to worry. But let us say no more of what is to be done with you just yet. First we have to accommodate you aboard this vessel. A task for which I think we will need our friend Frenchie."

Apparently, nothing could have delighted Frenchie more than settling me into my new cabin. His lean face positively beamed with pride.

"Finest accommodation on board," he said, patting a settle that stood between two empty chests. "All this furniture belonged to a previous passenger, miss. Captain's hoping to sell it all at the Cape; so you'll be quite cozy until then."

Cozy was certainly the word. Like everywhere below deck, the cabin was stifling hot with a smell it was best to ignore; but it had a sweet little cabin bed, Dutch tiles and a window you could really see the sky through. It also had all sorts of cunning little drawers worked in here and there and, as a finishing touch, a patchwork quilt with nutmegs and cloves worked into the design. I was sure it was the finest cabin on board, and certainly much better than hanging in a hammock. I had been blessed in my new friends aboard ship. Whatever happened next, I must remind myself of that and offer prayers accordingly.

Dr Lemuel had escorted me to the cabin and then left Frenchie to get on with the main business of settling me in, promising to be back in due course. I asked him again not to write to Father, but all he would say was, "We'll see." In the meantime, Frenchie had been very busy, coming and going with all sorts of things:

sheets, a nightshirt, a bowl of pease porridge, sticks to clean my teeth. The famous bucket and vial of cordial were brought in too.

"To save you from having to visit Saucy Sue in the night," Frenchie grinned. Apparently, I was also to eat all my meals in my cabin and basically stay out of the crew's way at all times.

"And you're to drink your lemon juice every day," Frenchie informed me. "Dr Lemuel says this is to be a healthy crew. He had the captain bring live sheep and chickens with us, and we're to take on fresh fruit at every port. He's a real modern man of science is our doctor." Frenchie beamed proudly, as though he had graduated in physic himself. He clearly admired Dr Lemuel immensely. I felt again that the doctor was a man to be trusted.

"You're to have these clothes too," he added, throwing something on the sea chest. A flush came across my face as it came to me that these were *boy's* clothes: baggy sailor's breeches, a striped shirt and a kerchief. I couldn't be expected to dress as a boy. Father would be appalled.

"I can't wear…" I began, but Frenchie merely held up a very long strip of white linen with a look of satisfaction.

"And this is to wrap around your top half. You won't want that corset again until we make port. Maybe not even then." He winked. "It's hot where we're going."

My blush deepened until I felt I was on fire. How could a young boy stand there and speak of such things with such a lack of embarrassment? It wasn't natural. But I was the one out of place here, not him. Despite growing up in a maritime household, I had no experience at all of life at sea. If I wished to stay, it would be best to do as I was told, however odd the instructions.

"Thank you," I said demurely, taking the cloth from him. I sincerely hoped my figure could be contained by a mere strip of cloth. Mind you, if I was never to leave the cabin, what would it matter?

"Ah, I see you now have everything you need, Mistress

Rosewood."

Dr Lemuel put his head around the cabin door. The sight of him brought back everything that had happened in the captain's quarters. I suddenly felt very small and alone, and the tears I'd been holding in earlier welled up again.

"Do I really have to stay in here all the time? Can't I go with you?"

The doctor shook his head. "Trust me: the surgeons' cockpit is no place for a young girl. Not unless you wish to see a great deal of blood."

I had no such wish. But it didn't change my desire to follow the doctor, if only to escape the silence of my own company. How could I express how it felt to be alone and fleeing for my life, the only female in a crew of seventy men, in the middle of the open ocean when I'd never been in so much as a fishing coble before?

"But there's nothing to read," I said, tears leaking from my eyes. It was ridiculous that of all the miserable things about my situation, I should pick on something as unimportant as a lack of books. But reading had always taken my mind off things; it had been a door to another world outside my own.

"There now, there's no need for that." He took a couple of strides across the room and I felt a fatherly hand touch my shoulder. "There was I thinking a young woman would ask for a comb or some embroidery thread. A curiosity indeed. Here." He passed me a handkerchief. I took it and blew my nose. "I think a wish for books can easily be remedied, can't it, Frenchie? I believe I may have one or two things in my chest beside Mr. Woodhall's *Sea Surgery*."

"Really?" I sniffed.

"Absolutely. I shall look them out forthwith."

I wiped my nose again. "Thank you."

"My pleasure," he said. "And keep your chin up, Mistress Rosewood. You're under the protection of the East India

Company now."

My life at sea began the next day with Frenchie bringing in a dish of gruel. Sad to say, much of it ended up in the brass pail, but my new friend said the sickness would soon pass, and in a few days I'd have the sea legs of true Jack Tar.

"Can't I go up on deck for some fresh air?" I said when I'd got dressed. A stifling cabin that smelled of regurgitated gruel was not my idea of a healthy environment.

Frenchie scowled. On his cheery face, it looked like something out of a Punch-and-Judy show.

"Don't you be getting me in trouble with Captain Robinson. You go up there, you'd better stay out of the way, or he'll make me kiss the gunner's daughter. And that's not so pleasant on the old backside, miss."

"I'll be as good as invisible." Maybe, I thought, I would see Kit up there and have a chance to begin putting things right between us.

"Very well, but you heed what I said, miss. Oh, and Dr Lemuel's going to look you out some books later on, but he's officer of the watch right now. A man of many talents is our Dr Lem."

"Tell him thank you," I said. "Or maybe I'll see him to thank him myself."

It was hard to find a square foot of deck that no one was using. I chose a spot right against the bulwarks on the main deck, where I could hold on to the cables and see the rolling grey of the waves all around us. I had never seen the sea from on board ship before and I couldn't get over how flat it was. There was no landscape or marker to indicate our progress; only the angle of the sun and the instruments of the mariners. England, I supposed, was behind us. Holland too. Had I come far enough to have escaped Van Guelder yet? I tried to feel for the pull of the lodestone, but all I could feel was the lurching of my innards and the rise of bile with every salty splash against the boards. Far ahead of us was another ship of the East India fleet, behind us nothing. Maybe I was safe. I would plead with Dr Lemuel again not to write to my father. As long as no one knew where I was, no one could find me. I hoped.

I didn't see Kit on deck. Perhaps it was his turn to rest in his cabin. Although the uneasy feeling came to me that in a crew of seventy souls, he could easily avoid me. Dr Lemuel was around. I saw him up on the quarter-deck, but I felt sure that to go and speak to him there would most definitely count as interfering with the running of the ship. The rest of the deck was filled with boys scrubbing the timbers and men singing to the sound of a fiddle as they hauled on the complex criss-cross of ropes. I felt half-naked and conspicuous in my boys' clothes with only a kerchief tying back my hair. But not one man looked at or spoke to me. They must have been under strict orders. Instead of conversation there was only the endless, "Way-hey, boys," the feel of salt on my lips and the glare of the sun.

The first morning set the pattern of things to come. Life at sea turned out to consist largely of hours of monotonous boredom. Staying out of the way was my chief pastime. I soon became used to the clanging of the bell every half hour, the daily heave into the bucket, and the hours stood watching the wind and weather. I learned that salt pork only came once a week, that Saucy Sue was the sailors' nickname for the formidable figurehead where the ship's privy was located, and that it was not good to be at sea at that time all women must endure. Incredibly, my guide to surviving the last matter was Frenchie.

"You'll be wanting these, miss," he said one morning, seeing me white-faced and attempting to hide the spoiled sheets.

I was grateful for the wads of cloth he passed me, but the knowing look he gave me as he did so made me wonder just what sort of an upbringing he had had. Home and family were not topics we discussed, and I had no wish to pry. After all, I certainly didn't want to discuss my home life.

The surgeon had kept his promise to bring me some books. On the second day, he knocked at my cabin door and presented me with a selection of essays, poems and memoirs in several languages, all bound in the same leather bindings.

"I trust these will keep you company." He gave a slight bow.

"Oh yes. Thank you so much. Dr Lemuel: what is to happen to me? On the voyage, I mean. I really must get as far from home as possible. My very life could be in danger."

He eased himself into the settle with great composure, considering the swaying of the ship.

"Now, Mistress Rosewood. I told you not to worry about that. We have your case in hand. The captain knows a very respectable lady at the Cape who is in need of a companion. Surely that would be far enough, and safe enough too? You speak Dutch well, do you not?"

I gave a little nod and tried not to shiver. The very sound of Dutch gave me nightmares at the moment, but every Dutch speaker was not Van Guelder.

"And I won't be found? Dr Lemuel, I can't have anyone knowing where I am. You won't write to Father, will you?"

He stroked his chin.

"That is less easy to promise. This is a complex dilemma. Perhaps if I knew a little more of your story? This lodestone you spoke of; can you tell me more? As I said, it interests me."

"I don't want to talk about it." I had been desperate in front of Captain Robinson. I couldn't face the nightmare now.

"Your father will be worried," Dr Lemuel's tone was gentle. "Fathers often are, believe me."

I swallowed. Was Father worried? I wondered if my family had gone home from London now, or if they were still looking for me. What had they said to Mr. Van Guelder about my disappearance? Did they think I was dead?

"Give me longer to get away," I said. "Please. And don't let Kit – Mr. Blackthorn – write either." Tears came to my eyes when I thought of Kit. I had seen him about his work several times now, but he never looked me directly in the eye or said more than, "Good day, Margaret," as formally as a village schoolmaster.

"You and he are close." It was half a question.

"Were," I said bitterly. I didn't know if the brother-and-sister days would ever come back now.

"Give Mr. Blackthorn time," said Dr Lemuel, squeezing my hand. "Pride is a terrible thing, Mistress Rosewood, and a man hates to have it wounded. You've struck a blow at his sense of honor, but an honorable man always comes round in the end."

I hoped so. I hoped sincerely that Kit and I could be friends again. But later I thought about Mr. Van Guelder's wounded pride too. I had struck a far worse blow at that. I was his betrothed – his property – and I had slipped from his clutches and made him look like a fool. If ever he caught up with me, I doubted even a crew of seventy men could shield me from his anger.

The port of Madeira proved to be a welcome break from the miles of open sea. From the harbor, I stood and looked up at flower-sprinkled hills and white churches. Hollyport seemed a distant memory, and I began to hope for the first time that I had truly escaped my marriage. In the company of Dr Lemuel, I watched the men take on board the additional oranges and lemons we would need for the voyage east. At this point, said the doctor, our journey began in earnest. The winds would sweep us outward from the coast of Africa, and from there on to the Cape and my unknown future life. The way he spoke of it, it sounded like an adventure. I almost believed it was possible to enjoy it. If only I could make it up with Kit again. And be truly sure Van Guelder would not follow.

Three days out of Madeira, the wind began to drop. I saw the sails go from fat to floppy in the space of a watch and overheard the sail maker's mate speak of a good time to make repairs.

"It's nothing to fret about, miss." Frenchie gave a cock-eyed smile when I worried aloud that we weren't making speed. "When we come to the doldrums for real, you'll know about it. This will be over in a few days. Have some mutton pudding to take your mind off it. Cook's special treat of the week. Put some color in your cheeks."

I wished I could smile too, but I couldn't. Not with the *Hopewell* standing dead in the water. I tugged more than ever at the betrothal ring that stubbornly refused to come off my finger. A feeling was creeping up on me. A feeling I had not had since we had left England.

Two days later, the wind got up again. The sails swelled once more and the men on the tops busied themselves with the cables. Coming onto the deck for my daily dose of fresh air, I was about to sigh with relief, when a shout went out from the crow's nest, ringing the length of the ship.

"A sail! A sail to stern! Alert the captain!"

6

The Flying Dutchman

She was behind us in the water, just off the starboard side: a smaller ship and faster, flying the English colors. She must have caught up with us while we'd been becalmed, and with our greater bulk and weight, would soon overtake us.

"Straight out of Greenwich, by the look of her," I heard one of the men say. "Anyone would think she'd followed us."

My heart leaped to my throat. I mustn't panic. Those were just idle words. The ship could be anything. A naval vessel or a slaver headed for the Windward Coast. It probably had nothing to do with us.

"She's signaling us." Frenchie's voice piped up at my side. The cabin boy had come to stand alongside me, balancing his lean figure on the gunwale while he hung onto the ropes. The other ship had raised flags in a pattern of colors and symbols. "A passenger wants to come aboard. I wonder what that's all about, eh?"

I had a terrible feeling I knew only too well what it was about. That feeling that had been growing on me, the one I thought I'd left behind; it was the tug of the lodestone. It was only faint now, but it was getting stronger, much stronger than it had been back in Hollyport. Could it be that Dr Lemuel had written after all? Or Kit? No, there simply wasn't time for anyone to have received news and followed so soon. This was the power of the lodestone. Just as he had promised, my betrothed was using its uncanny properties to prove he could find me anywhere. He was coming for me.

The ship drew alongside us. By this time, the captain was on deck and so were most of the officers too. The sea anchor was lowered. From the smaller vessel, a boat was let down by ropes. I climbed up on the gunwale beside Frenchie, grasping tight to the cables. Through the glare of sunlight on the glittering sea, I could just about make out three figures in the boat. Two sailors rowing and... I caught a glint of gold from the third man's bright blond hair. He was dressed in dark cloth, a high-sided hat held on by one hand, a black ribbon tying back his hair. I prayed for it not to be true, even now for the worst to be all my own imagination. There was a millstone in my chest. Something was pulling at me, harder, harder.

A sudden jerk of magnetism pulled me forward so hard I had to dig my fingers between the cords of the ropes to stop myself falling into the sea. Lumps of tar forced their way under my fingernails. My arms ached and shook with the effort of holding myself back. What was he doing to me? This was twenty times worse than it had ever been before. Was it my fear causing this? Did I fear him so much that I was powerless to resist him? Even as I strained, I felt a queer desire to throw myself into the dark-clad man's arms, even if it meant drowning to get there. I had to find something to stop me.

"Mistress Rosewood? Miss?" Frenchie's pretty-boy face was looking into mine with concern. Suddenly, he seemed much older than twelve. "Are you alright? Are you in trouble?"

"An evil man, Frenchie," I said through gritted teeth. "In that boat. He's coming to take me away. He has...power. Something uncanny." Another tug almost pulled me overboard. "I need something to hold me down so he can't take me."

Frenchie's face set with a grim determination I had not thought was in his character, and for a minute his voice sounded different.

"A man, eh? Huh! I should have known." He spat.

Then he squared his shoulders and went back to his usual swagger.

"You come with me, miss. Main mast. Built with a silver piece beneath it. Nothing evil can pass silver, miss, that's a fact. I'll make you safe there, don't you fret."

I wasn't sure I trusted in his maritime superstition, but the ship's main mast was almost as thick as me and surrounded by a mass of strong ropes. If anything could hold me down, that would be it.

"Very well." The boat was almost to the *Hopewell* now. I could make out Mr. Van Guelder's high cheekbones, his perfectly straight nose. And was it my imagination, or was he looking right at me with a dangerous sneer on his lips? I could almost hear my heart thumping. I didn't know if I dare let go of the rope. "You're going to have to help me," I said.

Frenchie grasped me by the forearms.

"Come along, miss."

I released the rope and instantly a great surge of magnetism yanked me out towards the sea. Frenchie strained and dragged me back towards the center of the deck, panting hard. He barely seemed any stronger than I was. His arms and chest were baby-soft. How was this going to work? Close by, the bo'sun's whistle sounded and men moved into place to haul the boat aboard. Frenchie gave one final heave towards the mast. Sweat stood out on both our foreheads. All around the great oaken pillar, about level with my hands, a ring of pegs secured the cables. Coils and coils of heavy rope hung like giant skeins of yarn. The pull of the lodestone yearned.

"Tie me." My voice sounded breathless and husky. "Tie my hands to the mast. Please, Frenchie, hurry. He's coming."

"Belay that down there!" A cry rang out from the quarterdeck. "Mr. Blackthorn, remove the passenger."

Brisk footsteps strode towards us and I heard Kit's soft bass in my ear:

"Margaret, do you want to ruin me? What in the name of Drake's drum do you think you're doing?"

He took hold of my shoulders. At the same time, Frenchie slipped with the knot and I lurched forward into Kit's buttoned chest. Frenchie pulled me back by the shirt and started tying again. Kit gave a look of baffled disbelief.

"It's Mr. Van Guelder, Kit. You've got to believe me about him."

There was a clap of gunshot behind us and the smoke and smell of black powder as the marines discharged their salute of welcome. A cork-heeled shoe, black with a silver buckle, planted itself carefully on deck, followed by a stockinged calf.

"The knot!" I was gripping frantically with both hands, my fingers slippery around the pegs. Frenchie grunted as he pulled tighter. My fingers bent back into a contorted position. I bit back a yelp. The man from the boat strode across the deck, tall and forbidding.

"Welcome aboard the Honorable Company's ship *Hopewell*, sir." The captain's voice rang out from the quarter-deck. "Captain William Robinson at your service. May I ask your business with the East India Trading Company?"

"*Meneer* Holman Van Guelder of Amsterdam." A shudder ran the length of my body as he bowed to the ship's company. His eyes flicked straight towards me. Beneath the veneer of politeness was a murderous flash of pure anger. A sickening mixture of fear and desire coursed through me. My twisted fingers strained against Frenchie's knots. It hurt like crazy.

"My business is not with the Company. Indeed, I have no interest in it." He strode up the deck, coming perilously close to me. "The fact is that you, sir, are harboring my betrothed wife and it is my right as a gentleman to take her back. You will please release to me that young woman, Mistress Margaret Rosewood." His eyes flashed towards me again: cold blue diamonds. "I would not be deprived of my wedding rites."

"Don't, Kit, don't," I begged. Kit's hand hesitated on the rope he had been about to untwist, his eyes going from me to Van Guelder and back. "Look at him. He's not normal."

"That is well, but what proof have you of this, sir?" For the first time, I felt glad of Captain Robinson's bluff manner. "In the absence of the young woman's father, the learned doctor and I are responsible for her welfare aboard this vessel."

"Indeed."

I had not noticed Dr Lemuel standing so close to the captain. There was a note of excitement, almost challenge, in his voice.

"There are certain mysterious circumstances surrounding Mistress Rosewood's arrival with us, which I for one would like cleared up before I release her to another's care."

"Proof?" Van Guelder's nostrils flared. "I hardly think a member of the Gentlemen Seventeen of Holland need prove himself to a mere sea captain. Nor to some interfering Sawbones. Release my wife, sir! There is proof enough on her finger, in the form of the betrothal ring I gave her; there is proof enough, sir, in her own heart. She will fly to my arms swiftly enough once those ropes are untied."

He turned and faced me directly. I felt my fingers strained to breaking point as the force of the lodestone pulled my whole body forward. My mouth was dry. My arms were shaking.

"Come, Margaret, my love." His voice was soft and dangerous. "Your family members are anxious to see you return home. We must not keep them waiting."

"Sir, I must demand proof before I give the order." That was the captain's voice.

Van Guelder held out his hand to me.

"Do not trifle with me, Margaret. Now, come."

I shook my head. Kit, suddenly released from his inaction, moved to stand in front of me, his shoulders squared. Behind the mast, Frenchie hung onto the ropes.

Van Guelder's face contorted with anger. He bit his lip, slowly, savagely, until a drop of blood appeared on it. His hand tightened around the ivory sword hilt.

"Mr. Van Guelder, I must insist..."

It happened so quickly, I never saw it all. There was the metallic rasp of a drawn sword. An order from Captain

Robinson, followed by another from the master-at-arms. Kit's cutlass flashed as he drew it, and clashed as he tried to parry Van Guelder's slice to the ropes. My wrists burned; Frenchie pulled. A single cut rope flew up and whipped my face. And then a wrench and a surge of pain brought bile to my throat as I jerked forward, held only by my hands.

"Arrrgh!" The cry ripped out of me. A numb chill grabbed the back of my neck and made me retch. Something awful had happened. Something to my hands. And I was still being pulled forward. My face was salty wet. The deck was swimming in unreal watercolor, like a painting with something spilled on it.

"Arrest that man!" The command came from a thousand miles away.

"Marines, prime your muskets!" From deep under water.

"Margaret." Mr. Van Guelder's face wavered in front of me, pale and perfect and cruel. Swords crossed and re-crossed. "You alone are my wife. One heart; one flesh; one soul. There is no separating us."

From a place hidden in the pain and confusion of weapons and commands and running feet, I heard myself gasp:

"Never...be...your wife."

"By God, you will!"

The marines had primed their muskets and were advancing. More drawn cutlasses flashed at either side. Kit took a blow and staggered to his knees. Van Guelder drew himself up to his full, towering height. His eyes lit on Frenchie – silent behind the mast – with a look worthy of Satan himself. Before anyone could stop him, he had grabbed the lad by the hair, forcing the pretty face to look into his own, pulling out the lodestone and pressing it into Frenchie's hand.

"He's going to try and take his form," I thought. But the thought was without emotion, as if I was watching everything from beyond the veil. Pain: it was filling every corner of my mind. My fingers wouldn't move. Why wouldn't my fingers move? I thought I could hear Dr Lemuel's voice from somewhere, or was it my father? I tasted salt on my lips, heard throbbing in my ears.

"Hell's teeth!" That was Kit.

"Frenchie!" Was that Mr. Solomons?

Frenchie had fallen to the deck with a thud. Van Guelder was standing over him, one hand gripping the mast. His face was shaking, shuddering, about to burst. It was Frenchie's face. No, it was his own face. It was Frenchie's again. This was too unreal. I couldn't bear it. Van Guelder gave a groan and for a second had no features at all.

A chorus of curses in various languages went around the deck.

"Steady, boys, steady," called the master-at-arms. "This ain't a natural foe. Nothing in haste, now."

The several faces of Mr. Van Guelder seemed to be fighting a war with each other. He gasped, his fingernails ripping splinters from the mast. Suddenly, he reeled back and spat blood from his lips.

"*Vrouw!*" he snarled, with a Dutch curse. His cold eyes shot Frenchie a look of utter contempt. He raised the sword over the cabin boy's fallen body.

"No!" One of the young marines had gone in too soon. The musket misfired and shot a hole in the yard-arm. With a savage bellow, Van Guelder caught him by the collar, swung him round and forced the lodestone into his hand instead. Arms flailed. Boots kicked. Two identical faces swore and spat at each other.

"Hold fire!" yelled the master-at-arms.

The two identical marines tumbled over and over across the deck, getting nearer and nearer the bulwarks. One was going limp in the other's arms. One was brandishing a hangar. A petty officer ran in, followed by the bo'sun. There was a jumble of men and bodies.

"Man overboard!"

The two marines had fallen backwards into the water, arms

about each other's throats. The rest of the detachment ran to the bulwarks, muskets in hands. I sank to my knees, the magnetism suddenly gone. The pain in my hands was excruciating. I felt sick, feverish. My pulse was getting faster and faster.

"Margaret! Margaret, wake up!"

"Mistress Rosewood, can you hear me?"

The back of my neck was hot and cold. Kit and Dr Lemuel were kneeling by my side on the deck. They looked pale, frightened even. Kit was crying. Dr Lemuel laid a hand on my forehead. I could feel the sweat between his fingers. Then he looked at my hands.

"Dear God!" He bit his lip.

Kit scrubbed his eyes, fierce.

"No. Don't say it. There has to be something else you can do."

The doctor shook his head. He did not seem to want to look at Kit or me. He stood up.

"Mr. Solomons, will you please fetch the..." He lowered his voice so I could no longer hear what he was saying. Mr. Solomons came out from behind the mast with an arm about Frenchie's shoulder. The lad stumbled beside him as they both walked off in the direction of the hatch. Dr Lemuel took off his coat and rolled up his sleeves.

"Kit." My own voice sounded weak and watery. "Can you untie the ropes now? My hands hurt."

"In a little minute. Just hold steady." Kit smoothed back my hair. The kerchief had fallen off.

"I'm sorry I spoiled things for you with Father and Captain Robinson. I didn't mean to. I just couldn't...I couldn't."

"No more of that now." Kit leaned his head against mine. I could faintly taste the flavor of his tobacco. "I'm the one who should apologize for letting that fiend anywhere near you. I should have listened to you, Margaret. And I'll tell you now, he won't touch you again. You'll have every man's word aboard this vessel. Here." He took a bottle from somewhere about his person.

"Have a drink of this."

I sniffed the bottle. "Father doesn't let me drink rum."

"Just this once. For me."

Dr Lemuel was tying something round my forearms. It bit into my flesh. I heard him call some of the mast crew to come and help him. Men knelt down to the back and front of me.

"Kit, what's going on?"

"Just drink this. It's going to be all right, Margaret."

He tipped the run into my mouth. It burned my throat and made me cough. The deck blurred again. Someone took hold of my legs.

"Just remember, I'm right by you." Kit put his arm round my shoulder. He was shaking.

"Kit?"

"Bite on this, if you will." I felt a leather strap being pushed between my teeth. Mr. Solomons came hurrying to hand something to the doctor, his eyes blinking furiously.

"Mmmm?"

"This will only take a moment, Mistress Rosewood. Breathe deeply and think of those charming curiosities. There's a good girl. Ready, men?"

The deck was spinning. My mouth tasted of wet leather. From somewhere I heard Frenchie's high voice: "Aye, Dr Lemuel," and then Kit's, hoarse and broken: "I'm sorry, sweetheart. I'm so, so sorry." There was a slice to my wrist like a bitter shard; the bite of shark's teeth tearing. Then the entire ocean rushed to my head and everything went black.

7

The Black Bottle

I opened my eyes. I closed them again. I was sinking into a great goose-feather bed, sinking deeper and deeper. The feathers were covering my face, my mouth. I was going right through the bed and out of the bottom, through the floorboards, into the depths of the earth.

No, I wasn't sinking. I was floating. I was flying above the deck of the *Hopewell*. I could see men on the fighting tops and the first mate at the wheel, all as tiny as specks of dust. My arms were outstretched in flight like wings, but as I looked, I saw that the ends of them were on fire. The flames were creeping up my wrists. I could hear my arms crackling like logs in a hearth. Sparks were flying out, and clouds of grey smoke. My arms were burning; I could feel them. The ends were crumbling to cinders and blowing away; scattering over the sea. I cried out.

"Easy, easy." Dr Lemuel was dabbing my forehead with something damp and cold. I could see his face with its dark eyebrows lit by bobbing lantern light. He put a spoon in my mouth. I closed my eyes.

I opened them again. It wasn't Dr Lemuel; it was Kit. He had black shadows under his eyes and little golden hairs on his chin. And it was daylight, not night-time. Mr. Solomons was with him. Kit said something to Mr. Solomons, but it sounded like the howling of the wind, not words. Then Mr. Solomons began peeling off the ends of my arms in one long peel, like the peel of an apple that you throw over your shoulder to find out who you will marry. I wanted to cry out, but my mouth wouldn't open, and the ends of my arms were too far away. They were leagues away, in distant lands. I would never reach them, never see them again.

"She's still in a fever." How had Dr Lemuel got here again?

And where was Kit? Captain Robinson was in the cabin now, arms folded over his calico shirt. Why had Captain Robinson come? Was I to be sent home now?

"Will you bleed her?" The captain scratched the side of his hawk-like nose.

"I'd rather not. Half a dish of oatmeal burgoo is all I've managed to get down her. She's too weak."

"Is she leaving us, Doctor?"

"Not if I can help it. But I'll have to increase the laudanum."

I wondered who they were talking about. I couldn't see anyone else. I wanted to talk to the captain. I needed to ask him to stop the ship's rats from eating my arms. They were there; I could feel them gnawing. Surely the captain couldn't just stand there and watch them do it?

"Do whatever you feel, Lemuel. You know I hold you in the highest regard. Poor child. To come to this so young. Thank God her father is not here."

The spoon went in my mouth again. I swallowed. Blinked. For a moment, a rat dressed in the captain's uniform wavered in front of my eyes. Then it disintegrated into swirling spirals and stars and triangles.

I woke up. I was lying in my own cabin bed and it was daylight. Dr Lemuel was sprawling on the settle opposite my bed, asleep. His shirt was open to the middle of his chest, his head tipped back in a snore. He didn't look to have shaved or washed for some time. Ranged around the washstand were things that had not been there before: rolls of bandages, sheets of grey paper, bowls and bottles that clinked together with the rolling of the ship. On the end stood one black bottle with a spoon by it. It was half-empty.

My arms hurt. Somewhere just above the wrists was the ceaseless throbbing I had felt even in my dreams. I wanted to lift them, but my limbs felt dull and tired. I was shivering, even though the sky through the window showed a shimmering blue. There was a sheet over me. I tried to feel it, but I couldn't. My fingers didn't move when I told them to. I couldn't feel them. All I felt was throbbing, throbbing. The walls of the cabin creaked and cracked, and everything smelled of sweat and strange cordials.

"Help me." My lips moved in the shape of the only words I could think of to say. My tongue felt enormous and seriously out of practice. I could barely hear the dry rasp of my voice. "Help me?"

Dr Lemuel gave a snort and sat up with a jerk. He looked at me with unfocused eyes, blinked, and hurried over to the bed.

"Mistress Rosewood." His voice was hoarse with sleep. "My dear girl. You're with us at last."

He felt my forehead with the back of his hand, peered into my eyes, sat me up and put a cup of water to my lips. At last? How long had I been lying here? I searched my memory for the last thing I could recall, but it was like charting an unexplored wilderness.

"Where's Kit?" Hadn't he been with me?

Dr Lemuel began to spoon some sloppy oatmeal burgoo into my mouth.

"Mr. Blackthorn will be much relieved to know you're improving. He's been here almost every moment he could spare from his duties. And poor Frenchie has been like a ghost around the place, waiting for you to wake. For a stowaway, my little curiosity, it seems you're not without friends."

Kit and Frenchie. That was it. Something to do with Kit and Frenchie. And ropes. I was standing on the deck with Kit and Frenchie and there were these ropes...

"Van Guelder!" I jolted upright, spilling oatmeal over the sheet and my chin. He had been here. On board ship. I could see him. His face. His eyes.

"Easy, now." Dr Lemuel put a hand on my shoulder. "He's

gone. The sea has taken him." He looked for a moment as if he would say more, but he only gave a pale smile and repeated his words. "The sea has taken him. He will not come back."

I shivered into the sheet. "My arms hurt."

"You shall have some more medicine shortly. Have some more burgoo for now." He spooned more of the oatmeal slop. It tasted like mashed sawdust. I didn't want to eat it. My arms were on fire.

"What's wrong with them?" I tried to lift the dead weight. The ends were covered with bulky dressings in the shape of stars and smelled of cheap wine as I brought them nearer. Even doing that was exhausting. There was something wrong about the length of the arms. I couldn't see my hands.

"Dr Lemuel?"

"Hush. You mustn't excite yourself. You're not yet strong."

I didn't want to be hushed. I wanted to make sense of what I was seeing, and I couldn't. I stared down the incomplete length of my arms. No hands. No hands!

"My hands!"

"Hush." Dr Lemuel put a hand to my forehead again. His expression was one I had seen before more than once. It was the way the masters of Father's ships looked when there was storm damage with large bills to pay for repairs. My stomach clenched.

"I'm afraid your hands were in a state beyond repair. I had to amputate."

No. This wasn't happening. Not after everything else I'd been through. I was only sixteen. This wasn't meant to happen to me.

"But you are a strong young woman. You're going to mend. Mr. Solomons and I are giving you the most modern and effective treatments. You will recover."

No hands. Who recovered from that? Who wanted to recover from that? Visions of ugly street beggars loomed in my mind. Useless. Disgusting. Unwanted. What place was there for a girl with no hands, who couldn't bake, sew, write down the accounts? Who couldn't even dress or feed herself? What could I possibly be to anyone now other than a burden? It would have been better if I had died in my fever and never woken.

I turned my face to the wall.

"I want my medicine now."

It might have all been some terrible nightmare, but it wasn't. As the days and nights lurched on in an endless repetition of damp dressings and changing faces and clanking bottles, the one thing that didn't change was the absence at the end of my arms. I tried not to look at the ugly stumps that replaced my hands, but the medicine that dulled my pain made me see things that weren't there, and in my dreams the stumps grew to the size of mountains, spurting out red flame and rocks. Sometimes Van Guelder's face would appear in the flames, and he would grab me by the hands and pull me towards himself until they tore off and I woke up screaming. There was always someone there to calm me down – Dr Lemuel or Kit or the silent Mr. Solomons – but they couldn't put my hands back and I had nothing to say to them.

Mostly I slept. It was easier that way; I didn't have to think about the future and what was going to happen to me. There was no hope of being a lady's companion now. For all I knew, we had passed the Cape long since anyway. I no longer had any notion of time passing. Weeks, or even months, could have gone missing and I wouldn't have known about it. All I saw from the mullioned cabin window was the sky in different shades – vivid blue or swirling purple or featureless black – and the lashing of the spray on days when the sea was rough. It was hot, I knew that. But it had been hot before. And I knew from my dry mouth and the way Dr Lemuel kept dabbing my forehead and making me sip from the ship's precious fresh water supply that a lot of the heat I felt was coming from inside me; from the pain that was always present even when it felt like my body belonged to another person. I suspected the truth was that my only future lay in this cabin, and that the captain may soon be able to sell his furniture after all.

Van Guelder had done this to me. Van Guelder and that thing around his neck. I should have known I would not be able to outrun him, even at sea. What was it he had said to me? *There is nowhere you can hide from your appointed husband. I will always know where you are.* Even now I felt his presence, although the waves had closed over him long since. He was here in the pain and the injury and the emptiness in my heart.

"He's long gone," Kit said to me, arm around my shoulder as I shivered and swallowed my spoonful from the black bottle. "That's the honest truth, sweetheart. There were plenty of marines took a shot at him, but it was the sea that got him. A wave came and not a man saw him rise. The boat went back to the sloop without him. You're free of him."

But that wasn't how I felt. True, there had been some sort of struggle at the time. Trying to take Frenchie's form had somehow caught Van Guelder out for a while. In my more awake moments, I thought I knew why that was, but the moments didn't last long enough for the thoughts to stick. Thinking was altogether too much of an effort. It was much easier to give in to the hollow feeling of doom. The betrothal ring I hated may have finally come off now that there was no hand for it to sit on, but its sentiments had been branded on my soul, as permanent as any sailor's tattoo. *One flesh. One heart. One soul.* If he was dead, than he had made sure my soul had died with him.

My friends tried to keep my spirits up. Kit brought me strange insects or tiny, captured sea creatures, and assured me that "the lads aloft" were all wishing me a speedy recovery. (I doubted it, since I'd been all but invisible to the crew before, but I didn't say so.) Frenchie swabbed and tidied with a will, and generally had a smile for me. I couldn't help wondering, though, if the smile was forced, since I'd been the cause of his grim misadventure with Van Guelder. An experience like that had to leave a mark. Even Mr. Solomons occasionally stuttered out the need to think for the best, while steadfastly avoiding eye contact. But all I really wanted was oblivion. And, if nowhere else, I found it in the bottom of the black bottle. The more I took my medicine, the less real the world around me became. Lanterns became hilltop beacons, curtains the branches of ancient forests. My life drifted into a realm of dream, only occasionally inhabited by real people. I saw creatures a medieval scribe could scarcely have dreamt up: men with fish for faces or with knives growing from their navels. When the illusions faded, I felt cold and sick. The cabin was stifling, its smell rank. The familiar faces leered down at me with grotesque expressions. I wanted them all to go away. I wanted everything to go away, including myself. I wanted another spoonful to take away the pain.

"I can give you no more of this."

Dr Lemuel had finally removed my dressings for good, and the sight of the wrinkled stumps underneath was enough to make me want to throw myself overboard. I looked up at him, pleading, but his square face was set in the sort of look I remembered from Father when Susanna and I wanted new ribbons from yet another peddler woman.

"I have seen many a strong man recover from the knife, only to become a hopeless dependant, swigging on a bottle of laudanum for the rest of his days. That will not happen to you, my dear Mistress Rosewood. I will not allow it. We must reduce the dose from today."

Reduce the dose? A cold hand closed over my heart; the walls of the cabin crept closer to my bunk, causing me to gasp for air. No. I needed that medicine. I needed it. Dr Lemuel could not take it away.

"Come." He gave a smile I had not seen for some time. "It is time to forget about sickness. Where are the books I gave you?"

Books? Was he mocking me? I had no hands. How could I hold a book?

"I don't know." I huddled into the bolster at my head. The doctor was taking away my medicine and now he was taunting me with pleasures I could no longer enjoy. I didn't want any part of this.

"Let me see." The surgeon rummaged in the leather satchel he carried around with him. It was currently hanging from one corner of the oaken settle, half-open and stuffed with medical equipment. "Aha! This will do nicely." He eased his weight onto the edge of the bed. It sunk slightly.

"I believe that after all that has passed, it is time for a little honest education, Mistress Rosewood."

He opened a small, square book onto his lap and began to turn the pages. I cast a glance at it, wishing he would go away. It was a hand-written journal of some kind. The script was neat and flowing, with long "S"s, scattered with occasional blots or faded circles where the sea spray looked to have got to it. Was this Dr Lemuel's own journal? I eased myself up onto my elbow and leaned in towards it, my unwashed hair flopping over one side of my face.

The journal was magnificent. Birds and plant-life had been sketched in inks with vivid colors – the sort an artist might use – along with people in strange dress with haughty expressions. The folk were no Europeans; that was for sure. This was a record of a distant land. Observations and notes filled the margins, along with dates and measurements, all in fractions of inches. The names of the plants and birds were ones I had never heard of. Dr Lemuel turned another page. Here was a chart or table with lists of words in columns, surrounded by yet more drawings. A new language, perhaps? I didn't recognize it.

"I mentioned to you once that I am a collector of curiosities, Mistress Rosewood. It may interest you to know that this is my field journal from an earlier sea voyage I made. I spent some time in a rather remote region."

My eyes flicked wearily over the book. The sketches were incredibly detailed. The birds seemed to fly off the pages, all brilliant reds and greens.

"The sort of region," the doctor paused, "that one does not find unless one is looking for something else."

The colors of the cabin suddenly flared as vivid as the birds. I sat up, ignoring the rush of pain.

"Lands beyond the edge of the map?"

"I thought that might catch your attention. Yes, those very lands. It seems I am fated to stumble upon them. A trifle inconvenient and not the sort of thing one would mention to the Royal Society, but fascinating from a scientific point of view. Hence my interest in your experience, Mistress Rosewood."

Recognition flared up. And with it a tinge of anger.

"The lodestone. You already knew about that? You knew what it could do?"

Dr Lemuel shook his head. "No, indeed. I can neither be credited with that knowledge nor blamed for withholding it. So there is no cause for that flash I see in your eyes, my dear Mistress Rosewood. Sadly, my knowledge has been of little use in preventing what has befallen you. But I do know that the lands where such things as that stone are found do exist, and that they are subject to the same laws of reason and nature that govern the lands more commonly known. It may behoove us all to learn a little from them, if only because we never know when our travels may lead us there." He raised an eyebrow. "In my experience, more often sooner than later."

My non-existent hands twinged. It was an odd effect I was still getting used to.

"I think it's too late for me to learn anything."

"Nonsense. The journey has only just begun." Dr Lemuel's face took on its fatherly look. "Come; let us study these field drawings, just for a short while."

The colors really were very pretty, especially on the flowers. I would not have thought the ship's surgeon to have such an eye for the beautiful, or the skill to represent it. I edged a little nearer. I hadn't forgotten the medicine, but I thought I might be able to put it off for a little while.

"Very well, then," I said.

For a short time every day after that, Dr Lemuel and I studied the field journal together. It was hard to concentrate – harder than I would have believed when I used to devour the contents of Father's few books by candlelight in the winter months – and I nearly always slept afterwards; but I became a little stronger every day and managed to go without my spoonful for just a while longer each time. I became used to strange words like *Nardac* and *Quinbus Flestrin,* and began to find it quite acceptable that trees could be the size of dandelions or horses the size of shrews. In my dreams now, I saw tiny palaces with the moldings and cornices Dr Lemuel had sketched, and their tinier inhabitants, leaping and creeping in high or low heels. Sometime, I must confess, I saw them in the corners of my cabin too, but they were much more welcome than the nightmares that had gone before. I smiled at them and they generally went away.

"I wish I could have drawn like this," I said, as we bent over the pages together. "Father once let us have some paints to decorate a sea-chest for Kit, but Susanna took over before I had a chance to do anything. But inks must be so much better to use; you can get all those fine details. Look at that butterfly!"

I sighed. I would never get to draw anything. I would never even get to write records of shillings and pence or a list for the larder. Since when could a person do anything worthwhile with only stumps for hands? I had lost all the usefulness I ever had. I was as insignificant as one of the tiny creatures in Dr Lemuel's book. Only more so, because at least their world was in proportion. In their homeland, they each had a place and a function. My world had no place for me at all. Not in any part of it of it that I knew of, anyway.

As the weeks went by, Dr Lemuel brought not just the first field journal, but a second, in which corn was the height of elm trees and berries the size of woolpacks. Truly grotesque were the sketches of that land's enormous inhabitants, and yet he spoke of many of them with great fondness and regret at parting from them. One day, he also showed me some of his "particular curiosities" as he called them, which he could not bear to be parted from, even at sea. Giant wasp stings, like black scimitars, and tiny fleeces so fine against my cheek they felt like baby's hair.

"You must learn to be open to new possibilities, Mistress Rosewood," he said. "And to inquire, always to inquire. There is always something to learn. Even the strangest of creatures has a reason for its appearance and behavior. It may take some time to understand it, but careful thought and observation will always serve you well."

Gradually, I became more alert. I started to sit up more and to take short, swaying walks around the cabin. I still had pain – even in parts of me that no longer existed, such as my fingers, not to mention other parts that had been lying in bed for far too long – but the dryness in my mouth had gone and I stopped seeing apparitions everywhere.

"Looking well this morning, miss," Frenchie said when he came to empty the pail in the close-stool. The sky through the cabin window was kingfisher blue, a color I had never seen before in anything but that bird's plumage. The ship was barely rocking. It was actually a beautiful day, I thought, and wondered how long it had been since I had thought that last.

"Dr Lemuel says I'm to bring you some chicken broth today. They've slaughtered one of the fowl for you. Aren't you the lucky one?"

I looked at my arms. They were healing well. Dr Lemuel had done a good job. There would always be scars and I wasn't sure I would ever get used to them ending just above the wrist, but at least they were healthy.

"It's better than burgoo." A sudden thought occurred to me. "I never thanked you for helping me, Frenchie. It must have been awful for you when..." My voice faded away. I still didn't like to think of anything connected with Van Guelder. Sweat prickled my forehead and the back of my neck with the simple effort of trying to form the words, but I needed to say this. "I mean, you didn't have to get involved at the mast but you did and it wasn't your fault that Dr Lemuel had to..." My eyes went back to my arms again.

"No trouble at all, miss. We honest sailors are always happy to serve."

I could see I was embarrassing him but I wasn't sorry I'd spoken. It was time I considered other people again. I would thank Dr Lemuel and Kit too. And Mr. Solomons. That would scare him.

I ate the broth with a relish and then surprised everyone by asking for more. In less than a fortnight, I was back on normal ship's rations. The sickly feeling was almost gone; and I was finding I could stay awake for longer and sleep more peacefully when I needed to rest. I started looking forward to my lessons with Dr Lemuel; so much so that I began to experiment with ways I could turn the pages of the book without the aid of fingers. That way I could be ready with a question or two about the natural history of Flanflasnic or the correct handling of miniature sheep. A nose, or a toe, or the stump of an arm did a reasonable job, I found. It was a bit of a struggle, especially when there was the lurching of the ship to contend with, and the first few attempts exhausted me. But the sense of achievement on opening to a page of crimson birds and giant, fern-like leaves made bubbles rise inside me and my tired chest swell like the rolling waves.

"Our patient seems to be improving, Mr. Solomons," said Dr

Lemuel.

From the slight crease in the corner of his mouth, I could tell that he was actually as elated as I was, even if he pretended not to show it. After all this time in his care, I knew the enigmatic surgeon a little better now. There was always a lot more beneath the surface than he cared to show. His eyes went over to me as I sat on the bunk, legs up, with the book at my feet.

"I think we shall soon be able to dispense with the black bottle for good. Be thankful for it, Mistress Rosewood. Be thankful."

Kit was all smiles when he next came to see me.

"Why, look at you, Margaret! You'll soon be able to come back on deck."

He looked sun burnt and tired. There was skin flaking off the end of his nose and white patches under his eyes. It would be good for him to be able to stop worrying about me, and think only of sails, masts and rigging. But going back on deck: I hadn't considered that.

"I don't know, Kit." I wasn't at all sure about going back to the last place I had seen Van Guelder. The nightmares had stopped now and I didn't want them to start again. Besides, there was the thought of being seen in public, in front of the men, without my hands. I would feel eyes staring even if no one was looking my way. And I now had no way of holding on if the sea got rough. I could fall, even drown.

"Ah, but I do." There was a firmness in Kit's voice that reminded me he was second mate. "And I know Dr Lemuel will think the same. There's a special occasion coming up soon and you wouldn't want to miss it."

"Special occasion?"

I had long since given up wondering where and when in the world we were, but I was pretty sure Christmas must have passed us by (Father didn't hold with celebrating that anyway) and my seventeenth birthday with it, which was nothing special either. We had never celebrated birthdays at home.

"Aye, a very special occasion. Isn't that right, Frenchie?" The cabin boy was standing right behind him, folding clean linen.

"Absolutely, Mr. Blackthorn, sir!" Frenchie gave one of his old-style grins. After all the sick-room austerity, that grin felt like an old friend. Kit smiled back, showing his crooked teeth.

Clearly, there was a conspiracy going on. Even Mr. Solomons seemed to be involved.

"The sea air is very beneficial at this time of...er...year," he said. "I believe it is time you changed out of your...that is Frenchie will assist you to..."

If I hadn't been able to guess what he was trying to say, I would have worked it out when Frenchie began brushing and plaiting my hair; and then (with a typical lack of embarrassment) helping me into the sailor's outdoor clothes he had laid aside for me. They were baggier than ever after my illness, but a bit of cord here and there did the trick nicely. And as Frenchie said: "It's better than the clothes you came in, miss. You don't want nothing tight in the tropics. Not if you want to breathe."

"What exactly am I getting dressed for?" I said, but Frenchie only shook his head.

"You'll have to wait for Dr Lemuel to find that out. No lesson for you today, miss. It's a big day."

That was as much as I could get out of him, however hard I tried, so I had to be content with watching the turquoise sky against the dark background of the cabin's oak paneling. Eventually, Dr Lemuel appeared, his thick hair tied back with a chocolate ribbon, his nutmeg waistcoat buttoned up, in spite of the stifling heat.

He offered me his arm.

"Are you ready, Mistress Rosewood? It's time for you to cross the line."

8

Crossing the Line

I had no idea what to expect. Dr Lemuel helped me up the steep stairs, through the hatch and onto the deck, supporting me by holding both my elbows or my waist where necessary. I had been so long in my cabin that the white sunlight brought tears to my eyes, and for a moment anyone might have thought I was blind as well as handless. Gradually, normal vision blobbed back through the pulsating circles of color: bare feet on the rigging, brown backs and unshaven faces, white sails mended with stitches, and the bluest sky I'd ever seen. The sea was like sapphire; I hadn't imagined it could look like that. Away to starboard were islands of emerald, and little boats bobbing on the waves, and the fins of sea creatures diving.

"Where are we?" I said.

"The Indian Ocean." Dr Lemuel helped me up the stairs to the quarter-deck. I was sure I had no right to be there, but I had no choice. "And more importantly for you, we are at the center of the world. The *Hopewell* is about to cross the Equator."

Captain Robinson was standing at the helm in his waistcoat and shirt-sleeves, his hawk-nosed face shaded by a straw hat. Kit was with him, and a thickset man I recognized as the first mate. I made a wobbly curtsey, which must have looked ridiculous in breeches.

"Mistress Rosewood." The captain's voice was as stern as ever. I trembled. "It seems you have escaped a time-honored nautical tradition. My second mate informs me that you were unconscious during our first crossing of the Equator, and so missed out on all the attendant ceremonies due to those who cross the line for the first time."

"I was ducked head-first in the ocean on my first crossing of the line," Dr Lemuel whispered in my ear.

"This simply will not do. We must rectify the situation immediately and have you cross the line in style this time. Mr. Blackthorn, what do you suggest?"

Kit clasped his hands behind his back.

"The men and I have prepared a little something appropriate to the occasion."

They were going to duck me in the ocean? Kit and Frenchie and the rest had cajoled me into getting dressed for that? How could they?

Kit gave a nod, and from somewhere behind me a fiddle struck up the tune of, "Come My Own One, Come My Fond One," a song I knew well from Hollyport harbor. Hearing it again, I could almost smell Peg's cooking and the seaweed at low tide. It was all I could do to blink back the tears. A muscular, black-skinned sailor and a slighter fellow with thinning copper hair came to the rail of the quarter-deck, each carrying something in their hands.

"For you, miss. From all the men," the black sailor said. He held up his gift as high as he could reach from the main deck (which was somewhere around my knees). "The ship's carpenter made these in his own time."

"Real silver, that is," the copper fellow added, holding up its twin. "Nothing evil can pass silver. Be safe from that devil and all his kind now."

"Each man donated a silver penny or sixpence from his wage," Kit said in my ear. "Mekuria and Conlan here have been in charge of the collection. It was all their own idea. The men don't like to see anything unnatural aboard ship. They've rather taken your side."

"Well, Mistress Rosewood, aren't you going to put them on?" It sounded like Captain Robinson was actually smiling.

I didn't know what to say. There was a big lump rising up my chest and into my throat. Hands. The sailors had made me hands. Wooden hands plated with silver sixpences and pennies.

They flashed and glittered in the strong sunlight. There were leather straps so I could strap them to my arms, and buckles to fasten them with. They must have taken hours of work. I sniffed back tears, trying to think of any words that would be enough to say thank you. There weren't any.

"Let me help you with those."

Dr Lemuel knelt down and took one silver hand at a time, buckling the straps tightly round my arms while the sailors waited. They felt a little awkward and heavy, and I winced slightly at the discomfort, but it was a discomfort I was proud of. There was friendship in those hands, tenderness and care. I could feel its warmth as strongly as I could the flaring sun overhead.

"Welcome to Neptune's Kingdom, Mistress Rosewood." The captain's gruff voice softened just a touch. "Glad to see you back on your feet again. Lemuel's done his job well."

I looked down the length of the *Hopewell*, all the way to the bowsprit and Saucy Sue. Everywhere I looked; steadfast, sun-baked faces were looking back at me and smiling. In the amidships, aloft in the rigging, all the way out in the bows. Men I had been certain could not have cared less for me if I was a weevil in their biscuit had given their own wages to buy me just a little bit of hope and dignity. They had remembered me, and now I was part of the crew. We were sailing together in sapphire waters and there wasn't a cloud in the sky. Summoning a smile I'd forgotten I had, I lifted my silver hands high over my head in a triumphant salute. A roaring *huzzah* went up from every part of the ship. The fiddle struck up again, along with the drum and fife. And the singing went on for a long time.

I was no longer a nobody aboard the *Hopewell*. Kit was right: in my absence, the men had formed some sort of anti-Van Guelder league, and I had suddenly gone from being a piece of luggage to being their princess. In the next few weeks, as I grew stronger, I found I no longer had to rely on Dr Lemuel alone if I wanted to go above and take the air. Any number of strong and surprisingly gentle hands was more than willing to take my elbow. It was amazing how many safe places could be found for me to stand in, places that had certainly never existed before. Everywhere I went; I was greeted by, "Good day, mistress. How's your health today?" and here and there with the touching of forelocks and a few shy smiles. Some of the bolder specimens went even further than that. Copper-topped Conlan introduced me with great tenderness to his pet rat, and one of the marines showed me at considerable length how to clean and load a musket, "because not everyone knows the correct way it must be done." I did notice that all of them kept half an eye on Kit whenever they spoke to me. The princess was evidently to stay an untouchable princess, and I imagined woe would betide any man who overstepped the mark.

Dr Lemuel still kept watch over me, as did Mr. Solomons, but my dose from the black bottle had gone down to almost nothing. I spent the time in my cabin experimenting with my new hands, and with my toes and mouth, to see what I could manage to do alone. Getting dressed was a battle that more often than not ended in an exhausted tangle, and attempting to comb my hair led to some ridiculous contortions that I was glad no one in Hollyport was able to see. Not to mention the animal mess I made trying to eat... But I made a little improvement each day, and when I ended up in tears (which was fairly often, given the level of frustration) Frenchie was generally there with a smile and a damp rag to wipe up with.

"Doing well there, miss," he would say, and since he so obviously meant it, I ended up having to agree.

My lessons continued too. Now that I was on the mend, Dr Lemuel naturally spent more time on his other duties. Some of the crew had fallen sick with an illness they'd caught on one of the emerald islands, and he and Mr. Solomons were kept busy with the medicine chest, not to mention the famous bucket. But, whenever he could spare the time, he would come and tell me more of his travels and his views on scientific discovery, until I knew the pages of his journals by heart.

Nor was that all my lessons consisted of. A few weeks after I got the silver hands, he began testing me on French and Dutch, and on calculations in shillings and pence. I hadn't needed to use any of those since I'd been back in Father's household and, since I'd been ill, I hadn't imagined needing to use them again.

"But that is a falsehood, Mistress Rosewood," he said, after listening to me rattle off French poetry and Dutch prose, occasionally slipping in the odd word of Lilliputian just for entertainment. Frenchie, who despite his name spoke not a word outside English, guffawed over every new sound until the doctor threatened to make him leave.

"No knowledge is without its uses, and whatever our circumstances, we must always be prepared for the moment when it will prove valuable."

Mostly, though, I spent my time taking Dr Lemuel's earlier advice, and put my mind to careful observation and thought. Now that I was able to go up on deck again, there was a lot to see. The sea was now clearer than I had even known it, and I was able to spot brilliantly-striped fish swimming fathoms beneath me. Close to shore, there were creatures that the sailors called turtles, with shells on their backs and fins like arms. I was able to observe the ports and islands we called at, more frequent now that we were coming to the part of the world we were to trade with. I saw white beaches and low houses, slender trees with shock-headed tops, and towering rocks covered with greenery. Bright birds and playful monkeys joined the ship's menagerie, and our dull rations were cheered with fruit so densely sweet, its taste followed you into your dreams. Hundreds of small boats crowded with men and their families filled bays and harbors; and the mish-mash of smells that make up human life floated up to greet us, along with the chatter and work cries and arguments of a whole dictionary of different languages.

Much of what I saw and heard and smelled was a whole world away from Hollyport, and yet it was not so different either. Men still fished as they did at home, though some of them did it while sitting on poles in the sea; and women still cooked and tended their children. The floating market we saw, with fruit and vegetables crammed into a fleet of tiny boats, may have been different from the quayside market of Hollyport, but the buying and selling, the bargaining and cheating were just the same. I began to think that what Dr Lemuel had said was true: that the strangest of lands could be found to follow the same patterns as the most familiar of homely surroundings.

I didn't like to actually go ashore. Despite the sailors' gift, I still felt ashamed by what I saw below my elbows, and the thought of strangers staring, not to mention the perilous landings necessary to reach some of the ports safely, put me off the idea of setting foot anywhere but the deck of the *Hopewell*.

"You'll have to disembark some time, Margaret," Kit said to me, as we lowered anchor in the Bay of Bengal. The men were to enjoy extended shore leave at the Company outpost of Fort St George in Madras. From the ragged state of their clothes and the sunken look on many of their faces, I could tell they were ready for it.

"Some time, but not now," I said. Nothing had really been said about my future since the accident. I was trying to put it out of my mind. If I could just stay on board, maybe this ship would sail on forever, and I would never have to face the troublesome question of a life on land.

Dr Lemuel's arithmetic tests had reminded me, however, that my passage on board the *Hopewell* wasn't coming for free. Someone – probably the doctor himself – must be paying for my food and medicine. I had already made the captain lose the chance of selling his furniture. I had to repay them somehow. I owed them that much, at least.

"Have you still got my ring?" I said to Dr Lemuel, as he stood on the watch before disembarkation. He had never offered it back to me. I was glad for that – the thought of it filled me with sick-making horror – but I could not imagine that he had thrown it away with the...well, I couldn't bear to think of that either, but I was certain he would not have discarded it.

"I think you should take it and – you know – trade it ashore," I said, when he raised his eyebrow at me. "For you and Captain Robinson. To pay for my passage."

"You know how much passage aboard an East Indiaman costs, do you?" His mouth curved in an amused smile.

I blushed. "Not really. But I know that food doesn't come from nowhere. And I'm hardly much use as an able hand before the mast."

He ruffled my hair, sun-bleached at the front where the kerchief tied round my head by Frenchie failed to cover it.

"We shall see. We shall see. Are you sure you will not step ashore with us? The glistening white walls of Madras are a sight to behold for a traveler, although a trading house manned by bored and tipsy officers perhaps is not."

My whole upper body tensed, but I managed to give a polite nod.

"No, thank you. Would you be so good as to tell me what you found there when you come back? I should like to hear your tales."

But when he did come back – after I'd spent three lonely weeks with Frenchie and a skeleton crew – he brought back more than tales. He had something to show: several sets of clothes from Madras itself. By the light of the cabin window, he held up baggy breeches and long-sleeved tunics in colors so startling a strolling player may have hesitated to wear them. All were cut from the most deliciously fine cloth and hemmed with a needlework I could only admire for its intricacy.

"Made by local seamstresses," he told me as I gazed with wide eyes. Was this what my ring had bought? Such beauty for something so abhorrent? "The captain now has several bolts of the same cloth in the hold. It will fetch a fine price in London."

"And I expect these will fetch a fine price too" I said. "In the next port. Oh, well done, Dr Lemuel. It's a first-rate investment."

"Nay, Mistress Rosewood, these are for you. No arguments," he said as I opened my mouth to protest. "The men would take it ill if the princess of the *Hopewell* was the only ragamuffin aboard." I squirmed to hear myself so called, even in jest, but Dr Lemuel merely raised the familiar eyebrow. "Your Dutch gold bought well. This is a mere token; a gesture of fatherly concern, if you like."

"I didn't mean for you to..."

But there was to be no arguing. The butterfly-bright clothes were not for sale under any circumstances, and the nods of approval I got around the ship while wearing them made me feel as if I were a princess indeed. We were coming to the East Indies truly now. The wind was warm, and the sunsets so magnificent that I was sure even Queen Anne in her palace had nothing to look upon with such richness of color and such splendor of design.

If there was nothing to observe out at sea on any day, besides the endless flat blueness (or grayness if it rained) I now took to observing the crew. I found that if I sat quietly and merely watched and listened, there was much I could learn without even trying. For example, I saw that the carpenter's and sail maker's men worked well together; but between the gunners and the marines, who had little to do, there was a constant one-upmanship. They were forever competing, whether at cards or fish bone carving or mending their own clothes. I saw that the men in the tops respected Kit because he was fair and listened to them, and wasn't afraid to put in a bit of hard work himself. I saw that proud, dark Mekuria and copper-haired Conlan were the best of friends, despite their very different appearances.

Indeed, there were many such friendships across a seventy-strong crew, where Dutch, Finnish, Brazilian and Virginian were all part of the mixture. Dr Lemuel's lessons had made it much easier for me to pick up snippets of the different languages I heard (although sometimes what I heard did not bear repeating). And it was this medley of languages that recalled to my mind something that had been there for a long time, but which I'd hardly thought of recently, since getting over the struggle towards health.

I thought of it in my cabin at night. The sun blazed in the day now, but night fell more quickly near to the Equator and brought a hot darkness. My bunk was stifling, with nothing to listen to but the endless creaking and cracking of the ship. I lay with my eyes open in the dark, testing myself on Dutch maritime vocabulary for something to think about. And that was when I remembered what Van Guelder had said in the struggle on deck. The word he had used when he'd tried to take Frenchie's form and hadn't been able to maintain it. *Vrouw*, he had said. *Woman*. At the time, I thought he had been referring to me, but he hadn't. It seemed so obvious now that I felt like slapping myself, had I been able. So much for observation! I couldn't believe I was such a fool as not to realize something that had been evident the whole voyage.

"You're a girl, aren't you, Frenchie?"

My friend had just come into the cabin with the morning breakfast tray. A piece of island fruit and half a ship's biscuit was all my ration could stretch to at this stage of the voyage.

Frenchie's cheeks colored deeper than one of the sunsets we had seen from the deck. The tray fell to the floor; the fruit rolled down and then up the cabin with the tilting of the ship.

"I'm sorry – I mean – I won't tell anyone."

Frenchie fumbled around on the cabin floor for the piece of fruit, eyes anywhere but on me. I swung my legs over the side of the bunk and picked up the fruit between the balls of my feet. It was a trick I had just learned and now seemed as good a time as any to use it.

"On my honor, Frenchie. I'm right, though, aren't I?"

There was the ghost of a nod. How old was she really, I thought? Not twelve, that was for sure. Sixteen? Seventeen? Older?

"I don't mean any harm. It's just that – well – Kit said we're bound for Tonkin now. Almost the last port. I don't know what's going to happen to me…"

I still hadn't steeled myself to the idea of leaving the *Hopewell*. Could I disembark when we reached Canton? As far as I knew, none of the crew was to remain East. And I knew no one in China. It would take a very special person to take in a crippled girl. The only other option was to turn around and head back for England. But that brought me back into fear and uncertainty, not to mention guilt. I didn't want to think of it.

"Make good time with a fair wind, miss," Frenchie mumbled to the oaken planks. I had better concentrate on what I was doing now. Telling Frenchie just how important she was. Letting her know I didn't think badly of her. I took a deep breath.

"So – the thing is – I just wanted to let you know: your secret's safe with me. You've been a good friend, Frenchie. The best. You saved my life and I don't know what I'd have done without you. There. Now will you shake hands and I'll promise to never mention it again."

Frenchie sniffed and stood up, sweat standing out on her hot face, and made a wobbly attempt at her familiar grin. She *was* pretty for a boy, but rather plain for a girl. I wondered how long she had lived as a boy, and how long she was likely to, and whether Dr Lemuel and Mr Solomons knew. I decided they probably did.

"Not wearing your hands yet, miss," she pointed out. She took the silver hands from their place in one of Captain Robinson's chests and waved them about like Punch and Judy. A snigger burst out of me. Frenchie snorted like a horse. The next minute, we were both in helpless fits of giggles. We rolled around, she on the deck and I on the bed, laughing and stopping and laughing again. I would miss her so much if we had to part. She had been the sunny heart of this voyage so far.

Eventually, we managed to stop giggling. Frenchie sighed and wiped her eyes. Then she tossed her head, trying to mimic an officer's look.

"You don't get rid of me that easily anyhow, miss."

But it turned out she was wrong. The day finally arrived when the weary *Hopewell* found her way into the Gulf of Tonkin. It was a basking hot day of a tropical spring. The harbor was alive with the coming and going of local vessels, their sails like the fins of fish, each cutting its own path through the busy shoal. Noisy sailors in conical hats waved their arms, warning off any others who came too near. Between them, tiny houseboats bobbed, oblivious to the danger. And behind all that, the low, white buildings of the trading station, the Company flag flying high above their roofs.

"I will need to have several words with you, Mistress Rosewood, when my business here is concluded," Captain Robinson said. He had summoned me to his quarters in the stern shortly before disembarking. The great bay windows behind his chart table, with their several mullioned sections, looked streaked and salt-splattered in the tropical sun.

"Captain."

I bobbed a curtsey, my throat tight. I knew what the words were likely to be about. I had begged once again to stay with Kit's party, who were to take first watch aboard the *Hopewell* while everyone else went ashore, but I couldn't put off the evil hour forever. I had already tried pretending to be exhausted whenever Kit or Dr Lemuel tried to raise the subject. I doubted Captain Robinson would have their patience. He was a man used to giving orders, and I was aboard his ship and subject to his commands. Whatever he decided upon would be my fate, like it or not.

There would be no getting out of it this time. The thought went round and round in my mind as I stood on the near-deserted deck after they had gone ashore. All around me in the harbor, I could hear the shouts of the Tonkinese and the cries of the elegant seabirds overhead. What would the captain want to do with me? Send me back to Father? In some ways I yearned for it. I missed my family so much. But to go back to that life…? Even the captain must have realized there was no future in it for me. I could never become a housewife now. No man in his right mind would take me. And I couldn't become a burden on Father. I just couldn't.

But to leave me in Tonkin or Canton? How could he do that either? I didn't like the sound of those bored and tipsy officers who manned the Company stations. Men who hadn't seen an Englishwoman for years may be prepared to overlook imperfection, but at what price? I shuddered.

And then there was the matter I dared not speak of, even in the privacy of my own cabin. Kit had assured me many times that the waves had closed over Van Guelder, but could you ever truly be rid of a man like that? The sailors had called him unnatural and I agreed. There had been something of the Devil about him from the start, and I knew full well that that old adversary was forever walking the earth, seeking folk to devour. Dr Lemuel may have done his best to teach me the ways of reason, but my heart still said: "Keep running. Don't stop. Not ever."

Perhaps I was praying extra hard. I don't know. I do know that I was desperate above all things to keep sailing. And two days later when Dr Lemuel came aboard to take over the watch, I saw a chance to do just that.

"There's been a change of plan," he said, as he clambered out of the jolly-boat and over the gunwale. Kit and the others were already standing by with belongings knotted in bundles, ready to disembark. "The special items of furniture the captain wanted making will not be ready for another two months, the porcelain not for another three weeks. Some internal dispute. So the captain hopes to make good his losses by loading a sloop with products to trade around the South China Sea. He is in negotiations with the Tonkinese now as to as suitable vessel and has charged me with selecting a crew."

"You are to command, Doctor?" Kit asked.

The surgeon ran a hand through his thick hair, now longer than ever.

"For my sins."

A buzz of questioning drowned out anything else I might have heard at this point. The men were keen to know all the details, both those who wished to put themselves forward for the enterprise and those who would rather stay in port. I couldn't interfere with that. I was not a mariner. But eventually I understood as much as I needed to know, which was that Dr Lemuel was to command a crew of fourteen to trade between local ports and Kit was to be his first mate. Everyone else was to stay in Tonkin.

"And that includes you, Mistress Rosewood," the doctor said, when I tried to turn my pleading eyes on him. "It is high time you went ashore. A sloop will not have the comfort of the *Hopewell,* and you will not have the benefit of Frenchie and Mr. Solomons to attend to your needs. There is no place for them aboard. This is a working vessel. Mariners only."

"But a whole two months without you or Kit?" I had never been very good at wheedling but I tried my best now. "Captain Robinson placed me under your supervision. You can't just abandon me. It's...dereliction."

"I will hear no more of this."

But he did. I made sure he heard of it as often as possible –
and Kit too. Kit, I thought, might be easier to work on. I could see
uncertainty in his blue-grey eyes when he talked about my
staying in Tonkin. But all he said was:

"You'll be fine with Mr. Solomons and the captain. They'll be
taking lodgings, and the captain's bound to have servants. You
could do with some home comforts after all you've been
through. I'll take you ashore myself and see you safe. Don't look
like that, Margaret. You know it's for the best."

I began to despair of ever getting through to them. Perhaps I
was being stupid and pig-headed after all. What could I do on a
working vessel? I would be in the way the whole time. But it
turned out that not everyone saw it that way. Just as I was
thinking that I was going to have to face the scrutiny of Tonkin
after all, big Mekuria and his men made an announcement. They
refused to sail on without me.

They came to Dr Lemuel in a stiff-shouldered bunch the day
before the sloop was due to sail.

"Begging your pardon, sir, but we've been talking and – well
– our little princess, if you'll excuse the expression, has brought
us fair winds and good weather all this way. The lads will be
hanged if we make sail without her, and that goes for every hand
aboard this vessel. It'd be tempting Fate, sir."

"Mekuria, what have I told you about these superstitions? It
really is beneath your dignity." Dr Lemuel gave a sigh of
exasperation.

"With respect, sir, the lads and I know what we've seen and
heard on this voyage and we're keeping Mistress Rosewood with
us."

No amount of reasoning from the Doctor could make them
change their minds on this matter. As far as they were concerned,
I was their ship's mascot and lucky charm. Besides, they said, I
gave the men a reason to get out of their hammocks when the
bell struck, and the Good Lord knew they needed that with all

this extra work the captain had put upon them.

I wasn't sure about the hammock part. Or about the lucky charm, come to that. But I made sure Mekuria got an extra-big smile when Dr Lemuel wasn't looking. He had done me a bigger favor than he knew. Now I would get aboard the sloop for sure.

I won't pretend that was entirely the end of the matter. There were still a number of strong words spoken (not to mention a few on-your-head-be-its and don't-blame-me's). But the tide, you could say, had turned in my favor. On the seventh day of May, after many tearful goodbyes and promises to meet again soon, I got my wish. I sailed out of Tonkin harbor aboard a sloop of fifteen souls, bound for the many ports of the South China Sea.

9

Pirates of the China Sea

The sloop was called the *Reward*. She was a small vessel, lying low to the water, with one mast fore-and-aft rigged, which meant that the sail hung in a line from bow to stern, like on the fishing vessels back home in Hollyport. She only had one cabin, which by rights ought to have belonged to the ship's master, but now belonged to me. To save space, I had to share it with Dr Lemuel's medicine chest, log books and navigational equipment.

The first three days were cramped and hectic, and I could easily have regretted begging to come along, but I didn't. I was relieved to simply be at sea again. I had spent a grand total of one hour ashore in Tonkin, which I remembered as a frightening confusion of lanterns and conical hats, chickens and strange cures. During my mercifully brief visit, I had shuffled through the streets, half-hidden against the damp linen of Dr Lemuel's shirt, praying for it to be over. The fact that I now had no one to help me dress and not enough space to so much as open a book (had I been allowed to bring any of my books in the first place) seemed less important than the fact that we were once more surrounded by water and moving forward, away from towns, villages, and any hint of betrothal.

We had taken on some new crew members in Tonkin: a local sailor named Loc and two other men. Loc was the shortest man I had ever seen, and no one but his two companions spoke a word of his language; yet within a matter of hours he had everyone – big Mekuria included – jumping at his every word. Kit found it hilarious and said there ought to be a Loc aboard every vessel. He claimed he would have the entire royal and merchant navy running smoothly within a week. It was one of Loc's men who came to my cabin daily to bring my breakfast, take out the chamber pot, and strap on my silver hands. He did it all with extreme politeness and discretion, but I missed Frenchie's grin and cheery comments. I hoped she was getting on well with Mr. Solomons in Tonkin and that we would be together again soon.

There was every chance of the journey being a pleasant one. We were due to call at a number of islands, and in-between them was miles and miles of what the sailors promised me was the most beautiful ocean in the world.

"We'll give you a space to stand where we can, miss," Conlan said. "There's all sorts to see out here. Sharks now, they're the foe of the honest seaman and a bad sign, though I don't doubt but we'll spy one or two. But dolphins, they're the sailor's friend. You can spot as many of those as you like."

"Sea stars, they're pretty," offered another sailor.

"Purple jellyfish, that's what you want to see. With crests like great big sails."

"Crabs that can crack nuts in their pincers."

"Birds no bigger than your thumb."

But I never got to see any of it. I woke in my cabin on the third night to the sound of crashing and thudding, and the feeling that the whole world was tumbling over the edge of a chasm and lurching back to the brink again. The lantern beat against the ceiling until its glass doors smashed. The cot-bed where I was sleeping swung out dangerously towards the paneled walls. I screamed.

"Hold fast there, Margaret!" Kit appeared at the doorway in silhouette, lit from behind by wavering orange beams and soaked to the bone. "She's a sturdy craft; she'll weather it. Only stay in your cabin, whatever you do."

I had no intention of doing anything else.

"Thanks," I managed, as the door crashed shut. The bed swung back the other way with a jolt, causing my face to miss the panel by inches. Beneath me, something in the cargo thudded and smashed. My guts lurched somewhere above my head. I buried my face in the pillow and prayed every psalm I could think of.

We had run into a storm. A bad one. It hadn't stopped by the morning, or by the morning after that. Chests slid. Crockery broke. Water slopped everywhere. There was nowhere safe for me except in the cot-bed. Loc's man had tied me into it with ropes, so that I swung like a ham on a butcher's stall and jerked with every lurch of the waves. I was constantly looking up to the long pole from which the bed hung by curtain rings, and to the brass hooks that fastened the pole to the beams above. With the constant creaking and straining, I couldn't believe they wouldn't break at any moment.

I was wrenchingly sick. Worse than I had been since my first days aboard the *Hopewell*. I was almost glad that regular mealtimes appeared to have been lost somewhere off the China coast; there was nothing I could get to stay in my stomach. Loc's man managed to stagger in occasionally and crumble something into my mouth with as little movement or eye contact as possible, but he soon learned to keep a bucket in the other hand. After a few days, there was a permanent ache in my middle and a taste of acid in my mouth that I thought would never leave. The world was reduced to a never-ending lurch, lurch, lurch, without fresh air or sunlight. The cabin stank.

"So much for my being the ship's mascot," I groaned to Dr Lemuel, when he came in looking for charts and dividers. "The men must be calling me a Jonah by now. They might as well throw me overboard and have done with me. At least I won't be sick any more once I'm dead."

The doctor's lip curled slightly.

"That is hardly a reasonable point of view, Mistress Rosewood." His voice sounded rough and weary. "I will make you up some ginger cordial when I have the time. We must outrun this storm sooner or later."

He opened one of the roped-down chests and piled several

charts on a table, tutting and sighing over the pitiful state they were in. Even with the most secure boxes, the water had managed to leak in from somewhere. He sat down at the table, leaning closely over the charts, his lips moving silently as his fingernail traced a journey. I saw him work out calculations on his fingers, grunt, consult a log book, put it down. He moved one chart out of the way and leaned over another. I heard him mutter something about north-north-east and lines of longitude.

"Are we lost, Dr Lemuel?" I said.

"Not lost." He began to measure with a pair of dividers, and then stopped to check his findings against another chart. I could see two lines scored from his mouth to his chin. They made him look much older. He turned to me and gave a smile that didn't quite erase them. "Blown off course, merely. But we know the co-ordinates we are trying to reach. That is something."

The storm stopped eventually. We came out of the squall and the sickening waves to something approaching calm. I was able to totter out of my cabin and stand on deck without fear of being swept to Davy Jones. The wind was warm again and the sky was back to kingfisher blue. Meals returned to three rations a day, and Loc's companion was able to perform his full Tonkinese courtesies to me without falling over.

But the *Reward* was half the ship she had been before. Water had seeped into everything and it would be months before we would be rid of the smell. The main sail had a rip in it. The biscuits were soggy. I don't think anyone could have told what color the paintwork had been before, had they not remembered. In spite of the heat, my stumps ached from all the damp. My silver hands had survived, but the shine had gone from the coins and they were black about the edges.

As for Kit and the sailors, they looked as if they had spent a week wrestling giants. There was not a man without black shadows under his eyes and bruises on his body. One or two looked ready to fall asleep at their posts, and there were several harsh words on that subject from the second mate that I had rather not have heard. It was a punishable fault at sea, I knew, to neglect duty for any reason, but I was sure a week in their hammocks would have served all the crew much better than a constant round of watches.

At first I was glad of the warm wind. It dried out the timbers and blew away some of the staleness. But it soon became clear that no one else was happy about it. The men shook their heads, and Kit and Dr Lemuel debated long and hard over the chart table when they thought I was asleep.

"It's blowing the wrong way," Kit said when I finally cornered them for an explanation. "Clear to the east and no sign of letting up. With the *Reward* in the state she is, we could just drift. And we're off course as it is."

"It's where we may drift to that concerns me," said Dr Lemuel. "The authority of the East India Company is not recognized everywhere, and we are coming to lesser known waters."

"Lesser known?" My chest tightened. "Then we are, in fact, lost?"

The two men exchanged grim looks.

"No," said Dr Lemuel, firmly. "We know our course and will do everything to return to it."

But this time he did not smile.

The wind didn't change. It kept up in exactly the same direction and the *Reward* limped along with it. The looks on the men's faces became grimmer, and tempers began to fray. I started to wish Dr Lemuel had not made me work so hard at languages, as some of the language I heard was pretty foul, and one or two men were gagged with an iron bar for several hours as a result. Dr Lemuel spent more and more time scanning the horizon with a quadrant and spy-glass or consulting the ship's compass. Kit looked like a walking corpse.

It amazed me that the men hadn't changed their minds about me and decided I was a bad omen after all. But if they had, they were keeping it very quiet. Generally, if they spotted me, there would be nudges in the ribs and a sudden cease in cursing, followed by nods and smiles.

"Don't you fret about this old wind, miss," they would say. "We blows one way and then the other, but we gets there in the end."

But if by chance they didn't see me coming, I would catch a lot of talk about ill luck and not boding well. I don't think it referred to me, and there were mercifully few complaints about Kit and Dr Lemuel either, but it felt like everyone aboard was simply holding their breath, waiting for something bad to happen.

It happened on the tenth day. The lookout had spotted an island chain the day before, and, though we still didn't know where we were, there was serious talk about trying to put in there for provisions and repairs. I knew better than to get in the way of sailors' debates, and had taken to my cabin, sitting on a roped-down sea chest to try one of my latest experiments. Since the storm cleared, I had found a piece of chalk rolling about the boards and discovered that, if I gripped it between my toes and the ball of my foot, I could get a reasonable control over it to make marks on the cabin wall. I had started keeping a tally of the days that passed, and over the last two days I had been trying to add other symbols as well, to show the weather and the sailors' mood.

It took a lot of effort for a small effect. I forgot the ship and became completely lost in what I was doing, as with one foot braced against the chest for balance, and the other stretched out from beneath the turquoise hem of my breeches, I scraped the chalk along the oaken panel. So it was perfectly natural that I screamed and dropped the chalk when, out of silence, the ship's bell clanged, as strident as the Last Trump.

"All hands on deck now!" Someone yelled. "Weapons at the

ready!"

Running footsteps followed hard on shouts and commands. The door of the cabin flew open and Dr Lemuel burst in, heading straight for the sea chest. He pulled out his pistols and hangar, and began to strap them about himself, cursing under his breath.

"Do not leave this cabin, Mistress Rosewood." He turned round to look at me, his dark eyebrows meeting in the middle. I had never seen him look so severe. "Stay put until Mr. Blackthorn or I tell you otherwise."

"I wasn't going to..." Seeing the kindly surgeon like this upset me far more than any of the noises I could hear outside. Was he angry with me? "I don't understand. What's happening?"

"There's a boat on fire in the water. And two other sails fast approaching from that island. I fear we have let our vigilance slip." He tugged his sword belt tight. "Damn my eyes for letting you come aboard. Stay out of sight."

He strode out and the door banged shut again. Tears burned at the backs of my eyes. Dr Lemuel had slammed the door in my face. He had practically cursed me out loud. I had been trying so hard the last few days to be as good a crewmate as I could in all the difficulties, to be supportive to the men and not get in their way. And now that it looked like the *Reward* was really in danger, he treated me like a disobedient puppy that needed locking up. And *swore* at me. The oath still resounded like a slap in the face. My Doctor Lemuel – the man who saved my life – never used language like that. It was more like something from one of my fever dreams than the life at sea I had come to know.

Something exploded outside. Cannon? A musketoon? The linen bindings round my chest suddenly felt much too tight. What was happening out there? These two ships: what were they? A boat on fire in the water, Dr Lemuel had said. Were we about to burn alive? My chest tightened still more. I fancied I could already smell the burning tar and hear the rotten planks crackling with sparks. I had to get out of the cabin. I had to see what was going on.

But not so as Dr Lemuel could see me. If he wished he had never brought me aboard, I was not going to afford him one glimpse of me. I would look out, that was all. And if it really was that bad, I would save myself as best I could. If that meant jumping into the sea, so be it.

The door was firmly shut. I was going to have to turn the handle. That was not so easy, since my silver hands were rigid and impossible to grip with. Usually, I like to grip things with my forearms, but in this tiny cabin there was not the space. I would have to do my best. I took hold, slipped, took hold again. I knew that rushing would only make it harder, but the pounding in my temples was saying, "hurry, hurry," in a way that was difficult to ignore.

The handle turned. I pushed the door open and put my foot in the gap to stop it from closing again. On the small sloop, the door opened straight onto the quarter-deck. The noises were already louder and more threatening than before. I pressed my body up against the woodwork behind the door and peeped through.

Kit and Dr Lemuel were easy to make out. They were standing on the quarter deck with their backs to me, drawn swords in their hands. Kit's hand was shaking. The rest of the crew was posted at various points around the ship, all with cutlasses, marlinspikes or some sort of weapon. But what I couldn't understand was why everyone was so inactive. Not a man among them was working the ropes or standing in the rigging. If there was danger, shouldn't we be fleeing it?

Then I saw. Every man was looking with set features at two Chinese junks that had drawn up at speed on either side of us. Each junk bristled with cannon, both the large and small kind. Spears and mirrors glinted. Tattooed men with beards and bare legs shook weapons and blew on conch shells. And every eye aboard the *Reward* was drawn to a man with a many-tailed flag in his hand and what looked hideously like a necklace of human heads. He was standing on the gunwale of his own ship, so close he could easily have stepped across to ours. He was a good head taller than his men, and his beard was not black like theirs, but red. When he spoke, it was in a language I recognized: a simplified version of Dutch.

"You have entered the territorial waters of Flood Dragon." His voice was so loud that I could hear every word from my hiding place. "If you wish to pass with your lives, my lord Flood Dragon demands that you pay tribute of everything you value in your hold. If you refuse, then know that this is only a thousandth of the fleet my lord commands. There will be no mercy. You have seen already that my lord does not hesitate to swallow his own ships with fire. He will swallow you just as easily. Take heed."

"Orders, Doctor?" Kit's voice was unnaturally level. "Captain Robinson stands to lose all if we surrender."

Dr Lemuel cleared his throat several times.

"And what of that other precious cargo we carry? Could you stand by and see her fall into enemy hands? Speaking as a man, Mr. Blackthorn?"

"As a man, sir, no." Kit looked down. "But the powder," he said. "You know full well that it's all waterlogged. And we've seen what their cannon can do. Are you then suggesting...?"

"That we do the only thing we can, yes. Tell the men to throw down their weapons and kneel."

Kit hesitated. "And if the pirates do not keep their word, sir? Forgive me, but they are not renowned for their honesty."

Dr Lemuel squared his shoulders. "Protect Mistress Rosewood."

"Aye, sir."

Kit's voice cracked. He turned towards Dr Lemuel and the two men grasped hands for a moment. I thought I heard something about, "it's been an honor," and, "if the worst should befall," but they spoke too low to be sure.

The *Reward* shuddered. Eight or ten grappling hooks had

clamped onto the gunwale at either side. I couldn't bear to see any more. As I took my foot from the door, I heard Dr Lemuel shout in Dutch, "We surrender! We surrender!" and Kit bellowing, "All hands throw down your weapons! On your knees! Kneel!" I flung myself into the corner of the cabin. There was a taste of blood on my lip; I must have bitten it without knowing. Pirates. Any moment now they would be aboard, overrunning the vessel to search for anything of value. They would come for the medicine chest, I knew they would. Pirates always stole medicine. They would take my hands, my precious hands. They would take... Would they take me? Muscles I hadn't previously known I possessed tensed painfully. What was it that pirates did to girls? I had a fairly good idea in mind. My notion of the exact deed was hazy, but I knew it would be far worse than a passionate kiss on the inner arm.

Dr Lemuel's oath in the cabin just now came back to my mind. He was right to curse. It had been the worst kind of mistake to let me come on this mission. Why in the name of sanity had I begged for it? I could have been safe in the captain's lodgings in Tonkin now, being fed by maidservants and laughing with Frenchie. Now Dr Lemuel and Kit...the doctor and Kit...

Tears were on my face before I realized I was crying. How could I have been so selfish? I had done nothing but make trouble for Kit, Dr Lemuel and the rest of the crew since I'd stowed aboard in London. All that time the doctor had wasted on me when he should have been tending sick crew members or taking his watch at the helm. All those hours of sleep Kit had lost watching over me, waiting for me to wake. Because of me, Frenchie had almost ended up like that man outside the Dolphin and had risked having her secret exposed to the whole crew. And somehow I'd made Mekuria and Conlan and the rest feel sorry for me and love me, so that they'd demanded I come with them on this insane voyage. If it wasn't for me, they would be fighting the pirates now. They might have managed to save the cargo.

Now they were allowing those appalling men to come aboard and… I couldn't get that necklace of heads out of my mind.

I was sobbing now. Tears dripped from my chin, and my nose ran, but I couldn't be bothered to wipe anything away. It was all my fault. Everything that had happened was my fault. I *was* a Jonah. I should have been thrown into the sea with Van Guelder: one flesh, one heart, one soul, just like he wanted. I deserved to be swallowed up. I deserved to be obliterated. They were all better off without me. And the sooner the better.

Harsh voices were shouting now on deck, in a language I didn't know. Footsteps were thudding. I couldn't take any more. I stared straight ahead through the mist of tears. Dr Lemuel's medicine chest was right in front of me, standing on top of a much bigger chest. I shuffled towards it and forced the lid open with my feet. All the glass vials of unguents and cordials were sitting in square compartments in the upper section. And in the top right-hand compartment, the one thing I needed more than anything now. The black bottle. Most of its contents were gone, but there was still enough in the bottom for a sizable dose. Or two or three.

I took a deep breath. I cared nothing for caution now. All I wanted was to be gone. I bent over the chest, grasped the stopper between my teeth, pulled, and spat it out onto the cabin floor. Then before I had time to think, I bit into the neck of the bottle, closed my lips around it and tipped back my head.

The laudanum burned down my throat like molten iron. I felt the top of my head lifting away, heard a thrumming in my ears like a crazy harp. I gave a cough and the empty bottle fell from my mouth onto the boards and rolled aside.

The door crashed open.

10

Flight and Fall

"Good God, Mistress Rosewood, what are you about?"

Dr Lemuel took hold of my elbow and hauled me to my feet. The cabin walls rushed towards me with frightening speed and then ebbed away like the tide, leaving blurs in the corners of my vision.

"Hurry. There is no time to lose. I have told the pirate captains you are my daughter. They have granted you safe passage along with me. Of a sort." He hastily grabbed a few essentials that were lying round the cabin and shoved them into the satchel hanging from his shoulder. "Come now before they change their minds."

"What about Kit?"

My own voice sounded slurred and seemed to be coming from someone else. I sniffed loudly. I wanted to sleep, to melt into nothingness. Why hadn't he just left me to punish myself in peace?

Dr Lemuel gave me a sudden, intense look and opened one of my eyes with two fingers.

"You have, haven't you? You've drunk the laudanum. Foolish girl!" He took out a handkerchief and wiped my nose as if I had been a five-year-old. He wasn't terribly gentle about it. "Foolish girl," he said again, pulling down my sleeves as far as they would go. "Keep your hands covered. And take my arm. Look only ahead. We may survive this yet."

"Kit...?" I murmured again, but Dr Lemuel didn't reply. He took an iron grip on my arm and walked me through the doors onto the quarter deck. The pirates were everywhere. Dragon tattoos snarled on bare backs; swords, spears and polished muskets glinted in every direction. Whatever Dr Lemuel had said about looking only ahead, I couldn't keep my eyes focused. They rolled about in their sockets, glancing aimlessly over this and then that. I would catch a glimpse of what looked like a tuft of human hair hanging from a sword hilt or a sea monster leering from a shield on someone's arm. I could no longer tell if what I saw was real or if this was one of the nightmares from the bottom of the black bottle. And I couldn't help looking for Kit and the others. I thought I saw Loc with his hands tied behind his back and his face to the deck. But I wasn't sure. Dr Lemuel was marching me as quickly as I could stagger, towards two men standing in the prow. Pirate captains. The vivid reds and blacks of their armor, combined with the smell of burning wood, made me wonder for a moment if they were on fire. They were wavering in the breeze. No; one man was simply holding the flag I had seen before. A stern face, neither male nor female, fluttered in the midst of its many tails. The other captain had a mask with eyebrows and a square mouth full of teeth. I felt myself being sucked into its hungry gape. It was going to eat me up. My knees sagged. My body was heavy all over.

"Please get in boat. Food is within," said the masked captain in bad Dutch.

Dr Lemuel bowed in the manner of Loc's man, on both knees, head to the deck, and pulled me down to do the same. The web of ropes and yardarms reeled. The grain of the deck's timbers swirled like cyclones. He dragged me to my feet and pulled me forward again, towards the *Reward*'s prow. Looking over the side, I realized we were being expected to climb into a vessel that was no more than two large planks held together by a rude cabin. Its one sail was the shape of a crab's claw. It was so low to the water that the waves were washing through it. I didn't want to get in. I wanted Kit. I wanted to lie down and go to sleep.

"Dr Lemuel, I..."

"Hush!" The doctor's voice hissed in my ear. He climbed overboard into the canoe (for that was all it was) and held up his arms for me. I felt one of the pirates take me round the waist and lower me down. The feel of his dirty hands on me made me want to scream. I hoped like anything it wasn't the man with the severed heads. Dr Lemuel grabbed me from the other side and lifted me into the canoe's excuse for a cabin. I turned and looked back at the *Reward*. Half-naked pirates were already manning the capstan and tiller. Our crew was being marched in two parties over the gunwales into each of the pirate junks. In the middle of the line, just stepping up to cross over, was Kit. His back was straight and his pigtail was sticking out behind him, stiff and proud. As I looked, he glanced round and our eyes met. A smiled forced its way over his lips and he gave me a wink. The next moment, he had stepped over into the junk with his hands in fetters.

It was too much. I could cope with anything except more kindness and bravery. My shoulders heaved as Dr Lemuel pushed me down under the shelter, packing his satchel in alongside me. Why didn't Kit fight to stop this? Why didn't any of them? How could they just stand there, shuffling along like sheep at a market? I wasn't worth going to a pirate ship for. Couldn't they see that? They had to do something. It couldn't end like this; it just couldn't.

"Kit!" I sobbed. "Kit, come back!"

But it was no good. The canoe was already drifting away, surging on the waves. The *Reward* fell astern. And my head was throbbing. My eyes closed, opened, closed again. Everything around me was going as soft as velvet.

"Kit..."

My head was too heavy. It sagged towards my chest. With an effort, I forced my eyes open. There was a bag of rice in a corner and a bucket of fish in cheap vinegar. I slumped onto the bag, its coarse cloth grazing my cheek. The waves under us swelled and subsided. I thought I could see Kit's tarred pigtail, bobbing just above my head. I reached out towards it, but I had no hands to grasp it with. It faded away. The sea swelled and the world smelled of fish and rice.

I woke to the sound of a crackling fire. My head was fuzzy and felt ten times its normal size. I was shuddering without control. My arms were sore, as if something had been digging into them for a long time.

"Frenchie, I need my medicine," I said sleepily.

"That you most certainly do not."

The briskness of Dr Lemuel's voice recalled me to the present. I wasn't on the *Hopewell*; that was months ago. Only where was I? I tried to sit up. A lopsided vision of rocks and scrub whirled round and round my head.

"I feel ill," I said.

"Hardly surprising, since you drained a bottle of finest laudanum just less than seven hours ago."

The doctor's tone was as matter-of-fact as ever, but his hands were gentle and fatherly as he tucked his coat round my shoulders. I took several deep breaths. The whirling vision settled down somewhat. We were sitting on a rugged island with heath under us and an overhanging crag above our heads. It was dusk. In front of us was a small fire and some roast eggs, and beyond that a beach that didn't seem to be the right color. I looked down at my sore arms. There were score marks on them and my silver hands were missing.

"You fell asleep with your hands on. I took them off for the time being to make you more comfortable. Here." Dr Lemuel put a flask to my lips. "Drink some water. You shall have some eggs presently."

I looked out at the wild scene ahead. Around us was nothing but rock and heath in various scrubby shades of green-grey. Birds were flying in to roost for the night but there was no sign of people. Across the sea, I could just about make out some shapes that may have been more bumpy islands, looking very much like this one. It was not a cheering sight. I dropped my gaze back to the heath.

"Why is the ground moving?" My voice was a dull monotone.

"It's not. You have been at sea so long that it simply feels that way. It will settle down in time. Rather more time in your case, given your foolish action."

I wrapped my arms round my knees. I didn't want to think about what had happened back on the *Reward*.

"Well, why is the beach black? Or isn't that real either?"

"Ah." A little of its old spark came into the surgeon's voice. "I believe that is due to the action of a volcano: a mountain capable of spurting forth fire. In time, the molten rocks it spits out turns to black dust and sand. This whole chain of islands may have fire beneath its surface. Although I hope not to encounter it during our brief stay. Fascinating it would certainly be, but not very comfortable."

I felt that I didn't care if any number of mountains spat out fire on me. It would be the least I deserved for what had happened to Kit. I heaved a sigh.

"We're marooned, aren't we? And it's all my fault."

Dr Lemuel turned sharply towards me. His heavy brows and the solid line of his nose stood out in the firelight.

"There will be none of that talk in my presence, Mistress Rosewood. Defeat is the enemy and we must fight it within as well as without. Besides, you are hardly applying reason to the situation. One is not marooned when one is provided with an escape vessel and a supply of food. Which, I might add, we have not yet had cause to touch, thanks to the bird life of this charming if rather lonely island. We have every hope of reaching human habitation, if we put our minds to that end. In the meantime, we have fire and shelter and the comfort of encouraging companionship. And do not dare lay the blame for this on yourself, my dear Mistress Rosewood." He sighed to himself. "That lies with me."

I knew that wasn't true, but my head was too muzzy for me to argue. I was sure I had only heard half of what the doctor had said. I had a vague idea that we were lonely and that we had to put our minds to fire and shelter. Or was it bird life? I tried to recall the bird life in the journals Dr Lemuel had shown me aboard the *Hopewell*. Birds in lands beyond the edge of the map. Those lands that could only be reached by those who were looking for something else. Those were the places Dr Lemuel had said he was fated to stumble upon. Places, he had said, as real and reasonable as any land we had visited with Captain Robinson. Where our travels might one day lead us, sooner rather than later.

"Where actually are we?" I said.

"Latitude forty-six degrees north, longitude one hundred and eighty-three. Or we were when we left the *Reward*."

"And where is that when it's at home?"

The doctor shrugged and gave a half-smile.

"That I cannot say. Maps become uncertain in this part of the world."

The next few days were very much like the first. Every morning, the doctor strapped on my silver hands and helped me into the covered hut at the centre of the canoe, where the stink of fish got progressively worse every day and the bag of rice got smaller and less comfortable. And every evening we would find ourselves sitting on the beach of some scrubby little island, eating roast eggs and fish if we were lucky or ill-cooked rice if we were not. Together we would watch another breathtaking tropical sunset, knowing that for another day we had no hope of finding human life or even of getting any more rice.

The only difference between the days was that I became less sleepy and more agitated as the effects of my dose from the black bottle wore off. Sometime I thought I saw things in the dark – mostly severed heads or that teeth-filled mouth of the pirate's mask – but mostly I would keep remembering Kit's brave smile, especially last thing at night. The memory tormented me over and again. As soft stars came out over the never-resting sea, and lumps of black shale stuck into our backs, I would toss and turn, wishing and wishing that I could have done something to save him. The combination of guilt and laudanum-visions was a heady mixture, and not one that was likely to keep my spirits up. On a couple of nights, it was all the doctor could do to stop me from getting up and fleeing into the forest behind us.

"Hush, Mistress Rosewood," he would say. "Fix your mind on tomorrow. We will sail on and we will find help. We are making progress every day."

But, even as I struggled to fight the effects of opium, I could tell his confidence was counterfeit. We had been traveling for five days now and the food was running low. We couldn't live on rice and birds' eggs forever, and the chain of islands had to end at some point. I could see the doctor's mind was on what lay beyond – whether the refuge of a mainland or endless open sea – and not on his surroundings at all. In the past few days we had encountered enough curiosities for a lifetime: monkeys that could have sat in the palm of your hand and moths as big as your fist, blue-tinted jellyfish and floating coconuts. The old Dr Lemuel, the surgeon of the *Hopewell*, would have been studying their every detail, measuring and comparing, scratching in his journal until the last of the firelight faded. Now he only sat staring through his perspective glass, trying to count degrees of latitude on his fingers and sighing in frustration.

"Is there anything out there?" To be honest, I didn't really care any more – I had given up hoping, and had enough to do simply fighting off the twitchiness that screamed *more laudanum* – but the silence between us had gone on for hours and, with no other company available, was fast becoming irritating.

"No." He shut up his glass. "Only a cloud. We should find better shelter. It may rain tonight, and tropical rain is heavy."

"That cloud out there, do you mean?" I could see a dark sort of blot above the sea, drifting in our direction. Something occasionally winked and glittered from the lower side of it. "It's moving quickly, isn't it? How come it's going in the opposite direction to the wind? You wouldn't think it would be able to get here."

In an instant, the doctor had his perspective glass out again. He stared through it for several minutes, and turned back to me. There was a dancing gleam in his eye.

"My dear Mistress Rosewood, you are a perfect genius. I knew I would make a natural philosopher of you, and now you have outshone your tutor. Quickly; on your feet. We must build up this fire to make a beacon. What a mercy you are wearing such bright clothes! Everything must be done to attract the attention of that...that..." He smiled to himself. "That flying curiosity."

For a moment, I had absolutely no idea what I had said to make him so excited. I could still see nothing out there but a large, dark cloud with an unusually glittery underside. For all I knew, that final detail may well be another vision from the bottom of the bottle. But Dr Lemuel had already stuffed our few belongings in his satchel, and was grabbing any bits of brushwood he could find to throw upon the fire. The surge of heat made me get up and step back before my Madras finery (now no longer quite so fine) caught ablaze. The flames' reflection danced in the silver sixpences on my hands.

"Ho, there!" Dr Lemuel waved his arms at the cloud. "Parlay! Truce! Take pity on two abandoned travelers!"

The cloud was coming on at speed. Now that it was nearer, it looked more solid and less like a cloud at all. There were roofs of some sort, and things moving about on the top of it. For a moment I had an idea of heavenly castles in the clouds, of the Celestial City coming down like a bride to meet her husband. But a moment later, all changed and my thoughts strayed closer to Hell. Something had made me stare and stare in horror so I couldn't tear my eyes away. It was that glittering surface beneath the cloud, or rather – I could see more clearly the closer it came

– that glittering rock, rough and sparkling like it had been dusted with diamonds. My throat tightened so I could scarcely breathe. I had seen this thing in my nightmares a hundred times since the *Hopewell*. And now it was here, huge, filling the sky. The lodestone. Van Guelder's lodestone, only a thousand times the size it had been before. Was this a laudanum-dream too, or was I actually seeing it? I could sense its power. It was exerting a repelling force from its great height against the surface of the sea, pushing out waves in ripples by the strength of an unseen will. Nearer and nearer it came. Soon there would be no escaping it.

"Over here; over here!" shouted Dr Lemuel.

Perhaps this really was a dream, and I would wake up in my cabin on the *Hopewell* to the sight of Frenchie bringing in a dish of burgoo and a shot of lemon juice on a tray. The flying mass was coming on by the minute now. It couldn't be real. It had balconies on it and stairs, for crying out loud. Above the lodestone, on the main body of the…cloud? Island? How could a cloud suddenly have become an island? How could an island be flying in the sky? I could see more detail now. The balconies and the stairs ran all the way up the outer surface of it, criss-crossing what looked like the walls of a vast city. Between the balconies were windows with wooden lattices, roofs with upturned edges: all piled on top of one another higgledy-piggledy. The very top of the wall shone with the azure tiles and curling roofs of several guard towers. Silver pagodas stood out at equal distances from one another. Towering above all in the distant centre of the city was a glass dome held together with a lacework of silver and lacquered wood.

And there were people. Surely it couldn't be real if there were people? Bare-legged fishermen hung lines from the lower balcony, nudging one another and pointing as they noticed us. Women and infants stared from the latticed windows. Higher up, a boy and an old man ran up the stairs. They all had lacquer-dark eyes in white faces and quilted coats in the Chinese style. They were all looking our way.

"Help! Help!" yelled Dr Lemuel. "Take us up! Take us up!"

It suddenly hit me what the doctor was trying to do.

"No!" The strength of my voice was not equal to the force of my emotion. I heard it waver. "You can't give me up to that. Please. Please. Don't let it take me."

I could hear a growing sound of music from the flying island. It sounded like bells, only sweeter and mellower, floating down from somewhere above the upper windows. On the balconies, I could now spot painted lanterns with tassels; I could smell the fragrance of spiny-leaved shrubs and herbs growing in finely-blown jars. The harmonies of the bells were achingly beautiful, like the song of stars. A part of me that still knew reason yearned towards the island. If ever there was a place of wonder, this was it. It defied even the most amazing pages of Dr Lemuel's previous notebooks. But I couldn't get my mind off the lodestone. It was the just the same as Mr. Van Guelder's, only huge. It had come to get me, where he had failed. A stone of that size, of that tremendous power, could reduce me to nothing in a heartbeat. Where could I possibly hide from a thing like that? I started backing towards the rocks and the forest.

"Mistress Rosewood! No!"

The doctor grabbed me by the shoulders with both hands. Tightly.

"Have mercy on us! I beg of you!" he yelled to the island.

"No!" I tried to wriggle out of his grasp but he held on tighter. I could smell sweat and see it standing out on his neck and forehead.

A man in an indigo robe with silver stars on it and wide, fur-lined sleeves had come down the stairs to the lower balcony. He gestured with his hands and called to Dr Lemuel in a language that sounded like singing. The doctor called back in a language I didn't know, and which I don't think the man in the starred robe knew either. But he nodded to Dr Lemuel and beckoned with his arms, talking away.

"I believe they want us to go nearer," Dr Lemuel said, straining against my writhing and flailing.

"I'm not going anywhere!" I kicked against his sea boots with my bare feet, but it only hurt me and had no effect on him. "Don't take me there, Doctor. Not up to that."

"You are hysterical, madam." His voice was infuriatingly calm. "When you come to your senses, you will see perfectly well that you will starve if you remain on this island. Now come along." He began dragging me towards the black beach.

"I'll starve, then," I said. And I dug my heels in harder.

But I couldn't struggle hard enough against Dr Lemuel's grasp. I had never been that strong anyway, and five days of roast eggs and rice hadn't done much to improve matters. Dr Lemuel was a full-grown man and a seasoned mariner to boot. Within moments, he had lifted my feet clear of the ground and was carrying me to the shore. The island above had slowed in its flight. The men on the upper balcony were turning a winch. A thick double chain with a triangular frame at its center was being lowered slowly, carefully. It reminded me unexpectedly of a garden swing we used to have in the kitchen garden in Hollyport. It passed down in front of the other balconies, past the windows with their herb gardens and staring housewives, until it hung below the base of the wall altogether. Just beyond the place where it swung was the island's underside and the lodestone; huge; inexorable. I set my jaw.

"I'm not getting on that," I said.

"You shall sit on my lap." Dr Lemuel calmly ignored my words and sat on the seat, then heaved me into position. The seat wobbled with the weight. The iron chains creaked. "Like the daughter I told the pirates you were. Just like my own little daughter, bless her heart. If she could see her papa now..." His voice softened and he sighed. Then he cleared his throat and held onto my waist with one hand and the frame with the other.

There was a clanking overhead and the seat began to rise. The beach dropped away beneath us in rhythmic jerks. From far above us, mixed in with the music of the chimes, I could hear the grunts of the winch-men, pulling, pulling. More clanks. We rose faster, more smoothly. The island where we had sheltered fell behind us; we were flying over the sea. I realized that the flying island must be continuing forwards and upwards in its flight, at the same time as the winch-men were pulling us up. We were a long way up now. The breakers against the shore became white lines on the water. The chain turned some more and we jerked to the height of the first balcony. A fisherman with a white beard gave us a solemn nod. Dr Lemuel's heart pounded against my back.

"Don't look down," he said.

I didn't really want to. But I didn't want to look up either. We must be passing level with the lodestone now. I was convinced I could feel its massive energy; repelling, repelling.

My eyes watered in the wind. The island was gliding over the sea now, gaining height like a soaring albatross. The wetness of a cloud enveloped us; then rushed away behind us, leaving us breathless and damp. Somewhere out ahead was the shoreline of a new country.

"Stop wriggling," said Dr Lemuel. "Can you not see they're struggling to raise this seat as it is?" He was gasping for breath. I wondered if he was afraid of heights.

"I want to get off," I said.

"Get off where?" His voice rose to a squeak. "I can assure you we are already off the map. Is that not enough for you?"

"I want to get off. Let go of me."

"Never." He tightened his arm about me until my ribs hurt. "My sweet child, if I let go of you now, how could I live with myself?"

"If that lodestone takes me, you'll never live with yourself. Please, Dr Lemuel. If you really care for me, let me go"

"Lodestone?" He looked behind him. A whole crowd of men and boys were standing on the lower balcony, holding out their arms to us. High above, the winch-men's faces were red with effort. "Mistress Rosewood, I truly believe you are mistaken if you imagine this island to be any sort of..."

But in his moment of distraction, I kicked and wriggled as hard as I could. A faint voice of reason begged me to stop, but all I could think about was getting away from the lodestone. The doctor's grip on my waist loosened. I leaned forward with as much force as I could muster. His hand slipped. My heart lurched up to my throat. What was I doing? There were hundreds of feet between me and the fast-approaching land.

"Mistress Rosewood!"

The doctor snatched at the Madras cotton, but it was too late. One minute the seat and Dr Lemuel's lap were beneath me; the next my heart was as huge as my whole body, threatening to explode in fear as I plunged through cloud and air and nothing, sheer nothing.

"Mistress Rosewood!"

The cry that ripped out of him was swept high above me. Other voices – gasping, exclaiming – were sucked into the clouds, along with a lingering harmony of heavenly bells that I felt would haunt me for the rest of my life. Then there was nothing but the wind in my ears and terror in my heart.

I wondered if death would be quick. If it would be painful or more like waking up in the morning to find yourself in a new place. From my reading, I had a pretty good idea of what that place would be like. There would be a river, and beyond that a golden gate through which the redeemed alone could pass. Would my mother be waiting for me on the other side, I wondered; and would she be pleased or upset to see me there so soon? Would I have to answer for my deeds? Perhaps my hands would grow back in the Heavenly Jerusalem. Only I didn't feel ready for heaven now. I wanted the flying island I had fallen from. I wanted to live. But the ground of a new land was rushing up towards me at dizzying speed. It would all be over before I knew it.

There was barely time for images of my sisters and Father and Kit and Frenchie to flash through my mind. Down, down I fell. I had no breath, no strength. The landscape beneath opened out, broadened, flew towards my face. A ring of mountains and a shoreline with boats, forming a border round a flat countryside of fields and orchards, rivers, bridges, lonely temples. A little, gray-roofed town with wooden walls and gates. At the town's center stood more walls forming a circumference to some important structure; strong walls, with castle towers rising from them at intervals. Their many-layered roofs curled white like glorious wedding cakes. I was falling within the bounds of the castle walls. A complex of elegant, low-roofed buildings inside glittered with hints of gold, even in the dull light of an overcast day. A vast, splendid garden surrounded the buildings, landscaped with trees, pathways, lakes and rocks.

I didn't want to die. I tried to pray, but none of the prayers I knew would come into my mind. All I could remember was one verse in the psalms about angels bearing you up in their hands lest you dashed your foot against a stone. I was about to be dashed against something now. Was an angel watching me? Was I one of the ones who dwelt in the shadow of the Almighty and could expect such protection? Conlan had said back on the *Hopewell* that my silver hands would guard me against evil. Could that possibly be true? Would they save me now?

I was falling into the garden. A lake was looming beneath me, surrounded by trees and moss-covered rocks. Its surface was scattered with flat leaves, its clear depths swimming with orange fish. The roof of a small house curled beside it, half-hidden in the trees. It stood partly on land, partly in the lake, held up on low stilts. On the side nearest the lake was a kind of wooden veranda where a man was sitting cross-legged in the shade. He was wearing a loose, cross-fronted coat or robe (I wasn't sure which) in a fine, blue print. His hair, which was black and looked to be receding at the front, was tied up on top of his head. It was impossible to tell what age he was. He was staring across the lake, not really looking at anything in particular. Perhaps he was simply enjoying the view.

I saw him for a second and then I didn't. A world-encompassing splash filled my ears and thumped right up my nose, threatening to break it apart. I plunged down among the stems of floating flowers, thrashing my arms and coughing for air that wouldn't come. Above me, everything was green and blurry and full of bubbles. The impact of the water stung my skin and pressed down on me like a ton of ballast. My lungs were burning. My nose throbbed. I couldn't breathe. Fish closed in around me.

There was a second, thunderous splash in the water above. I could feel a rush of movement towards me, the water parting, strong arms grasping me under the armpits, strong legs kicking. The light surged towards me, faster, faster. Water sprayed everywhere and cold air kissed my face.

I coughed as if my lungs would burst. My stomach retched, trying to bring up lake water, from my mouth, from my nose. Someone was dragging me to the edge of the lake; wading through the water; heaving me onto shore; laying me on wooden boards. I heard him pant and cough. His voice was definitely not that of an old man. Droplets of water flicked onto my cheek. I opened my eyes.

The man from in front of the house was kneeling over me. He was gasping hard and water was running down his face. I could see now that his black hair was not receding at all, but done up in a strange fashion that pulled it back tight from the forehead and fastened it in a topknot at the back. A whole lock of it had come undone and was lying wet over his high forehead. In his dark almond eyes was an expression of pure wonder and amazement.

"*Anatawa kamisama desuka soretomo rei desuka?*" he said.

In response I could do nothing but stare back. I had no idea what the young man was saying.

11

Lord of the Secret Empire

"*Anatawa sora kara ochitekita.*"

The man looked up to the overcast sky that I had fallen from only minutes before. There was no sign now of a flying island or a giant lodestone, or indeed of anything more unusual than drifting cloud or birds on the wing. His gaze went down to my bare feet, now tangled with pond weed, and along to my carven hands. They were waterlogged again and not very clean, but the sixpences and pennies were still recognizably silver.

"*Gin no te.*" His own hands hovered over them, as if he were afraid to touch them. "*Do-yu imidesuka? Anatawa rei desuka? Iinasai.*"

There was an urgency in his voice. Possibly even a command. Whoever he was, his awe at having seen a girl fall from the sky into a lake hadn't in any way hindered his self-control. He sounded as if he expected to be answered, and quickly. But I couldn't.

"I don't..." I tried to say, and choked on the water still filling my windpipe.

The man raised me up to a sitting position, while I gasped and coughed and tried to get my breath back. In the lake, his grip had been painfully firm, but now he touched me so lightly I could scarcely feel it. He talked to me the whole time, softly but determinedly. There was a rich tone to his voice, a dark honey tone, which complemented the sharp syllables of the tongue he spoke. I only wished I knew what he was saying. The language was one I had never heard before, even on the *Hopewell*.

"I don't understand." I finally managed to find a breathy version of my voice. "Do you speak English? *Parlez-vous français? Spreek je Nederlands?*"

The man's eyebrows came together in a look that I thought

was concentration rather than anger. How old was he, I wondered? Two and twenty? Five and twenty? His face, sharp-featured and well-looking enough as it went, was smooth and showed only the faintest hint of a moustache. But his features, though Eastern, were not like any I had seen in the ports. With such a severe forehead too, it was hard to make an accurate guess. He was kind, though, I decided, looking in his ebony eyes and seeing warmth in their crescent moon shape. Kind and authoritative. I thought that I could trust him. He had just saved my life, after all.

"I..." I looked up to the now island-free sky. Wherever the flying land had gone, it didn't look like it was coming back. Perhaps it was unable to stop flying; it hadn't stopped to pick us up, after all, just slowed a little. Perhaps the people weren't so friendly after all and had taken Dr Lemuel prisoner. Whatever had happened, I could truly say I was off the edge of the map now. I had absolutely no idea where I was. And I had no friend to help me either.

"Pardon me, sir...squire...master... Look, I know I don't speak your language and I'm sorry to trouble you, but..." The man's face was so intent, I could almost believe he understood me, despite our different languages. "I don't know where I am, and I'm a very long way from home. I literally have nothing. No one. Not even my hands." I looked down at the silver sixpences. The man's gaze followed. "I don't want to be a burden. But if there's somewhere I could go. An almshouse. Anything."

I couldn't believe I was reduced to begging. Father would have been appalled. But after all the terrible adventures I'd been through, I couldn't afford to care about social niceties. My heart was still pounding from the fall, and I was shivering with shock and cold. I was wet all over. All I wanted was a warm blanket and something to eat. I could worry about the rest later.

The man wasn't shivering, although he was just as wet as I. He was sitting very still, watching, examining. If I listened hard enough, I was sure I would hear him thinking. He sat back on his heels and put his fingers to his lips, pinching them together, knitting his brows. Then in one decisive move, he stood up and called something out across the garden. The tone of authority reminded me of Captain Robinson aboard his ship. I didn't doubt that someone would come in answer to the call.

I was not wrong. In a matter of minutes, a gardener in a loincloth had come running from the trees and thrown himself at the man's feet. I heard more words spoken, crisp and commanding, and the gardener rushed away, bowing. My rescuer watched him go, then crouched beside me and spoke again. He seemed to be trying to explain something. He gestured back to the house behind us and made signs with his hands like he was giving a gift. Then he waved towards the castle towers and put his hand on his breast.

"The castle? You're going to the castle?" I said.

I wasn't really sure. The little pantomime could have meant many things. Knowing which one to choose would be an art in itself. The young man repeated it again, slower, more forcefully, adding further gestures. He spoke precisely in his dark honey voice. I could see a hint of frustration in the set of his brows at my inability to understand, but he kept it well under control. This was a man of discipline, a man who could not only give orders but could keep to them himself. After my months at sea, I respected that immensely.

It was not too long before the sound of voices and running feet could be heard among the trees. More servants – men and women – were hurrying as fast as they could along the stony path that led out of the artistic arrangement of botanical life and towards the lakeside house. The bare-legged ones among the men carried boxes or baskets slung from poles across their shoulders. The senior servants (I presumed), who were dressed in a fashion closer to that of the young man, barked out orders, to which the lower servants responded with many bows. Several women, their faces to the ground, hurried inside the house and busied themselves about something. A man of better dress than the rest stood by while maidservants put an embroidered cover round the young man's shoulders. The young man tried to shrug it off and pointed towards me. A woman in grey scurried in my direction, wrapped me in a quilt and scurried away again, without a single glance at my face.

Such a bustle of activity – seemingly out of nowhere – baffled me. I tried to catch the eye of the man who had pulled me from the lake, but his attention was taken up with talking to the senior attendant at his side. I could see him making economical hand gestures and scowling slightly, giving some complex order. The other man seemed more concerned that he should not catch cold and kept trying to entice him away. Eventually, he gave in and walked away, still giving commands. I tried to swallow the panic that came with seeing him leave. A whole flock of servants was still scurrying round me, some bowing to me or trying to tell me something, but I was not at all sure where I fitted into the picture.

I was still wondering when what looked like two person-sized butterflies glided through the swarm. They knelt before me on the veranda's wooden boards, their hands to their faces in gestures of supplication. After blinking several times, I realized they were in fact two young women. They wore elegant silk robes covered with floral patterns and tied with heavy sashes to form bows at their backs. Their hair was piled high on their heads and fastened with combs and long pins. Their faces were like those of painted statues: unreal perfection. I was suddenly aware of what an absolute state I must look after the storm and the marooning and the plunge from the flying island. Certainly, I would be nothing like the princess of the *Hopewell* now; more like a tinker from a traveling fair. And these two might be princesses themselves, for all I knew. Unless they were idols come to life. I had never seen women so artfully arrayed.

"Please forgive my ignorance," I said. I tried to stand up and curtsey, but the quilt was in the way and my knees seemed to want to do a different thing to the rest of my body. I wobbled and fell back to the boards.

The rounder-faced of the two young women put her hand to her mouth and giggled. The other – a little older with serious eyes – gave her a sharp look and they both bowed again. Then they stood and took my elbows on either side of me, bowing and gesturing towards the house. I understood that we were to go inside.

The sliding doors that led within were open now. It looked dim but restful in there. Open squares in the wall let in the view around the lake on all sides. As we came to the threshold, my attendants removed their shoes (and looked in vain for mine) and then bowed me into what I supposed was my accommodation. There was nothing to do but follow and see what I found there.

I couldn't believe my eyes.

It was as if the whole place had been designed with me in mind. Everything was at ground level. The floor was covered with soft straw matting, and the only furniture, beside an elegant vase in an alcove, was a small table barely higher than my ankles with a cushion beside to sit on. Eagerly showing me through a sliding paper screen into a second room, my attendants were keen to point out a lacquered chest, a doll-sized dressing cabinet already set with combs and mirrors, and a low bed, barely inches from the floor. The chest, I was soon made to understand, was filled with fine silk clothes, and the bed was made private with a free-standing screen, painted with a scene of cranes and willows. The older attendant pointed out each thing in turn, speaking in slow, single words as if I were an infant. I knew she was naming the objects, but I was too much in awe to take in the sounds.

"Is this your home?" I said. "Am I to stay here?"

I had never seen such a place. Here, I thought, I could live comfortably without my hands. With everything so low to the ground, I could easily sit and use my feet to eat, to dress, to turn the pages of a book. There would be no discomfort or embarrassment at all. I would need no aid to climb in and out of my bed. I may even find some useful task I could do to repay my hosts' kindness. I must do all I could to show my gratitude and make an effort to understand my new surroundings.

I shivered. I was still soaking wet and the quilt was slipping. The serious-faced woman gestured towards the back of the house and said something that sounded like *o-furo*.

"*O-furo?*" I repeated. The younger one giggled again.

I had no idea what the word meant, and probably would never have guessed until I was led to a room at a lower level, where a bare-legged servant had just finished filling what looked like an open barrel with steaming water. Beside it stood smaller pails, stools, and a rack of clean cloths. A delicious smell of cedar filled the air.

"*O-furo,*" said my attendant again.

I was not used to taking a bath. In Hollyport they had been something of a luxury, and at sea pretty near impossible. But after my plunge in the lake, the smell of hot water was wonderfully inviting, and at any rate, my attendants gave me no choice. They were quickly helping to remove my wet clothes and fix screens for my privacy. The sopping garments were taken away, one by one. Where to, I hadn't a clue. The two women were too busy stripping me to a bare bodkin for me to even try and ask. There was some consternation when they came to my hands; like the man in the lake they eyed their silver surface with an awe verging on worship. But when I asked them to unfasten the buckles, and made a few gestures to go along with my words, they seemed to understand. They laid the hands aside on a stool with reverence, before seating me on a second stool and picking up the cloths and pails to wash me. Within minutes, they were scrubbing my back and swilling away the soap scum with fresh water from the pails. Then they took me by the elbows and helped me into the tub.

It was hot. At the first dip of my toe, I wondered if they intended to make a pottage of me. Sitting down caused me to let out a muted, "Ahhhh," and to feel around to see if my back still had skin on it. But there must have been something medicinal in the bath water. After a few minutes, the shivers stopped and the pounding I had felt in my head since falling from the island began to calm. I breathed in the cedar-scented steam. I had come to a good place. Whatever happened next, I would remember that and try to be thankful. When it was time to get out, they dressed me in a quilted gown, heavy but comfortable. My silver hands were replaced. My newly-combed hair hung wet over my back. I felt clean for the first time in months; a new person.

When we got back to the upper rooms, a meal was waiting for me on a wooden table-tray. At least I thought it was a meal, although it could just as easily have been a work of art. Five real porcelain bowls arranged in a symmetrical pattern held doll-like morsels of shellfish, vegetables cut into shapes, fragrant rice and lake-clear soup. I had never seen food so daintily presented, and I was afraid to spoil it with so common a response as eating it. Neither did I know how. Despite the progress I had made with my feet while on board ship, the two delicate sticks laid as my place-setting baffled my imagination altogether. I could see there was much more I would have to learn before I could handle myself here.

My attendants did not appear to see a problem in my helplessness. The more serious of the two took up the sticks in one hand, picked up a morsel of food between them with extra-ordinary dexterity, and preceded to feed me as if I were a baby. I had no objection to the food; it was as clean and fresh as I now felt. Vinegary rice and a sip of soup were followed by a bite of fish and a flavor of the garden. Sweet pickles that made my tongue sing with pleasure cleansed my palate. A bowl of something hot and green to drink warmed my insides. But being fed in this manner, after so much other courtesy, was embarrassing. I was only a mariner's daughter, after all.

"I'm deeply grateful," I tried to say between mouthfuls. "But really there's no need. Simple food and shelter for the night will suffice. Perhaps if I could explain to someone. Who is mistress here? Or master? What about the man I saw first: where is he now?"

I half-expected another fit of giggles, but my attendants stiffened and fell silent. Outside the open door, where rain had now begun to fall, there was a second swarm of people and activity. A procession was coming along the path of flat stones. At its head was an escort of men in painted armor, each with two swords apiece in their belts. Then high-ranking servants like I had seen before, in various types of cross-fronted jacket or gown. And following that, a box-carriage of black and gold, borne on the shoulders of two strong men. As the procession reached the flight of stairs to our door, the carriage was lowered and its door opened. A young man stepped out, a lacquer hat covering his top-knot, his clothes of fine silk in shades of spring green. The outer layer of his outfit had enormous jutting shoulders that would have screamed power and intimidation were it not for the gentle look in his ebony eyes. For just a moment, he caught my gaze, and my heart gave a strange flutter.

It was the man from the lake. But he looked so different now. Regal. Elevated. As he stepped from the carriage, a servant hurried to hold an umbrella over his head. Those waiting lowered their heads to the puddles as he passed.

Others hurried to remove his shoes, to place an armrest by the spot where he would sit. Two pages moved to stand silent on the step, one carrying a golden sword, the other a folding fan with crimson tassels. Two members of the guard came to sit cross-legged on either side of the armrest, their expressions fearsome. My attendants had already flattened themselves to the matting.

The young man sat down. At a signal from the guard, an old

woman in plain dress was hurried in front of everyone and flung herself on the mat, visibly shaking. I couldn't imagine what her purpose was until the man from the lake began to speak. To my surprise, she repeated his words in old-fashioned Dutch, although I had to strain to make it out. Her accent was so strange and her voice quavered so much.

"I am the Lord Shimatani Yasutaka. It gives me great honor to welcome you to my home."

His rich voice was all courtesy and composure. The old woman, on the other hand, was about as composed as I would have been had I been asked to attend Queen Anne and Louis the Sun King both together.

"If indeed you are a spirit, please condescend to accept my reverence, and my sincere hope that the hospitality I have offered pleases you. My family has not been so honored since ancient times."

A spirit? Was that what he thought? It was so unexpected a notion, I didn't know what to say. I supposed people might have such ideas in foreign lands. I thought back to my prayer for an angel as I fell from the flying island. The idea that someone might see *me* as the angel seemed insane, but his lordship looked perfectly sane to me. His lordship. I swallowed. I had never been this close to a man of rank before. A couple of times, I had been invited to sit and sew with our local squire's wife, in the company of other tradesmen's daughters, but this was something on another plane altogether.

"My lord."

I really ought to be curtseying now, as deeply as possible, only I was on the floor, and my gown was the wrong shape, and the table was in the way. Should I try bowing as I had seen the servants do? I lowered my head over my rice bowl.

"I am your lordship's humble servant, Margaret Rosewood, from England. And, please my lord, I'm not a spirit. Just a poor, lost girl, far from home and friends."

"Lift your head, please. I wish to see your face."

I looked up. His ebony eyes were searching me, right into my soul.

"Not a spirit, you say. You scarcely seem of this earth to me. You fell from the sky. Your hands are of silver. You are clearly no servant of mine, or of this empire. And there are no travelers in this land. Not for a hundred years."

There was a question in his voice. Did he think I was hiding something? I racked my brains for how to even begin explaining who I was or how I had come to be there.

"Please, your lordship. These silver hands are not the ones I was born with. I lost mine in...an accident." I wouldn't say any more about what had taken place on the *Hopewell*: Van Guelder, the saw, Kit's tears. I had to stay in control of my feelings at all costs. "These are their replacement. The maidservants here will tell you, they can be removed. As for how I came to be in your lordship's land..." A jumble of confused memories tumbled through my mind: a giant lodestone, fishermen on balconies, the music of bells, Dr Lemuel's agonized cry. How far dare I trust my senses about what I had seen and heard in the sky? No one else had seen the island. I had simply plunged from above into a lake full of fish. "I'm not sure." It seemed the safest answer. "I fell; I know that. But I don't know where I am now. Is this one of the lands beyond the edge of the map, my lord? If you will permit the question."

There seemed to be some confusion about how to translate the last part of my speech, and about what should be said in response to it. One of the armed men turned to speak to Lord Shimatani for some time, and the old woman looked close to having an apoplexy. In the end, I was given to understand that the name of the country was something like the Sunrise Empire, and that the castle (in whose estate I now was) was called Tokushiro.

"The Castle of Protection was the name my ancestors gave to

it." There was pride in Lord Shimatani's voice. "It is a noble fortress in a good land, and the manor my grandfather built within its walls has no equal for tranquility. Its people are loyal to my family, hard-working and virtuous. If you truly have no other home, you are welcome here and assured of safety. But..."

He made a signal to one of the attendants, and the sliding door to the garden was shut, leaving the waiting servants to devise their own entertainment, unless their duty was to remain kneeling in the pouring rain.

"I said there have been no travelers in the Sunrise Empire for a hundred years. That is the truth. By decree of our overlord, no one comes in or goes out. And my honor as a man of rank demands that I am loyal to him. I cannot let it be said that Tokushiro harbored a foreigner."

The warmth inside me began to drain away. I wished there was something I could hold onto for security. But holding was not a possibility for a woman with no hands. Lord Shimatani saw my air of anxiety and his mouth curved into the slightest of smiles. He gave me a look I couldn't quite place.

"For myself, I cannot believe there isn't something of the spirit world about you. As far as this estate is concerned, you are a sky-spirit, and you will be treated as an honored guest in reverence to the countless spirits who live amongst us. But it would be wise not to put this to the test. Even members of my own clan may not view you in this light. Therefore you will remain in this house rather than the main manor. It is a favorite of mine, built by my grandfather to house a lady he favored, and the part of the gardens it stands in is particularly private. You may walk here without fear, although the coming rains may keep you indoors for some time. I trust it is to your satisfaction? I have tried to provide everything necessary for your comfort, but if there is anything further you require...?"

"No, my lord. Thank you. It is more than satisfactory."

I didn't know what to say. I couldn't believe someone would

provide all this just for me.

"The lady's maids I have sent you – Sakura and Miyuki – will tend to your everyday needs. They are entirely trustworthy, as are all members of my personal guard." He indicated the two men in armor. "You need have no fear of them betraying your presence beyond these walls. If you wish, you may also retain the services of Ume as an interpreter."

The old woman found herself covered in confusion on having to speak her own name. I wasn't sure I wanted to put her through the anxiety of having to maintain her role, but having someone to translate would be very helpful, at least to begin with. As from tomorrow, I would apply Dr Lemuel's lessons and try to learn the language.

"One more thing. We must give you a name, sky-sprit." Again, warmth glowed in Lord Shimatani's ebony eyes. "You will be know as O-gin; the silver lady. It seems appropriate."

His lordship rose, and the guards on either side of him did likewise. I wondered if poor Miyuki and Sakura would be able to lift up their heads soon. I tried once more to make a similar bow, but Lord Shimatani shook his head.

"It is I who should bow to you, O-gin. My ancestors revered the spirits. Allow their descendants do likewise."

"You do me too much honor, my lord," I said.

"I think not." The hint of a smile returned to Lord Shimatani's lips. "We will speak again, O-gin. Please take the greatest care of your health."

"God-speed, my lord," I said.

12

The Floating World

I had fallen into Paradise. Or so I decided the next morning, when I woke to the sound of the heron's cry and the scent of green tea. The paper doors slid back on a world where water mirrored leaf in startling clarity and the silence of stones had a language all its own. I had come to a place of dreams, where each new day brought fresh wonders.

Even the growing humidity and frequent downpours took nothing away from the glory of it. The climate meant a constant fight with invading insects, but I could cope with that for the glory of the view. It made me think of the blissful bower of *Paradise Lost*, watered daily by a mist that went up from the earth, and tended by the innocent pair. Of course, the gardeners that I saw tending this particular bower were not quite naked and were often seen running from the rain with straw mats pulled over their heads, but it was close enough for me. I couldn't get enough of the landscape. The panels remained open all day, even late into the evening, when the room was lit by paper lanterns and by tiny insects that looked like green sparks. We would sit and listen to the pattering of rain on water, and when it ceased, the music of frogs.

"Does it always rain like this?" I asked Miyuki on the second day.

"My lady has come during the season of rain," was the reply. "After this comes summer. It will be hot for my lady then. She will need to rest."

Miyuki was the giggly one with the round face. Of the two, she was more accommodating of my clearly strange desire to serve myself with my feet or forearms where I could. Watching me pick up the eating-sticks between my toes for the first time brought a look of awe, horror and hilarity in equal measures. But the second time I tried, she made no move to stop me. I soon learned that her real talent lay in fashion. It was she who picked out the gowns and sashes I wore (*kimono* and *obi*, as I soon learned). The cloth they were cut from was exquisite. Miyuki chose ever lighter weaves as the weather grew warmer, always in colors and patterns that subtly complemented one another. My hair too, when I glimpsed it in the dressing mirror, showed me I was in the hands of a true artist. It had been so long since it had been dressed at all that I marveled at what she could do with pins and flowers. That was one area in which I was happy to leave everything to her.

Sakura was the serious one. It was she who strapped on my silver hands each morning with a reverence verging on worship, and insisted that I be referred to as "my lady" at all times, despite my explaining that I was a commoner. I think she polished the sixpences too; someone certainly worked hard to restore their shine and make them look something like the gift they had originally been. In spite of the presence of Ume, she continued to speak to me slowly in her own language, pointing and naming with admirable patience. For this I was extremely grateful and tried to show it. My first aim was to learn my new tongue as quickly as possible.

If Sakura appeared stern, I discovered she did have a softer side, which she kept for the little sparrows that perched in the wisteria and a grey cat that wandered in from time to time. Her whole face would change on their arrival, and when she thought I wasn't watching, her tender touch and voice revealed quite a different woman within.

At first I tried to get to know Ume too. The poor old woman seemed completely ill at ease sharing a house with a sky-spirit and two sophisticated lady's maids. I kept hoping I could reassure her in some way. And I was keen to know how she came to speak Dutch if, as Lord Shimatani said, there had been no travelers in the empire for a hundred years.

"There were travelers once, my lady," was her stammering reply when I tried to ask. "My late-and-sainted grandfather was a Dutch merchant. He had a wife here, children. That was long ago. Times have changed. The land is less open but more peaceful, yes. No more wars. But, please, I must beg my lady not to trouble her servant further."

Apparently, it was not appropriate for me to speak to her directly. Miyuki and Sakura seemed to think the same. A merchant, especially a foreign merchant, was not considered highly in the Sunrise Empire, and I was a lady now. It was a shame, because I would have loved to know more of Ume's grandfather and how he had found this land. Not to mention the fact that I was of trading stock myself, and probably much closer to Ume's class than theirs. But I was O-gin now, a visitor straight from the heavens, and anyone who gainsaid that (even I) was going against the word of Lord Shimatani himself.

I hadn't particularly expected a visit from his lordship any time soon. When he had said that we would speak again, that could have meant anything: in a week, a month, even longer. I imagined feudal lords to be pretty busy managing their estates, settling disputes and entertaining important visitors. Since he had set everything up for my comfort, he didn't need to be present in person.

But I was wrong about that. He arrived on the afternoon of my first full day in the house. He was without his entourage this time. He came with just a maidservant and a guard, walking between the trees, although it was raining hard. There were damp patches on the front of his kimono from the drips of his servant's umbrella by the time he came through the door, but he didn't look at all put out. His eyes betrayed nothing but courteous attention.

"I hope you are well, O-gin."

I inclined my head as we knelt on the matting, the table between us. Even in that posture, there was an air of calm authority about him. It was impossible not to feel safe.

"I am, your lordship. Thank you. You have been most generous."

"It is an honor to provide for you." I could tell he meant it. "If there is anything else you need, please let me know."

"I will, my lord, but I am extremely satisfied."

The conversation went on a little longer in the same vein, interpreted haltingly by Ume. Then he rose and took his leave, saying, "I will return tomorrow."

It was a short visit, considering he had to cross all the formal gardens to make it, but I appreciated his kindness. And he kept his word. He came back the next day, and every day after that. His daily visit became part of the routine of my new life. Our conversation was usually the same: polite inquiries after one another's health. He would ask if I was comfortable and I would assure him I was. Sometimes our exchange stretched to the weather: a topic I found was as much a favorite in my new country as it had been in my old one. How long the rains would last before summer came for good was a question both he and my household staff were more than happy to discuss.

"Some weeks yet, my stewards tell me," his lordship said. "Summer will come at an auspicious time, I hope."

He usually arrived at about the same time each day, either late afternoon or early evening. Sometimes he had a guard or two with him, sometimes a handful of servants to carry his umbrella or his carriage; more often he came alone. Miyuki and Sakura generally retreated behind the sliding screen, leaving only poor old Ume to tremble on the mat between us, stammering out her best attempts at translation. Although I had only picked up a few words and phrases so far, I preferred to listen to Lord Shimatani's voice, with its subtle richness, than Ume's trembling squeaks. If I listened hard enough, I felt sure I could understand everything in time.

There was a lot of listening in my new life as O-gin. And a lot of observation too. In my heart, I thanked Dr Lemuel for his lessons every day because I certainly needed them. So many things were new and strange to me, from the taste of bean curd, to the sight of my first raccoon-dog, to the many little rituals and courtesies that punctuated each day and which I often despaired of ever grasping. I wanted to absorb it all. I wanted to embrace my new life with both arms. But I couldn't get there without hard work. I had to think in Dutch and come to terms with Ume's antiquated dialect. I had to listen for the rhythms and patterns of the tongue spoken around me. I had to concentrate in order to grasp just why I must never look in the kitchen or what the doll-sized houses by the rock garden were for.

It was tiring. I loved my new house and everything in it, and still couldn't believe it was all mine. But I still felt a little like an idol in the Madras temple Dr Lemuel had once described to me, being dressed and fed and taking in everything around me without any means of letting my inner feelings out. It was a difficulty that grew on me more as the days passed.

I was unsure how to tell Lord Shimatani about this. He had been kind and generous beyond the point of belief; I was afraid to offend him. But when I thought of the warmth in his ebony eyes and his gentle touch by the lake when he had rescued me, I believed that he would listen. The least I could do was to try.

The next time he came, it was just as the rains had cleared. He brought with him a smell of cedar wood: he must have come from his own bathhouse. That was one new experience I was fast coming to enjoy, and to wonder how I ever did without it.

"Are you well, O-gin?" He looked tired tonight. There were dark shadows beneath his eyes, giving him a vulnerable air.

"Yes, thank you, my lord." I had practiced this phrase to say to him in his native tongue. He broke into a smile at the sound. I noticed that his top teeth overlapped slightly and a boyish spark appeared in his tired eyes. Suddenly, he looked much younger.

"I have a request to make, though," I said, lapsing back into

Dutch. "My lord did say I could ask for anything I needed."

The smile changed to a look of concern.

"What is it? Do your surroundings not please you? Your maids? Your clothes?"

"No, my lord, it all pleases me very much. It's just…" I struggled to find the words. "I feel somewhat confined. Not by the house," I added hastily. "And I don't mean because of the rains and having to stay indoors. But more because of being unable to speak my own tongue. Or have my own occupation."

"You miss your home? The place you came from?" He sounded regretful, even hurt.

"A little." I dreamed of Kit and Dr Lemuel often, and sometimes of my father and sisters too. But I didn't like to confess that, with all the upheavals I'd been through, I'd lost the concept of home somewhat. Tokushiro was the nearest I'd come to it for some time.

"It's more like… I feel like there are things trapped inside me that I can't express. I need to let them come out. I need something to do. Does my lord understand what I mean?"

For a moment, a boy's openness showed through his look of calm control. He lowered his eyes to the straw matting.

"Yes," he said quietly. "I know that feeling."

"I'm not ungrateful, your lordship." God forbid that he should think that.

"No, no, of course not." He looked up, the perfect nobleman again. "An occupation. It is hard to know what to suggest. Riding would be unsafe for you and the usual occupations common to ladies – flower arranging, archery, playing the harp – might be…"

He glanced at my false hands, stiff and immobile.

"I can do things with my feet, my lord." I hoped that didn't sound too bizarre. "And with my mouth and arms. They supply the loss. And these silver hands are not altogether useless. I was very fond of reading before I came to your lordship's lands, but

I suppose here..." Reading was no good if you couldn't understand the language the books were written in. Unless they were all woodcuts and engravings. "I do like pictures, my lord. When I was on the...in another place, I studied them every day."

"Pictures, you say? Art?" The hint of a smile had returned again. I found myself willing him to show the sparkly-eyed, boyish smile he had earlier, but he didn't. "I, too, am a great lover of art."

His eyes went to the slender vase in the alcove, delicately painted with branches in blossom, and to a scroll of calligraphy that hung above it. They were the only ornaments in the house, but the way they set off the view of the lake with its willows and maples showed exquisite taste. I should have known.

"I am patron to many artists and craftsmen. Even now, there are several at my own manor. Perhaps something can be arranged. I will give it some thought."

It did not take long. I was coming to realize that, once Lord Shimatani had said he would do something, he did it without hesitation. A few days later, another visitor arrived at the lakeside house. Unlike the high-ranking men I had seen here, whose hair was scraped back from high foreheads into a stiff topknot, this man was simply bald. Instead of a sword or an umbrella, he carried a square basket full of cylindrical pots. There was a pleasant, unassuming expression on his face and, when he bowed, he introduced himself as Master Seika, an artist and calligrapher. Lord Shimatani, he said, had instructed him to give the honorable O-gin tuition in painting, and he was here to begin her lessons.

I didn't know what to say. "Come in," seemed as good a start as any. With the help of Miyuki and Sakura, I managed to offer what I hoped were suitable courtesies and offers of hospitality. While food and tea were brought, Master Seika busied himself unpacking the tools of his trade. The pots contained brushes, ink sticks and seals. A vessel was filled with water to wet the ink stone and make up the ink. From beneath oiled silk, he drew out several scrolls of paper, waiting to become our first attempts.

"I'm afraid I will be a poor student to you, Master Seika," I said, as Miyuki plied him with offers of food and drink. "I've never painted before – not properly – and I'll have to hold the brushes in my feet. I don't want to cause offence."

Ume, on the mat, stuttered out her translation. She was going to have to act as both interpreter and chaperone. From the looks of her, an artist was only fractionally less intimidating to her than a member of the nobility.

"Not at all; it is the greatest honor." Master Seika inclined his head.

My eyes strayed over to the brushes and inks. Already, I could feel how they would slide between my toes. I wanted to do this. I really wanted to. How had Lord Shimatani known when I hadn't even known myself? Even through the difficulties of translation, he had heard me and understood completely.

"The way of the artist is a spiritual journey," Master Seika said. "I suggest my lady thinks less of technique and opens her mind to possibility. The rest will follow naturally."

For a moment, I was back aboard the *Hopewell*, recovering from my amputation. I smiled.

"Another teacher of mine said something very similar."

"Then he was a wise man," Master Seika said.

"Yes," I agreed. "He was."

We began lessons that very afternoon. The ink stone rubbed up to create a jet-black ink with an intoxicating smell. Master Seika showed me how to mix it with different amounts of water to produce degrees of shade, and how three simple strokes could become a bamboo pole. He had me try each brush, demonstrating with the sure hand of an artist how to create bold strokes, a wash of grey, or with the tiniest brush, marks as fine as the needles of a distant pine.

"This is a traditional form of painting," he said. "I think my lady will enjoy it. With water-ink painting an artist can put to paper what he sees, and also the feelings and truths invoked by those sights. It is simple but meaningful."

"Yes, I see."

I did see. I saw the minute I held the brush between my toes and swished it against the paper. The sweeping line it made was elegant; a line the brush seemed to want to make of its own accord. But at the same time it was something that flowed straight from my heart. This was nothing like the last time I had used inks – lifetimes ago it felt – scratching with my quill in Father's ledger. This was more like song, like poetry. In a land of foreign speech, I had found my own language.

"In time, Lady O-gin will learn the strokes of calligraphy too," Master Seika said. "Calligraphy and painting are two facets of the same jewel. With brush and ink, we can create pleasure and pain, and hold in our hands for a moment the beauty of the fleeting world."

I sighed with happiness. "I can't wait."

"You honor me with your gratitude," was all Lord Shimatani would say when I tried to thank him for what, to me, was a priceless gift. "I simply wish you to be happy here, O-gin. I wish you to feel...at home."

I was enjoying his lordship's visits now. I became used to the sure tread on the wooden boards, and the sight of him kneeling across the table from me with his top-knotted hair and his wide shouldered garment. I liked the way the heraldic crest embroidered on each shoulder shone within its encompassing circle. I even became used to his severe hairstyle and began to see it as dignified and manly.

Every day, he stayed just a little longer. He had begun to slow his voice in my presence, to pause between phrases, and to gesture with his hands so I could follow his words.

"I wish to make you happy, O-gin," he said yet again on one visit.

I blushed. For some reason, his saying that made me feel strange inside. I couldn't decide if it was a good kind of strange or a bad. I decided to choose a topic of conversation myself.

"How is your work going with the register of inhabitants?"

He had told me about this on a previous visit, when I had asked him what he did with the rest of his time. Apparently, he needed to know exactly who lived on his land, how much they all owed him in taxes and how much rice crop his fields could produce. It sounded familiarly like the account-books at home.

"It is a slow process." He sipped from the small bowl of tea that Sakura had served him. "My retainers are hard at work, but there is much to do. I wish to get the best I can out of my lands – I need to do so, in fact – but I do not wish to over-tax the people. They cannot afford it. I have only been lord of these lands a short time, since my father passed away. I fear they are not as well-managed as they could be."

"I see."

The news that he was new to his position surprised me. He looked as comfortable in his role as if he had been lord of Tokushiro all his life. I wondered again what age he actually was. Perhaps he was younger than I thought.

"Well, I'm sure my lord will do all things well," I said with an encouraging smile. "He has a good heart."

I thought I saw a trace of red creep up his neck and face at this. He fingered his collar and poured some more tea.

"Unfortunately, it comes at a difficult time. The matter of my marriage is long overdue and my uncles are pressing me to finalize the arrangement as soon as possible. It is a heavy weight to consider both at once. Forgive me. I should not burden you with my troubles."

"Not at all. It is the least I can do to repay my lord's kindness.

And I agree: betrothal is a difficult time. For all concerned."

Unbidden memories of my own nightmare marriage arrangement thrust themselves into my mind. I tried hard to suppress a shudder. At least Lord Shimatani's bride – whoever she ended up being – would not have to face the kind of horrors I had run from. She would have a very different sort of betrothal: a good start to married life with a husband who would treat her generously and with understanding. I wondered if she would appreciate how blessed she was to be in that position.

"Is everything all right, O-gin?" Lord Shimatani's rich voice softened; gentleness came into the ebony eyes. Obviously, I had not suppressed the shudder well enough.

"Bad memories; that's all." I shrugged them off. "So tell me who your uncles recommend."

"Shall we play as we speak?" he said. "Do you remember the board game I taught you yesterday?"

He had Miyuki fetch the board and stones. I had enjoyed the challenge yesterday, although my intuition was no match for his lordship's military strategy. I liked the fact that he didn't hold back because I was a beginner. He had watched with interest as I pushed the stones from square to square with the tips of my silver fingers. Now he scooped up his pile of black stones and set the first position with the deft movements of an expert, his eyes more on my face than on the board.

"Perhaps in the strategy of the game we shall learn something we can apply to the complications of matchmaking," he said.

"We can only hope," I said.

As I tipped the first white stone from my foot to my silver palm, I stole another look at Lord Shimatani's face, while he began a speech on the various noble families he could be allied with and the relative merits of their daughters. His features were as open as a boy's; his eyes alive with intelligence. He wasn't striking as Van Guelder had been, or full of honest warmth like Kit, but he had the kind of face one would not grow tired of easily. I couldn't help thinking again that his bride would be a fortunate girl indeed.

My painting lessons continued nearly every day. From shades and strokes, I progressed to the forms of leaves, the shape of water, and the symbols used to write a woman's name. Master Seika was a patient tutor. If the ink blotted, or I ended up with a toe print, he would calmly return to the beginning of the lesson and we would try again. His bald head bent over the table beside me, and his ink-stained fingers working the brush, became as much a feature of the house as Sakura's bird-feeding or Miyuki's giggles.

Whenever he demonstrated his art to me, I was in awe. The simplest stroke in his hand could become a man or woman, a horse or tree, stark and yet bursting with life and significance. I admired his work intensely and longed to produce something even half as good. And yet he was full of praise for me too, in his quiet way, and I started to think I'd found an occupation I had a real talent for.

"My lady O-gin surprises me," he said, examining a painting I had made of the sky and the water. It was a day when, for once, it wasn't raining, and we had taken our table out onto the veranda. "She sees something in this sky. A secret thought, perhaps. Or a dream just coming to birth."

I looked at what I had done. Without meaning to, I had turned the cloud into a naïve depiction of the island in the sky. There was the faintest hint of the roofs of pagodas and different levels of balcony. The top was rounded like a dome. I felt my face color. Why had I painted that? It was almost like admitting that I was a sky-spirit after all, and that this was my true home. I was definitely not going to show this picture to Lord Shimatani. I belonged here now, not up in the sky.

But maybe I had been thinking of the flying island without realizing it. The more that time passed in the Sunrise Empire, the more I started to believe that what I had seen in the clouds was a true experience and not at all the nightmare I had first imagined. The island had been real, just as Dr Lemuel had once tried to tell me: as real and reasonable as any lands more commonly known. In fact, as reasonable as the Sunrise Empire itself. I thought of the music chiming in the sky. I couldn't regret falling now, knowing the place I was to fall to, but maybe the island had been quite harmless. Could I possibly believe that, when I had seen and felt the power of its giant lodestone myself?

I turned to Master Seika with a nervous smile. "It's a flying island. It...er...floats in the clouds." In other circumstances, I might have been embarrassed to admit this. Certainly to a man such as Father, I would have been. But Master Seika often painted fox spirits or ancient gods as if they were part of the natural landscape. It seemed to be the way here. So I wasn't surprised by his reaction, which was to stroke his chin and peer into the painting without looking up.

"A picture of the floating world," he said. "Quite the fashionable thing in the capital nowadays, or so they tell me. Although the depictions printed there are certainly not for the eyes of young ladies. But this... So fleeting and yet so beautiful. A world apart. My lady truly has an artist's soul."

I didn't like to contradict him and say it was a place I had really seen. There was far too much "sky-spirit" talk already for my liking. Besides – I thought that night as I lay on my bed, with sectioned curtains hanging down to screen out the humming insects – in a way Master Seika was right. Tokushiro itself was a kind of floating world. A place apart. It struck me that, for the first time since Mr. Van Guelder had come to dinner in Hollyport, there was no need to run for my life. I was protected: by my secluded home, by the castle walls, by the Sunrise Empire itself. No one had come in or gone out for a hundred years. That meant no one outside the empire could find me. Truly, I had fallen beyond the edge of the map. I was safe. Free. I could breathe the air of my new country in peace and learn to enjoy its delights.

But as sleep stole up over me like a warm mist, the last thing I saw in my mind was not the lake with its masses of lilies, or the subtle stroke of a brush on paper, or the colors of a new kimono.

It was Lord Shimatani's smile.

13

Fear in the Night

Sometimes there were earth tremors. I would wake in the night, imagining I must be back aboard the *Hopewell*, to find my mattress shuddering and the kimono Miyuki had hung up for the next day trembling as if possessed by an invisible lady of a nervous disposition. Or I would be about to take tea when the lacquered bowls would begin knocking together, causing Sakura to hurry to the table with scowls and apologies for what was spilled.

"I regret this awkward situation, my lady," she would say, as I pushed back what I could with the tips of my silver fingers and assured her it didn't matter. "The earth is troubled in his digestion today. We must bear with him."

Generally, the tremors passed quickly enough, with nothing more to show for it than a few spilled drops of tea or a brush pot rolling on its side. With so little furniture, and that so near to the floor, the chances of anything actually being damaged were small. According to Miyuki, worse tremors were possible but hadn't happened for some time.

"And so we give thanks for the small tremors, my lady," she told me, smiling. "They keep the big ones away."

So far that had been the case and I hadn't worried about it. A few shakings of the earth were a small price to pay for everything I had gained on the Tokushiro estate.

It wasn't until one evening – a good few weeks into my stay – that there was anything that looked like trouble. It hadn't been a happy day. There had been an enormous downpour the day before. The lake had looked like a water world under siege, pierced by a million silver spears. The grey cat was found under the veranda shivering and looking half its usual size. Sakura had spent most of the afternoon drying it and coaxing it with fish ends. When the rain had finally stopped, the air was thick with humidity. There had been no more rain since, and by the evening of the second day, every breath was charged with need of a storm that wouldn't come. Miyuki complained of a headache. Sakura was already frustrated by her efforts with my false hands, which were becoming soggy in the wooden part and refusing to polish properly. She gave a sharp answer to Miyuki, who promptly started to cry. Ume hunched further into herself, her face set with suspicion.

I just didn't know what to do with them. Perhaps if my own day had gone better, I might have had the resources to take control as mistress, as I often had in Father's house at Hollyport. But it hadn't. Master Seika had caught a cold in the damp weather and had been unable to come. I had tried to paint without him, but I couldn't remember the strokes of the character I wanted and had thrown the brushes back in the pot. Lord Shimatani had called, but only for a brief moment. He wanted to use the break in the weather to exercise his horse. And after that, he was having something done to himself that involved piercing the skin with needles, which he told me was very good for one's health, but which sounded absolutely disgusting. I hadn't found any pleasure in the news that a party of nobles, including ladies, would soon be coming to visit. His lordship had only been asking my opinion on plans he had for their entertainment, but I couldn't help feeling that a load of courtly ladies strolling and pleasure-boating about the gardens would force me to live the life of a hermit if I was to keep my privacy. The more his lordship told me of the party, the more I wanted to push the first lady I saw off an ornamental bridge.

"Oh, do what you like with them. It's your castle," I had said at one point.

Lord Shimatani had stopped and looked at me.

"Are you unwell, O-gin? You do not seem yourself."

The gentle tone of his voice made me feel guilty for being so irrational. I couldn't think why it should bother me so much what his lady guests did. Frustration at my lack of reason made me snap more.

"I'm fine. My lord. I'm a spirit, aren't I? Why should there be anything wrong with me?"

I regretted saying this now. The conversation had ended politely enough. Lord Shimatani had gone off with his groom and I had gone back to my bickering maids. But I couldn't help feeling that I had spoiled things between us, just when we had been getting to know one another. On top of everything else, it was too much. Suddenly, all the effort to make myself fit into a new status in a new country, where everyone looked and thought differently from me, and expected me to be like them, seemed too much like hard work for not enough appreciation. I was sick of it. I was sick of sitting on my knees, eating raw food, and being molly-coddled by painted dolls that couldn't even get along with each other.

I stood up to my full height, glaring imperiously at my three servants.

"I'm going to bed. Take the night off. I don't want to see you here."

I could manage this much in my new language without translation. I flounced and shuffled into the bedchamber (it was impossible to storm out of a room in a leg-hugging kimono) and shut the sliding door with my feet. Let them ponder over my words themselves, I thought. For a moment, I allowed myself to wonder how seriously they would take my instruction and what they would do with a night off anyway. A brief vision of Miyuki and Sakura flirting with tipsy guards popped into my mind, but I soon dismissed it. They would probably go to the main mansion, back to whatever chambers they had occupied before. If they wanted to gossip about me to the other maids, I could hardly stop them. Ume, I hoped, would go back into the town, where at least she could feel at home for one night. When you looked at it like that, I had done them a favor. A night to themselves for once. And, for me, peace from their whining, so I could hear my own thoughts at last. It was about time. I dropped down on the mattress-bed and flopped back with a groan.

I dropped off to sleep a lot sooner than I expected given the stifling heat, but my dreams were troubled. I was standing on the deck of the *Hopewell* with Frenchie. The wind was blowing her sandy hair about her face and she had that familiar grin I remembered so well. I tried to say something to her, but the wind carried my voice away, and even I couldn't tell what I had said. She leaned closer to me and, as she did so, her face began to bulge all over like a pot on the boil, as if something were trying to burst out of it. I screamed and put my hands over my mouth – my real hands – but my screams were silent. She began to speak: her voice was deep and indistinct and seemed to come from anywhere but her mouth. She cursed me in Dutch and threw herself backwards over the bulwarks into the sea. How she managed such a leap, I could not comprehend. I rushed to the side of the ship and leaned over. It was no longer Frenchie in the water. It was Mr. Van Guelder. His hair was made of seaweed; there was a starfish stuck over one of his eyes. He spurted out water like a whale and laughed at me with his cold, blue mouth.

"You didn't imagine I was dead, my love? I cannot die. I am you and you are me. I am always with you."

He lashed a great tail like a seal and leaped high in the air. Seaweed covered my face and I couldn't get it off.

Then I was looking at a place I had never seen. An island in a busy harbor, covered with low, dull buildings like those of the East India factory in Tonkin. Men walked to and fro in the somber clothes of Dutch merchants. A narrow bridge connected it to the mainland, passing under a tall gate. Men with dour faces, dressed like the guards at Tokushiro, marched towards it, scrolls in hand. In a dizzying motion, I was swept inside one of the buildings. Only, once I got inside, it looked like nothing so much as my own house by the lake. Everything was overturned. Tea bowls were broken. Make-up brushes and ink sticks were scattered among bits of broken mirror and the rags of torn-up sashes. The grey cat was dead. Someone was standing over it, pulling a sword from its lifeless body. He turned round. Van Guelder's eyes met mine, ice blue and glittering with fury. He was wearing the short kimono and baggy breeches of the Sunrise Empire. He put the sword to my throat; I could feel the cold steel.

"You have betrayed me, Margaret," he said. "Living in another man's house, eating his food, employing his servants. You are my betrothed and I will have you. By God, I will have you yet!"

Then his hands were round my neck. He was shaking me, shaking. The paper walls of the house were tearing. Things were falling on me: boxes, splinters of wooden beams. And from somewhere, I could hear a scream. A desperate, cut-to-the-heart scream that went on and on. No matter how hard I struggled, I couldn't stop it...

I was in bed. The walls and screens were lashing like topsails in a storm. The dressing mirror had broken. And it was I who was screaming. I was sitting up, holding out my mutilated arms and screaming in harsh bursts that wouldn't stop. In a shaft of moonlight, I could make out the shadow of a man against the rippling screen. He was holding out a sword. The screen flew back. I flung my arms across my face and screamed fit to sear my throat.

"O-gin!" He gasped my name. "Are you hurt? Where are your servants?"

The screams subsided into shuddering, coughing sobs. Somewhere beyond the screen, a lantern flickered and bloomed into light. Lord Shimatani called something out in his own language, too quick for me to follow. He pulled back the sections of curtain by my bed and knelt at the side of the mattress. The sword was still in his right hand, its blade decorated with engravings, the hand-guard formed of two golden dragons. He put it carefully into the scabbard hanging from a cord at his side.

"Are you hurt, O-gin?" he said again. He put a hand on my shoulder, hesitantly, as if the touch might harm me. Its warmth flowed down my whole arm. "Was it the earthquake that scared you? It is passing now. You are safe."

"My...my betrothed." I gulped. "He was here. He was..." Sobs swallowed my words. The dream was too vivid; it wouldn't fade. Van Guelder was in this house. Somewhere in one of those dark corners he was there, with a sword in one hand and the lodestone in the other.

Lord Shimatani turned round and called out commands to people I couldn't see. More lanterns were lit. A table was brought in with rice wine and a kettle of hot water. I was shaking and couldn't stop. His lordship took the thin quilt from my bed and placed it round my shoulders.

"Do you want your hands?" he said gently. The wide sleeves of my gown were hanging, limp, where the stumps of my arms ended. "I could have someone find them and put them on for you."

I shook my head. Heavy, damp hands and straps were the last things I wanted now. They were too much a part of my dream, part of a past I thought had gone forever. They brought Van Guelder close. Too close. I shuddered and huddled into the quilt.

Lord Shimatani made a signal to his attendants. The screen closed and, one by one, the voices beyond it stopped. There were just the two of us in the house, in the company of burning lanterns and bowls of wine and water. The earth still moved slightly but the tremors were subsiding; the sobs of a child lulled to sleep by its mother.

Lord Shimatani unfastened the cords that held his sword and

laid it down on the mat, tucking his feet into a more comfortable position. His hair had come loose and cascaded down his back like a black waterfall. He fixed me with his warm ebony eyes.

"Tell me," he said. "What is this fear? I want to know."

My heart was still thudding against my chest. How could I get all I had been through into mere words and sentences? The betrothal. Losing my hands. The twisted adventure of a journey that had brought me here. And the man – the fiend – who even now crouched in the shadows of my mind, waiting.

"I don't..." My voice was still hoarse from screaming. I swallowed back the tightness in my throat along with the wine I was offered, and tried to breathe.

"I am concerned for you, O-gin." His lordship's rich voice was urgent. "Whatever it is that frightens you, it is making you ill. Is this what made you unhappy this afternoon?"

"No, no." I could hear my own voice rising in panic. "My lord, forgive me. I regret this afternoon." My command of the Sunrise language was still minimal. How was I to express this? "It has nothing to do with my fear now. This is about a man...a man..."

I mustn't start crying. I took a deep breath. Lord Shimatani brought his hand to rest on my shoulder again. For a mad moment, I actually wished he would embrace me, but the urge calmed and passed.

"What man? Tell me," he said.

"The man to whom my father betrothed me."

His hand tightened but he said nothing. Now the first words were out, the next ones tumbled after them in a rush.

"Far away, in my homeland. My father invited him to dinner."

I couldn't have stopped the flood of words now if I had wanted to. The whole tale came out, in breathless pants at first, but gradually with more conviction. Lord Shimatani listened, thoughtful, stopping me at points with questions or suggestions as to what I meant to say.

The tale went on for some considerable time. When

description became difficult, he brought paper and brushes, and I sketched with my feet the outlines of people, places, emotions. I used the tone of my voice and the expressions of my face. He did the same: getting up to act out pantomimes of what he thought I was suggesting and checking my response to see if he had it right. By the time I had finished, we both needed a refreshing sip from the wine bowl. I took mine between my forearms, glad that my sleeves covered the scars. The shivers had stopped but I was aware how much of my frailty I had exposed tonight. His lordship would not think me a spirit now, if he ever had truly done so before.

"You are brave to tell me this." Lord Shimatani rested his elbow against his knee, a bowl in his hand. "Many would say you acted dishonorably in fleeing your father's choice of a husband. But I see this is not so. The man is a demon. Whether living or dead, he must not haunt you again. As from tomorrow, I will assign a portion of my guard to protect you. No evil thing will touch you in the Castle of Protection. You have my word."

"And will you...keep this matter to yourself?"

I didn't want anyone here knowing about Van Guelder. Not Miyuki or Sakura or Master Seika. I was still their Silver Lady, their sky-spirit. It would be degrading to have them hear of my shame.

"With whom would I discuss it?" A flicker of lamplight sparkled in Lord Shimatani's eyes. "I alone am master here. My horse or my hawk may get to hear of it, but they are unlikely to discuss it over a bowl of *sake*." His voice grew soft. "I want you to be safe, O-gin. Safe in this house and safe on this soil. No one who enters my estate will hear one word of you that they do not need to hear. And no one outside it even knows of you. No one knows."

I dropped my gaze, letting it wander to rest on an ivory toggle that tied Lord Shimatani's purse to his sash. It was carved in the shape of a man and two clothed rats bearing a bag of rice.

Somehow, it was easier to look at the little details than at my host.

"But you know the truth about me now. You know I'm not a spirit. I'm not even nobility. Not even gentry. I shouldn't be here, in this house like this. I should be your servant."

"O-gin." The intensity of his voice made me look at his face. There was a light in the eyes that made my heart rise. "The spirits sent you to me. I truly believe that, and I would not dishonor them by turning you away, now or ever. This house is your home. And I *will* protect you."

I fell silent. Only the fluttering of the paper lanterns and the occasional groans of the house covered my embarrassment. I had no idea what to say. This conversation was giving me feelings I didn't recognize, feelings that made me want to both run away and hear more at the same time.

"Do you miss your family?" he asked suddenly. "Your sisters. Your father. Do you miss them?"

"Yes," I said. "Of course." It would be lobster season now in Hollyport. The lines and pots would all be out, and strawberries would be turning ripe for picking in the woods. I wondered if Susanna was still as keen to be courted; if Martha had grown tall in my absence."

"I also have two sisters," Lord Shimatani said. "One lives with her husband in another province. The other must remain in the capital with my mother until she is wed. I will see them only every other year now I have taken up my father's title."

"Must remain?" I said. There had been something of regret and loneliness in his voice.

"It is the law of our land. To ensure the loyalty of all his nobles, our overlord commands that we live one year close to him in the capital and the next on our own lands. The women of our families must stay behind when we return home to our estates. When I marry, my wife and children will live in the capital too."

I began to wonder if Lord Shimatani's bride would be such a lucky girl as I had thought after all. What was the good of gaining a husband to whom you could turn for support and companionship, only to lose him again for half your life? If I had such a man, I would want him close to me at all times.

"It sounds an expensive way to live," I said, recalling his lordship's land register and our earlier conversation about balancing the books. Even with the little I had seen of the Tokushiro estate, I knew it was home to a vast number of servants and retainers. If even half of them had to travel to and from the capital every other year, finding food and lodging along the way, the trip was going to cost a pretty penny every time. And from what I had observed so far of life in the Sunrise Empire, I imagined it all had to be done with great style and dignity. Economy wouldn't come into it.

"Terribly expensive." His lordship sighed. "And it is my people who bear the burden of the expense. That is why I must find a way to work the land more effectively. Otherwise they will sink into the worst kind of poverty. Sometimes I despair. I want to honor the ancestors who have gone before me as lords of this place, but I wish I could hear their advice more clearly, my father's especially."

"And you miss your mother and sisters too?" I spoke as carefully as I could. We were straying into very personal matters now. Without my realizing, my heart had started to race again.

Lord Shimatani nodded.

"My sister O-matsu especially. She always knew how to calm my mind. She plays the harp beautifully and writes the most moving poetry. I miss her gentle conversation. I miss them all."

"I am a poor substitute, my lord." I gave a half-smile.

"No." His ebony eyes became intense again. "You are my honored guest and – excuse my awkwardness, but – with you I feel I can speak as freely as if to my own sister. In fact, I would be privileged if, in private, you were to call me by the name my family has for me."

"Is that entirely appropriate, my lord?"

He broke into the youthful smile I had been longing for. Something inside me leapt to see it.

"Most inappropriate. But I would like it all the same. My name is Taro."

"Taro." I tried it out, copying his inflection. It seemed the right name for the person he was tonight.

"It is a name for a first son," he said. "Although in fact I am the only son, and considerably younger than my elder sister."

"How old are you?" I had dared to ask the question at last.

"Nineteen years."

Nineteen? Was that all? He seemed so self-controlled, so confident. That meant he was only two years my senior, since I must have passed my seventeenth birthday by now.

"And how old are you, O-gin?" he said, as if reading my mind. I told him.

"I see." He seemed pleased. "It is hard to tell with your strange, foreign beauty." The word *beauty* made me blush. I didn't correct him, though. It hadn't occurred to me that Taro might find me hard to read too. He already seemed to know me so well.

"And what did you say your people call you?" he said.

"Margaret."

He found this much harder to say than I found *Taro*. It sounded like a completely different name when it came out, but his attempt warmed my heart anyway.

"It's all right. I like O-gin," I told him. "It is who I am here. Who I am with you, my lord. Taro." I blushed again.

The blush was apparently infectious. Taro swallowed and struggled to set his face to that of a patron. "It pleases me that you feel this way. I hope you look on Tokushiro as your home."

"I do, my...Taro. But what about when you go to the capital? You must stay a year, you said." The shadow of Van Guelder, that had faded while we talked, began to loom again, as large as ever. "What will become of me then? I can hardly travel with you." I did not dare add that Taro might well have a wife to consider by that time. At the moment, he was on his own estate during the dull rainy season. He had time for the needs of his secret guest. But once other obligations and distractions came along, and especially when he was in the city, I would be all too easy to forget.

Taro became serious.

"You must not worry about such things, O-gin. I have said I will protect you. I will do so. I do not travel until next spring. When the time comes, I will ensure there are measures in place for your safety. But that is far away yet. You must think of the present, and of health and happiness. Do you understand?"

I nodded slowly. Taro stifled a yawn. It was the small hours now; we had talked half the night away.

"You should sleep," he said, stretching his shoulders. "I will be on my guard against demons." He lowered his voice. "Don't be afraid, O-gin. The nightmares are over now."

I wriggled under the quilt and closed my eyes. The curtains were drawn closed. Taro's breathing came soft in the half-dark, broken only by the rustle of silk or a quiet yawn. In and out, came the breaths. In and out. I drifted into a sleep whose dreams I did not remember, only colors of pale orange and grey. When I woke, heavy-eyed and slightly swollen about the throat, Miyuki and Sakura were removing the wooden shutters. A bird cry pierced the sound of falling rain. I looked about. My chamber had been tidied after the chaos of the previous night and Taro was gone. Only the fluttering in my heart told me he had ever been there.

14

The Weaver and the Cowherd

The rainy season gave way to summer. The trees were heavy with insects that cried, "mi-mi-mi," all the day long, and the lake came alive with swooping wings. In the early mornings, I was able to have my table brought out onto the veranda, where I sketched the shapes of graceful willows and practiced the strokes that made up *tree* and *water*. At noontime, as Miyuki had predicted, I was forced to retreat to the house's shady interior, where I dozed, surrounded by screens and curtains to keep away the insects.

I was able to walk in the gardens more. I wandered the winding paths that suddenly opened on picturesque views, which Taro had told me were meant to represent famous scenes. I took time to contemplate the moss-covered stones, the banks of irises and floating lotus plants, and to gaze down on streams from crimson bridges. Crossing a bridge, Master Seika said, represented a journey from the earthly world to the heavenly one. I could think of no better place to consider such a journey than in the beautiful gardens of the Shimatani estate.

However, I no longer walked alone. Not even when I was in the company of Miyuki and Sakura. Taro had been serious about his intention to give me a guard. The day after our night-time encounter, I had been briefly introduced to Colonel Akita, one of the Shimatani's most noble retainers and the man who would be responsible for organizing my protection. The colonel was a thin-faced man with a thin moustache who spoke little (to me, at any rate) but let it be known that his *samurai* (as he called his warriors) were men of deep honor and faultless military training who would give their lives for whatever cause Lord Shimatani laid on them. As the days went by, I accepted their presence: silent men in colorful armor, sitting along the veranda or walking two paces behind me, their hands on the hilts of their two swords. "They make me nervous," I confessed to Taro. "I feel as if I'm being watched. Sakura wants me to put up screens all the time, but I can't paint if there's nothing to see."

"Any man caught watching you will have a short life," Taro said warmly. "Remember, these men are here for your protection. The demon won't dare show his face to the warriors of the Empire."

We had spoken little of Van Guelder or other personal matters since the night of the earthquake. I still referred to Taro as Lord Shimatani or His Lordship in the presence of Miyuki and Sakura. But increasingly Ume found herself dismissed when he visited, and when she was out of the room we knelt close together, a table the only thing that separated us. On the first visit after the earthquake, I unaccountably found myself blushing when he spoke, and put my sleeve to my mouth as I had seen Miyuki do many times.

"Your hands are becoming tarnished. Let me see."

Taro's gaze had fallen on the wood-and-silver fingers I had raised to my mouth. He held out his own hand for a closer look.

In return, I held out mine, letting the sleeve of my kimono trail towards the matting. It felt strange to have him take my hand. I could feel nothing but a change in weight where the straps circled my arms, yet it was still a deeply intimate gesture. My throat tightened.

"The wood is rotting. It seems the spirits have not yet discovered lacquer." The corner of his mouth curled in the hint of a smile. I realized he had made a joke. "A patron of the arts should not have his noble guest clad in bad handiwork. That hardly seems honorable."

I took my hand back and hugged it to my chest. Memories of the Indian Ocean flooded into to my mind. Good memories. I didn't want them spoiled by critical words, however true.

"These hands were made for me by...friends."

They had been my friends, those men. Truer friends than I

could have thought were possible. Sometimes I hardly dared wonder what had become of the sailors of the *Hopewell*. The necklace of heads still found its way into my dreams from time to time.

Taro knit his brows together and looked out at the lake.

"And would you accept a gift from...another friend? If he were to offer it?" His voice had suddenly become gentle.

Perhaps it was the summer humidity, but there somehow didn't seem enough air in the room. I looked down at the hem of my kimono, running my silver fingers along the stylized bamboo leaves that edged it. Then I looked up and tried for a smile.

"From a friend. Yes," I managed to say.

As the year turned to the seventh month, Sakura told me there was to be a festival. On the seventh day, the rice laborers would have a holiday. Shrines were to be processed through the streets of the town to the local temple, which was patronized by the Shimatani family.

"A joyous occasion, my lady," she told me, with an enthusiasm I had not known her to possess. "An auspicious day for the town and for all the villages around. And of course his lordship and the noble families will feast too. The mansion will be filled with music and flowers. Such scenes of splendor! A pity my lady must remain hidden and cannot see it."

She was delighted when Taro sent a servant to bring us rare varieties of morning glory, in pots to stand on our veranda.

"A favorable sign of summer," she said. "His lordship honors us by sending a flower so appropriate for the season." She caressed the velvet petals as they opened to the sun, revealing five-rayed stars within. Clearly, this was a side to Sakura that I had not seen before.

As I didn't know what the festival was for, I found it hard to join in her enthusiasm. I had to confess to neglecting my own religion sadly since I came to Tokushiro. Back on the Hopewell,

Captain Robinson had led us in a service each Sunday; here all I managed was to ask God's blessing on my family and friends before I dropped asleep, not knowing if they were living or dead. My guardian angel, if I had one, must have given up in disgust. From what I had gleaned so far, religion here sounded a far cry from the Low Church faith Father had brought me up in, but in the absence of fellow-believers I would have to make do with what was available. I decided to ask Master Seika about the summer festival.

We were working on the shapes of bamboo again at the time. In true drawing-master fashion, he made me complete the full exercise to his satisfaction before he allowed himself to answer. Then he washed the brushes and replaced them in the pot. There was a sound of swallows over the lake and the gentle ripple of orange fish swimming.

"The legend of this season is a beautiful story," he said, "and one that will appeal to my lady's artistic soul. It is said that there were two young lovers – a weaver and a cowherd – living on opposite sides of the river. Because they were forbidden to meet, the only way the young woman could tell the young man of her love was to write her thoughts on a strip of paper and tie it to a long branch of bamboo, holding it out across the river." He picked up a stem we had been sketching and twirled it in his fingers. "The young man received the note with joy and wrote back, arranging to meet on the seventh night of the seventh month. When the night came, he crossed the river in his boat. But – alas! – The meeting was discovered and the two young lovers were punished most severely. They were put to death, and their spirits banished to the heavens, where they were placed on opposite sides of the River of Stars. Only on the night of their meeting – the seventh night of the seventh month – can they meet again if the night is clear, and be reunited once more."

"That's so moving," I said. "Is there more?"

I was really interested now, and not just in the story itself. I couldn't help feeling there was something about it that went beyond mere legend. A young man and woman communicating secretly; any union between them ultimately forbidden by every convention possible. It felt so familiar. The tragic ending saddened me, yet oddly I felt excitement growing.

"It is also said," Master Seika continued, "that whoever writes their dearest wish on a strip of paper on this auspicious day, ties it to a branch of bamboo and raises that branch high, will have that wish carried away by the wind and granted. Many houses in the town will bear bamboo poles on the day of the festival, and many branches of trees will become the bearers of messages. Does my lady wish to try this?" He smiled.

"Perhaps."

My mind was still swirling with thoughts brought on by the story. A paper message. A way of saying what was in your heart. I wanted to send a message to Taro. Something to tell him of my...gratitude? Friendship? Was that what I felt? Was that what was making me listen a hundred times a day for footsteps at the door? I didn't know, and I certainly wasn't going to mention that in a letter. It would be best to avoid anything too specific. And to stick to something I could manage.

I would put something on paper to thank him for the morning glories. That would be appropriate. I couldn't write poetry as his sister did – certainly not in a language that was still new to me – but I could paint with inks now. And I could write a word or two if Master Seika helped me. I would make it for a gift. For a surprise. After all, Taro himself had said that friends could accept gifts from one another.

Master Seika approved my choice to paint the morning glories wholeheartedly.

"It is most appropriate that you should paint this flower, my lady," he said. "The morning glory is the symbol of the Shimatani house. His lordship will take it as a great compliment."

I had noticed that in the circles on Taro's scabbard and on the jutting shoulders of his over-garment there was a five-petalled flower, heraldically stylized. But I had not realized that the flower it was meant to represent was a morning glory.

"Then you must teach me to paint it as well as I can." I grinned. "And I want to write Lord Shimatani's name. Can you teach me that too?"

The characters used to write a man's name, Master Seika told me, were quite different from the feminine writing he had shown me so far. But in honor of Lord Shimatani, he would teach me them immediately. He was sure I would master them quickly enough. We set about discussing and planning a design. I described the arrangement I wanted. Master Seika compared the merits of different brush sizes and debated the possible introduction of color into this particular piece. By the time we had finished, Miyuki had been in and out with several servings of rice crackers, and Ume's back had nearly given out with maintaining her posture of humility. I hardly noticed the figure walking among the trees, and it was only by sheer luck that all was tidied away before Taro came in through the open doorway.

"You have a secret." He gave a sly smile, as I tried to get my breath back and look like a dignified hostess whose sole concern was the preparation of tea.

"Only a good one, my lord," I promised.

He beamed back. I loved it that he smiled now. I loved the way that his not-quite-perfect teeth and boyish spark transformed his face from that of a serious aristocrat to that of a friendly young man.

"I'm sorry you must miss tomorrow's festival," he said. "But really it is best for your safety that you stay hidden. You may celebrate here, of course. Do spirits celebrate the festivals?" He raised an eyebrow.

I smiled too. "In our own way. I wish you great joy for the occasion. Will you be visiting the temple?"

He nodded, serious once more. "My revered father's shrine is there. I must take time to honor him. I hope to find wisdom for the running of my estate, and for my future."

"I will pray for you," I said, suddenly realizing I meant it. I really cared what happened to Tokushiro. And I really cared about Taro, too. I was surprised by just how much.

"Thank you." He made a slight bow. "O-gin," he said in a different voice, "I have something to ask you. Will you wait for me? It will be quite late, but I would like to spend the last part of the festival with you. The sky should be clear. Perhaps we may see the two lovers?"

"I should like that." My heart skipped several beats. I hoped I still looked normal. Of course, there wasn't anything new about a visit from Taro. He had visited me scores of times now. But I knew this wasn't the same. And I wanted it. I hadn't known until he asked, but I wanted it badly.

"I will wait," I said. "By the bridge, perhaps?"

"I will have the stone lanterns lit," Taro said. He cleared his throat. "Would you care for a short game now?"

Neither of us raised the subject of the festival again. We placed stones on squares, sipped tea and discussed the weather. But as I pushed my pieces across the board with silver fingers, I kept glancing at Taro's face. His eyes had an ardent glow in them, and every now and then he would give a sigh, stare out at the lake and compose himself again.

The festival day dawned with a kingfisher sky. The sun soon burnt off the morning mist, promising a beautiful – if baking – day. Although I was going nowhere, Miyuki was determined that I must be dressed for the occasion. She picked out the finest silks Taro had provided. Sashes and accessories unrivalled in good taste were selected, along with hair pins that would make a princess jealous. She made up my face with white powder and a cherry kiss of a mouth. Susanna would have fainted with awe to see the transformation. Miyuki wanted to paint my teeth black too (which was apparently the height of fashion) but I decided to stop short at that.

"My lady looks so beautiful." She gave her familiar giggle. "She is fit for her husband now. Or her lover."

"That's enough," I said. I hadn't revealed tonight's plan to anyone. Taro and I were just meeting as friends, I was sure of it, but the fact remained that he was lord of this estate and soon to be betrothed, and I was a young woman alone. What my own situation was in terms of betrothal and wedlock, I no longer knew or wanted to think. There was enough on my mind as it was.

The heat was solid, something to wade rather than walk through. I had just about mastered the art of walking in a kimono by this time, and had learned too to deal with the kind of shoes women of the Empire were expected to wear: something resembling pattens on stilts. Together, Sakura, Miyuki and I balanced our way along the gravel and down the slopes. We took a path away from the lake and sat under some pine trees, kicking off our shoes and tucking our feet out of sight. Sakura and Miyuki had brought fans – which I couldn't wield – and they took it in turns to fan all three of us while whoever was left provided entertainment.

It turned out Sakura had a sweet singing voice, and her rendition of local songs was quite a treat, even though many of the words were too poetic for me to understand. Miyuki sounded more like a cat being tormented, but I let her have a turn anyway. I sang a few songs of my own too: a psalm we had often sung before bed in Hollyport, and a ballad about a willow tree and a young woman taking leave of her sailor sweetheart. They seemed so much a part of the tides and ships of the English coast that it was strange to hear myself sing them under the tranquility of Taro's pines. Yet it was pleasant too. I felt my maids and I had never been so happy together. In a way, they had become my new sisters, and I was glad of their company. I hoped our companionship would grow in strength from now on.

It was only when the heat got really unbearable that we decided to turn back to the house. Sakura put up a painted umbrella for shade, and we tottered back to our veranda. There was something waiting for us there. On the shady side, where the lake ran under the stilts of the house, were three round packets, wrapped in leaves and lying on a larger leaf that had turned yellow in the sun. I told Sakura to pick them up, but she shook her head. There was hesitancy about both the maids that made me uneasy.

"What are they?" I said.

"Rice balls, my lady." Sakura bowed. "Left as an offering."

"An offering?" I had no idea what she was talking about. "To whom, exactly?"

"To you, my lady." Miyuki made a similar gesture on the other side. "As a visitor from the realm of spirits, people wish to honor you."

In spite of the stifling heat, I felt a chill creep across my heart.

"You discuss me outside these walls? Who knows I'm here? If Lord Shimatani hears of this..."

"No, no; no one discusses you, my lady." Both maids went into a flurry of bows. "But the kitchen staff, the gardeners, the low-caste servants who carry water for my lady's bath: they know they serve the silver-handed spirit. They wish to pay their respects."

"I do not need this kind of respect," I said stiffly. "It is inappropriate."

My mind was besieged with images of servants whispering the word *sky-spirit* from mouth to mouth. How many servants knew? Which ones? How discreet were they likely to be?

I turned to our guard for the day, a pleasant-faced young man who had followed us up the veranda stairs.

"Has any gossip reached the town? Sky-spirits, silver hands;

this kind of thing?"

"Not as far as I am aware," he said. "My lady, if you are concerned, I could send a message to Colonel Akita. He is dining at the house of a friend today, but one of the men could go."

I wanted to summon an army, but the voice of reason brought me back to Taro's reassurances. *No evil thing will touch you in the Castle of Protection. I will protect you.* I had to stay calm. The idea of guards bursting in on the grave Colonel Akita and his friends at the whim of an irrational woman did not sound so wise.

"Do not disturb the colonel in his visit," I said. "Tomorrow, if you will, advise him of the increased need for vigilance." I hoped that sounded confident and the sort of thing someone in my new position was expected to say. "And thank you for your concern. Please carry on."

The guard made a military bow.

"All for the honor of Tokushiro," he said.

The incident put something of a damper on the rest of the day, and I became impatient for the evening to come. After supper we ate peaches and plums – a gift from Taro's orchard – and waited for sunset to turn the maples and willows to silhouettes. The soft darkening of the sky brought out a hazy moon from which the sun seemed reluctant to part company. Only gradually could we make out the pale points of stars, repeatedly obscured by clouds of insects. I could smell the warmth of earth and water, still holding onto the scents of day. I wondered how Taro would look: if he would be worn after the long day; if he would be dressed formally like the lord of the manor he was. I hoped he would smile. I hoped he would have words to say that were just for me.

Eventually, we could no longer see anything in the water but dim shadows. The fish were hidden in its depths. I noticed a servant in a loincloth walking with a lantern in his hand. My pulse picked up. I stood and tried to smooth down my skirts.

"I'm taking an evening stroll," I said to Miyuki and Sakura. "I want to be alone for a while. The guard will watch out for me."

The guard, I was sure, would also keep a distance if he saw his master coming and say nothing of it. I took a path round the side of the lake, where trembling bamboo whispered to lotus leaves. A stream wound off between two banks; over it arched a bridge painted in red. The sound of night insects hummed and the green sparks of fireflies danced over the water. I had never seen fireflies before coming to Tokushiro and they still seemed magical to me. Moths fluttered round stone lanterns that looked just like little houses. It was the perfect summer's night. Only one thing was needed to complete it.

He was there. The formal clothes of the day had been replaced by a simple blue-and-white kimono, just like he was wearing the day he found me. I could see by the lantern that he did look tired, but he was smiling. As he came nearer, I caught a scent of incense and, faintly, of rice wine.

"You came," he said. "I was afraid you might be too tired after such a hot day." He gave an order to the guard, who disappeared into the trees. I came closer to him in the lantern-light and he gasped. "O-gin, you look beautiful! I wish there was more light so I could see you properly."

I had forgotten about my make-up and all. My hair, I knew, had come slightly undone since the morning, but the silk Miyuki had chosen was still the same and must have looked splendid by starlight. I hadn't even stopped to think what effect it might have on a man.

"Just as well you can't, my lord. I wouldn't wish to succumb to the sin of vanity." I was trying to be serious but I couldn't help my mouth twitching with an uncontrollable smile. He had said *beautiful* again.

"Ah, well, if you put it that way. I wouldn't wish to hamper the progress of your soul," he said, strolling on. "Shall we walk?"

We chatted about the day so far. Taro told me about the temple, its gate crowded with flower-vendors beneath the gaze of thunder-gods, and the processions of the cheering villagers around their local shrines. He spoke of the visitors he had entertained in his golden hall and the truly abysmal poetry some of them had offered over drinks. I gave an impersonation of Miyuki's singing that made Taro laugh. We strolled together along the lantern-lit path; over stepping-stones; past rock sculptures and raked gravel; under dark maples alive with insect-song, and back to the bridge again.

"We mustn't forget to look at the stars," I said.

"But of course. Since it is the landscape of your homeland." There was that slight lilt to Taro's voice that let me know he was teasing. "Here." He turned me gently by the shoulders. "We must look for Orihime, the brightest star in the sky."

I had no trouble finding my way around the heavens. Anyone brought up in a mariner's household or who had spent so much time at sea could hardly fail to know a thing or two about astronomy. The name Taro used wasn't one I was familiar with, but I knew which star he meant.

"There," I said, pointing.

"Ah, yes. That is our weaver. Now we must find her lover, Hikoboshi, further down across the River of Stars."

He was still holding my shoulders. I could feel his breath, warm against my cheek. My neck gave a little quiver as I pointed out the star we were looking for.

"It is a fine night for them," Taro said. "The magpies will build a bridge for them and they will cross and share a night of happiness."

He sighed; making my skin ache with a longing no one had ever told me existed in a woman, although I thought I could guess what it was.

"O-gin." He let go my shoulders. I turned round to look at him. "I would like to say something."

"Yes?" That pounding in my heart had come back again. Even the insect chorus was obliterated by it. All I could see were the soft depths in Taro's eyes. He swallowed several times; I saw his Adam's apple bob. Silence. I felt I would die if he didn't say what he had to say. I waited; he frowned and sighed to himself. For all his aristocratic poise, whatever was on his mind had him flummoxed.

"I am glad you came," he said at last. "You have made my castle a happy place this summer. I am grateful."

"Oh. Yes. Thank you." My innards sank. I had been so sure he was going to say something else. "I am grateful too. You have given me a beautiful home. Way beyond anything I deserve."

"I...er...you do me great honor." Could it be that he was using formalities to cover the awkward moment? "Would you like to see the new summer tableau I have had made? The scents will be exquisite by night."

By the time I got back to the house, it was very late. Taro insisted on walking me all the way to the door, and on picking one of the morning glories as a parting gift, "for a friend." Its petals were shut, and in the heat I doubted it would last the night; but I touched its velvet to my lips and cheek, breathing in the night perfume.

Indoors, Sakura was yawning and ready for sleep. I had her bring paper and inks to my chamber before she left me for the night. There was one more thing I must do before the festival was over. I had never tried to write English with my ink brush, and I imagined the results would hardly be those to delight a schoolroom. But what I had to write now needed to be in a form that no one here would recognize. I knew I was speaking a forbidden thought; yet tonight of all nights, it had to be said.

There were so many wishes I could have made. I counted them silently as I struggled to rub the ink stone and persuade my brush and toes towards my old handwriting. Kit's safety. Dr Lemuel's return from the flying island. The wellbeing of Father and my sisters. Was I just being selfish in that this was the wish I wanted above all others? More than anything I had ever wanted before?

There were three guards at their post when I stepped outside. I offered greetings to the nearest, showing him the bamboo plant where two strips of paper already hung. Miyuki and Sakura, I guessed, had already made wishes. He smiled to himself and shrugged at the strange markings on the paper, but went to hang it up as I had asked. In the darkness of my chamber, I imagined the paper fluttering in a gentle night breeze. What guardian angel would come to carry the thought away? What heavenly throne would see fit to answer the prayer I had put there? As I lay there, the words I had written- smudged and grey in poor writing – blinked on the backs of my eyelids. My midsummer wish.

"To cross the bridge and be with Taro forever."

15

"Everything to me."

The moment I woke, I knew it hadn't just been a romantic sensation of the night. I was in love with Taro. The certainty of it was so strong; I couldn't understand why I hadn't known it before. As Miyuki helped me to the soup, rice and salt fish that were now my usual breakfast, I was convinced she would see the emotion threatening to burst my chest apart. I loved him. I loved him so much. And I had no idea what I could possibly do about it.

The family with the noble daughter would be here any day now. Taro had planned poetry parties and archery contests, and a display of wrestling by local champions. I knew he would have to make an arrangement with his bride. He was an aristocrat, a feudal lord. It was his duty to make a good alliance and gain heirs to his family title. That was the way it was, in my country as well as his. Taro knew I was not really a spirit from the heavens. I was a master mariner's daughter seeking sanctuary from my marriage contract. The two of us could never be together. The dream-world of the River of Stars had vanished with the morning sun. The reality of life was something altogether different. I knew I must keep my thoughts to myself and express friendship alone. It was the only way.

I worked on my morning glory painting. Master Seika was pleased with my progress and complimented me on my developing techniques. He didn't know that each stroke of the brush was now an expression of the love I felt for his master. The outline of the delicate petals was a caress; the curling vine was my desire to cling to Taro and never let go. As I practiced writing his name over and over again, it started to become part of me. The characters radiated Taro's quiet strength, and every touch of the brush felt like an intimate gesture.

Taro himself was unable to visit so often. His relatives had arrived in advance of the auspicious visit. The preparation took up most of his time, and his uncles, he said, would be suspicious if he was seen to be sloping off to the garden when he should be in discussion with them. The day after the festival, he sent a servant with the gift of a brush-stand, decorated with carvings of cranes. Knowing I could not read his language, the note he had attached merely bore a picture of the stars in the sky as we had seen them. I hadn't known until then that he had any skill in drawing, but the positions were accurate enough for the Royal Society. I tried not to feel too much excitement at the gift, but failed miserably. Only the thought of a beautiful bride could force me to the desired level of gloom.

The next day, he called briefly to tell me that the family was on the way. Messengers had ridden ahead.

"I have told my relatives there is a taboo that prevents anyone crossing this most revered part of the gardens at the present time. You should be quite safe, O-gin. I want you to know that."

"Thank you." I couldn't help drinking in every aspect of his appearance: the shape of his eyebrows, the way he held his hands. Features that had seemed unremarkable a day or two ago now made warmth flood my whole body. I was certain everyone could see what was happening to me. How was I ever going to keep this to myself?

"Is there something concerning you, O-gin? You should tell me now and I will do everything I can to make all things well for you. Colonel Akita has had nothing to report. Is there something he has failed to tell me?"

I wondered whether I should mention the incident of the rice balls, but decided against it. Taro had enough to think about at the moment. He didn't need my irrational fears.

"No, nothing. I'm a little nervous about the visit, that's all. But I should be quite happy by the lake as usual."

"The lake." He smiled wistfully. "How little I expected such a spirit to tumble into it from the sky that day." He reached out and put a tentative hand on my shoulder. "Please take the greatest care of your health, O-gin."

It sounded like he was saying goodbye.

The visitors arrived the day after that. Master Seika came hurrying along the white stone path with an air of secrecy. The guards were miserable, knowing they would be avoided by their peers for having broken the taboo. On the surface, everything was much the same as it had been before. I painted and strolled and made observations of the weather and the natural world. Miyuki arranged my hair, selected seasonal flowers for the vase and giggled. Sakura scolded and petted the cat. But now we would occasionally catch a strain of music or a murmur of female voices coming from another part of the gardens. One night an explosion of fireworks could be seen and heard, lighting up the curling roofs of the guard houses. There would be rumors brought along with the food trays, of the main hall alive with the sound of harp and flute, rarefied with the fashionable patterns of ladies' kimonos and their exclusive perfumes.

And there was no Taro. I waited night after night, watching the sky change from azure to crimson to indigo, but there were no footsteps on the boards, no dark-honey voice beyond the screen. I had Miyuki put the board game away in its box. In the moonlight, I lay silent on my bed, my practice papers of Taro's name lying on the pillow beside me.

After seven days, I couldn't take it any more. I knew Taro meant for me to stay hidden, but I could no longer bear to be on the edge of a party I couldn't see. I hated not knowing what was going on or what Taro was doing. It was time I saw the aristocratic world he lived in. I needed to know for myself what sort of a bride was taking him away from me.

There was plenty of cover in the landscaped gardens. The expert gardeners Taro employed had ensured an artful blend of shrubs and rocks that took the eye line smoothly from one level to the next. It guaranteed varying levels of hiding place. If anyone did see me, I decided, I would wave my silver hands at them. Then they would have plenty of ghost stories to tell their friends about the spirit who haunted the lake of carp. If people thought I was an *evil* spirit, I reflected bitterly, maybe they would leave me alone.

I sneaked out while Miyuki and Sakura were airing the quilts. I didn't bother to check if a guard was following. I just went as quickly as the pattens-on-stilts would allow, heading in the direction I had last heard harp music and delicate laughter. I took a turn here, a twist there. Scene after scene opened out around me. Path after path strolled through ever-changing foliage. Taro's gardens were huge! I hadn't grasped the size of them at all, even with what I remembered from my fall.

I kept under cover, diving into azaleas and long grasses whenever I heard the sound of footsteps. Eventually, I could see a glimpse of the mansion buildings from behind trees, joined wall-to-wall by covered walkways. Lacquer and golden flowers gleamed from walls and roofs, set off by the simplicity of pine beams. The roofs curved with lines that were sheer poetry. I should have known how beautiful it would be. Much more beautiful than anything I was ever likely to inhabit. Should I go nearer? Was it worth the risk? I hesitated on the pathway, trying to find the courage.

A peal of laughter from beyond a rhododendron bush stopped me in mid-step. I plunged into the bushes and peered out from between the leaves. There, on the other side, was a group of ladies sitting in the shade of some plum trees. One was playing a two-stringed harp. The others had books or fans in their hands. Perhaps they had come to the plum grove to read poetry together. Or to exchange high-class gossip. As I watched, one of them whispered something confidentially and they all giggled. Each one had lacquer-black teeth in a pure white face:

the exact look Miyuki had wanted to give me. The sunlight glittered off jeweled hair combs and sash accessories, and they all wore kimonos worth a dowry in themselves.

But what struck me most was the delicacy of their hands. Their fingers were childlike in daintiness. The way they gestured and the deportment with which they used their hands – to pick up a fan, to adjust a comb – had a beauty and poetry all its own. I could well imagine how elegantly they would wield the sticks to taste an artistic meal or place white stones on a game board. And how a husband would take delight in having such a hand caress his cheek, his neck, the hollow of his chest.

The sky was clouding, promising future rain. I didn't know if Taro's proposed bride sat under the plum trees, but it didn't really make a difference. No father was going to travel this far with his daughter only to take her home again. By the time the visit was over, Taro would be married. He would have a jeweled butterfly for a wife; a woman with beautiful hands, real hands. She would know the courtly world he lived in inside out, and would have a sophistication I could never hope to match. He might continue to provide for his "sky-spirit" friend, but things could never be the same between us after this. I suddenly realized how much my head was aching with the heat. I didn't want to see any more.

I spent most of the day lying in the dark surrounded by screens. I wasn't hungry. Even my favorite pickled ginger couldn't tempt me to kneel at the table. The cat came and lay on the bed beside me and I found its compact warmth comforting until its fur made me sneeze. Sakura started fussing that I was coming down with a summer pestilence and wanted to send Ume for the doctor. I told her that was nonsense and I would be fine by the morning, but it didn't sound convincing even to me. Sakura vented her frustration by ordering Miyuki to prepare meals that would restore the balance of the five flavors, before leaving me to my misery.

My paradise was coming to an end and I didn't want to be here any more. I couldn't bear to be so near to Taro and never see him; or worse still, to see him as a husband, glowing with the joys of his new wife. For that one crazy moment on the night of the festival, I had actually believed he was going to say he loved me. That was never going to happen. Taro was a man of honor and his first duty was to his ancestors and his people. A person with so great a sense of obligation would never allow himself to have feelings for anyone outside his own rank. I might be his friend, his confidante, his silver-handed spirit. But I could never be his bride.

I started to fantasize about escaping Tokushiro. I imagined that Dr Lemuel would come back on the flying island, waving at me from the lowest balcony. The pulley-men would lower the chain-seat to my veranda, and he would call:

"Come now, Mistress Rosewood. This is no time to dawdle."

Then I would go up and watch it all sink away: the lake, the willows, and my lovely house. My paintings and brushes would still be on the table, left behind along with my possessions and all my friends. Tears prickled at my eyes and nose. It didn't matter how many times I pictured it. I knew Dr Lemuel wasn't coming back. And I knew I could never leave the Sunrise Empire. Not now.

There was only one other option. I must take it quickly before I lost my nerve. The painting of the morning glories was nearly finished. When it was complete, I would ask Colonel Akita's guards to have it delivered to Taro with a note. I would make a request of him, and pray that he would be understanding enough to grant it.

Of course, I needed the assistance of Master Seika. He was practically radiant the day the painting was finished. His faded brown face glowed with satisfaction and pride.

"My lady has proved herself a worthy pupil. Lord Shimatani
will be delighted with such a gift."

I was not sure his lordship would be so delighted when he
saw what was to accompany it, but I had to go ahead with my
plan. I cleared my throat.

"Master Seika, could you translate a letter to Lord Shimatani?
And please." I could feel my heart thudding. "Could you keep its
contents completely private? That applies to you too," I added,
looking at Ume.

I could see them both wondering what on earth I was about,
but Master Seika only said:

"It is my honor to be of service in any way I can."

And Ume just bowed. She had no one to tell, in any case.

I had no knowledge of the form letters took in this country, so
I dictated it much in the style we used for writing to Father's
clients at home. I would let Ume and Master Seika work out the
best translation they could between the pair of them. When it was
finished, Master Seika stamped it with a seal and rolled it up.
What it said, more or less, was this:

To the Lord Shimatani Taro Yasutaka
My Lord:
I hope you will accept this gift of a painting by way of thanks
for the beautiful morning glories you sent for the summer
festival, and for your many other acts of kindness to your
humble servant. As your lordship's marriage is fast
approaching, I beg that you will consider my position and see
fit to house me somewhere other than your lordship's estate. I
humbly suggest a quiet temple where I could live in seclusion,
or a remote dwelling in the mountains. You have been most
kind to me in my distress and I pray that you will remember
me with goodwill.
I wish you great joy for your forthcoming marriage.
Your most obedient servant and devoted friend.

Margaret Rosewood
(O-gin)

The painting was rolled up with the letter and both were presented to the *samurai* guard with detailed instructions. When he was gone, I lay down on the bed, and cried and cried.

The rest of the day was miserable. I pretended I wanted to take tea and listen to more of Sakura's songs, but I don't think my forced smiles fooled anyone. They could all see how puffy my eyes were, and hear me sighing time after time. In the end, I gave up and went back behind the screen again. Miyuki came and sat beside me, her round face pouting with sympathy. A tear left over from somewhere slid down my cheek and she dabbed it with her sleeve.

"Many tears will flow in life, my lady," she said. "It is better to let things go and understand that everything passes."

She knew. She must have done. There was no real privacy behind paper screens. And it wasn't difficult to work out what was going on when I was radiant one day and sobbing the next. Anyone who'd ever been in love would know the signs. But I was ashamed to be so transparent. I lay my head down on Miyuki's shoulder.

"You'll always be with me, won't you though?"

She put an arm round me without speaking. This was how it was going to be from now on, I thought. Just me and my maids, alone, with nothing but the sound of the wind in the pines to keep us company. Should I ask Sakura to pack my belongings now? If I was to go, I wanted to be gone quickly. I didn't want to linger, where the lake and the bridge and a thousand other things spoke to me of a life I could never have. I took a breath to say so to Miyuki.

There was a commotion at the door. Running footsteps, screens sliding, a man's rich voice speaking in an urgent tone.

Miyuki hurried out, but I didn't want to get up. I wanted to stay screened, hidden. I couldn't speak to Taro; not now. Maybe he would think I was out. Maybe he would go home again. I shook my head. How desperate could my wishes get?

A shadow reared up, right beside me. Taro's voice, shaking with emotion, sounded so close that it made the paper of the screen vibrate.

"O-gin, come out. I need to speak to you."

I didn't move. I barely even blinked.

"O-gin. Margaret."

He must have been practicing my name in private. This time, he had it almost perfectly, and he spoke it with a kind of tenderness I had never heard in his voice before. Hesitantly, I pushed the screen aside. Taro's face was white. Strands of his lacquer-black hair had fallen from his formal top-knot, over his eyes and cheeks. His eyes spoke a tale of urgency.

"You cannot leave."

"Don't say that." I shook my head, willing tears to stay out of my eyes. "You know it isn't right for me to be here. Not when you become a husband."

He reached out a hand towards my hair. I flinched.

"Please, Taro. We are friends."

"Friends do not ask to be sent to the mountains." He scowled.

Why was he making this so hard for me? Was he really so unobservant?

"I have to go. You have to find me another safe place."

"You think you will be safe in the mountains?" He interrupted. "In a temple? Who will protect you from the demon? Monks? Bamboo cutters?"

"I don't know," I said miserably. "But I can't go on living here."

"This house is not good enough for you?" he said. "Everything I have done…"

"Of course not."

"Then I am the one you do not wish to see again?"

The tears wanted to come again. I had to keep them away.

"I do wish to see...that is, I want to see you, but..."

Taro had gone very still. His ebony eyes were fixed on me, staring.

"In the name of mercy, O-gin! Say it!"

I could barely speak for the lump in my throat. I fixed my eyes on the straw matting. When my voice came out, it was like the squeak of a cricket.

"I think I'm in love with you. I'm sorry."

Tears welled up and turned the matting to a pale yellow sea. I pressed my lips together, my face burning with the pressure of silent sobs. The silence seemed to go on for hours. Then, out of the tear-blurred emptiness, came Taro's voice, warm as dark honey and frank as a schoolboy's. He might even have been smiling.

"You're sorry for that? Have you any idea how long I've been in love with you? Since the moment you first fell into my lake, with your pale eyes and your silver hands. I only had to take one look and I knew I would give my life for you. You are everything to me, Margaret. Everything. Oh, don't cry sky-spirit. Don't cry."

I felt Taro's arms wrap around me. I laid my head against his chest, sobbing and breathing in the scent of aloes, cinnamon, cedar wood. The fine silk of his kimono soaked up the tears. I could hear the beating of his heart; feel his sighs through my cheekbones. He laid his cheek against my hair. His breath was warm. I didn't want to keep anything in any more. I started to kiss him where my lips touched his clothes: on his chest, his collarbone, his shoulder. I heard him heave a deep sigh. Softly, Taro took my face in his fingertips, lifted it up, and kissed me on the lips.

It was as though the world had stopped and started again, the same as before, yet wondrously different. As though there was suddenly a new color in the spectrum or a fifth point on the compass. Taro was kissing me. He tasted of wine and peaches. I could feel the softness of his lips, the down of a faint moustache. My insides leaped up and down. I pulled him closer and kissed him back.

The next minute, we were kissing like crazy. We couldn't stop. We kissed on the lips, the cheek, the curve of the neck. Even when – once or twice – we clashed teeth or got our noses stuck in each others ears, we didn't let up. It was as if all the kisses we hadn't given each other in the last months had to be given now or both of us would die. Taro's hand slid inside the back of my hair. My combs fell out. I was breathless and dizzy and my lips felt numb, but I didn't want it ever to end.

Eventually, we had to stop just to breathe. Taro wiped away what was left of my tears with a handkerchief from the sleeve of his kimono. I didn't want to cry any more. That was past. We both smiled at each other, feeling shy. I didn't know what to say.

"What about your bride?" I said at last.

"She is here." Taro looked at me. "You are the only bride I want, Margaret. My sky-spirit bride. My beautiful O-gin."

"But is that even possible?"

I thought about Taro's family. Even now they were expecting him to ally with the visiting family any day. The laws of his land said I was an illegal fugitive; the social rules known in every land stated aristocrats did not marry tradespeople. Could a man really claim he was marrying one of the spirits and be taken seriously?

Taro set his face to that of a warrior.

"It will be possible."

I remembered what I had observed before on several occasions: that once Taro put his mind to something, he did not hesitate to act until it was done. Still, this seemed a task beyond even the most determined mind.

"It will be possible," he said again, drawing me close and kissing me on the forehead. "I have to go soon, Margaret. My guests are still here. The painting was remarkable, by the way. In the right circles, you could earn quite a reputation as an artist."

"Truly?" I snuggled closer to him.

"Indeed. And I have a gift for you, too. I am expecting its delivery any day. Perhaps you could look on it as a betrothal gift?"

I loved the way that, in spite of all his authority, he went so shy when he mentioned anything to do with his feelings for me. I beamed at him and he gave the boyish smile I treasured so much.

"Yes," I said.

I knew I was accepting a proposal. The second in my life, and yet so completely different from the first that it hardly deserved the same name. Excitement and fear welled up in my chest. I couldn't imagine how it would be possible, but I was going to be Taro's wife.

We talked just a little longer, and then Taro had to slip away, back to the manor where his noble guests were waiting, still expecting a marriage alliance they were never going to get. As he got up to leave, Taro turned back. And gave me a long, lingering kiss.

16

A Chill to the Blood

I couldn't wait to see Taro again. The waiting, I discovered, was a hundred times harder now we had kissed than it had been before. This didn't quite make sense. Surely the fact that we'd let our feelings out ought to make waiting easier? But it didn't. I had no interest whatsoever in the artistic way the summer vegetables were arranged on my dinner tray, the health of the cat, or whether summer thunderstorms would damage the wisteria. All I could think of was how another kiss with Taro would taste, and when he was going to come again.

In actual fact, I only had to wait a couple of days, but they felt like years. I heard his step long before I saw his silhouette emerge from between the maples. My chest tensed. I had Miyuki bring my fan and place it between my fingers, while I desperately tried to look ladylike and unconcerned. I needn't have bothered. Taro came along the stepping-stones by the lakeside two at a time, and the minute we were safely behind a screen, he cupped a hand to my cheek and kissed me in a way that said he had been counting the hours just as desperately.

"You are beautiful," he breathed. "I love you, Margaret."

We spent a few glorious minutes getting re-acquainted with each others' lips. Then we sat back on our heels in the old, modest postures. There were things we needed to talk about, and neither of us could possibly concentrate with our hands in each others' hair. I wrapped myself in the beautiful sight of Taro, lordly in his dark blue kimono, his back straight, his legs crossed underneath him. The cuffs of his sleeves had pictures of cranes in flight on them. It was going to be very hard to stay demure.

Taro took a breath, his face serious.

"I am going away for a few weeks. A hawking expedition. I have invited my noble guests to accompany me, along with my uncles and cousins."

"Why?"

My heart dropped to deep six. This was not what I'd been expecting. I had entertained a vague hope that Taro would send his guests away this morning and we would have the gardens all to ourselves again. Of course, I knew that was a touch unrealistic, but this? Hadn't he just proposed to me?

"It is necessary," he said gently. "My uncles are becoming suspicious. I must be seen to be seriously considering the alliance, until I have time to form a plan. Out in the countryside, riding on horseback, I will think more clearly. It will give me space to decide. And there will be fewer eyes to pry on you while I do so."

"But..."

"That is not all, O-gin. A lord's hawking expedition is more than a pleasurable hunting trip. It is a chance to inspect my lands, unofficially, without being hindered by ceremony. If I can see for myself how things stand with the farm laborers, I may get a better idea of how to make the land more workable. To improve life for all Tokushiro's inhabitants. That will be more important than ever if...when..."

"If we marry?" I dared to suggest.

"Indeed." He flashed a nervous smile. "Somehow the two must come together. I have been reading through the paperwork again. I fear the accounts and records tax me greatly."

I had noticed the shadows under his eyes again. Poor Taro! He worked so hard, and all I did was paint and learn vocabulary. Now he had spoken of marriage, I wanted to be more than just a burden to him. I wanted to be a partner, someone who could work alongside him.

"Perhaps," I began, "if Master Seika would teach me to read numbers, I could help you. I used to keep my father's accounts at home, you know. He always said I had a head for figures."

Had I gone too far? I could see by the look in Taro's eyes that he was uncomfortable. Aristocratic brides were not meant to tot up debit and credit in double entry and know how many silver coins could be exchanged for a feudal note. That probably showed terrible breeding. But there again, how many aristocratic brides fell out of the sky? There was hardly going to be anything typical about my marriage to Taro, if it ever came about.

"It is not such a very great burden." He spoke quickly. Had I offended his dignity? I was going to have to be sensitive in future. "I have a number of clerks and accountants, beside my stewards. They do much of the work." He sighed. "But I must read the records. Since I began this register I have had headaches almost every day."

"Maybe my lord needs spectacles?" I smiled.

Taro gave me a shrewd glance.

"Trust the sky-spirit to think of that! Such foreign imports are sold in the capital. I will consult my physician. He may be open to the idea. A pair could be ordered and swiftly delivered along the main highway with little trouble. That road is well-maintained. Official messengers ride its length in a matter of days."

A sudden chill ran through my blood. Foreign imports? The Sunrise Empire traded with the outside world? So it was not completely sealed off after all. The second dream I had dreamt of Van Guelder – the one with the Dutch merchants and the *samurai* on the bridge – seared my mind.

"I thought you said there were no foreign travelers in the Sunrise Empire." I had to force the words through my tight throat.

Taro's eyes softened. He moved to put an arm about my shoulders.

"Hush now; there is no need to fear. There *are* no travelers. In the whole land, there is one trading port, and merchants may not come ashore. Our overlord sees to that." He kissed me several times. "No one is going to harm you. I am leaving Colonel Akita in charge here. Your protection is his sacred duty." His fingers traced my jaw line. "And I will have your gift delivered to him, too. I wish it could have come sooner; I would dearly have loved to see your reaction. But that pleasure will have to wait." He sighed. "Along with other pleasures."

We kissed some more. Whenever I was in his arms, comfort and protection radiated from Taro's very heartbeat. I wished that I could wring it from him. I didn't want him to go. There was a seam of unease at the heart of paradise that I just couldn't dig out. Several weeks were a long time. I knew I would not feel completely safe again until Taro came back.

It was hard to settle after he was gone. Master Seika suggested that I begin a second painting and we decided on a bridge by moonlight; but somehow none of the preliminary sketches would go right, and had it not been for fear of wasting paper, I would have torn them up with my toes. I cautiously began learning numbers and the correct way to record accounts. It was by far my easiest lesson, but it was dull work. I found myself staring into space more than once. There was another earth tremor and several thunderstorms. Sakura began to complain aloud that the weather did not match the almanac. Ume caught a fever and had to be quarantined. Despite their class-induced standoffishness, I could tell Miyuki and Sakura were secretly as concerned for her as I was. Although I only needed her services for complex translations now, she had become part of our little family. There was a great sense of relief in the house when she returned, and a lot of surreptitious worry about the lingering cough she was troubled with at nights.

"These last days of summer are melancholy, are they not?" said Miyuki. She was sitting beside me, fanning me as I lay on the bed in the mid-day heat. "The poets call autumn a melancholy season, but at least it has the beauty of fading glory. Lord Shimatani's gardens are transcendent in that season. My lady will enjoy them greatly."

"I trust I will," I said.

I couldn't imagine autumn right now: the golden colors and the smell of leaves. The lengthening nights. Would I be Taro's wife by then? I prayed for it every night, before I even prayed for my sisters or Kit. It simply had to come true. There was no way I could go on living if I couldn't be his. I wished Taro would come back. I wished he would walk through the door this very minute.

"My Lord Shimatani will come home soon," Miyuki said.

I looked at her and smiled.

Three days later, a lacquered box arrived at the house. It was inlaid with pearl and had a scene of a garden depicted on it. Inside it was a poem. Despite the best efforts of Master Seika and Ume combined, the translation became a bit scrambled on its journey from formal poesy to antiquated Dutch. But I understood that it said something like this:

Spirit without hands
Insubstantial as starlight
I long to touch you.

The public recitation of this (in both languages) was followed by a distinctly embarrassed silence. Of course, I was pretty sure by now that everyone knew about me and Taro. There was a limit to what a paper screen could hide, and frankly it wasn't much. But this was the first time our relationship had been spoken of openly. Taro must have been feeling confident of our future. Maybe the country air was working its magic. Maybe we could finally see the day when I could go with him to the hawking lodge and see falcons stooping and wheeling in the open sky. I had to assume now that Taro was also a poet, as well as an artist, horseman, swordsman, falconer and goodness only knew what else. I felt pathetic in the face of such accomplishment. Was he sure I was really the one he wanted?

Beneath the poem, and packed in with straw, was the gift the box had been built to contain. Miyuki exclaimed with joy and admiration when she lifted it out, and even Sakura nodded several times with evident approval. As for me, I had no words in any language to express how I felt. The gift was priceless. I couldn't believe such a work of art could have been created in so short a space of time.

It was the replacement silver hands Taro had promised me. Only it seemed wrong to call the humble offerings strapped to my forearms by the same name as what came out of the box. The silversmith, whoever he was, had produced hands the likes of which the poor sailors could not have imagined. They were exquisite, perfectly-formed things. All the little creases and fingernails and everything were in just the same places as on real hands. The fingers were held in elegant postures, as if they were about to pluck harp strings or pick flowers. Engraved lightly on the back of each hand were cherry branches in blossom.

I swallowed. Yet again he had seen into my heart. Now I would have delicate hands like the ladies beneath the plum trees. I would be genteel, a fit bride for Lord Shimatani. Perfect for our wedding day. I pressed my lips together, trying hard not to cry.

"Try them on, my lady; try them on." Miyuki could no longer contain her enthusiasm.

"Very well." I tried to sound like the future Lady Shimatani. "But after that I'm going to save them for best. For when Lord Shimatani comes." I willed myself not to blush on speaking Taro's name.

Miyuki blushed for me.

"You will look very beautiful," she giggled.

Sakura carefully unfastened my old hands, and Miyuki put the new ones on. Compared to the waterlogged wood I was used to, they felt like wearing air. They were so light; the silversmith had made them hollow. At Miyuki's insistence, I struck several poses with them, letting my sleeves fall gracefully over the silver wrists. Sakura brought the mirror. I could sense her longing to polish and shine already.

"The old hands are beginning to smell," she said in a tone that suggested she questioned my judgment in the matter of false appendages. "Is my lady sure she wishes to keep them?"

"Yes."

I stopped posing and looked at the new hands soberly. It was true that the old ones smelled of damp and mold, and now had a tinge of green to them, but they were a gift of love. I thought about the hard work and sacrifice made by the men of the *Hopewell* while I had lain sick and struggling to live without laudanum. I remembered the honest faces of Conlan and Mekuria on the day I had crossed the line. Where were they now, those brave men? Prisoners of Flood Dragon? Food for fishes? I couldn't just throw their hard-won gift away.

"Put these hands back in their box," I said.

"And the old hands, my lady?"

"Put them in a box, too. And lay out the bed. I'm going to lie down."

I could feel I was about to get emotional again. I needed to be alone. I went and lay on my mattress, feeling a faint breeze as it wafted across the open house and stirred the curtains. I wondered if another storm was coming. In my mind, I could hear Conlan's voice, as clear as on that day in the Indian Ocean:

"Real silver, that is. Nothing evil can pass silver. Be safe from that devil and all his kind now."

And then Taro, gentle and shy:

"I have a gift for you. Perhaps you could look on it as a betrothal gift? I love you, Margaret. No one is going to harm you."

Both pairs of hands were gifts of love, both given by men who wanted to protect me and show me I was valued. How could I choose between them? It was impossible. I shook my sleeves down to the elbows and looked at the scarred stumps of my arms. This was who I really was. Not a flawless bride or a sailor's lucky charm. Just Margaret Rosewood, trying her best to make a life for herself out of what was left behind. Bride and stowaway; scholar and Jonah; sky-spirit and maritime maiden. All these things and yet none of them. I sighed and shut my eyes. Life was too complex to reason out right now. The weight of the summer heat covered me like a blanket. I let my mind drift until I fell asleep.

I heard the commotion even before I woke up properly. Miyuki came running up to my bed on her knees (an odd look by any standard), her voice ludicrously high-pitched with excitement.

"My lady! My lady! Lord Shimatani is here!"

"What?"

I sat up, my hair tumbling all over. Taro, here already? He wasn't expected for two weeks at least. And here I was with my hair down and no hands. I tried to think through the fog of sleepiness.

"He is here with Colonel Akita, my lady," Miyuki added.

"He is what?"

I got up from the bed and bird-stepped to the main entrance of the house. Looking down the stairs I could see right down the stepping-stone path as it wound between the trees. Taro was indeed coming, on foot along with the Colonel, who was in full armor. My heart gave its usual leap, but the joy that usually went with it was strangely absent. I had never seen Taro's face so grim and stern. He was wearing riding gear: narrower breeches than normal tucked into boots and greaves; narrow sleeves with bracers on the wrists. He strode into the house without even removing his footwear. Instinctively, I knelt.

"Get up, Margaret," he said.

He had never used my real name in public before. It made me feel naked.

"Is something wrong, my lord?" I said.

"Get up. You are to leave this house. You don't need anything," he added, as Sakura made a move to fetch my belongings.

"May I ask the reason why?" I couldn't think straight. Was he taking me to the manor? Were we to be together now? But then, why was he so angry? And so *rude*?

"You may not ask. Come. I am in haste."

Behind me, Miyuki began to wail. Sakura shuffled after me, crying, "Your hands, my lady!" But Taro took me by the bones of the elbow and marched me out of the house. I scrabbled at the threshold to step into my shoes and still keep up with his irate stride. Was I still asleep, I wondered, and this was a bad dream? I waited to see if I would wake up soon. I didn't.

"Taro," I said, trying to keep my voice from being overheard by the colonel and the house-guard who were now marching behind us. "Have I done something to offend you? I loved the hands, truly I did. I just wanted to save them for our wedding day."

He turned on me with such a look of scorn and fury that I wished I had never spoken.

"Indeed? Well, there is to be no wedding. There is no place for foreigners in this country. Your stay here is over."

I didn't understand. Tears welled in my eyes; obscuring my view and making me trip. Had his uncles made him do this? Or his overlord? Was it something to do with my offer to help with the accounts? I was only trying to be helpful; I didn't mean to offend his honor. But he had sent a poem; he had given me a gift. I thought he loved me. Maybe this was all an act, and in a moment he would embrace me and tell me everything was all right.

"Taro, I love you," I began.

"Be silent!" he snarled.

I gulped. Sobs hiccupped in my chest. I searched Taro's face for any sign of pity, but there were no tears in his eyes. The ebony moons were cold with disdain. Colonel Akita's face wore its usual look of expressionless duty; I could tell nothing from it.

He dragged me the full length of the gardens, a punishing distance in feminine apparel. I became breathless from having to take twenty steps to every one of his. My stilted pattens tipped on the stones and turned my ankles. He didn't even look at me. I was pulled along the strolling paths, over the red bridge where we had watched the stars, between rock sculptures and stone lanterns. I stumbled through silent gravel gardens and heaving orchards, beside miniature mountains and tiny trees. He hauled me through the plum grove, now bereft of the ladies of the delicate hands. The vista opened out to show a full view of the golden mansion standing proud before a pond where herons fished. The layers of roof on the main hall curled up to the heavens; its many walkways and side-wings branched off into the trees. Gilded décor glinted in the late summer sun.

Taro's palace. My heart ached for the beauty of it. For so long, I had only seen partial views and heard descriptions. The reality was way beyond my naïve imaginings. It was grandeur and simplicity in a way that seemed to speak with Taro's own voice, calling me into its halls. And yet Taro's hand was bruising my elbow, dragging me away from the entrance with the roughness men reserve for disobedient dogs. What had I done to make him like this? He said he loved me. He said I was his only bride.

I could barely walk now, but he didn't let up the pace. He hauled me away from the mansion, towards the walls and the imposing main gate of the castle. These must have been the walls I had seen from my fall: thick enough for men to patrol in double file; housing viewing platforms, stables and guard quarters. Men in armor were stationed at every level: sitting, standing, pacing. They fell to their faces at their lord's approach.

Close by the gate, two grooms were holding a horse: a black gelding. It was wearing a coat of red tassels, and flaps decorated with golden waves and fish. Taro strode over to it and gave a grunt of satisfaction. He turned to Colonel Akita.

"Give me your helmet. And your flag."

"My lord, that is highly irregular." It was the first time I had heard the colonel speak at all since we left the house.

"Do you wish to keep your honor?"

Colonel Akita took out the helmet he carried under his arm and bowed, holding it out level with his forehead. The design was an elaborate affair in black, gold and red. It had a great half-moon balanced on top, and a face mask with fierce eyebrows and a mouth full of teeth. At an order from one of the senior men, a guard moved to kneel beside him. Another came running from with guard house with a vertical flag on a pole bearing three crests of the Akita house. They fastened the helmet on Taro's head and the flag to his back. The effect reminded me sickeningly of the pirate captain.

Another man brought a hooded cloak and tied it round my shoulders, pulling the hood over my head. It was far too warm for summer and uncomfortable.

"I don't need this," I said to Taro.

Cold fury blazed through the eyeholes of the mask.

"You will do as you're told. For once."

He mounted the gelding, rather less smoothly than I would have expected. His foot wobbled on the flat shoe of a stirrup. Somehow, I had imagined Taro to be the perfect horseman, like the knights of old. Another dream shattered. I could feel my heart literally breaking, I was sure. What else could hurt this much?

"Lift her in front of me," Taro called to the nearest guard.

It was the young man who had hung my wish on the bamboo tree. I caught a look in his eye that could have been fear or confusion as he grabbed me round the waist and lifted me to the saddle. It was made of wood with high saddle-bows and was certainly not made for sharing. Only the smallest part of it supported my nether quarters, and that part hurt. Taro wrapped an arm round my waist with a grip like a bulldog's jaw. All the guard looked uneasy now, even Colonel Akita. One or two of them glanced to the stables, where their own horses stood.

"How many men, my lord?" said Colonel Akita.

"None." I could hear the intake of breath. "No, wait. You." He turned to the young guard. "Ride to the inn at the port and tell them to expect a guest."

"My lord?" He looked utterly baffled.

"Are you deaf?"

The man threw himself to the ground, then picked himself up and ran to the stables. Moments later, there was a drumming of hoof beats. Men rushed to open the gate.

This made no sense. Why was Taro traveling alone with no guard and no entourage? Where were his guests and his uncles? And where on earth was he taking me? The whole thing seemed so underhand and out of character. I had thought honor to be written on the very soul of the Sunrise Empire's aristocracy. If he despised me so much now, if he wanted to send me away, he could have done that from the comfort of his own palace with one wave of his fan. Why bother to remove me himself?

Was this an elopement? The thought suddenly flashed across my mind. Perhaps this actually was an act and we were riding towards a secret wedding. But wasn't that underhand too? Unless it wasn't a wedding, but something much more carnal. Muscles in uncomfortably private places tensed with horror. It couldn't be that, could it? No; if he meant to use me for pleasure, he would have done that at Tokushiro. Besides, this was Taro I was talking about. Taro wouldn't treat me that way. Would he? I had believed he would never hurt me either. I had believed he would always be gentle and kind.

"Ha!" He called to the horse. It whinnied and broke into a trot. I looked back as the gate of Tokushiro Castle receded behind us. I was being carried away from the only home I had, and the man I had thought loved me was a heartless deceiver. Words from *Paradise Lost* sprang to my memory:

> *They, looking back, all the eastern side beheld*
> *Of Paradise, so late their happy seat,*
> *Waved over by that flaming brand, the gate*
> *With dreadful faces thronged and fiery arms*

Dreadful faces like that of a fierce mask, I thought, trying not to look at the snarling lacquer mouth. At least our First Parents had left the garden hand-in-hand. At least they still had each other's love. I no longer knew if Taro was my Adam or my punishing angel. As the movement of the horse jolted my rear into pounding agony, I could no longer hold back the tears.

"Hush." The voice at my ear was muffled by the mask I was unable to look at. "Do not attract attention by your sobbing. Be silent."

We were beyond the castle walls now, riding down an avenue of two-storey wooden houses. The well-dressed servants at their doors bowed as we passed. I couldn't possibly let him see how scared I was to be out in the open like this for the first time since the markets of Tonkin. And how utterly hollow I felt to find my beautiful life was nothing more substantial than a shadow on a paper screen.

"You will remain still and silent until we reach the inn," Taro said, tightening his grip on my waist. My heart ached at the touch. I wanted to feel tenderness again. I wanted to nuzzle my head in the space between his collar bones, to drink in once more that comforting smell of cinnamon, cedar wood, and a hint of rice wine. Without meaning to, I found myself leaning into him, tilting my head towards his shoulder, closing my eyes...

Shock jerked me upright. Surely my senses were not deceiving me? There was no smell of incense. No cedar wood from the bathhouse. No rice wine. There was nothing. Not even a tang of sweat from the summer heat or a hint of lacquer from the armor.

I lifted my eyes to Taro's neck, searching the layers of silk and woven bamboo. Glinting under his jaw bone were three links of a brass chain.

"Oh yes, my love," said the man beside me.

17

The Road to Misery

It was the moment I had dreaded for months. I had seen it in my worst nightmares over and over. The merest thought of it had been enough to reduce me to tears. But now that it had come, all the fear I might have felt was suddenly replaced by hot, furious anger. I beat on Van Guelder's chest, my arms going like windmills, regardless of the pain or the risk of overbalancing.

"Where is Taro? What have you done with him, you fiend? You demon from hell!"

He drew me closer with a grip of iron and hissed in my ear:

"I would not attract such attention if I were you. Remember you are a foreigner in this land. And foreigners are unwelcome."

I looked about. We had gone down several dog-legs into the outer part of town, where short curtains split in two over the doors of houses proclaimed various shops and trades. The towns-people were all on their knees with their heads to the ground. Whether they thought they were bowing to Taro or Colonel Akita, I couldn't say. Taro had said the people were virtuous and loyal. But that was no guarantee of their loyalty to an unknown woman muffled in a hooded cloak. A woman with European eyes and chestnut hair. I tucked my arms back under my clothes.

"That's better," he said. I swallowed hard. His dangerous, mocking tone made a travesty of Taro's voice. "It is good to see your intelligence has not deserted you completely. I doubt the Shogun would be as generous and forgiving to you as I."

"Who is the Shogun?" I said.

He made a sound of contempt. "You don't even know where you are, do you?"

"The Sunrise Empire," I said flatly.

"The Sunrise Empire?" He snorted. "Is that what your little King of the Castle told you? This is Japan. It is a hostile nation, full of heathens who would kill a Christian as soon as look at one."

"Well, you should be perfectly safe, then," I muttered.

I couldn't believe he could insult Taro's country so cruelly. I had been treated with nothing but kindness and hospitality here. It was a beautiful land: home to spiritual art, courteous manners and honorable codes of conduct.

"You know nothing about this land!" I said.

"Oh, don't I?" His breath came through the mask, hot and menacing. "Three days as a customs official; two months as a rice merchant; four weeks as a riverbank gardener, merciful God! Have you any idea how despised those river people are? I should have died of shame were it not for the fact that I had tracked you down at last."

"You came from the island in the harbor." I blanched as I remembered my second dream on the night of the earthquake. "The trading port with the Dutch merchants. I saw it in a dream."

"I hope it ate at your soul!" he retorted. "You have tormented my dreams night after night. Picked up on an island in the Laccadive Sea by a Dutch vessel bound for Nagasaki; no thanks to your friends on the *Hopewell*, who I wish may meet with the Kraken for their treatment of me. Slinking from town to miserable town of this cursed empire. The only thing driving me on: the pull of the lodestone from my radiant, disobedient bride. And when I finally discover her whereabouts, what do I find? Not only has she turned native." He looked in scorn at my kimono. "But she has offered herself in marriage to a self-important pup with more fawning toadies than the Queen of Sheba!"

My anger exploded out of me.

"He is not a pup! He is Lord Shimatani."

"He had better not have anticipated his wedding night with you. My love." He laced the last two words with irony. "I have waited long to be truly one with my bride. I will not be disappointed again."

"How dare you? Taro would never treat me like that."

As I spoke, I remembered with a pang of guilt that I have been on the verge of believing Taro would treat me exactly that way. I had doubted him and everything he was. I had betrayed him. And all the while, he was suffering at the hands of Van Guelder.

I sensed, rather than saw, a triumphant smirk inside the mask.

"You will be pleased to learn that he fell like a stone when I finally took his form. I had expected a little more resistance than that, but it seems that the men of this land, for all their outward ferocity, are really as weak as women."

"We women are not as weak as you suppose," I muttered.

It struck me that I actually believed that now. I was not weak. How many strong men had Dr Lemuel told me failed to recover from amputation? Yet I had not only survived without the black bottle, but settled into a new land, becoming mistress in my own home, and learning a new language, along with new skills of painting and calligraphy. It may be wise, I realized, to keep this revelation from Van Guelder. If he wished to think me weak, so be it. Perhaps I could use it to my advantage. Out loud, I said:

"If you despise this land so much, why do you speak its language?"

"I don't," he said. "It is this vile body. It refuses to let me speak anything else. I will be glad to wash its taste from my mouth. As for you, if I catch you so much as thinking in it once we are under the Dutch flag, you will regret it bitterly."

"I wouldn't dream of it," I said in Dutch, my eyes flashing.

Inside, my heart was hammering against my ribcage. In his hatred for Taro and his country, had Van Guelder let something slip? When he had been in the form of the rakish aristocrat from England, he had spoken both English and Dutch with ease. "His sort is ludicrously easy to control," he had said. But Taro was not that sort. He had discipline and strength of character in abundance; in no way was he weak. Taro was fighting him! The thought came to me in swell of emotion. I had to be strong. I had to control my own fears and despair, and meet Van Guelder head-on.

"Give the body back, then," I said.

"I think not." I was glad the mask hid his mockery of Taro's features. That cold irony made me sick. "I intend to pass from this country without hindrance. And you will come with me. In meekness and silence."

He spurred the horse on to a canter.

We passed through the town gate without inspection. Outside, there was only one road that led in two directions: one going past the temple to the mountains and the main highway, the other to the coast. Which took the rider to Taro's hawking lodge, I didn't know, but since we took the coastal road, I guessed it wasn't that one.

Once we got past the first few farmsteads, the road became a raised path in a sea of rice paddies and groves of trees. We passed by laborers bent double, up to their knees in the harvest, and farmers carried in open carriages by bare-legged servants. As we came to sparser ground, scattered with flowers and grazing horses, our fellow-travelers became more varied. Men trudged in the opposite direction with baskets of fish or seaweed suspended from poles across their shoulders. Travelers with small packs and conical hats hurried by. Mules complained under the load of boxes and barrels. A lone man lumbered down from a village on the back of an ox. An official messenger thundered past on horseback, bells jingling on his harness. All stopped to do homage to the high-ranking *samurai* of uncertain lineage, while tactfully ignoring his prisoner/companion of ill repute. Here as elsewhere, a gentleman's business was his own. Tongues may wag in private but silence was prudent in the open.

Did all this land belong to Taro, I wondered? All these people, with their various lives and trades and duties? All this terrain: the fields, the villages, the distant forests? Was he responsible for them all? No wonder he got headaches! I couldn't allow Van Guelder to abuse his form and keep him helpless and unconscious. His people needed him. I needed him. No, that was not right. I wanted him. I wanted him so badly it hurt. But that was simply my selfish desire. I had been better brought up than to put that first. Besides, I had done a dreadful thing in letting myself believe Van Guelder was Taro. I didn't know if I even deserved him any more.

The further we traveled, the harder it got to hold my thoughts together. I was sweltering in my cloak and hood. Sweat ran into my eyes, insects buzzed and stung. Every so often, Van Guelder tipped a splash of lukewarm water into my mouth from a gourd at his side, before swigging from it himself, but the benefits wore off almost from the moment I swallowed. Taro's thoroughbred sweated and panted. Van Guelder breathed heavily through the mask. My rear parts were unbearably saddle-sore, and I swayed in exhaustion every time Van Guelder shifted position.

I thought I was about to pass out when I smelled the unmistakable salt tang of the sea. The familiar freshness in the air was so much a part of childhood and everything that was innocent and good, that I had to fight the urge to cry. We had reached a fishing town, where straw-roofed houses nestled in a bay, overlooked by tree-topped hills. I could see sailing boats out on the water, a small fleet unloading by a pier, all the familiar bustle of buying and selling, bargaining and cheating. It wasn't Hollyport, but my blood rose to see something I understood so well.

On closer inspection, the "town" didn't quite deserve to share the title with Tokushiro or even Hollyport. The town wall was nothing but a tottering fence of bamboo, its watchmen apparently more interested in gambling than actual watching. The main street was nothing but grass, boasting inexpertly scrawled shop signs and old men eating noodles at tables. The general surly air of the place put a chill like cold fingers on the back of my previously sweating neck.

Standing by his horse outside fly-ridden stables, and looking as if his very reputation was being ruined simply by being there, was the young guard Van Guelder had sent ahead. He bowed when he saw us coming, although I caught a glint of unease in his face.

"The inn is here, my lord. I have had the host ready your room."

He indicated a dilapidated building of several storeys, the upper ones of which looked as though they were about to come down on the lower ones. It boasted one or two names on the door, mostly of the type rich farmers or merchants might have. Beneath the signs, a couple of girls in garish kimono fluttered fans and eyelashes at passers-by.

"My lord, are you sure about this?" the guard asked in an undertone.

"Do you question my orders?" The young man looked offended at the very idea. "Very well then."

Van Guelder handed me down to the guard before dismounting himself, in a shaky fashion that was most unbecoming to the Sunrise warrior class. My legs instantly gave way beneath me. The guard made a move to hold me up. Van Guelder – I noticed through my own exhaustion – was swaying where he stood.

"Sell the horse to pay for the room," said Van Guelder. "Have the saddle and all the equipment brought to me."

The man took in a breath.

"My lord, I am not a merchant." Had it been possible to challenge his superior to a duel, I believe he would have done so. "Besides, who but my lord could possibly afford it? This is a…" He looked around the town with contempt. "An inferior place."

"Then tell the innkeeper to hold it as security. I no longer require it. You may then return to your garrison."

There was stark pity in the young man's eyes as he rose from his final bow and glanced over at me. I wanted to yell out:

"This is not Lord Shimatani! You must find him and help him! This man must be stopped!"

But I feared as much for the guard's safety as for my own. I had heard that, in this empire, a man of honor could be ordered to fall on his own sword. If Van Guelder knew of that custom, I had no doubt he would use it to his own advantage.

Van Guelder took my elbow, not at all gently. He dragged me past the bamboo carriages cluttering the road, ignoring the entertainment girls' suggestive invitations. The next minute, we were out of the horse-dung scented street and into the dimness of the inn.

It seemed we had stumbled upon the Sunrise version of the Dolphin. Men with flushed faces reclined with wine bowls in one hand and pipes in the other; alternately drinking, smoking and singing along to the sound of twanging music. Girls like those outside in the street minced round the tables, refilling drinks and complimenting their guests' manhood, in voices so feminine they had to be faked. The music turned out to be coming from a corner, where another girl sat on a cushion and plucked what resembled a three-stringed guitar. Whatever the song, it was evidently very popular. And so was its singer. The men swayed as they sang, and some leaned way too close to her for propriety.

A girl who reminded me painfully of Miyuki came tottering towards us, bowing repeatedly.

"If our honored guests would condescend to step this way."

Van Guelder pushed me ahead and I limped into the room the girl indicated: an interior space lit only by lanterns and whatever light filtered through the paper screen from the next room. Hanging above its one cushion was a picture of clothed frogs playing lutes and harps. Van Guelder sank to the cushion with a groan, pulling off the helmet and leaning his head against the flimsy wall. I felt like simply slumping with my face on the matting, but I made the effort to kneel in the demure posture I had learned in this land. Alertness was my only hope against Van Guelder's plot. I had not known so many parts of my body could ache at once. My ears throbbed with heat and with the movement of the horse, which I could still feel even after dismounting.

"Our honored guests will take some refreshment?" the hostess said.

Van Guelder grunted and waved a hand. The girl bowed several times and proceeded to come in and out with tables of food, wine and the full trappings of a tea ceremony. Between her many exits and entrances, the inn's host came groveling in with the horse equipment, his greasy face sweating as he babbled out apologies.

"If only we had known your honored self was coming sooner, we would have sent out for better food. Would you like me to throw the other guests out, sir? They are nobodies, mere nobodies. I assure you, revered sir, that the Inn of the Thousand Autumns will do everything in its power to accommodate so august a personage..."

"Silence, dog," Van Guelder said. The man shut his mouth like a clam and pressed his bald forehead into the matting. "I am not to be disturbed, do you understand? I have a private meeting arranged here and it must remain private."

"Absolutely, Your Worship." The man bowed up and down like the handle of a water pump.

I kept my eye firmly on Van Guelder. Flush-faced and with strands of sweaty hair stuck to his forehead, he looked less like Taro now. But I didn't think it was just his disheveled appearance that made the difference. It was the face itself. The nose was less sharply defined; the eyes had lost their glow. And there were startling pale patches beneath the eyes. He looked ill. Did that mean Taro was ill too? Or was Van Guelder starting to weaken? I held myself upright by force of will and kept watching.

Eventually, the host and hostess left us. Van Guelder knocked back a bowlful of the wine, ignoring the fish dish (which had barely stopped wriggling) and angrily balled up fists full of rice.

"Would you pour me some tea, Mr. Van Guelder?" I said in the most polite voice I could manage. "And unfasten my cloak, please. No one can see me in here."

"Do it yourself," he said, between mouthfuls of rice. "You seem used to helping yourself in this country."

In response, I held up my arms, so that my sleeves fell back, revealing the withered stumps. His eyes widened. I realized that, until this point, he had failed to grasp the fact of my loss of limb. A mixture of disgust and outrage flashed across his face, along with something else I could not define.

"Your hands!" he said.

"Amputated." I shook the sleeves back down. "You see, I am no longer a perfect bride. I fear I will be a disappointment to you after all. I am only fit for the..." I forced the word out. "Heathens."

"Oh no, my love." He shuffled across the matting. In a swift movement, he unclasped my cloak with one hand, and cupped my cheek with the other. Taro's mouth curled into the customary ironic smirk. The effect turned my stomach. "You may not break our betrothal bonds so easily. It is your soul I crave. Your soul and your submission. Hands are neither here nor there. In fact, being without them may be an advantage. Now you can no longer push me away."

Before I could protest, he pressed me up against the flimsy wall and kissed me savagely, hungrily, until I felt my lips begin to bleed. Tears flooded my eyes. These were Taro's lips against mine. The same lips that had touched me when he said he loved me, when we had said our last goodbye. His kiss had been the sweetest thing I had ever tasted. Now it was foul, a bitter punishment.

"Is that what you like?" Van Guelder said in my face. "The kiss of a heathen lord? By God, you will have me in any form I choose! I would take you now, were it not for the fact that everything must be done correctly. Past experience has proved that anything less than the bond of marriage is ineffective. We must be one in every sense: in law, in spirit, in body, in mind. And then..." He closed his eyes and gave a shuddering sigh. "Oblivion!"

I sank to the matting, feeling every pain in my body as a separate agony.

"I won't do it," I said.

"You will!" Beads of sweat stood out on his forehead. "Or live out the rest of your days as a starving beggar on the streets of Batavia. Oh yes," he said, catching the question in my eyes. "That is where we are going: to the Van Guelder spice plantation in all its glory. And that is where I will leave you to die if you fail to pledge yourself to me with your whole heart. You will have no friends there. No more jack tars and slit-eyed popinjays. How will you manage then, without the hands to even feed yourself?"

"God will help me." I looked up, defiant. The eyes that met mine were filled with scorn.

"A child's notion! God helps only the strong. The weak may cry and cry but no one comes to their aid. Believe me."

Was there a hint of bleakness, even of hurt, as he spoke those words? Had I just seen a crack in his cynical façade? He reached into his kimono breast and drew out the lodestone on its chain, turning it over and over in his hand.

"Now sit up and get behind that screen. I am expecting a visitor."

I scrubbed my nose with my sleeve and took the bowl of tea he shoved towards me. Such a tiny drop of so strong a liquid did little to cure my thirst and nothing at all for the throbbing in my head, but it was better than nothing. Van Guelder watched with a mixture of fascination and disgust at the way I balanced the bowl between my forearms and leaned forward to sip. The cold eyes gave me frost burn. The bowl shook; tea spilled on the matting. I couldn't let him beat me down like this. I had to be strong. But I was so tired and my heart was a millstone in the ocean. What would Taro say when he came home and I wasn't there? He would think I had left him.

The door slid open and the hostess came bowing in again.

"Our honored guest has a visitor."

I shuffled back behind a screen, crudely painted with fishing boats. From my position behind it, I could see most of what was going on. The hostess bowed in a greasy-haired man wearing the loincloth and short coat of a fisherman. He put his head to the ground before Van Guelder, before grinning up at him, showing missing front teeth.

"My lord, are you the one I was to meet regarding the transport of the Dutch cargo?"

"I am." Van Guelder continued to finger the brass chain as if he couldn't care less, although sweat trickled down his forehead and his face was salt-pale. "At what hour does the ship sail?"

"At sundown." He bowed and grinned again. "I hate to mention so vulgar a thing, but an honored taskmaster can be relied upon to reward his faithful servant. If I may congratulate you on your prosperity..."

"There is an exceptionally fine horse in the stables here." Van Guelder cut through his prelude to avarice. "I'm sure you and the innkeeper can come to some sort of arrangement between you. You may convey this superior equipment to the captain for our passage." He patted the saddle and smiled. "Three shrewd business minds such as yours are bound to make the best of this generous offer. I hear the Shimatani are always on the lookout for good horses."

I stiffened with anger. He proposed to make Taro buy back his own horse! Van Guelder just laughed to himself, and the other man smiled with him. What kind of criminal was he, anyway? A pirate? A smuggler? He wasn't loyal to Taro; that was for sure. Perhaps he served a rival clan. I seethed. Smuggling was going on right under Taro's nose. Just when the province was most in need of a sound economy. And what was the Dutch cargo? A cold finger stroked my spine. Was that me? But I couldn't leave the Sunrise Empire. I would never see Taro again.

"Expect the cargo in this room at sundown," Van Guelder said. "Two parcels. You may leave us now."

The man made several more slimy courtesies and shuffled backwards through the sliding door. I crawled out from my hiding place. Van Guelder dangled the lodestone on its chain and spun it first one way and then the other.

"Not long to wait now, my love. Do you not feel the attraction between us? You will not resist me. We are destined to be one."

"I feel nothing," I lied.

In truth, parts of me I couldn't control screamed out for the twisted resemblance of Taro sitting before me. The pull of the lodestone was growing. The longer we were together, the closer Van Guelder and I would be bound. He was right. I couldn't resist, not for ever. Sooner or later, I would become exhausted and relinquish the struggle. I would surrender.

No. I had to gather my strength and fight. The magnetic force was nothing like as strong as it had been on the *Hopewell* the day I lost my hands. Back then I had barely been able to stand up for it; this time I hadn't felt it coming to me until I was captured. Surely that meant something. Was Van Guelder actually weaker now? Or was I stronger? On the *Hopewell*, fear of Van Guelder had consumed me. Now there were other emotions in my soul: love for Taro and fears for his safety; knowledge of who I could be and what I could do; passion for this beautiful country and all it had come to mean to me. Could I somehow use all that to stop me falling victim to the lodestone? Could I find a way to resist before it was too late?

Minutes blinked by. Shadows moved round. The song of one singing-girl was replaced by another. Every change brought me closer to being carried away from the Sunrise Empire forever. But what could I do? I couldn't run. My feet were fat with blisters, my body bruised and shaken. Neither could I scream for help. Unless news of the silver-handed spirit had spread to the coast, I stood more chance of being finished off as an illegal traveler than being worshipped as a god. I knew nothing of the Shogun, but turning me over to the feudal lord in this case would mean turning me over to Van Guelder. I looked at him. His stare seemed to be eating me up in anticipation of our wedding day. Blankly, I took the parcel of raw fish and seaweed he passed me as if it were my last meal before going to the gallows.

No plan came to my mind. A distant temple bell announced sundown. Van Guelder put the fierce-masked helmet back on his head and drew an enamel box from a pouch at his belt. It looked like – and probably was – a snuff box, decorated with a picture of shepherdesses. But instead of containing powdered tobacco, it held only a lock of fine, fair hair. He pressed the lock to the lodestone, breathing in and out with heavy breaths. I stared. That hair. I had seen it before; in all my nightmares, in fact. The hair of a drunken son of a peer. "Ludicrously easy to control," Van Guelder had said. So easy that he could fell the poor man from the other side of the world, using only his hair? I shuddered at the heartlessness of the man who would be my husband.

But if he changed form that meant... Taro! Taro would be freed! He would come looking for me. Regardless of the danger, I leapt up and made a charge for the door.

A pair of sinewy arms stopped me. I fell forward and found myself looking into the toothless face of the smuggler. He gave a sly grin on seeing the pallor of my skin, the lightness of my hair and eyes.

"The Dutch cargo is ready to sail?" he said, with a glance towards Van Guelder. "Come, my lord, quietly. The boat is waiting."

"Taro!" I screamed, unable to stop myself.

In an instant, a ringing slap to my cheek made the room ripple. The smuggler cupped a dirty hand over my mouth. It stank of fish and strong tobacco.

"No noise," he hissed at me.

Van Guelder swayed towards him and closed his free hand around the smuggler's throat.

"Lay your filthy hands off her. She will be silent if I say so. Now lead on and be mindful of your place."

Van Guelder's words came out in a curious jumble of Japanese and English, but the smuggler's face showed he understood the meaning. He loosened his hold on me, while still keeping a hand over my mouth, and marched me through the debauched merriment of the inn. Out in the street, dusk had turned everything grey. A few lanterns were burning, and dogs barked behind bamboo fences. But, beside a drunken night watchman, there was no one to see us pass. If this was a smuggling town, I thought, an inattentive neighbor would be a good neighbor.

The man dragged me between the rows of wooden houses and down to the harbor. A single-sailed fishing boat was waiting between the sleeping boats at anchor, a lantern glowing at its stern. I struggled in the smuggler's arms as he waded out. It did no good. He simply tightened his grip, thinking no doubt of the value of Taro's horse. Two equally dirty and gruesome fishermen reached down from the stern and pulled me aboard. Van Guelder clambered after me, still clutching the lodestone. The water lapped at the side of the boat. Its hull bobbed in a motion I hadn't felt since I parted from Dr Lemuel. It was not something I had expected to feel again. Tears stung my eyes. I looked back at what could be seen of the town. Somewhere beyond its border hills was Tokushiro: the castle, the gardens and my lakeside house. They would wait for me there but I would not return. I would not be there when Taro came home. I hadn't been able to think of anything to do to save myself. It was too late.

The boat pushed off from the shore. A wind caught its sail and carried it out into the bay. As we rounded the coast into the open sea, I could see a barquentine waiting in deeper waters, flying the Dutch flag. This was the ship from which the smugglers unloaded their illegal goods, no doubt. I caught a glimpse of its name plate in a bloom of lantern light: *Rotterdam*. It was the vessel that was to take me to Batavia and marriage. And the end of my own identity forever.

Swiftly, too swiftly, we sailed towards it. Pigtailed sailors looked down from the bulwarks. They signaled to the smugglers, who made a countersign. Van Guelder stood up in the stern of the fishing boat, swaying. He pulled off the helmet. Golden hair spilled over his shoulders. His face was death-pale, his jaw tight with inner tension, but the perfectly straight nose and cold blue eyes were recognizable instantly. His chosen form. He took a deep breath and spoke hoarsely in Dutch:

"Gentry of Amsterdam and Batavia seeking safe passage. Take us aboard. And tell your captain there is a lady in the party."

The sailors lowered ropes and a jolly-boat. There was nothing I could do. I had been sold to a Dutch captain for the price of a fine saddle. Within moments, I was on deck and being escorted to the first-mate's cabin. Van Guelder followed close on my heels, in whispered conversation with the captain. I noticed he gasped when he spoke, as a sick man will, but he stood as upright as ever and his eyes were still cold and determined. He pushed me into the cabin ahead of him. It had white paintwork and a hanging cot, and not much in the way of comfort. The first mate was evidently a Spartan amongst mariners.

"Only one night alone for you, my love. For decency's sake." He smirked and leaned heavily on the gun carriage that stood by the cot. "I have told the captain to lock the door so you do not stray. I would not wish to lose my bride on my wedding eve."

"Wedding eve?" I strove to keep my voice normal.

"Why yes, my love. There is little point in delaying it any longer. I have requested that the captain perform the marriage ceremony as soon as we are safely out at sea. With a good wind, we should be man and wife tomorrow. By the time we arrive in Batavia, we shall be quite one."

He leaned towards me and kissed me sensuously on the side of the neck. His unreal lack of smell wafted under the tumble of my hair. It made me shiver.

"How I shall count the hours until then! Every minute will be torture." He straightened up, casting an almost sorrowful glance at me through his sickly pallor. "Be merciful to me at the last, my love. You are my only salvation. And tomorrow when we become each other at last, my hell will end."

He closed the door.

18

Van Guelder's Curse

I sank to the cabin floor, pulling my sleeves over my head. One night only. That was all I had before I became Mistress Van Guelder, and my soul was swallowed up by my husband and the power of his terrible lodestone. I was friendless aboard a Dutch vessel, bound for the capital of the Dutch spice empire in the Pacific. Everyone I knew and loved was far away. I had lost my home, my friends, my beloved Taro, even my silver hands. I was locked in a cabin until my wedding day, and there was no one I could turn to for help. The captain had been bought with the promise of gold; the sailors had no reason to trust me. If there ever had been a guardian angel, it was now back in paradise, blocking my return with a sword of fire. Perhaps Van Guelder was right. Maybe God really was on the side of the strong.

"That is hardly a reasonable point of view, Mistress Rosewood," said the voice in my memory.

I sat up. Of course. Dr Lemuel was right; he always was. I had to look at this scientifically. Van Guelder had spoken those words in bitterness. He was angry with me because of my relationship with Taro and – could it be he was threatened by it too? My heart began to quicken. Inquiry, careful thought and observation. That was what Dr Lemuel had taught me. Even the strangest of creatures has a reason for its appearance and behavior. Were my instincts about Van Guelder's appearance and behavior today correct? I had to think hard.

He was angry, yes. But he was pale and tired too. Anyone could see that. Almost sickly, one might say. And that had to be due to changing form. What else could it be? He had taken several different forms on his journey across the Sunrise Empire; he had said so himself. For the most part he would have targeted the weak-willed and the easily tempted. But he had over-faced himself in his decision to take the form of Taro. I thought back to the *Hopewell*. Van Guelder had been unable to take the form of Frenchie because she was a girl. He had reeled and cursed, and been forced to turn on the marine instead. There were some things the lodestone simply couldn't do. Or couldn't do in his hands, at any rate. It channels its master's will, he had told me once. But what if another's will were stronger? Taro had fought Van Guelder for control of his form, I was sure of it. His strength had forced Van Guelder to speak only Japanese. It had worn him down and exhausted him with the effort of maintaining the shape. Even taking on his most comfortable form – the heir from the *Dolphin* – had taken something out of him. Van Guelder would never be weaker than he was tonight. If ever there was a time to act, it was now.

But there was something else too. Something that had not occurred to me until today. A magnet does not only attract. It repels. If Van Guelder was seeking to attract the outward features (or in my case, the innermost soul) of others, then what was he seeking to repel? His last words before he closed the door echoed in my head; they had been strange and unexpected. Van Guelder wanted to escape something as desperately as I wanted to escape him. And if I could only be strong enough…

My mind was abuzz with ideas. I had to take deep breaths in order to keep fixed on Dr Lemuel's famous reason. A plan was forming. One which could see me free of Van Guelder for ever.

I stood and knocked on the door by kicking it with the stilts of my shoes.

"Ahoy!" I yelled in Dutch. "Assistance needed! Ahoy there!" On a ship such as this, there were bound to be several officers' cabins together, along with rooms for dining and examining charts. And since we would be into the dog watch by now, a few sociable drinks would be in order for those off duty. I had no doubt that someone would hear me.

I was not wrong. A lad of about ten, whose original home

appeared to be somewhere on the west coast of Africa, opened the door and peered round. By the formal cut of his clothes, I imagined he was the captain's servant. Or his slave.

"Captain Bakker says to keep it down," he said. "There are men trying to sleep."

"I need to use the privy," I said. "And there's no one to help me undress for bed. I can't do it myself." I deliberately let my sleeves fall down to show my ravaged arms. The boy swallowed hard and looked everywhere except at me.

"We don't keep maidservants aboard this ship, miss. And Captain says no one's to go near you."

"What about my husband?"

"He retired to quarters. But Captain says you're not to leave yours until the morrow."

Captain Bakker said rather a lot, I fancied. I wondered how many more repetitions of the same phrase I was likely to get. I gave a sigh that made me sound like Miyuki. The boy squared his narrow shoulders, but I saw pity in his eyes.

"It's my wedding day tomorrow," I said, in the most wistful voice I could manage. "And I'm so tired." At least I didn't have to pretend that part. Any fool could see I was exhausted. "Please let me at least use the privy. I just want to go to bed and sleep."

Acting the part was almost making me cry for real. I actually was in dire pain and ready to collapse. All I wanted was to be back in Tokushiro and away from this ship. It was a fight to hold the tears in, and I think the boy could see it. He took several deep breaths through his nose, and didn't seem to know what to do with his hands.

"Very well," he said hurriedly. "You may use the officer's privy. I will show you where to go. But look lively or Captain Bakker will be displeased."

He took a lantern and showed me the place where the officers' close-stool was. On the other side of a wooden partition, I could hear a flute and hautboy being played, and several male voices talking at once. I indicated the sash of my kimono. The boy held it at arm's length like a rotten fish, and pulled on the knot with his face turned in the opposite direction.

"How long will this...er...take?" he said.

"I don't know," I said, summoning up a look that made him squirm. "Why don't you go back to pouring the captain's rum and brandy, and then come back to me? I'm only on the other side of this wall." I gave a nod to the painted panels.

He glanced in the direction of the music and then back to me, as if uncertain where his first duty lay. I made a move to hitch my skirts with the stump of my arm.

"Hell's teeth, miss, I'm going! But you mind what Captain said. I'll be back when I've filled his glass."

He ducked through a door in the partition. The moment he was gone, I let my skirts fall again. Now, where was Van Guelder? I closed my eyes. For once, the pull of the lodestone was a blessing. Yes, I could feel it already. The insistent yearning plucked at my breast. All I had to do was follow it, and Van Guelder was certain to be there.

A step or two; a couple more. I was in the corridor between cabins. I looked up and down the length of polished oak. This door was the one I wanted. This was where he was. I pushed against the door, all my injuries throbbing. I hoped he really was as weak as I had reckoned. Otherwise, I was going to need an almighty excuse for being here. Even Van Guelder couldn't believe the lodestone had pulled me through cabin walls.

But the snores I heard told me I had been right. I let out a ragged breath, with silent prayers of thanks. The flickering stump of a candle inside a lantern showed Van Guelder sprawled across a cabin bed, still in Taro's kimono. He lay on his back. One arm hung limp over the wooden rail. His head was tipped back in complete insensibility. If he ever resembled the man whose form he had stolen, he did so now. His face was grey and clammy; the tender part beneath his eyes was bruised purple.

For a moment, I caught myself feeling almost sorry for him. Were I a man now, armed with a sword or cutlass, there would be nothing to stop me from plunging it into his heart. It would be no less than he deserved and a pitiable death.

But I was not a man; and Father had taught me the Commandments better than that. I had not come to take life. I had come to take something else. Something Van Guelder should never have owned in the first place.

I stepped out of my shoes. The candlelight showed the glint of the brass chain round Van Guelder's neck. The lodestone hung heavily to one side, luckily the side nearest me. I tried my best to fix its position in my mind; then lowered myself to a sitting posture on the floor, balancing myself with my arms behind me. This was going to be the hardest thing I had ever done. Surely the toes that had learned to wield chopsticks and paint calligraphy could manage to unclasp a necklace? I sincerely hoped so.

Leaning back onto my arms, I raised my feet higher and higher. I had to take the brass chain between my toes, to pay it through until I found the clasp, to unclasp it and to pull it away from Van Guelder without dropping it. And I had to do it gently. If Van Guelder woke now, all was lost.

He maketh my feet like hinds' feet. I recalled the words from the Psalms. *How beautiful upon the mountains are the feet of him that bringeth good tidings.* My feet needed to be everything that was graceful now. I would worry about good tidings later.

Every fraction of an inch was torture. The muscles in my arms, legs and even my stomach ached and shook with pain. My blistered toes slipped with sweat. The candle flickered and smoked like it was about to go out. Van Guelder snorted and twitched; every time he did, I was convinced it was the end. I had to wait, heart thumping, until he was completely still, and then begin the whole process again.

Worse still, the magnetic pull was growing stronger by the minute. I didn't want to go gently. I wanted to seize the lodestone with both feet, and then seize Van Guelder and melt into his arms. The instinct repulsed me, but I couldn't deny its power. I had to resist. Oh, but it was hard! I was tired, so tired. I had to force myself to go on, to try again.

When I fall, I shall arise. The once-beloved words from *Pilgrim's Progress* came back to my mind. That was right. I must be strong. I wasn't going to let my Apollyon get the better of me this time.

Eventually, I had the clasp between my toes. By this time, my arms and legs were shaking terribly. All I wanted was to collapse and give in to the magnetic drag on my soul. But I had to go slowly now; this was the hardest part. I felt the clasp cautiously with my toe, working out where I would press, how I would turn. Then I tried. Nothing happened. I tried again. My foot slipped and I lost my grasp. Agonizingly, I pushed myself higher and took hold of the chain again. The shadows on the cabin wall leaped madly from large to small. The lantern was going to go out at any minute.

I took a deep breath and made a third attempt at the clasp. It came loose. I let out a shuddering sigh and pulled the rest of the chain through my toes. I mustn't let it fall now; a stone of that size would make a terrible bang on the floor. I had to bring it down and get it round my own neck. Every muscle I had ached and quivered. I was sweating all over. My heart threatened to burst in my chest as I looped the chain over my loose hair and fumbled with the clasp once more. My legs were in agonizing contortions, my rear end devoid of all feeling. If I could just get that bit inside the other bit… I was nearly there.

Done it! I collapsed back, panting. The pull towards Van Guelder stopped in an instant. The stone hung heavy round my neck, the chain's links tugging on loose strands of hair. I had done it! Now I had to get out, if I could get my shuddering limbs to move and my pulse to stop deafening my ears. Quickly, before that slave boy came looking for me. I hauled myself to my feet, swaying, blood rushing to my head, and turned in the direction of the door.

Everything plunged into blackness, with a choking smell of poor tallow. The lantern had gone out. I groped madly for the door, gasping for air, and tripped over my shoes. Pain jarred my knees as I fell to the deck. Behind me, Van Guelder gave a violent snort and was silent. There was a rustle of bed sheets and a creak of timber.

"Who's there?" a hoarse voice cried. "Bakker? Speak out, man. What do you want?"

I tried to hold my breath, but my heart was beating too quickly, and in the darkness of the cabin, my breath sounded louder than ever.

"Speak, I say." From the rummaging sounds behind me, I guessed he was trying to find candles or flints. "Don't creep up on a man like that." He broke off into a fit of coughing and groaned.

That small sign of weakness gave me a seed of strength. I had the lodestone. I had it round my neck and he didn't. He couldn't control me any more. I was my own woman. In a tone I had learned from Taro, I called out:

"It is I, Mr. Van Guelder: Margaret Rosewood. I came to tell you that I won't be requiring the captain's services in the morning. Or indeed at any other time. I intend to remain a maiden. I'm sorry to disappoint your hopes after all this time, but you simply can't force someone to give themselves to you, body and soul. That isn't how love works."

"Margaret?" To my surprise, his voice was one of almost tender desperation. "You came to me?"

"I am leaving you," I said firmly. "I intend to keep to my cabin until we reach Batavia. It is over, sir. You no longer control me."

"What?" I could hear the tremor in his voice, the scrabble amongst his clothing. Fear rose in my chest again. "What have you done with it, you witch? Give it back to me!"

His heavy tread sounded on the deck, lurching with the sway

of the ship. I struggled to get to my feet and turn so he was no longer at my back.

"Curse this dark!" he said. "Where is that flint? You will give the stone back to me, Margaret, or you will live to regret it."

"You will stay away from me, sir." My voice rose to a high pitch as I fumbled for the door with my forearms. "The sailors will hear and, however much you paid the captain, he will not tolerate disorder aboard his ship."

"He will tolerate whatever I...ow! What was that?"

I had no idea, but Van Guelder had cried out as if he were stung. I fumbled desperately behind my back for a door handle, but all I could feel was endless paneling. If only I could see something. Having to face him in pitch darkness was worse than any fate. I could hear him flailing and stumbling mere feet away from me.

"Ow!" He cried again and cursed in Dutch. There was more bumping about and clanking of pewter, followed by the sound and smell of a flint being struck. Yellow light bloomed up the walls of the cabin. The bed was visible again, beside a built-in chest of drawers. And in front of them stood a man with his face turned slightly away from me, just closing the glass door on a lantern above his head.

A man I had never seen before in my life.

To say he was ugly would not be true. But he was certainly plain, as plain as any dull farmer's boy or slow-witted apprentice I had ever seen. The face was square and heavy-set, the face of a thousand forgettable Dutchmen in their late twenties. All that stood out in it were a wide mouth and a clump of rusty curls about the forehead. He was the sort of man I could have passed by in the marketplace my whole life and never known he was there.

Was this Van Guelder? This Lowland nonentity was the cruelly handsome rake I had fled to the world's end to avoid. He turned from the lantern towards me with a flash of blue eyes and an attempt at his familiar sneer. But on those homely features, it just looked pathetic.

"Don't look at me like that," he said. "Don't give me that look of pity. Do you think that's what I want? All I want is oblivion and escape from this hell I live in. Give me the lodestone now!"

He lurched towards me and stretched out his hand. The next minute, he snatched his hand back with another cry of pain.

"Ow! What is this cursed devilry? Margaret, give me the lodestone. Ow!"

He had fallen back again, about a foot away from my body. I could see the anger and frustration rising in his face, but there was nothing he could do. Every time he tried to touch me – and every time I flinched, expecting he would – something pushed him back. It looked for all the world as if he was fighting with the air. The lodestone must be doing this. Now that it was about my neck, it was channeling my will. And what I willed more than anything was to repel Van Guelder.

"It's no use, Mr. Van Guelder," I said, as he collapsed back to the bed, coughing and gasping. "The lodestone is on my side now, and you of all people know how powerful it is. Perhaps God really does love the meek after all, as the Scripture says: *Blessed are the meek for they shall inherit the earth*."

"Huh!" he snarled. He wrapped his arms around himself and stared at the deck. "What do you know about inheritance? You: with your kindly father and merry sisters. Making friends every-where you go. Having every man you meet fall in love with you, from common seamen to nobles of the Orient. Yours was a charmed life from the start. I'll tell you what happens to the meek in the real world."

He flashed cold blue eyes at me, daring me to interrupt. But I would not have done so in any case. This new Van Guelder held me in morbid fascination. It was like seeing in a true mirror after years of looking into a warped scrap of metal.

"My father was a member of the Gentlemen Seventeen, a

director of the *Vereenigde Oost-Indische Compagnie*. All he cared
for was foreign trade and fat purses of guilders. In his mind, he
had sent me to Batavia and mapped out my career in the spice
trade before I was even born. And when his son turned out to be
a shy, studious boy with no head for commerce whatsoever, he
decided that son was a disgrace to the name of Van Guelder. He
beat me with the birch rod to teach me manliness and locked me
in his cabinet to teach me to value the commerce of Holland. By
the end of it I loathed my very life. And it was all for what? For
being the very creature you would have me believe God created.
I vowed to be that creature no more, to escape him at all costs."

His eyes glinted with evil memories. I listened in silence.

"What a day it was when I stole my father's precious stone,
his trophy of the far-reaching power of Dutch trade! How I bent
my will to studying it, to experimenting and learning its powers!
The first form I took was that of our gardener. I cannot tell you
the release I felt on escaping myself for the first time. I walked
into my father's study and insulted him to his face. The man lost
his position, but what did I care? I had a power now that my
father never possessed. I used it all the more, growing stronger
every day. I planned one day to use it to take my vengeance on
him, but nature robbed me of that chance. He was carried off by
a consumption, curse him! Even in death he mocked me,
taunting me with what I was unable to do."

"It is a wicked thing to take revenge," I said. "It's a good thing
you were stopped."

"It was my right!" he shouted. "You have no idea of the hell
he created *here*." He beat on his breast. "No idea of my
suffering."

"I lost my hands, Mr. Van Guelder," I said. "I would have lost
my life, were it not for a very skilled surgeon. I have been forced
to flee across oceans, leaving behind those loving friends and
family you spoke of. I have faced storms, pirate attacks and
marooning. I have fallen from the sky. And just when I had found

a home and happiness, you stole it from me. Don't tell me I know nothing of suffering."

"There was no need for you to suffer at all." His voice became taut. "All I asked was that you be obedient to me. Was that too much to ask?"

He looked up. The blue eyes were no longer cold; they were awash with pain. There was a human being in there after all. He twisted one of the rusty curls around his finger: tighter, tighter.

"Do you remember that first dinner at your father's house, Margaret, my love? The way you curtseyed to me; the demure look in your eyes. You were everything a maid should be. Do you remember how we spoke of poetry, of *Paradise Lost*?"

"You said it was an unexpected choice for a young girl."

"*Which way I fly is Hell; myself am Hell,*" he quoted. He stood up and began to pace, turning sharply and clenching his fists. "Don't you understand, Margaret? I need you. It is not enough: the taking of other forms, the repelling of these loathsome features. I need your soul, your goodness, your sweet nature. We must become one: one flesh, one heart, one soul. You must become my wife. Oh Margaret: take pity on me, for the sake of all that is good!"

Tears began to well in his eyes. His face tightened, his nostrils flaring as he breathed heavily. The dark shadows beneath his eyes stood out starkly.

I took a step backwards. He was more disturbing in this desperate state that he had been in his cold cruelty. He was like an opium addict, the addict I had almost become myself.

"I think I do pity you, Mr. Van Guelder," I said. "But I cannot be your wife."

"You must!" He stepped towards me, his hand stretching out. I shrunk against the oak paneling, hoping the lodestone would bite again if he tried to touch me. "Curse you, Margaret: you must wed me! Give me the lodestone now!"

My arm touched the cold brass of a doorknob.

"How could I wed a man who curses me? It is not possible."

He gave a cry of rage and sank to the floor. When he looked up again, he was weeping.

"Forgive me, my love. See what I have become because of you. Forgive me and know that it is I who am cursed, and will be every day I live without you."

I took a deep breath and let it out. How could I answer an addict?

"Very well, then. As a Christian woman and true daughter of my father, I forgive you, Holman. The Lord alone knows you're in need of mercy. But now I must leave. Captain Bakker's slave boy is coming to escort me back to my cabin. This has been a truly horrendous day and I need to rest."

"I..." he began, but I never heard what he was about to say. The ship's bell began to clang an alarm, and we heard men running from the officers' quarters. Van Guelder pushed past the invisible shield around me with indrawn breaths, and flung open the door. A relay of marines was taking muskets from the arsenal, the master-at-arms bellowing orders. Half-drunk wine glasses lay abandoned on the captains' table as officers rushed to the poop deck, hands on swords. Above our heads, the bo'sun's whistle sounded and drums beat an advance. And behind all that was the dull thud of gunfire.

"What is it?" Van Guelder yelled. "What's happening?"

He reached out and grabbed the collar of the captain's boy, who had just come running along the corridor, and pulled the boys' face into his own. The lad's feet dangled above ground; his eyes whitened with shock.

"What's happening?" Van Guelder said again.

The boy swallowed hard.

"Pirates," he said. "We're under attack."

19

Old Friends

Van Guelder ran back into the cabin and scrabbled amongst the cargo. He came out holding Taro's sword, the one with the dragon hilt. Even in the dim lamplight, I could see the deep groove and golden decoration that ran the length of the blade. It glittered. Van Guelder turned towards me. His eyes were glittering too, with cold determination that transformed his plain face into that of a warrior. I hardly knew whether to be frightened or impressed.

"Get into the cabin behind me," he said. "If they come, I will hold them off."

"Don't be crazy," I said. My pulse was so violent, I could hear it. I had seen pirates before and I doubted the finest sword in the world could hold them off.

Van Guelder screwed his features into an animal snarl.

"They will not touch you while I have breath."

He took a fighting posture with the sword outstretched in his right hand. He had to be insane. There was barely room to wield a butter knife.

"Do as he says, lady." The slave boy's face had gone clammy and he was shivering. He was just a child, and probably more used to polishing pewter than facing an armed attack. "I'll go with you."

"I'll go if..."

At that moment, there was a loud explosion from on deck. The pirates must have thrown a grenade. Van Guelder leaped back as pieces of iron shard peppered the oak paneling.

"Get in the cabin now!" he roared.

The boy didn't waste any time. His bare feet skidded on the boards as he hurtled through the door. I backed off more slowly, fascinated by the sight of the man I had hated and feared for so long standing now in the ill-fitting clothes of another, with a sword of princes in his hand, ready to face the entire pirate fleet if need be. Ready to face it for my sake. Was I right that he was crazed? Or, in his own twisted way, did he actually care for me?

The door to the poop deck flew wide open. A half-naked pirate rushed in, tattooed all over his body and howling a war cry that barely sounded human. He was brandishing a two-handed sword at the level of his eyes. I screamed.

Van Guelder was on him in a moment. Taro's sword sang as it sliced the air. It glanced off the other man's weapon and slashed a clean line across the panel by his ear. The man parried, whooping something in a language I didn't know.

"Amsterdam! Amsterdam! *Heldhaftig; Vastberaden!*" Van Guelder cried in return.

He was fighting like a madman. Of the two, it was hard to tell which was the more ferocious. But I had been right about the lack of space. The tiny passage outside the cabins was no place for swordplay. The swords struck the woodwork more often than they struck cold steel or flesh. Chips flew everywhere; angry moments were spent struggling to release a blade while the opponent tried to take the advantage. Taro's sword was undoubtedly the better of the two, but it was also the longer and of a different design from anything Van Guelder could have been used to. I could see already that he was bleeding. And I knew as well that he was more exhausted than I was: sick, even. I couldn't bear to watch and yet I couldn't tear myself away either. He was doing this for me. Putting himself in the way to save me. The very man I wanted as far from me as the oceans of the world could make us.

He stumbled. I don't know if it was exhaustion or if he slipped in some spilled blood. He collapsed to his knees. Taro's sword fell from his hand and clanged on the deck. My heart leaped right to the back of my throat. The pirate gave an evil grin, blood running down his brow. It was all over; he would come for me next. I screwed up my eyes so I wouldn't see the final moment, but I still heard the gasp and rattle of breath. I peeped between my eyelashes. He wasn't moving. Holman Van Guelder had gone.

He was gone. I was free. But it was nothing to celebrate. I felt sick and shaky. His life had gone, just like that. Oblivion. Or damnation. I had never wanted to witness that.

The pirate gave a cry of triumph and licked his lips, savoring his own blood. Behind me, the slave boy whimpered. The wicked eyes turned on us both in an instant. I shrank back, knowing there was nowhere to hide.

The outside door banged open again and another man's voice stuttered out some awkward words in the pirate's language, ending with a peculiarly English oath.

"Drake's beard; why can't you understand me? Take prisoners for ransom, you fool! Look at him now. Not worth a groat. Get on deck before Captain Hu has you flayed. *Qù! Qù!*"

I stared. The man who had burst in was English, without a doubt, although he was dressed just like a man of the East Indies, in mottled green and white. He was young and not all that pretty, with a fair pigtail at his neck. He bent down to look at Taro's sword, fallen by Van Guelder's side. I heard him give a low whistle.

"Now, that is worth a ransom. A king's one, I should say."

"Don't touch it!" I said. But at that moment the young pirate's eyes met mine. Something flipped in my stomach.

"Kit?" It wasn't possible.

"Margaret?" But that was his voice. Those were his eyes. "Margaret! God be praised! Oh, bless your heart, sweetheart. You're alive!"

He sprang from the corpse's side and ran to meet me, opening his arms for an embrace. But, as soon as he got within a foot of me, he leaped back.

"Ow! What in the seven seas was that?"

"Oh." I looked down at my chest, swallowing back the tears that had sprung to my eyes. Diamond dust glittered on a rock, hanging from a brass chain. "I think it must have been the lodestone."

It made sense. I had no idea how to use the thing. Van Guelder had experimented with it for years; all I did was to hang it round my neck. My strong desire to repel him had kept him at bay while he lived, but now that he was gone, it seemed the lodestone couldn't tell the difference between one man and another. It was just repelling, regardless.

I tried to explain to Kit, but it didn't come out well. I was still hiccupping with tears and shock. All I managed were some vague words about "stole it" and "channeling the will" and "because you're a man, don't you see?" One thing, however, Kit did understand.

"Lodestone?" he said. "You mean that blackguard Van Guelder is...?"

"Dead," I said in a small voice. I looked towards the corpse and then looked away, feeling I was about to be sick.

"That's Van Guelder? Seriously, Margaret?" He walked back and stood over the body again, examining the dead face from every angle, as if he couldn't get enough of it. If he was looking for a resemblance to the man he had once known, he would never find it. Eventually, he straightened up and curled his lip. "Huh! It looks like Apu had the right idea after all. Fiend!" He spat on the body.

"Kit, don't," I said. "You didn't know him. He was...he was a disturbed man."

"I'll say," said Kit warmly. But, after another black look at the corpse, he stepped away. "I suppose I'd better take the sword. Captain Hu will want to take that straight to Flood Dragon. It must be worth a fortune."

Flood Dragon? That was the name the man with the necklace of heads had given. The pirate lord. And Kit wanted to give him

Taro's sword? Was nothing right in this world any more? I staggered. I couldn't contemplate this. I had been through more in the last day and night than some people went through in a lifetime, and I couldn't take any more. My legs would no longer hold me up; my whole upper body was going hot and cold. I sank down with my head against the paneling, no longer able to stop the tears.

"Oh, I'm a heartless fool." Kit came to kneel beside me, as close as he could manage. "Come, can you stand? We must speak to Captain Hu and get you aboard the *Shengfeng Hao*. Ow! Can't you do anything to stop that?"

I couldn't. Even though I was desperate to feel Kit's friendly arms around me, the lodestone seemed to have the complete opposite idea. All he got for his efforts to help me up were more shocks and pains: to the arms, to the hands, to everything he tried. More pirates began to pour in from the poop deck. They ran in and out of the cabins, looking for plunder and prisoners and shouting in harsh dialects. I thought I recognized one of the men as Loc, but I wasn't sure.

"There's a boy in the cabin," I tried to say, but my voice didn't come out.

Kit just leaned past me and collared one of the pirates. I heard him say the words "Captain Hu" and "kinswoman".

Before I knew it, there was a crowd of pirates all around me. Several of them made attempts to lift me from the deck, but all their efforts ended in some variety of "Ow!" or worse, in whatever language they knew best. I wished they would leave me. All I wanted was to be alone with Kit.

But there was no chance of that. The crowd parted to let through a better-dressed man with a pointed beard and glossy black hair tied up on the top of his head. He squatted down by Kit, and they both began talking in a pidgin of different languages mixed together. Behind him came a girl dressed in a tunic and breeches of the Chinese style and carrying two short swords in her belt. I thought she bore a resemblance to the man with the beard, although she was much more delicate and graceful. Without a word, she took hold of me under the armpits and hauled me to my feet. The pirates let out several oaths and exclamations, and one or two made signs at me with their fingers. A couple pointed to the lodestone with a glint of what could only be described as greed in their eyes. The others cuffed them and shook their heads, making even more wary hand gestures.

But I couldn't concentrate any more. Everything was starting to blur around me. I swayed in the girl's arms. There was an icy throbbing at the back of my neck. Kit gestured to the bearded man.

"Tell her to remove the necklace, sir." He threw in a few more words I didn't know.

The man looked at the girl and muttered something in a low voice. I felt her fingers on my neck, catching in my hair. I saw the brass chain shining in her hand. Then Kit's arms went round me. I tasted the faint tobacco smell, with a hint of exotic flavors I hadn't remembered from before. It was so good to sense him again. The tears I had been holding back burst out of me. I buried my face in his Chinese tunic and sobbed. He lifted me up like a baby, hugging me into his chest. I could feel him shaking and sighing too. Neither of us spoke. He just walked out onto the poop deck with me in his arms and down the stairs to the amidships.

Around us, it was chaos. There was the flash of swords and spears in the lamplight; musket cracks; the Dutch captain in irons; a fleet of junks and sampans in the water. I held tight to Kit and ignored it. Someone helped him lower me to a boat. I felt the bobbing of the waves. Kit wrapped both arms round me and rested his chin on my head. The girl with the swords sat on the other side of me.

"It's all right, sweetheart," Kit whispered. "You're with us now. You're safe."

"Member family now," the girl agreed, in barely recognizable English.

"But I need to go back," I began.

"Hush." Kit rocked me like a baby. "You need to sleep. We can talk later."

The boat rowed out to one of the junks. Kit carried me up to its quarter deck and into another cabin. It had grille windows of dark wood cut into geometric patterns and smelled strongly of sweet ginger. I was vaguely aware of being plied with a warm drink; of small hands combing my hair and loosening my clothes; of two female voices talking rapidly in a singing dialect; of the constant background of cannon fire and the clash of arms.

But it quickly began to fade away. I was sleepy, so sleepy. All I felt was the rise and fall of waves and a soft bed beneath me. And soon even that had dissolved into darkness.

I slept for three days. I only woke to answer nature's call, to eat (mostly fish and a kind of porridge) and then to fall asleep again. In the brief moments I was awake, I saw that the cabin housed other sleepers beside me, including the girl who had removed the lodestone and an older woman I took to be her mother. It was decorated with round lanterns that had tassels hanging from them, and red scrolls of calligraphy similar to that of the Sunrise Empire. A heavy sort of breeze blew in through the window. The air was warm and muggy to say we were at sea. It made me feel sleepier than ever. Not until the fourth day did I remember I was still sailing away from Tokushiro. I got up in a panic, keen to learn where I was and what was going on.

"Where is Kit?" I said to the older of the two women.

In reply, she handed me another bowl of porridge and began a tirade of unintelligible speech. It took several spoonfuls and a number of respectful bows to get her to open the door to the deck and let me find out for myself.

Thankfully, Kit was only too happy to answer my questions. And he was keen to introduce me to several of my old *Hopewell* shipmates, who were all serving aboard the junk. Loc was there, and Mekuria too. Conlan, I heard, had died of a tropical disease. But the slave boy from the *Rotterdam* – whose name was apparently Theo – was now following Mekuria around like a shadow. Not an unwelcome one, it seemed either, judging from the big man's sorrowful smile. The men were all thrilled to see me, and several paid me compliments on my health, offering to personally see to anyone who might have harmed me since we parted.

"But how did you end up here?" I said. "That attack on the *Reward*: I thought those men were going to eat you alive."

Kit laughed. "No one could abide my foul flavor. No, I thought it was my last hour too, but Flood Dragon is much more reasonable than that. If you're worth something, he puts you up for ransom; if you're not, he offers you the chance to serve in his fleet. Piracy here is linked to clan loyalty, anyhow. All Flood Dragon's captains are loyal to the Ming dynasty and refuse to wear the Manchurian pigtail. It's all to do with who's on the throne of China. And unfair trading laws."

I found it hard to believe that the motley collection of killers who had attacked Dr Lemuel's sloop wearing necklaces of heads could care less who was on the throne of China. But Kit assured me it wasn't like that on Captain Hu's ship.

"It's more like a family, really. You've met Mistress Hu and Xing-Xing. They're the captain's wife and daughter. We fight to protect their honor as much as anything. And yours, of course. Speaking of which, the captain wants you to wear the lodestone again. Not that the men will try anything, but you can't be too careful."

"So I'm not a prisoner?" I said.

Kit shrugged. I eyeballed him severely.

"Ransom or serve in the fleet, you said. I can't see what good

I'll be to the captain and his noble cause." I flapped the empty ends of my sleeves.

"I told the captain you're my kin. He's happy to keep you with his own family for now, but he daren't disobey Flood Dragon." He screwed up his face. "The answer is: you're as safe here as you can be. Just wear the lodestone; there's a sweetheart."

"Very well," I said. "But I don't know how the lodestone works. The repelling effect may not last." He shrugged again. I decided to change the subject. "So you're not going home?"

"To England? Eventually, I hope. But for the time being the lads and I are content to serve here. Working a passage won't be easy if the Company finds out we've turned pirate."

He had to leave me to attend to the ship's business then. But it wasn't the end of the discussion by a long way. I soon discovered that Kit had questions for me too. And so did his captain. I shouldn't have been surprised. Naturally, they wanted to know where I'd been, who I'd been with, and how I ended up on the *Rotterdam*. Kit was keen to learn what had happened to Dr Lemuel and where my silver hands had gone. The captain wanted to know about the lodestone and the beautiful sword. He also asked several times whether I truly was Kit's kinswoman, as he had claimed. It made me wonder if my position aboard was really as safe as Kit would have me believe.

I didn't know what to tell them. I was sure now that the flying island had been a real place. But a place you could only get to if you were looking for something else. From what I knew of Dr Lemuel's previous voyages, it could be some time before he returned to commonly known lands. And the chances of ever finding the island again were remote in the extreme.

As for Tokushiro, my heart ached every time I thought about it. Was Taro looking for me now? Did he understand what Van Guelder had done to him, or did he just think I had walked out and vanished back to the realm of spirits? Every part of me craved his touch, his gentle voice. I longed to be back in the house by the lake, looking out over the willows and lily leaves, painting Taro's name with my brush. I had to get back. But how? There were no travelers in the Sunrise Empire. Van Guelder had smuggled me out. Who was going to want to smuggle me back in?

I told the captain what I could. That I had found myself in a strange country. That a great lord – the owner of the sword – had taken care of me. That Van Guelder had caught up with me there and tricked me away to force our marriage. I told more to Kit in private: about the way Van Guelder had stolen men's forms across Japan, and how his true self had been revealed when the lodestone was finally taken from him.

"Whatever he did in his life," I said to Kit, "I can't wish him torment in the hereafter. I just can't. He was pathetic, Kit. Without the stone, he was an empty shell. And he saved my life."

"And what about this lord?" Kit said. "Shimmy-what-you-may-call-him? Did he harm you? Did he – you know – press his advantage? Because if he did, I'd like to ram that fancy sword down his throat. After all you've been through, to be stuck in a foreign land where they've never even seen a mutton pie or a Bible…"

Without warning, I began to cry.

"Oh, Margaret! What is it, sweetheart?" Kit put a hand on my shoulder. "Something did happen, didn't it?"

"Yes; but not what you think," I said between sobs.

"What then?"

"I loved him," I blurted out. "I loved him and he loved me. We were going to get married. He gave me a house in a beautiful garden and new silver hands and inks to paint with and…and… He was the loveliest person I have ever known and if I don't get back there I think I'm going to die."

I put my head on my knees and sobbed like an infant. I didn't care. I wanted Taro and every wave we crossed was taking me further from him.

"You can't mean that," said Kit, incredulous.

"I do. I love Taro with all my heart and soul; and if you and Captain Hu can't help me find him again, I'll just have to swim for it."

I looked down at my severed arms and tight kimono. The possibility of swimming wasn't very likely, but right now I didn't care for logic.

"Don't you dare." Kit hugged me tight. "No one goes overboard on my watch." He gave several deep sighs and scratched his chin. "I don't pretend to understand this, Margaret, but if a man of that standard has proposed marriage, then it ought to be honored. I imagine Master Rosewood would say the same. But do you truly love him, Margaret? Will he make you happy?"

"Happier than you'll ever know." I sniffed, scrubbing my eyes with my sleeve.

Kit sat silent for a long time, his head in his hands. I thought he had gone into a daydream or something. Eventually, he shook his head and came to.

"I didn't expect anything like this, Margaret. And you don't know what you're asking for, in wanting to go back to that place. I'll speak to the captain, of course. But you need to know, the decisions aren't in his hands. My lord Flood Dragon decides all. But you'll understand more of that soon enough. It's his island we're bound for."

20

The Dragon's Lair

Flood Dragon's island was a little-known place; somewhere – Kit thought – off the coast of Taiwan. Apparently, he ran a legitimate business there making salt, but its main function was as the headquarters of the pirate fleet. All crew had to report there after a raid and declare their plunder, which would then be shared among the crews according to rank. Of course, the main prize on this occasion was the *Rotterdam* and those of its crew members who could be held to ransom at the nearest Dutch outpost, but the *Shengfeng Hao* was carrying its own share of treasure, Taro's sword being the finest example.

I was terrified by the time we got there. Kit had spoken to Captain Hu, but all he said to me was:

"I wouldn't set your hopes too high, Margaret. Flood Dragon is a powerful man and not used to being questioned. And the captain was planning to over-winter on the island. The storm season is coming on and no one wants to be caught out at sea."

Mistress Hu and Xing-Xing had spent all the time I was in their care giving me long lectures in what I gathered was a dialect of Chinese. I'm sure it would have done me a great deal of good, could I have understood what any of it meant. The captain's two young sons, who shared the cabin, had distracted me by clambering on my knee and showing me rattle-drums and wooden swords. But nothing ever took away my constant yearning for Taro and the fear that, even now, he was reluctantly considering marriage to his uncles' choice of bride. I had been given to understand that I was to be presented to the great pirate lord as soon as we made land. But I didn't really know what that signified, still less what I could say to convince him to let me travel to a land where no outsider was welcome.

The weather was muggier than ever the day we put in at the

island. From a distance, I had seen a rocky cove with dozens of
junks and sampans moored in and around a landing platform.
Above that, a path wound up the cliff face towards a high fence
of wooden stakes. Most of the crew were to stay with the
Shengfeng Hao, in order to make her safe and unload the cargo,
but Captain Hu and his family, along with Kit and myself, were
to go up to Flood Dragon's mansion, to present the sword and
our report on the raid. I was still unsure if I was going there as a
noble guest with a petition or as a prisoner.

The fence was heavily guarded. The guards were nothing like
as disciplined as Taro's (one man spun his knife around his hand
like a traveling showman as we arrived) but they made up for it
in ugliness and a generally threatening aspect. Luckily, they all
seemed to respect Captain Hu. They let us through the postern
door with deep bows and dour faces. Once inside, it all looked
like a grimmer, smaller version of Tokushiro, without the gardens
and the gold roofs. Vertical flags flew; wooden buildings of
various types stood facing the stiff wind. It was obvious that the
large house at the center with the curling roof was Flood
Dragon's mansion. The others, said Kit, belonged to the captains,
with some communal houses for the guards. The crews mostly
lived on the flatter side of the island, where they could work in
the salt business.

My legs shook, but my mind was on one thing. Taro. I had to
find a way to persuade Flood Dragon to return me to him. Could
I do that? Would I be permitted to speak at all? At any rate, I was
going to use every courtesy I had learned in the Sunrise Empire
to make a good impression and come across as the lady I had
become there. Surely that had to count for something?

"Are you wearing the lodestone?" Kit whispered across the
humid wind.

"Yes. Xing-Xing fastened it for me this morning. So don't get
too close."

Xing-Xing grinned at the mention of her name and made

bowing gestures with her hands, nodding towards the mansion.

"Lord Flood Dragon special friend. Always pleased to see."

Well, at least that was something, I reasoned. It would be useful if his friendship extended towards cabin-mates as well, but I wasn't going to count on it.

The mansion was a low building, with gray tiles and wooden lattice windows, just like those on the junk. It stood slightly raised up a flight of stairs, surrounded by the only bit of garden on the island. As we passed, I spotted miniature trees, raked gravel and carefully-placed stones, just like in Tokushiro. Guards stood under a porch, before a heavy door embossed with decoration. Behind them, servants hurried to announce our arrival.

We did not have to wait long. The great door opened and a robed servant bowed us in. Still more servants escorted us through several more doors and into a hall with a tiled floor and a dais at one end. Sitting on the dais, on a low seat beneath painted scrolls, was a middle-aged man, heavy-set with a drooping moustache and deep lines round his eyes and mouth.

I did not see him for long. The instant we were in the room, we all knelt with our heads to the ground and arms outstretched, even the little boys. Captain Hu held Taro's sword at eye level and presented it to Flood Dragon.

A rumbling voice spoke to Captain Hu in Chinese. He answered with what I assumed was one of the elaborate courtesies I had become familiar with in these waters. But I didn't know. The only Chinese I had picked up aboard the *Shengfeng Hao* were the translations for "hard about, there" and "no hands; so sorry." The men continued speaking while my forehead pressed against the cold tiles, making blood rush to my face.

"So: the crest of the Shimatani. And a hostage who has walked in the Sunrise Empire," said the rumbling voice.

For a moment, I didn't know why I could suddenly understand him. I thought that all the blood in my forehead had addled my thinking. Then I realized that it was because he was speaking Japanese. His accent was strange, but the words were definitely ones I knew.

"The able first mate owns her as kin, yet Captain Hu says she claims a home in the Shogun's land. Which is the truth, I wonder?"

Could anyone else in the room understand what he was saying? They had all gone very quiet. I decided to risk a reply. I lifted up my head a little.

"Your very humble servant, O-gin, Your Excellency. Please condescend to accept my very best wishes for your health."

To my bewilderment, he started to laugh. It sounded like the grunting of seals. I couldn't decide if this was a good thing or a bad.

"She speaks like child of the sunrise, yet she is pale as one who never saw the sun! I never thought to hear my mother's tongue from such a one. It has been many years since I heard it in a woman's voice. Come: let us hear some more."

My armpits prickled. This could be my chance.

"May I congratulate the noble Lord Flood Dragon on his prosperity and his victory in the water?" My mind raced, trying to get this right. "He has delivered me from the clutches of rival men of the waves, who stole me from Shimatani lands."

"Rival?" Flood Dragon's nostrils flared. He looked very much like the fearsome beast he was named for.

"Forgive my presumption, but yes." My heart was hammering. "Smugglers in league with the Dutch, working the coast near Tokushiro. I was..." Dare I say this? "I was promised in marriage to Lord Shimatani himself, my lord, and they took me away."

I daren't look up again, but I could hear him breathing hard through his nose. My decision to mention rival pirates had been a risk, but evidently one that had hit the right target. Only now I had to follow it up with something equally provoking.

"And how did you come to form alliance with such a one as Lord Shimatani?" Flood Dragon grunted. "You are no daughter of the great houses of Japan."

I took a deep breath and decided to dice with the truth.

"I fell from lands beyond the map, Your Excellency."

I dared another glance. Flood Dragon scowled, making the lines in his face even deeper, and stroked his moustache. "Lands beyond the map, you say? Many tales have I heard of them, and many times I thought I had glimpsed them when the sun was in the west. But never have I met any of their inhabitants. And you are promised to one of the Shimatani? A great family. My mother told me of them in her exile. Your native land must be illustrious indeed."

"It is an island in the sky, Your Excellency." Now I really was taking a risk. I couldn't believe I was actually claiming to be the sky-spirit Taro had named me. I knew nothing of the island in the sky, except that it had taken Dr Lemuel away on another of his fated voyages, and that I was unlikely to see it again. But I had to get back to Taro. Even if he never forgave me, I had to see him one more time.

I was going to have to push my claim a little further. I held out my arms, letting the sleeves fall back from my withered wrists.

"My people are different to those of the earth: born without hands, as you can see. And our scholars have made discoveries as yet unknown to the natural philosophies of other lands. I wear about my neck a chastity device. No man but my appointed husband may touch me."

I edged nearer to Kit as I spoke. He was still bowing with his head to the tiles, as were the others. When I got within about a foot of him, he jerked from the floor with a suppressed yelp. I felt terribly guilty, but I had to prove my story somehow. I had to get the pirate lord on my side.

Flood Dragon leaned forward with another seal-like chuckle.

"So, the legends are true. There is an island in the sky. And you are not this sailor's kinswoman?"

"No." It wasn't exactly a lie; Kit and I weren't blood relatives. Still, I was very glad he didn't know Japanese. "But I beg of you not to punish him, my lord," I added hurriedly. "The effects of sky dwellers on mortals can be overwhelming."

I could hardly credit the nonsense I was coming out with. I tried to push commandments such as *Thou shalt not bear false witness* out of my mind, along with related thoughts of fires and abysses.

Flood Dragon stroked his moustache again. He turned to Captain Hu, and the two spoke in Chinese for several minutes. Then he turned back to me.

"This talk of rivals angers me greatly. I am lord of these waters. They must be crushed, and swiftly. For bringing me this intelligence, I give you thanks."

"A thousand thank yous, my lord. May you live for ever." In the circumstances, I didn't think it was too exaggerated a response.

"As to what to do with a bride from the sky..." He looked again at Taro's sword, running his finger up and down the scabbard, over the golden morning glories. "This is a fine heirloom. The Shimatani were always known for their appreciation of the artist's skill. I imagine Tokushiro houses quite a collection."

"There was a saddle and horse equipment on board the *Rotterdam*," I said, not sure where this was going. "My lord will be very impressed with its quality."

"And for the return of a bride, they will pay more."

For a moment, I didn't know what he meant. Then I realized the situation I had put myself in. Flood Dragon wanted to ransom me to Taro. This wasn't exactly what I'd been hoping for. A quiet return via the *Shengfeng Hao* had been more what I'd had in mind. This way risked everything. I could hardly deny I was the official bride after what I had just said; nor was I about to impeach Taro's honor by admitting the Shimatani were financially embarrassed. It was rather like it had been when I was playing the board game with Taro: all my stones suddenly surrounded with no way out. There was nothing to do but play along and trust in Taro's generosity.

"Your Excellency knows a way into the Empire?" I dared to ask.

"Flood Dragon knows a way into all realms." He lifted his chin, resting an elbow on his knee. "I will send a flotilla by way of the Ryukyu isles. The spy clan there is always amenable for a price."

I had no idea where the Ryukyu isles were, and did not seem wise to ask. I had the feeling my future was drifting from my grasp again, but I was determined to keep control, come what may. I had proved myself stronger than Van Guelder. I had to keep hope alive and believe in myself. I had the lodestone now. It had protected me so far. It could do so in the future.

"Your will, my lord," I said, and bowed deeply.

The rest of the audience took place in Chinese. Flood Dragon spoke with Captain Hu again, with Mistress Hu and with Xing-Xing. (He did seem to have a special smile for her, I noted). Poor Kit was barely acknowledged. I felt I'd let him down terribly, but I vowed to try to make it up to him in some way, if I had the liberty. Eventually, with more bows and courtesies, we shuffled backwards from the hall and came back out onto the windswept hilltop. Servants from Captain Hu's household hurried to meet him and his family. A wrinkled old woman took me by the arm and coaxed me towards a house with the flag of a tiger flying alongside it.

"What was all that about?" said Kit. "I only got ten words of the whole thing. Is he letting you go?"

"In a manner of speaking." I didn't want to divulge too much about the conversation between the pirate lord and myself. I would have to end up telling the truth. "Is Lord Flood Dragon really half-Japanese?" I said to change the subject.

"Is that the language you were speaking? I thought I'd been transported to a Quaker prayer meeting!"

Kit gave his familiar crooked smile, but he was red about the neck and looked uncomfortable. I must have put him in a pretty awkward position with his new lord. Poor Kit! I really would have to tell him more by-and-by. It wasn't fair. Not after all he'd done for me.

But I didn't get the chance at that moment. As we arrived at the lantern-hung door of Captain Hu's home, the wrinkled old woman began to pull me inside. I looked back at Kit and shrugged. In my position, it was best to go along with whatever happened.

"Hang about. Where are you off to now?" Kit said, looking from me to the Hu family and back again.

Xing-Xing smiled at him and gestured in my direction.

"Member family. For now."

I wouldn't have exactly said I was a member of the family. More like a noble prisoner under house arrest. But the outward effect was very much the same. I was forced to endure more hospitality from Mistress Hu and her maids than I could rightly cope with. And Xing-Xing's incomprehensible lectures went on from morning to night. After a few days, I was sick to the stomach of dumplings, and my ears buzzed with the constant talking. At least I had a real bed to sleep in, though. After all my time at sea, that seemed like a luxury.

In the meantime, I discovered more clearly what my fate was to be. The *Shengfeng Hao* was to be re-fitted and provisioned as soon as possible. Then, along with a handful of other boats, she was to sail to the Ryukyu isles, where Captain Hu was to negotiate with a clan head there. It appeared the family trade of this clan involved certain dark skills which were available for hire: spying and infiltration being just two. I was to accompany them as the hostage to be returned in exchange for treasure.

"The Captain's not happy about it," Kit said, when he called to visit. "He's certain the storm season is almost upon us. But Lord Flood Dragon won't wait now a rival group has been mentioned. He wants them stamped out instantly. The chance to bargain with the Shimmy-tanners is just the extra plum in the pudding, as far as he is concerned. What in the seven seas did you tell him, Margaret?"

"Oh, about what happened in the Sunrise Empire. Taro, Van Guelder, that sort of thing."

I faked a smile and looked down at my knees. I had told a fair amount to Kit over the past days. As Captain Hu's right hand, and one of the few who spoke my language, he was my one official visitor on the island. But I had to admit to smoothing over my falsehoods somewhat, especially the one about us not being related.

"You know he's treating you as a hostage. That isn't what I wanted, Margaret. I was trying to keep you safe. To do what your father would have wanted me to do."

My throat tightened at the mention of my father.

"I know, Kit. But Taro will keep me safe." I hoped that was true. I hoped with all my heart that he would forgive me and that I could be his Silver Lady again. "And the lodestone will protect me too. That's still biting like a good guard dog." I attempted a smile. "I am grateful for what you've done. You've been like a brother to me, Kit. Always. And better than a brother. I'll never forget that."

"I could have been more than a brother." He looked down at his sea boots. We were sitting side-by-side on Mistress Hu's polished bench. His feet were planted firmly on the floor. Mine didn't reach. "You do know that before Van Guelder came along, Master Rosewood was going to marry me to one of you girls, to keep the business in the family. It would have been you,

Margaret. First born; first choice."

I gulped. I had never thought of that, although it seemed so obvious now. But, no; it was ridiculous. I loved Kit with all my heart, but I could never have looked on him in the way I looked on Taro. And he could never have looked on me as anything other than a sister, either. The notion was absurd.

"I did think..." His voice had gone very quiet now. "I did think when I found you again after all this time, that I would be the one to take care of you now. When they put you in that canoe with Dr Lemuel, Margaret, I thought you were lost for certain. All those months, not knowing if you were living or dead: I couldn't abide it. And now it's all happening again and there's no reason to it. Hang it all, Margaret, what do you want with a foreigner you barely know? Couldn't you have stayed with the fleet this time? With me?"

His voice cracked. I signaled to the wrinkled servant and she unclasped the lodestone. I put my arm about Kit's neck and kissed his forehead.

"You'll make it home one of these fine days," I said. "And Susanna and Martha will be waiting for you. You can tell them all about their sister's adventures. They can fill your pipe and pour your ale and make house for you better than I ever could. My home is with Lord Taro now. It always will be. I have to try and return there, at whatever cost. When you fall in love, you'll understand."

"How do you know I don't understand now?" he said gruffly.

I ruffled his hair with my long sleeve.

"Sky-spirits know everything, Mr. Blackthorn. The ship is your wife and the ocean your mistress. But Martha will forgive you. Provided you bring her a monkey and a box of nutmeg."

He looked up and gave a wry smile.

"Monkey indeed!"

I smiled back and we nudged each other like children until we both laughed. But, when I looked again, his eyes were sad.

21

Riding the Storm

Autumn was coming on for certain by the time we embarked. I had given up keeping a tally long ago, but Kit said he had been keeping a log by the stars every night, and he was sure it was nearly October. Down by the landing dock, the weather was sultry. Captain Hu looked grim and the men were silent. Apparently, typhoons and worse were common at this time of year. Lord Flood Dragon's revenge on the smugglers could cost us all dear if we were not careful.

Xing-Xing accompanied me down to the *Shengfeng Hao* and helped me into the familiar cabin. Mistress Hu and the little boys were to stay on the island for safety, but Xing-Xing was coming with us all the way. We looked like a couple of sisters that day. Both of us were dressed in Chinese tunics, breeches and soft shoes, our hair tied up in knots on our heads and fastened with long pins. I had the lodestone about me and Xing-Xing had her two swords.

I had watched her practice swordplay every day we had been on the island. When she had trained alone as much as she could, she had taken to sparring with the off-duty guards. And she had certainly given them a fair fight. She was quite as good with the sword as any man, and just as much a part of the ship's crew. I suspected that if her father had tried to leave her behind on this voyage, she would have swum after us. She would have made a good companion for Frenchie, could the two have ever understood one another.

"Empress of Heavens watching us," she said, gesturing towards the flag fluttering from the stern mast. A figure that looked like a relative of Flood Dragon – and not necessarily a female one – held up a glittering disc while being fawned over by fish and sea monsters. "Pray good passage."

I did pray. Many times. But it didn't alter the fact that, the further we journeyed out to sea, the wetter the wind became and the more the sea began to swell. I began to feel the nag of sea-sickness for the first time in ages. For once the reek of ginger in the cabin was welcome. By the third day, the tassels of the cabin lanterns were doing a bizarre dance. Out on deck, big Mekuria strained at the tiller, his muscles standing out like rocks. Something was coming and I didn't like it. I had heard of typhoons: how they could suck great funnels in the sea and drag a ship down to Davy Jones. But Kit assured me that the wind was still on our side.

"It's but ten days to the Ryukyu islands. We'll make heavy weather of it, but we'll get there. I'm not so sure about getting back, but that is no concern of yours."

He was right. If all went to plan, I would be going home to Tokushiro. I would never look on the outside world again. Only what would the world inside the empire look like when I returned? Would Flood Dragon's bargain impoverish Taro? I had wanted to help him with his rents, not make his burdens heavier. I ought to suggest that my silver hands be the things that were given in exchange for my life. They were unnecessary, a worldly vanity. Tokushiro needed a good rice harvest much more than it needed an expensive bridal gift. But I had wanted them so much. They were Taro's precious love gift. The promise of our wedding day. He had sent them with poetry. To ask him to return them would surely be an insult beyond measure.

There was just one night when the sky was clear. I had staggered out to visit the *Shengfeng Hao*'s version of Saucy Sue, giving a demure nod to Loc and his compatriot who were on watch. On the stern mast, the Empress of the Heavens flapped in shadow. I took a moment to look up and enjoy the view. The whole of the heavens was watching us. I could see the River of Stars, with Orihime and Hikoboshi waiting steadfastly on either side. That was Taro and me now. We were the weaver and the cowherd, separated by a vast expanse of water, yearning to find one another. I thought about my midsummer's wish: *to cross the bridge and be with Taro forever*. It hadn't come true for the ancient lovers; their tale had ended in tragedy. Would ours? Had heaven truly heard my prayer that night?

"Taro," I whispered to the night. "Where are you? I'm trying to come to you. I am, truly. Please wait for me. Please."

For a moment, I thought I caught the scent of the *o-furo* and wet foliage on the breeze. And a rich voice seemed to whisper back:

"I have searched for you. I have searched everywhere. Tell me where I can find you."

In spite of the lunacy of it, I wanted to call out our co-ordinates to the waves. I longed to send kisses to the wind with promises of eternal love. But the next moment, a roller washed overboard. Loc's man ran to steady me, his strong hands gripping my shoulders in the absence of the lodestone. When the wave settled down, there was nothing. No words. No voices. The whispers had gone, and all I could hear was the hiss of water and the creak of timber.

On the tenth day, we reached the island. By now, the wind and waves had angry plans of their own. Xing-Xing and I had spent a sleepless night in the cabin. Everything around us had gone up and down, up and down. She had lain by my side as closely as possible, holding onto me to stop me falling from the bunk. Now we stood side-by-side on the deck. The *Shengfeng Hao* could come no nearer the island. The coast was all caves and rocks, with precious little landing space even for a small boat. Captain Hu prepared to send out boats tied to the *Shengfeng Hao* by ropes. Men sat in them, preparing to row inland. The waves boomed in the caverns, and the screams of the sea birds seemed unnaturally piercing.

I watched the first boat go out. The waves lashed above the rowers' heads, soaking them to the bone. Every time they went under, I kept thinking they weren't going to come back up again.

"Must I go now?" I said to Kit. The prospect of being smashed to matchwood suddenly didn't seem very alluring.

"You were the one who longed for Japan," Kit said bluntly. "Xing-Xing will hold onto you; it's not as bad as it seems."

No indeed: it was worse. I had never had a great desire to be close to marine life. Now it was much closer than the most dedicated enthusiast could have wished. The boat reared and pitched. Waves slapped our faces, stinging our eyes and cheeks with salt. Captain Hu sat immobile in the stern while Kit and a man named Susumu – a Japanese exile from Batavia and the captain's interpreter – battled with the oars. Xing-Xing clung so tight I could feel her fingernails. And every few minutes would come a muffled "ow!" from any man who was flung too near the lodestone. The shore was unimpressive as shores went, but the relief of gaining it under my feet was such that it may as well have been the shore of El Dorado or Utopia.

Ashore, a passage between the giant rocks led to a village of simple bamboo houses. There, Xing-Xing and I were taken aside by women with gentle voices who spoke a dialect I could almost understand. The fire and the food were welcome after our drenching, but I couldn't keep my mind off Captain Hu's mission. I had seen him go into the largest house. Its door had been guarded by men clad entirely in black. This village was home to the spy clan. Its shadowy elders held my future in their hands.

All I could do was to wait. And wait. Not just for hours, but for days, as the whole pirate crew made itself at home in the village. The shadow men moved swiftly, Kit told me, and their network stretched far, but it was still some distance over land and sea to Tokushiro.

"The smugglers won't survive, though," Kit said. "That's been taken care of already. I don't care to talk of the clan's methods, but there are one or two folk who won't waken in the morning after a certain night visit."

I shuddered, recalling the smuggler's filthy hand on my mouth. It was not the method of justice I would have chosen. Flood Dragon was lord in these waters, though, and could choose his own punishments. I was glad not to have offended him.

"And have they sent a man to Lord Shimatani?" I said.

Kit nodded. "So I understand." He blew out a cloud of smoke from his pipe, and stared out across the dense woodland that stood further inland from the village square where we sat. "I suppose there'll be no going back now. The wind's got you bound for harbor."

"I suppose," I said, not looking him in the eye.

Time passed. We waited. The pirates got ever more restless. Fierce squalls had now begun to blow. Trees bent. Flimsy roofs shuddered. Dogs and children got under the women's feet, called into the shelter of the houses for safety.

"Must leave island soon," Xing-Xing said. It was one of the few clear things she had said to me between her interminable Chinese lectures. I could tell from her tone that she was frustrated. Her sword practice had been sadly hindered by the women's hospitality, and none of the men would let her into their combat secrets.

"We will," I said, trying to believe it myself. "You to Flood Dragon's fleet and me to Lord Taro."

I understood the sea was getting up something savage. Some of the sailors had rowed back to the *Shengfeng Hao* to try and keep her safe. A couple of the non-*Reward* ones gave me dirty looks as they passed. Apparently, Captain Hu was only waiting on Taro's reply before disembarking for Flood Dragon's island.

At length, it came. A man whose eyes alone could be seen in the blackness of his covered face appeared in the village as if from nowhere and made for the central house. From the shared living quarters of the women's house, I watched him enter at the door. I sat motionless, hardly daring to breath. Dogs ran over my legs. Wet washing dripped around me. Xing-Xing and the women talked on and on, regardless of their different languages. The door opened. Kit came towards our house at a run. I swept children and chickens aside and ran into the communal cooking ground, ignoring the turbulent weather. Rain slapped my hair to my forehead. Kit panted.

"Gather everything," he said. "We're going back to the *Shengfeng Hao.*"

"What?" I wondered if I'd misheard him.

"You too, Margaret. We're going back to Flood Dragon now."

"Lord Shimatani?" My voice rose, anxious.

"Never heard of you. And married already, so I hear tell. Get some proper clothes on, Margaret, before you catch your death; and tell Xing-Xing we leave on the next tide."

He strode off into the tropical rain. I couldn't move. This was a dream; it had to be a dream. Women crowded around me, their soft voices full of concern and interest. Children chattered and pulled at my clothes. I felt Xing-Xing's arms about me, propelling me into the house. In a daze, I watched her gather our bundles, bow to our hostesses, coax me along the path to the shore. Seabirds screamed in the caves and around the boats. The pirates heaved and hauled, cursing in every language around the China Sea. Waves lashed. Salt burned. The many tails of the Empress of the Heavens whipped like some form of divine punishment.

I looked about me. I was back on the deck of the *Shengfeng Hao.* It was tilting at crazy angles. Waves crashed over the bulwarks.

"Into the cabin, Margaret," I heard Kit say.

"But he loved me," I said in my smallest voice. "He said I was everything to him."

"The cabin, Margaret," Kit said in his first-mate's tone.

At the same moment, a dozen voices in as many tongues cried out:

"The moorings!"

Several people rushed to the gunwale of the junk, but it was too late. The sea anchor had come loose. A breaker the size of a house side rolled towards us. Captain Hu seized Xing-Xing round the midriff. Xing-Xing grabbed at the back of my tunic. She tried to pull me closer, but something held me back.

"Get that blasted necklace off her now!" Kit roared.

Xing-Xing's nails scratched my neck. The deck tilted violently. I felt something break loose, a bond broken. Kit slid across the deck towards me and crushed me between him and the mast. His heart thudded against my back.

"Hold on!" he bellowed, his voice raw. "Get on the tiller, someone."

Several men ran for the stern. Captain Hu strode to the quarter deck, snarling out orders in Chinese, and still dragging Xing-Xing with one arm. I saw her struggle to release a sword from her belt. She raised it high and rammed it vertically into the boards, then clung onto it with her full strength.

Kit tightened his grip and spoke into my ear:

"Now, wrap your legs about the mast, sweetheart, and hold on tight. We're going to weather this."

I didn't want to weather it. Taro didn't love me after all. Or he loved Tokushiro more. After all that he had said to me in the lakeside house. He wouldn't pay for me to go home. He had turned his back on me and taken his uncles' choice of bride. Another girl would lie in his arms under the starlit night. She would bear his ebony-eyed babies. He had said he never even knew me.

"Margaret!" Kit commanded.

The wave hit with the force of a giant's fist. My breath was pounded from my lungs. I felt myself lift from the deck. Suddenly, the will to live screamed inside me. I tensed my thighs around the mast as hard as I could, clinging on with my feet, wrapping my arms as far as they would go. Behind me, Kit's body flattened into mine, squeezing me almost to suffocation. The *Shengfeng Hao* spun in the water. I closed my eyes and gritted my teeth.

"Mother!" came a scream in Dutch. That had to be little Theo, clinging on to the ship somewhere with the rest of the crew.

The waves sucked us down, spat us up again. We were riding the back of a sea serpent. The water was up to our necks; it was fathoms beneath us, swirling at the foot of briny mountains. A man washed overboard with an agonized cry. Mekuria, at the tiller, grunted like a rutting stag. Captain Hu's voice turned to gravel as he barked his orders.

We weren't going to make it. We were going to die at sea. The waves would close over us and that would be it. Suffocation. Insensibility. No one to even bury us. Why couldn't we wash up on the beaches of the Sunrise Empire? Couldn't I sleep my last sleep in the land that had made me happy, and rise on the Last Day over Taro's roofs and gardens?

"Taro." I whispered the words in my head. "Why? Why wouldn't you take me back? I love you. I need you so badly."

A conch shell blew: strident, urgent, before its sound was swallowed by the gale.

"Land ho! *Yīzhí zǒu!*" someone yelled.

Another wave lashed. The junk creaked terribly. I was sure she was about to break up. From somewhere in the distance, I thought I could hear the sound of an immense bell, deep as the voice of Neptune himself. We rode up a great wall of water and down the other side, everyone crying out in whatever language and to whatever deity first sprang to mind.

"There," Kit gasped in my ear. "Lights. There's a town or something."

Through the squall, I could just about make out a beach with a sea wall, lit from behind by many windows. Figures were running towards the shore, waving lanterns. The conch sounded again.

"Bring her about! Bring her about!" Kit yelled.

A wave cut off his voice. It thundered against our heads, stinging eyes and nose, choking my throat. I felt his grip loosen.

"Kit!" I moved my lips but no sound came out. My nose streamed; my lungs ached. Another wave struck me violently from the side and knocked my head against the mast.

22

The Island of the Lonely Monastery

The first thing I heard as I slid out of dream was the bell again. Deep and sonorous, its vibrations went right to the pit of my stomach. It was the harbor bell, tolling for those lost at sea. And I was the one that was lost. I was drowned and listening to the sound of my own funeral.

Something rustled and moaned beside me. I fluttered my eyelids. It was light and there was a faint smell of incense and open spaces. Above me was a beamed ceiling; white walls surrounded me. Xing-Xing lay beside me on a sleeping mat, her arms and legs sprawled in all directions, muttering in her sleep.

I wasn't dead. I remembered now. Lanterns on the beach. Arms pulling us ashore. Shaven-headed men – or were they women? Coarse blankets; hot tea; covered walkways; shining symbols. We had been on the ship and now we were somewhere else. Someone had rescued us.

I sat up. Slowly. Every part of me was aching, including parts I never knew could ache. My head especially throbbed. I tried to touch it with my forearm and felt soft cloth. Someone had bandaged it; I couldn't remember who. I looked about the room. There was nothing in it, save Xing-Xing and myself on two sleeping mats, and a bowl of burnt-out incense sticks. On the wall behind my head was what looked like a constellation chart, done in inks on a scroll.

There was a rap at the door. Xing-Xing groaned and turned over in her sleep, squashing into me. A young woman with a shaven head (yes I was right; it was a woman) and dressed in a light blue robe put her head around the door. Her eyes were almond shaped and dark as two pieces of polished jet. Her skin was so white it could have been made from alabaster. She bowed demurely.

"The abbess invites you to breakfast," she said, in surprisingly good English. "If you will be ready shortly, I will show you where you may wash and then take you to her. Here are clean robes."

The robes she offered us were white, which did little to dispel my notions of my own death. I kicked Xing-Xing awake and tried to explain the situation to her, and she quickly helped me into my robe, before putting on her own. The effect was rather more angelic than I felt suited Xing-Xing's temperament, but then I didn't know how I looked myself.

By now there were two shaven women at the door. The second spoke to Xing-Xing in Chinese, and then the two led us down a passageway with many doors leading from it. Outside, I could hear the wind howling and the roar of the sea. Where were the others, I thought: Kit and the captain and all the men? We seemed to have been transported into a world of women only, and a strange one at that. The floor was of azure tiles, cold on our bare feet. At intervals along the white walls were circles of midnight blue with silver symbols at their centre. I thought one looked like a rising phoenix, another perhaps a tiger.

Our solemn hostesses led us along a covered walkway across a courtyard, exposed at both sides to the lashing rain that was still falling. A latticed door stood open at the other end and we followed them through. In an alcove just inside was a metal basin. Xing-Xing helped me wash, before we were led into a chamber lit by silver lanterns, where a fire burned in a brazier and a solemn-eyed woman of about five-and-thirty sat cross-legged on an indigo mat. Between her and us was a table, set with a simple meal. The woman held out her hands to us as we entered.

"I bid you welcome, travelers, to the Lonely Monastery. May the stars light your path! I am Serene Night, abbess of the nunnery here, and these are two of my close disciples. Please sit and eat."

She spoke in English; then repeated her words in Chinese. Xing-Xing and I looked at one another, uncertain.

"Our friends?" I said.

"Housed in the main monastery." The abbess inclined her head slightly. She had the same dark-and-pale coloring as the two nuns. Her robe, I noted, was deep blue and edged with silver stars. "Men and women live strictly separate lives on this island; except for those lay brothers and sisters whose work in the infirmary and in the rescue of travelers lost at sea demands their combined efforts." She indicated the breakfast again. "Please eat. We have already partaken of our own meal. Our vows do not allow us to eat the food of guests."

I still didn't know whether to trust her, but I was ravenous. Besides, there was a feeling prickling in my stomach besides hunger. It felt like memory, or maybe even recognition. There was something about these nuns that was vaguely familiar.

Xing-Xing was quicker to make up her mind. She sat down and tucked into breakfast, firing off questions ten to the dozen between bites. The two disciples sat at either side of the room – legs crossed, hands folded – trying to answer. I bit my lip. Despite having encountered all sorts of people lately, I still didn't like to be watched eating with my feet. I put on what I thought of as my O-gin face, and picked up the chopsticks between my toes, defying the abbess to comment.

The breakfast was a welcome treat. There was rice in coconut milk, fresh fish, omelets and fruit. I made the necessary compliments about the food and hospitality, knowing there were dozens of questions I was itching to ask instead. Only then did I dare attempt conversation.

"My Lady Abbess is an excellent scholar of languages", I said.

The abbess placed her palms together.

"Indeed, it is the foremost mission of this monastery island to provide hospitality to those stranded at the edge of the map. Our novices spend much time learning the tongues commonly spoken by merchant sailors: Dutch, Spanish, Chinese, Portuguese, English, Arabic. We pride ourselves on being a reputed center for the study of foreign tongues."

I paused; the chopsticks part-way to my mouth. *Edge of the map.* She had said *edge of the map.* Those eyes; that skin; those robes: I knew I had seen them before. And I had been searching for Taro with all my heart and soul; yearning to get back to Tokushiro. Looking for something else.

"And what, pray, is your native tongue?" I fought to keep the thrill out of my voice.

"Laputan. This island is a colony of the Empire of Laputa, and it is the teaching of Lunodi of Laputa that we strive to follow."

I glanced over at Xing-Xing, who was struggling to follow the conversation. Did this mean what I thought it meant?

"Laputa? I confess I have never heard of it."

"The Queen of Cities, if I may be so bold." The abbess smiled. "There the four quarters of heaven and the twenty-eight constellations are revered above all else. She floats in the heavens itself, by the will of her emperor. A benevolent mother to her children and a terror to her enemies."

I dropped the chopsticks.

"She floats..." I was just repeating everything she said. "Xing-Xing: the stone! Show her the stone".

We both fumbled and fought to disentangle the necklace from under my robe. Xing-Xing got to it first and held it out to the abbess, scowling and shrugging her shoulders at me. In the cold light of the meeting chamber, the brass chain glowed dully as it swung, and beams danced here and there from the lodestone's glittering surface.

"Lodestone of Laputa." The Abbess narrowed her polished jet eyes. Her voice sharpened. "Might I ask how you came by this?"

I gulped, and decided now was the time for several respectful bows.

"My former...my late betrothed husband." I looked at my

feet. "He had it. He said Dutch merchants brought it. He manip-ulated its power and used it to do terrible things." I wouldn't say what. Van Guelder was dead now. His secrets could stay buried with him. "I took it from him to save myself. Whenever I have worn it, it has repelled men. But I will gladly give it back to its rightful owner."

The Abbess's lips twitched with a smile.

"Repelled men, you say? That I would dearly love to see. Although if there were need of such power in this holy place, I should soon hear of it!" Her face became serious again. "This is Laputan crown property. None but the Imperial line may bind their will to the Great Lodestone, of which this is undoubtedly a fragment. To do so takes a lifetime of preparation, for the will of the emperor is the will of Laputa herself. She goes where he wills; the two are one.

That sounded awfully familiar. I nodded slowly.

"The emperor will be grateful for its return," the abbess said. "In the right mood, very grateful. Do you and your companions intend to return the gift yourselves?"

"I beg your pardon?" I had a feeling I had missed part of the conversation.

The abbess leaned towards me.

"The Queen of Cities makes regular visits to her children. How else may she receive their tithes and the petitions of her subjects?" She fixed her black eyes upon me. "It is many moons since we were last prevailed upon. We expect the call of the heavens any time now".

It had happened. I had sailed off the edge of the map. Almost right to the place where I had last left the uncommon lands. Laputa was coming! The island of chimes and silver roofs was not a place of nightmare, but the real and reasonable land of Dr Lemuel's philosophies. Its stone was not an evil but a natural phenomenon in service of its princes. And – best of all – the good doctor may still be there. We could be reunited and enjoy its curiosities together. How much we would have to tell each other and learn from one another! What sights we would see; what sounds we would hear; what new marvels discover!

But I couldn't anticipate it that way. I did want to see Dr Lemuel again. I had missed him terribly; I also needed to beg his forgiveness for my behavior on the swing-lift. But it wasn't the voyage I had been hoping for. That only led one way: back to Tokushiro, the garden house and Taro's rice-wine kisses under the summer stars. Inside, my heart broke afresh every time I thought about his noble bride and the splendors of their life together. What was it that had made him turn against me so completely? Did he blame me for Van Guelder's assault on his person? Did he think I had scorned his gift in my sudden departure? Was loyalty to clan and land just too strong in the end, even against a love such as ours? I wept every night as I lay on my mat in the cell with Xing-Xing snoring beside me. I might have found out I carried a king's ransom all along, but I would have thrown it into the sea for one more night with Taro.

And that was not all. It turned out none of the others were planning to go to Laputa with me. After the first day in the nunnery, Xing-Xing had demanded with characteristic bluntness that she be allowed to speak with her father. The news she brought from that meeting was that the men had been spending their time discussing with the monks the best way to get the *Shengfeng Hao* repaired and back out to sea as soon as the storm season was over. Allegedly, there was a port of Glanguenstald, or some such name, that they could sail to on one of the other islands, where it was possible at certain seasons to find a route back to ordinary lands.

"Honored Father wanting sail very much," Xing-Xing told me. "Return to fleet."

"But what about Kit?" I said. "Mr. Blackthorn? Doesn't he want to find Dr Lemuel?"

"Mr. Blackthorn sorry. Wants going home. Asking you come too."

"I can't," I said. "He knows I can't."

I couldn't be a wife to Kit or even a daughter to Father now. Not after everything that had happened. In England, the lodestone was nothing more than a trinket, and a dangerous one at that. It couldn't buy me the security I needed as a maimed woman. I had to return it to its rightful home.

"I'll try to speak with him before I go," I said. "If the abbess permits it."

The abbess agreed that I could go to Laputa with a party of nuns, in order to return the stone and seek my former guardian, Dr Lemuel. We were to request permission to go aloft the very next time the island city made a descent on the monastery. I would be permitted one meeting with my former companions in the Pilgrims' Cloister of the monastery before I left.

In the meantime, there was nothing to do but wait and listen to the great bell tolling, day in and day out, at each of the twenty-eight hours marking the nuns' day. I watched white-clad novices and pale blue initiates walk silently through the passageways between schoolroom and prayer hall, infirmary and refectory. Lay sisters struggled to collect eggs and coconuts in the squalling wind. In one room, the sisters practiced calligraphy. My toes ached to feel the brush and ink stick again, to trace the strokes of familiar words.

It was on a morning when, for once, the wind and rain had let up a touch that there was a commotion at the gate that separated the male and female sides of the island. A plain wall running the full width of the island cut it in two, so there was no temptation of intermingling. Just one gate – roofed like a tiny guard house with a lattice-work door in an arch beneath the roof – allowed men or women to pass between the halves. Even from way back on the female side, everyone could hear fists knocking and a man's voice bellowing with the full force of his lungs:

"Let me in! Let me in! I must speak with Mistress Rosewood urgently. Margaret: are you there?"

Kit's voice! I ran from the medicinal garden where I had been walking, my heart pounding. Initiate sisters crowded under the archway, shouting back through the shuttered lattices in shrill tones:

"It is not permitted. Go back. No man may enter here."

I ran faster.

"Kit! I'm here! What is it? Is everything all right?"

One or two of the nuns turned their attention to me now. White hands took hold of my shoulders, trying to turn me back from the wall. Kit shouted louder:

"Margaret: there's a man come. A shipwreck. Susumu says he...he had a box...morning glories." There was a scuffling and muffling on the other side of the wall. I could only catch some of the words. The monks must have been trying to drag him off their way. Kit's voice became fainter but he was still yelling at the top of his voice.

"Silver hands! He said he was looking for a woman with silver hands!"

My heart stood still. The nuns who had taken hold of me turned me round and began propelling me backwards through the gardens. My feet walked with them but the rest of me was frozen, as if in a dream. Silver hands. Silver hands. Those had been Kit's words; I hadn't been imagining it. A man had come. Could this possibly mean what I thought it did? The next minute, I had broken free of the nuns and was running, running until my lungs almost burst. I flew along the blue-tiled walkways, blurred past the silver phoenixes. I knew I shouldn't disturb the abbess, but there wasn't a moment to lose. I burst through her door without knocking. Her eyes snapped out of meditation: smoldering black coals.

"What, pray, is the meaning of this?"

"Forgive me," I gasped. "I humbly beg your pardon, Lady Abbess, but I must make my visit to the men's sector now. My future depends upon it."

"It is not yet arranged." The abbess folded her hands, in no hurry to do anything.

"Please." I got down with my head to the tiles. "I beseech you. A shipwrecked traveler has arrived and I think...I think..."

I hardly knew what I thought. I lifted up my head and glanced at the abbess again. Her features softened and there was a look of wisdom in her eye.

"You believe this traveler to be an acquaintance?"

"I have to find out," I said. "Please, Lady Abbess."

The abbess nodded slowly and smiled to herself.

"This is highly irregular, I hope you understand. However, I felt in my meditations just now that a change was taking place in the stars. This may be of significance. Go. I will send lay sisters to accompany you. Wear the stone that repels, for the time being."

Looking back, I could never remember clearly what followed. Xing-Xing took me to our cell. She fastened the stone about my neck, combed my hair, smoothed down my robe; but I may as well have been asleep for all I knew of it. All I could think of were Kit's words: *a woman with silver hands*. My heart pounded and the constellations on the wall seemed to swim. Before I knew what was happening, two lay sisters dressed in black had appeared. They walked me down to the wall, through the lattice-work door, and out across the wider gardens of the main monastery. A third ran ahead, so that by the time I reached the Pilgrims' Cloister, there were already black-clad monks standing outside to receive us. They opened the door to a warming room, dim with blue lamplight. I could see Kit within, and the man I remembered as Susumu. And half-sitting, half-laying on a pallet, covered with a quilt, was a young man, pale and grazed about the forehead, whose ebony eyes lit with fervor as they met mine.

"O-gin! I thought I should never lay eyes on you again."

"Taro!" I cried, and fell sobbing into his arms.

23

The Edge of the Map

For a long time, we simply held on. The familiar scents I remembered had been obliterated by the smell of medicinal herbs and borrowed clothing, but I couldn't forget the feeling of my head tucked into the crook of his neck, his cheek against my hair. I didn't know all the words he whispered over and over, but I felt the warmth of his breath and the clasp of his arms, and I knew he loved me.

I also knew I was in a monastery, being watched by three nuns, two monks, a pirate and my almost-brother. I disentangled myself, blushing. Taro – who outranked everyone in the room massively – did not blush, but continued to eat me up with his ebony eyes.

"Margaret," said Kit, hoarsely. "The stone. He touched you and it didn't repel."

I looked down to the pendant at my neck, across to Taro and then back to Kit. Hesitantly, I moved my elbow to brush against Kit's forearm. Nothing happened.

"It's gone," I said. The power had died. It looked as if the crazy boast I had made to Flood Dragon had come true after all. My true husband was with me and I didn't need protecting by a stone any more. My heart was as open as it could be; there was nothing in the world I wanted to repel right now.

I looked back to Taro; gazing, gazing. He had come. We had found one another. Kit cleared his throat.

"Is this Lord Shimmy-whatsit?"

I nodded.

"Your Lordship." Kit got on his knees and bowed. So did everyone else. I could see at a glance that there was respect in their eyes. Even battered and bruised, nobility couldn't hide itself. Not Taro's sort of nobility anyway. That sort that came straight from the soul. It was the kind of nobility that men from every nation and creed knew to esteem instantly. My heart swelled with pride to see it. I loved Taro more than ever.

But even a lord could not transgress monastery rules. There was a lot of whispering and questioning and, "Better tell the abbot/abbess". Within moments, monks on silent feet were hurrying with messages. The nuns remained, holding my gaze with forbidding expressions and shaking their heads every time Taro and I got close. I sighed. I was desperate to be alone with Taro. But this was a religious house after all. Perhaps the strictures were for our own good. The way I felt right now, it would be all too easy to throw virtue to one side and regret it later. Still, my senses ached for that brief moment in each other's arms.

Eventually, the consensus seemed to be that we could speak to each other for one temple hour in the warming room if we remained on opposite sides of the room and were watched by a monk and a nun respectively. Taro was under physician-monks' orders to stay in bed, and I was to kneel on the floor. But there was at least one concession to privacy. The religious folk, it seemed, did not speak Japanese (it not being a merchant tongue). In view of that, I thought the abbot and abbess were being more than usually generous, knowing we could say whatever we liked even if we couldn't touch.

For the first moments, we hardly knew what to say. Taro looked thinner than when I had seen him last. His cheekbones stood out more strongly and it was harder to see the boyishness in him. He was very pale, and by the set of his mouth, probably in pain too; but he sat with a straight back and his eyes glowed with what I knew could only be love.

"Sweet sky-spirit!" he sighed. "I have searched heaven and earth to find you. When I woke from the touch of that fiend, I thought you were gone to a realm where no man could follow."

I sniffed back the tears that had suddenly sprung to my eyes at the sound of that dark-honey voice in all its tenderness.

"Forgive me. He came to me in your form. He said I must leave the country. I thought...I thought you didn't want me. After he died, I tried so hard to get back to you; I truly did. They said you were married. They said you told them you had never heard of me."

The tears came out anyway. I couldn't stop them. Taro grasped the side of the pallet and leaned forward. The hand of the monk stopped his movement. I heard him give a frustrated sigh.

"No, no. You must not ask my forgiveness. I pledged to protect you and I failed. It is my honor that suffers for this. I should never have left you alone."

"What happened?" I dared to say.

"One of the falconers." He breathed out through his nose. "I knew there was something about him that wasn't right, but I did not recognize the fiend until he had his fingers about my throat and was pressing the stone to my hand."

"Not a fiend," I muttered. "A troubled man."

"Spirit-possessed?" Taro cocked his head, thoughtful.

"Perhaps." Who knew what had taken hold of Van Guelder in his youth? There were principalities and powers at work in the world, spiritual forces of evil. A boy like him could so easily have become their victim.

"Some spirit fought to control me; that I know," Taro said. "Even in my dreams, I did battle with it. I became as one of my ancestors of old, fighting to bring every warrior discipline to bear. When I woke, I was exhausted. I was lying in the hunting lodge, and my servants told me I had been in a fever for two days."

"You did fight him," I said. "You made him weak. He took me on a ship, but he was weak. I stole his stone. Then we were boarded. He died defending me."

Taro's eyes widened.

"Truly? This I did not expect. You stole his stone and then he defended you? You must tell me more of this later, O-gin. The immortal kind is indeed with you; I said that from the start."

"But what happened when you awoke?" I said.

"I sent riders to Tokushiro instantly. They came back with disturbing news: that I had been seen in the castle at the time I had lain ill. That I had acted unnaturally, as no man of rank should. That I had ridden unaccompanied to the coast with the sky-spirit. Some even said that I had been possessed by a spirit myself.

"I sent my cousin to Tokushiro in my stead, to take charge at the castle and reassert the family authority. My uncles took the burden of appeasing the visiting family. When they were gone, I sent men to search the coast. They took apart an inn where my shadow had been said to go. Their enquiries were met with only silence and the faintest hints of rumor. I could discover nothing. I feared you had returned to the sky and the world of spirits after all."

"Actually..." I began to say, but Taro pressed on with his story.

"By this time, I had recovered from my fever, but not from the rumors of my spirit-possession. And I needed to find you, Margaret. I could not let you go. I sent a second message to my cousin, telling him to take my title and the care of the estate for as long as it took for me to clear the mystery. The Shimatani honor must be upheld; that seemed the best way."

"And your cousin is married?" I ventured.

"He has both wife and child," Taro said.

"And knows nothing about sky-spirits."

"Indeed."

My heart glowed. There had been nothing to worry about, after all.

"And what then?" I said.

"I took a party of faithful *samurai* and went to the coast myself. We commandeered a ship to search the waters off Shimatani lands. By now, the storm season had come. My desperation to find you was so great that I cared nothing for my own safety. Once I even thought I could hear your voice calling to me, saying that you were trying to get back to me."

My chest jolted.

"You did; you did. I was on the *Shengfeng Hao*. I heard you say you were looking for me too."

I was burning for Taro's touch again. I glanced across at the nun. She gave me a stern stare, and I sat back.

"I can well believe it." Taro nodded. "My desire for you was so great, I'm sure it could be heard by heaven itself. We sailed up and down, searching for any sign. Then the storm struck."

I bit my lip.

"Waves such as I have never seen." Taro shook his head. "The crew was brave but so small a craft stood no chance of survival. All I could do was to cling to what I could and trust to the faithfulness of my ancestors."

"And you found yourself here?" I guessed.

Taro's eyes were wide with wonder.

"Yes. They tell me this is a religious house, a colony of a great empire. But it is no part of the great Sunrise Empire; that I know."

"It is not." I shook my head. "It is one of the lands beyond the edge of the map. You can only get to it," I blushed, "if you are looking for something else."

We gazed into each other's eyes, distracted, forgetful of time. I think we both knew what had drawn us here.

"This is a spiritual realm?" Taro said at last.

"My old teacher would say not," I said. "It is a real and reasonable land, ruled over by another land, which is due to visit shortly. A flying island." I gave a half-smile.

"The place you fell from?" Taro looked at me intently.

"The very same," I said. "And the home of this lodestone too." I looked down at the sun-like brass setting. "I am to return it to the island's emperor, as soon as the island arrives." I shrugged. "I don't know what will happen after that."

Taro squared his shoulders, his ebony eyes shining with suppressed pain and determination.

"I do," he said. "If the sky-sprit will consent to honor her word."

It was a simple wedding, and the strangest I had ever attended. Xing-Xing dressed me in my Chinese tunic and breeches and pinned up my hair. Then, accompanied by nuns, we walked together to the prayer hall of the main monastery. Under its domed ceiling, a row of blue-clad monks sat cross-legged and chanting; and round the opposite wall sat Captain Hu and his pirates. Kit was among them, fiercely blinking back tears.

Taro was dressed in his own clothes again, somewhat faded in the wash but still recognizably lordly. The crest of the morning glory gleamed at his back and shoulders. His hair was tied in a topknot. His face was still pale and taut, but he bore himself like a king, and smiled with his eyes as I walked through the door.

There was no ceremony: no hymn, no flowers, no throwing of shoes. We simply stood one on each side of the hall, facing the abbot. Above us, the midnight-blue ceiling shone with silver stars: the whole wheel of the twenty-eight constellations. With the help of Susumu, the abbot questioned Taro if it was his intention to wed.

"Yes," he said, in the language I had come to love. "This woman is my chosen wife. She is my equal partner, the balance to my qualities."

His rich voice lingered in the air. My chest swelled with emotion.

"And is it your intention to wed this lord?" the abbot said to me.

I looked up to the spangled ceiling. The weaver and the cowherd shone bright amid the constellations. They need never be apart now. The river could not separate them. I had crossed the bridge.

"It is. He is my husband for life," I said.

"Does anyone here object to this union?"

There was silence, broken only by Kit's sniffle.

"Then you are married indeed," the abbot said. "And may the stars light the way to your future."

For a dowry, I gave Taro the Lodestone of Laputa, on the understanding that it would be presented to the emperor as soon as we embarked. And for a bride-gift, he had two monks bring a box and open it: a lacquered box inlaid with pearl that had clearly been through storms and shipwreck, but was still the same box I recognized from Tokushiro.

"It was that box that nearly drowned him, you know," Kit told me afterwards. "He wouldn't let go of it. They had to pull him and the box from the sea together."

Inside the box were my silver hands; the beautiful silver hands Taro had sent to the lakeside house for me. The box had kept them safe from the wind and weather: the delicate fingers with their nails and joints and cherry blossom engravings were as exquisite as ever.

"I had my guard retrieve them for me," he whispered to me as he put them on me. He insisted on performing that task himself: a ritual of our new beginning together. "I wanted to keep a part of you with me always; I simply prayed that I would find the rest."

"And you did," I smiled.

He smiled back; the sparkly, boyish smile that made my heart grow full. He wasn't just Lord Shimatani; not just a nobleman with a kind and honorable heart. He was my Taro, and I was going to stay by him and work alongside him for the rest of our days.

He leaned closer to me. I could feel the buzz of his breath on my ear.

"I want to make love to you," he whispered. "I can't wait until we can leave this monastery and finally be together."

"Me neither," I whispered back. The thought of our first encounter made me feel nervous all over, but it was a good kind of nervous. I knew I would always be safe in Taro's arms.

The abbess allowed us one embrace. She also allowed one embrace between Kit and me. This would be the last time I would see him. I knew that full well. If he got away at Glanguenstald, then this time next year he could be in Hollyport, sitting to table in the brass-studded chair, with the smell of seaweed drifting in through the window.

"Tell Father I'm safe," I said. "Tell him I'm with a good man."

Kit held on tight.

"I will." He sniffed. "Always knew you were a lady, sweetheart. You'll do us all proud."

"I am indebted to you," Taro said as Kit knelt before him. "I wish you long life and prosperity. May you reach your home in safety."

Laputa arrived two days later. With the abbot and abbess in attendance, Taro and I stood on the beach. Together, we watched the waves lash the shore and spray salt in our faces, as a shape came down from the clouds, a mighty force attracted to the ground beneath our feet. Its underside glittered like diamond dust scattered over rock. Climbing the walls that surrounded it ran stairs and balconies, shielding the topsy-turvy houses with their roofs, lattices and hanging greenery. Black eyes stared from white faces. Baskets were lowered and monks rushed to fill them. On a higher step stood an official in a fur hat and starry robe, and behind him stood another. I squinted. Did that figure in the robe of strange cut belong to a man I knew? A man who had once saved my life? The abbot and abbess raised their arms high in petition.

"Lord and Lady Shimatani of the Sunrise Empire request an audience with His Celestial Majesty. May it please the Queen of Cities to take them aloft?"

Just as before, the swing-seat was lowered. Taro took me by the hand – the silver hand of a sky-spirit – and led me along the shale. Around us, the sea boomed and sea birds screamed in flight. But growing ever louder and more harmonious from above were the celestial chimes that floated down to meet us as we rose from the lonely island, our arms tight about each other, our hearts beating as one.

Author's Note

Silver Hands is inspired by three things:

"The Handless Maiden," recorded by the Brothers Grimm in their famous fairy tale collection
    Gulliver's Travels, Book Three (A Voyage to Laputa, Balnibarbi, Luggnagg, Glubbdubdrib and Japan) by Jonathan Swift
    And global history at the turn of the 18th century

Creating a fusion of the three has sometimes involved a balancing act as far as "authenticity" is concerned. Where there has been a clash of interests, I have generally followed my instincts as to what seemed best for the story. However, the following notes may be helpful.

The Handless Maiden

In the Grimms' version of the tale, the heroine is a miller's daughter, whose father accidentally bargains her away to the Devil. Her hands are cut off during the Devil's frustrated attempt to claim her. She then wanders the world, eventually arriving in the garden of a king, who marries her and gives her silver hands. They become separated when the Devil again intervenes, and the king must then wander the world until he finds his wife again.

My decision to relocate the "king's garden" to Japan was prompted by the idea of everything being at floor level, making it easier for a girl with no hands to learn to use her feet instead. From there, it seemed a natural step to make her father a master mariner instead of a miller. I also made the decision to defer Margaret and Taro's marriage until the end of the story (in the original they are already married and have a son) as it fitted in better with Margaret's personal development.

Gulliver's Travels

The course taken by the *Hopewell* and the sloop *Reward* from England to the point where Dr Lemuel and Margaret encounter the flying island is the same as Swift records in *Gulliver's Travels*, Book Three, including the dates. Descriptions of Japan, however, are altered to fit in more closely with the history of the time. As Japan was a closed country when Swift was writing, his information is likely to have come from out-of-date 17th-century sources and conjecture. Interestingly, Japan is the only place visited by Gulliver that is a real country. Perhaps, given its distance from Europe and "mysterious" closed state, it felt almost like an imaginary country to Swift. It is this idea that prompted me to give Japan the unique status it has in *Silver Hands*, as a place somehow between the real world and the lands beyond the map.

The Island of the Lonely Monastery does not feature in *Gulliver's Travels*. It is my own invention.

The World in 1706

1706 is the year the *Hopewell* departs in *Gulliver's Travels*. At the time, many similar ships made the dangerous voyage from Europe to East Asia and back on behalf of the Dutch and English East India Companies. The Dutch controlled the spice trade, and were also the only Europeans allowed access to Japan (via the man-made island of Deshima off Nagasaki). Their main outpost was Batavia (Jakarta) in Indonesia, where Van Guelder threatens to take Margaret. The English had outposts at Madras and Canton, amongst other places, mainly bringing back tea and porcelain. English ships sailed from London, between Tower Bridge and London Bridge.

Pirates were a real threat in the South China Sea. Chinese pirate fleets were huge, and were run like a floating mafia, demanding ransom from ships that crossed their territory. Pirate lords like Flood Dragon were similar to mafia dons, often fronting their piracy with a legitimate business on land, such as salt making. Flood Dragon is actually inspired by an earlier pirate, Coxinga (b.1624) who was a Ming loyalist of mixed heritage. His name is taken from an earlier Chinese name for Japanese pirates (flood dragons).

Japan in 1706 was in the middle of the Edo Period (1603-1867); the period during which Japan was ruled by Shoguns and was closed to the outside world. Although it was essentially a military dictatorship, with the warrior class as the ruling class, this was a time of internal peace and sophistication in the arts; characterized by strolling gardens (like Taro's), haiku poetry, and the woodblock prints of artists such as Hokusai. One theme for prints was *ukiyo-e* (pictures of the floating world). These depicted the fleeting pleasures of life, including pictures of geisha and courtesans – not something Margaret would approve! The system of hostages and alternate residence described by Taro was a genuine feature of life at the time, and was used by the Shogun to stop feudal lords rebelling. The story of the Weaver and the Cowherd is well-known in Japan, Korea and China; the Japanese festival celebrating it is called *Tanabata* and is celebrated on 7 July.

**TOP HAT
BOOKS**

Historical fiction that lives.

We publish fiction that captures the contrasts, the achievements, the optimism and the radicalism of ordinary and extraordinary times across the world.

We're open to all time periods and we strive to go beyond the narrow, foggy slums of Victorian London. Where are the tales of the people of fifteenth century Australasia? The stories of eighth century India? The voices from Africa, Arabia, cities and forests, deserts and towns? Our books thrill, excite, delight and inspire.

The genres will be broad but clear. Whether we're publishing romance, thrillers, crime, or something else entirely, the unifying themes are timescale and enthusiasm. These books will be a celebration of the chaotic power of the human spirit in difficult times. The reader, when they finish, will snap the book closed with a satisfied smile.